I. Back Drop
  — CANCER I...

H/1, man 100 !

a frame for flowers

- No small Talk
- Cut To The Meat
- No Meals
- Don't Talk To Self
- Don't state The obvious
- Each Character. Speaks differently !
- Show - Don't Tell
- Summarize Plot — 3 Sentences
- Enough Plot?
  Conflict ?

a frame for flowers

sean storin

*This book is dedicated to the courageous and cowards in the world...
we all know who you are.*

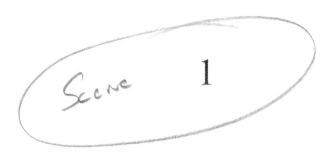

Scene 1

The white picket fence enclosing her yard accentuated the paradox: it was beautiful misery. The pointed white slats stood rigid framing a picturesque American household, but they served as a reminder of a wall that defined her world. She knelt at a six-by twelve-foot rectangle of fecund soil eager to give birth to the colors of life that spring would promise. But for now the dark earth would have to wait.

Her hands were dry and slightly cracked at the tips, flecked with dirt but smooth like china on the back. In the crisp, autumn air she could smell the slight chill. There might yet be an Indian summer, but the yellows were already edging the leaves, and the oranges, reds, and browns were sure to follow. Kate was thinking how the fall in New England never lets its residents forget they're getting older, but how its brilliant colors never make them regret it.

Katie Kelley was now thirty-seven years old—Mrs. Kate Bruno—and most days without snow or bitter cold she worked in her garden, which was the envy of the neighborhood. Kate filled every inch within the white picket fence with a lush painting of flowers and plants, colors and scents, textures and movement. This was her sanctuary in an often-darkened world, an oasis in a life whose challenge was not

1

always an explosion or crash, but more often a persistent drip that slowly devolved into an incessant pounding.

On this day, though, the summer was clinging by a finger, and although the air was cool, the sun's rays found their way to Kate's soft, blonde hair and warmed her neck and back. The family dog, a brown and black-furred German shepherd named King, sprawled out by the fence gate, eager to defend but committed to relaxation.

Her hands were busy, gently easing the bulbs of spring into the Stygian soil. In short, calculated strokes, she dug a hole with her trowel, lowered the bulb, and softly buried it beneath the dirt, patting the earth until it appeared as it was, with no indication of the flower in waiting. Each color predetermined and aligned. Each row carefully planned with each space as important as the flower itself. The bulbs would sit quietly in the ground and remain protected from the harsh winter that would sap the life above. Waiting calmly for the time when the world could see their color and understand their purpose.

Kate had no idea at that moment, that while she planned the painted picture for the following spring's terrain... she had just framed the flowers of her life.

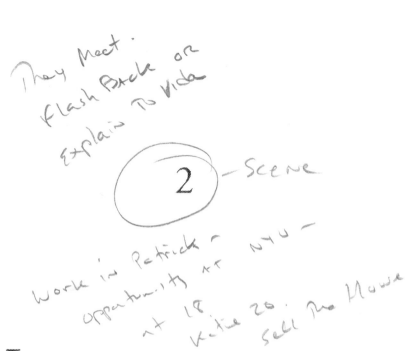

2 — Scene

K ate had always been <u>interested in gardening</u>. As a young girl, her Grandmother Eva and her mom had both been gifted, and every year their bulging, red tomatoes and flavorful squash found their way to neighbors' dinner tables, often in exchange for a casserole, cookies, or pie. Everyone felt it was a pretty good arrangement, but Kate viewed it as more than a barter system—it was a form of expression. She had tried to major in horticulture in college, but the small Massachusetts school she could get into (and afford) did not offer the major, so she pursued a <u>degree in English</u>. She loved to read.

Kate didn't really have much time to kneel in the garden until years after college. She met Frank Bruno one night on a study break at a local bar in Brighton. He was thin, but strong and handsome with a thick, dark mane and a tan, angled face. His powerful hands were big for his frame, and the veins made it obvious they worked for a living. His swagger projected confidence, and although he didn't look like her father at all, he did look like someone who <u>could protect you, and that reminded her of her dad.</u>

<u>Brighton and Allston had lots of pubs.</u> There was a sense of community as locals gathered for a pint or two and to share a laugh. People read the paper by themselves or simply listen to the local news from

3

the barkeep or fellow patrons. Everyone in a Boston pub seemed to have an opinion, and for those who took the time to listen, it was evident that most would brush up on the news prior to arrival.

Although he had glanced over several times that evening with a vague smile, Frank had not approached Kate and her girlfriends. The girls easily noticed the handsome Italian, and it became obvious the attraction was strong between Katie Kelley and the dark-haired man across the bar. It took a couple more cocktails and some crafty angling by one of her girlfriends to get into a position so the two of them could meet, but sure enough they stood just six feet apart when their eyes met.

"Oh my God, Katie… he totally wants you, he keeps lookin'. Just go say hi to him," said Kate's friend Molly, who she had known since sixth grade.

"I don't think I've seen him look once, Moll."

"He's a stallion," added Amy, another girlfriend who stood just behind her, "and he's in wicked shape too!" The three of them had been socializing at the Allston and Brighton bars since long before they were legal, and they always had fun together. Kate was pretty reserved, but Molly Coyne and Amy Harris loved to flirt with the male patrons and were more than happy to hook up with them on weekends. They both worked as hairstylists and teased Kate about her scholarly pursuits. Neither of them had any interest in college. They were friends Kate had known much of her life… they were neighborhood girls.

"Tan skin and dark hair, just the way you like 'em Kate—the anti-Irish!"

"Ya… I get it. He's cute, and if he's interested, he'll come over here!" Kate blushed,

"Just drink your wine cooler, ya lush, and stop staring at 'im! It will happen if it's supposed to," she continued with a laugh.

"Fuck that," said Molly, who had always had the mouth of a sailor. "I'm going over there to talk to the musclehead next to him, so I can plant the seed for you, Katie."

"Plant the seed, Molls," screeched Amy over the din of the bar.

"You go get 'im Johnny Appleseed," she continued, cackling with a slight slur as Molly marched across the bar.

4

Amy and Molly watched intently as she struck up a conversation with the muscular guy standing next to the man Kate Kelley couldn't keep her eyes off of.

"She's nuts," Kate proclaimed, as Amy giggled uncontrollably.

Kate felt a calming glow from the pint of Guinness she was sipping. She was one of only a handful of the girls (even the Irish ones) who drank the dark beer, but she honestly loved the taste. So did her younger brother, who'd introduced her to it.

Patrick Kelley was only eleven months younger, but the day Kate became legal was the day she became her brother's best friend. At such a close age, they were chided as Irish twins, and they had always been close like twins could be. Long before buying her brother Guinness beer at Mickey's Packy on Friday nights, Kate shared a deep kinship with her brother that spanned time and place.

The night Kate met Frank, she was at Irish Town Bar, a smoky and dark local known for its ability to assimilate newcomers to Boston's heavily Irish population. Irish Town was a happy venue, and, particularly early in the evening, a place where everyone seemed to be smiling. The thick, worn wood of the bar mixed with the shiny brass taps gave it the feel of a ship's galley, and behind the deck were the men who pulled and poured the ale into traditional pint glasses. The banners of Galway family crests filled the walls.

There was always music playing, and on that evening there were three older gentlemen playing traditional Irish songs. Their voices, drums, and fiddle filled the air with a melancholy hopefulness, and there was a sense of timelessness to the place that night, and every night.

Kate was lost in the music as she enjoyed the buzz of her beer. In the bustling bar it took a while for her to notice that Molly and Amy had slipped away. They had been lured to the bar next door by two handsome boys, leaving her all alone. Kate scanned the room looking for them and was suddenly concerned. The bar was all at once loud and filled with strangers, as her eyes darted into the corners in search of her friends. She knew the girls to be a bit unreliable, but they had never ditched her. After several minutes when they had still not emerged, Kate stood up and contemplated leaving. She couldn't believe they would abandon her. It was right then Frank Bruno moved in.

Frank's first words to her were: "If you're not with someone, we should hang out."

Short and simple, if not awkward and in some ways almost crude, but he had reached out his strong hand and when he touched her, it felt safe. Outside, the world may have been rushing and raging, but right there she felt safe. They talked in a way they might never again, and on that night, Kate found him to be irresistibly attractive and intriguing.

Her girlfriends never returned having gone off into the night with that weekend's love interests. She and Frank sat closely in a way that was more familiar than a chance first meeting and she could feel the warmth of his body when he leaned in to speak. Now and again he would touch her or his chest would press against her as revelers pushed by. Frank created a barrier between her and the bustling bar that sheltered her. Everything seemed to shrink into a tight circle, just she and this handsome man.

Kate was taken by him and a combination of the alcohol and his deep dark eyes led her back to his apartment. It was completely out of character for her but it just felt right. His voice soothed her and his body pulled her in like a magnet. She wanted to be closer to him and in the quiet solace of his simple apartment he took control of her. She was not the type to have a one night stand, in fact she never had. It was as if she knew she would be with him, she knew it was her fate. She gave in and their bodies came together as if it were meant to be. For that moment in time it was perfect.

The two dated steadily during Kate's first and second year at college. For much of the first year they went out for drinks, haggled for cheap tickets to Red Sox and Bruins games, and got to know each other's lives. Frank worked a lot of hours doing construction, but he paid for everything and made her feel special. He was not much of a romantic, in that he would not say things to make her feel pretty or confident, but he hovered over her in a way that said she is mine and I would kill to protect what is mine. On more than one evening, Frank demonstrated that instinct, exchanging punches with some poor fool who dared to look at or approach Kate. She found it silly, but could not help feeling like she mattered, that she was worth fighting for.

From early on Kate accepted that Frank was a very structured person who liked things, that is to say everything, to be in a certain order. He liked to check off lists and had a method for everything. He took the lead and dictated the pace and frequently demonstrated a short temper, but for Kate it was a safe ride in the passenger seat of a comfortable vehicle.

Before long, however, it seemed with each passing month their relationship became more regimented and formatted. To Kate this seemed like the natural progression and behavior of a responsible man looking to settle down. She found comfort in his patterns and idiosyncrasies. She could picture him as a provider and a father who could deliver a safe environment for children to be raised. She did not have much experience with other men and assumed this was all quite normal.

As months passed, the young couple moved in together, although they kept that hidden from Frank's family. With Kate's parents deceased, she had lived alone in their house for a number of years, but eventually sold it to help her brother pay for his expensive school. She had since been living alone in small flat. Kate was excited to finally share a place with someone and call it home. Frank liked it because he could keep her close.

Increasingly Frank preferred to stay in and watch TV with Kate, but when he did choose to go out, he did so with others instead of her. It took on a routine pattern, but to Kate that again felt natural. This is what you do. People get older; they get married and have kids. They were just becoming like everybody else. Kate's life slowly became more insular.

After a couple years at a local school, her brother Patrick was accepted to NYU in New York City. Most of Kate's knowledge of

New York was the Empire State Building she visited on an eleventh-grade trip, as well as the dreaded Yankees and, of course, the Mets who made the '86 World Series an event Bostonians wanted to erase from their memories.

Patrick Kelley had been a promising forward in the Massachusetts hockey scene, and several coaches and scouts (as well as every kid from the neighborhood) thought he could play at the collegiate level, if not the pros. But Patrick was not in love with hockey and did not lose too much sleep when a slapshot shattered his ankle and ended his career on the ice. Everybody in the neighborhood envisioned a future forward for the Bruins, but secretly, Patrick was more interested in designing a rack of clothing than racking up goals. With both of their parents gone, Patrick was the only close family Kate had, but at such a young age, they never thought twice about his going away to school, assuming the separation was just temporary.

Though she had never admitted it to anyone except her brother, Frank was not her first. Kate had lost her virginity to her teenage love on the twenty-fourth day of summer following high school graduation. She had messed around with a few boys from the neighborhood who were always trying to wear her down, but for three out of the four years of high school she went with the same boy. He was ideal: handsome, athletic, and smart as a whip. He was an altar boy and, moreover, a good Catholic, and although they kissed and petted frequently in hidden spots around the neighborhood, they both spoke of waiting until marriage.

Kate generally assumed they meant their marriage, but he never specified. He worked hard in school, got good grades, played two sports, and planned to go to college just like his parents. After making it past prom with her virginity intact, Kate figured it wasn't going to happen, but one night they found themselves down on Cape Cod at his summer home all alone, when his parents had decided to drive down the next day due to a raging thunderstorm. They shared the home that night like a married couple, and he treated her gently in a way she would never regret. She would never forget him, but he was the youngest child, and he went to college in California. A month later, his parents packed up and moved out there with him. California was clear across the world, and he was gone. She tried to hold on to hope, but she never saw him again.

When Kate got pregnant by Frank at twenty-two years old, she felt all alone. In Boston, Massachusetts, in 1988, she had to "do the right thing." So she did. She married Frank Bruno and dropped out of her college classes. The two had been dating some time, and Frank's mother and two sisters were always telling them to: "Get married already!"

It was pretty much what everyone expected. The whole thing went down pretty quickly, and they were wed at St. Leonard's Parish. All the Irish and Italian Catholics filled the church and got drunk together at the reception. Kate ended up giving birth to a baby boy six months later, but nobody seemed to make a fuss about the math. It just was. Things happen, and she needed to do what she had to do.

3

Frank Luis Bruno had grown up in a decaying town north of Boston, but later settled into life as a teenager in East Boston. His father moved them there so they could be near the North End and a heavy population of Italian immigrants. He ran with some kids in the neighborhood but in general, Frank kept to himself. He had two brothers to serve as built-in cohorts.

His dad, Emilio Bruno, was in construction, but eventually went to work for the City of Boston, managing a territory for the Department of Public Works. He oversaw several crews of heavy, blue-collar guys in light-orange vests, and they were thick as thieves. He wasn't rolling in the dough, but he had connections, and when you do, you don't pay for much. Every time Emilio Bruno got to drinking wine, you could hear all about his bloodline tracing straight back to Sicily. He had married his high-school sweetheart, Theresa Loccianso, and made it as a streetwise guy who could handle himself in the '50s, and a foreman who could get things done in the '60s.

Emilio was hard on Frank growing up, and when any of the Bruno kids got out of line, they were going to get a taste of the belt. The name Emilio is derived from the word rival in Italian, and in his house, he had no rival. He routinely referred to Frank as a dummy, and that made Frank's blood boil.

Unlike his social father, Frank Bruno was mercurial from early on. He wasn't much in the classroom, but he understood how life worked and could always get an angle on something to improve his position. He was a good athlete and excelled in baseball, but was tossed out of the Babe Ruth program after multiple altercations with other players, physical and verbal. When Emilio found out, he told everyone for weeks how: "My dummy son blew his best chance in life."

Emilio always said it with a chuckle, but Frank wasn't laughing. Frank hated to love his dad, although he did. His father once told him: "Making your kids tough is a father's job," and that made sense to Frank.

In the Italian-dominated North End, everything was brick, and there were no lawns and few porches to speak of. Frank always thought his dad chose East Boston because it was cheaper, but Emilio claimed to have chosen East Boston because he could have a porch to watch the world from. Everyone liked to sit on the Bruno's front porch, which was just five creaky steps up from the sidewalk.

There wasn't much in East Boston except people and the airport, but over in the North End, Boston's history boiled over. You could walk right up to the Old North Church where the famous "one if by land, two if by sea" night unfolded or visit Paul Revere's statue that commemorated the famous ride. Frank always hated to sit on the front porch in East Boston and preferred to walk the streets of the North End alone.

Growing up, Frank was a good-looking young man and never had trouble catching the eye of the ladies. All throughout his teenage years, Frank had worked out to exhaustion in his basement bedroom, endless hours spent honing his discipline in the mirror. He was the oldest of five, with two younger sisters and brothers to lord over. Frank had made the basement inhabitable, and at seventeen took possession of the only kid's room in the house that wasn't shared. His grandmother had to live on the first floor. His parents had the top floor, and his brothers and sisters both shared rooms on the second floor.

Frank always had some kind of job, and when he wasn't working, he was working out. He did endless curls and bench presses using the dumbbells he bought with money he earned doing odd jobs. His muscles grew strong and sinewy, and he took every opportunity to display his rippled arms and flat stomach, especially in the summer when his olive skin turned a deep tan. Frank had hazel eyes that sometimes looked green depending on what he wore, although the majority of the time that was dirty jeans and a tank top or dingy sweatshirt.

When he was nineteen, Emilio got Frank a job though a connection over at the Metropolitan Boston Transit Authority, the MBTA. Frank stuck it out for more than a year but hated it. The guys sat around and never did anything, and as he told his dad: "You're not making any real money doing that garbage work… not with guys like that." With Frank's deep Boston accent, it sounded more like:

"C'mon pop… ya nawt makin any real money doin that gahbaj wuhrk… nawt wit jamokes like that."

He and his siblings spent pretty much every Sunday at his folks' house, and that was expected. Nearly a year after he moved out, he returned one Saturday, tore down the front steps, and rebuilt a perfect six-step staircase. It took him nine hours. He had asked his parents for years to do it, and his father declined. Finally, Frank took matters into his own hands. His mother made his father pay him for it, and Emilio was pissed.

"God damn it, dummy, I told you I would get to it… now you cost me big time."

"What are you talkin about? Those stairs have been busted for eva! Besides, I didn't ask for the money," said Frank, shrugging his shoulders.

"Yeah… and you didn't know your mother would do exactly this… don't bullshit a bullshitter."

Frank smiled as he walked to his car and counted the money before he left.

Frank remembered that first night in Irish Town Bar a bit differently. He didn't recall any music or any of Kate's girlfriends. He did remember the grain of the wood on the bar and how he felt they used too much lacquer. He also recalled the blonde at the bar whose sky-blue eyes were easy to look at. He remembered just wanting to reach out and hold her, which is what he did. He walked right up, threw down his lines, and told her how it was. She was hot, and she was hooked. He would repeat the story about the night he met his wife and how he just walked right up to her took her hand and said: "You are going to be with me tonight."

They had been dating for two years or so and it was getting to be a grind, she was still the best option, but it was just a grind. When Kate got pregnant his mother told him it was a sign.

"This is how God sends you signs, Frankie. You got a sign that's all… so don't disrespect it."

Frank wasn't thrilled about the prospect of being married and a dad at twenty-five, but he knew it was how things were done. He married her and although he was just getting started with his career, he had squirreled away enough money to start a family. Frank was glad when Kate dropped out of college. He always told her she was wasting earning years learning how to earn. Kate never thought of learning in those terms.

4

After his stint with the MBTA then a year as a framer, Frank built homes for a guy named Jim Star. He began swinging a hammer, but within eighteen months, he stepped up from framer to foreman, and years later became the jobsite boss overseeing all the projects. Frank would still wear a tool-belt and couldn't walk past a crooked anything without stopping to fix it or at least complain about it. He was brutal on the crew and treated them like they were grunts at boot camp. Jim liked Frank because he worked hard and was a hard-ass on himself and everyone around him.

"These guys just gaw-ta work hah-da!" he would rail to his boss and aging owner of the company.

"I understand that perspective Frank, but just remember if you drive them off a cliff, you'll have no workers. So strike a good balance. Will ya?"

"Sure... no, I understand," Frank would say, not believing a word of it.

"Profits are up, Frank. Sprinkle some of it to your people, and they will pay you back with hard work."

"Yeah, you're right. If they get the Cuneo job done, I will... I'll take care of 'em. They just gotta get shit done and earn it!"

"It'll get done… it always does," said Mr. Star, with a sage look that was completely lost on his young foreman.

Frank was the best foreman Star could ask for: loved to work hard and fast and had zero tolerance for errors and lazy behavior. Jim's big issue was finding guys to stay on the job as Frank had a tendency of running them off before long or driving them to quit in a huff. He would tell Frank: "Life's a journey, Frank. Don't torch everything behind you. It can circle back and bite."

When Frank was in the office, he stacked papers in specific bins, he filed things in their exact place, and he answered the phone in one ring. When he was on the job, he paced the joint like a lifeguard always looking for things to save. When he worked on the job himself, he was obsessed: the grain of wood had to follow patterns that in his mind made perfect sense; nails had to align each spike to be driven in at the precise point to insure the hold; the shingles, windows, floorboards each had a pattern. It was not, however, artistic. It was perfection, the unattainable goal that drove Frank Bruno. Everything needed to be right, and if you can't get that, then get lost.

Jim Star was more than happy to relegate the vendor relationships to Frank, and over time, he worked less and less. Jim was looking to retire, and Frank was his natural successor. He and the cute gal in the office seemed to run everything just fine, and there just wasn't much to do. Jim planned to sell forty-nine percent of the company to Frank and then, eventually, let him buy it all. Star recognized that Frank had a predator's talent for negotiating. Most of the vendor relationships and subcontractors they worked with would describe Frank's approach as exhausting and dizzying, if not flat-out obnoxious, but like an unpopular bouncer at a popular nightclub, Frank was going to have the last word. Star Builders only did five to seven houses a year, but under Frank's management, the units clicked up and the margins got better. They were making significant money.

Frank was a bastard to pretty much everyone, but respectful to Mr. Star, the man who held the keys. He was also pretty cozy with Tricia McAllen, the receptionist and scheduler who worked in the office, but to everyone else Frank was a terror. To demonstrate he had no loyalty, Frank would lambaste Jim Star to Kate in private, but maintained a subservient facade to the white-haired man who signed his checks. On the jobsite, Frank's true persona emerged.

"Any you dicks gonna actually work today?" he barked as he climbed out of his muscular pickup truck, smoothed back his hair with his hand, and slid on his yellow hard hat.

There was no response, but a palpable pickup in pace from the six or eight guys in various spots around the site. It was a new home build for what Frank called "some yuppie scumbags" in Newton, and although they were on time and ahead of budget, the couple had wanted a large and terrifically heavy safe installed in their bedroom upstairs, and it appeared the crew had already framed in the upper level.

"Hey, Charlie... c'mere a sec," said Frank, tapping his pencil on a clipboard and biting his lip.

Over scrambled the lead installer Charlie, who had somehow managed to endure Frank's malevolence and stick around for seven years.

"I suppose you're gonna throw that 450-pound safe that's sittin in the garage on your back and just carry it up to the custom-ahs bedroom, huh?"

There was silence and a deep, hard swallow as Charlie realized they had made a mistake. He ran his long, thin fingers through the waning wisps of blonde hair he had left.

"Yer right Frank... ah we buttoned er up too quick, but no sweat, we can get this taken care of and make it right here quick," bumbled Charlie in a somber tone.

Charlie was 48 years old, had labored in construction for his whole life, and he knew little else. He and his wife had logged some tough years together, but they managed to get their daughter Alison into a good school, and by the looks of it, she was headed for a better life than theirs. That's why Charlie took the barbs and condescension from Frank on a regular basis: he didn't have options.

In reality, the crane they needed (and Frank knew was delayed) wasn't on site. He also knew they could remove the upper gable in one piece and fairly easily use the crane to bring the safe in through the opening. Charlie could have explained that without the crane available, it was probably smart to close up the house to the elements rather than let it sit open. But why bring the storm down on yourself? In Frank's eyes, it was a mistake that would create work and waste time. Everyone knew: this would cost them.

"That's it on O.T. guys," Frank yelled suddenly, addressing the entire site. "Cuz we not paying for you to work and rework the same shit you just screwed up."

He then turned and, in a still-audible tone that feigned discretion, he continued directly to his foreman, "And Charlie, you bald, stupid prick, ya better staht running this crew like you own it, or I'll get someone who can."

Frank shifted gears seamlessly and kept talking as though he had not just threatened his oldest employee's career. He went on, not to anyone directly, but rather as if delivering a public-service announcement to the group of laborers he considered expendable. He walked deliberately, navigating around the dirt-crumbled yard, stepping over wood scraps, boulders, and piles of sawdust as everyone watched from their various perches, hoping he'd step on a nail.

"Lots of waste here, guys... tons of waste! We measure twice and cut once," he recited condescendingly. Frank was the only guy who wore safety glasses, and the guys would all laugh at him behind his back, but not a one of them would confront him. He was still their boss, and besides, they didn't want to end up like that Polish kid who called Frank out a couple years back. The young framer asked Frank, "Why do you always have to be such an asshole to us?"

Frank's answer was to be beat the young man within an inch of his life and then fire him in a thunderous and humiliating tirade about how lazy "his people" were. Frank had beaten up a pretty tough kid and sent him packing in an instant. He knew the immigrant from Poland was illegal, so there wasn't going to be a police report. He sent a message right there to everyone: Do not cross Frank Bruno.

He made his way around the back of the house and down a grade to an opening into the basement where a bulkhead or walk-out would eventually be. He kept pointing out errors, from a slightly crooked joist to a loose piece of tar paper.

"Ahhh Charlie... will you fuckin please look at the pea stone in the basement and tell me how that is spread evenly? And by the way... your guys gotta put more tar on the foundation or those holes will leak... am I right?

He asked but didn't wait for an answer. He looked up at the framer who was peering over the edge to watch and thought he was out of sight. The young man's head quickly snapped back out of sight.

"Are you knuckleheads building a house or a fuckin fort in the woods?" he hollered to the young employee with no idea what his name was.

Charlie followed him around like a little dog, scratching down notes on a small, frayed pad of paper then nervously placing and replacing the square, yellow pencil behind his knobby ear.

"Sure thing, Frank... we're on it. I will make sure the stone is smooth and we'll recoat the tar," said Charlie, reviewing his notes.

"When do you suspect the crane will be here?" he asked, which drew a glare from Frank.

"I just want to be sure we open up the gable at the right time to avoid rain damage. You know... whenever is fine"

And so Charlie retreated, hands punched down into the pockets of his dusty, tan work pants, chewing on his thin lips and eschewing any conflict.

"The crane will be here when it gets here.... okay? Got it? You got that now?" Frank peppered Charlie, leaning into him.

"Tighten this up, Charlie, or your kids gonna need a fuckin scholarship for next semester," said Frank, bursting into hyena-pitched laugh. "I'm just bustin' your balls, slim... just get crackin."

And then he was gone, marching over to the familiar white Ford pickup truck and driving away with a spray of gravel in his wake. The most revered sight on the job to a work crew at Star builders was the taillights of Frank Bruno's truck.

a frame for flowers

"What an asshole," said a random framer to a withered Charlie Hess.

"Yeah," he replied in a nervous tone. "You could say that."

"Someday he'll get his."

"Oh yeah, that's written. The devil's got a special place for guys like that," replied Charlie, with a bit more conviction, as if the oxygen were returning to his body.

"Someday he will get his."

5

Kate and Frank had their share of arguments in the early years, but they were generally one-sided. His hair-trigger temper frightened her, so for the most part, Kate didn't argue too strenuously. When Frank got angry, he would punch things: the wall, the steering wheel, or other people. But the first time he actually hit her, everything changed. Like waking up suddenly in a prison cell, Kate's life had been instantly redefined.

When Frank's rage gathered momentum, there was no way to slow it down. It was best to get out of the way, but sometimes, that was impossible.

They had been married about eighteen months, money was pretty tight, and they had a colicky baby in the house. The argument that night was like countless ones before, but Frank had lost a major bid at work and had been out drinking. He was hours late and made a ruckus when he stumbled angrily through the front door of their modest South Boston apartment. As he entered, Frank dropped his keys and then knocked his head on the door when he bent to snatch them up. It was enough to trigger the rage wave.

"Fuck!" he shouted to no one in particular.

As Frank regained his footing, he grabbed at a stack of mail that sat on a small, rectangle table near the front door, acting as if it was all planned. He rifled through the envelopes, dropping certain letters to the ground as he went.

"Can we get any mo-a fuckin' bills?" he asked with a slight slur.

Kate emerged from the kitchen to see what he was doing.

"You're home late," said Kate, ignoring his commentary.

"What? Yah... so what?"

"Nothing, I just hadn't heard from you, and it's almost ten o'clock," she said, looking over to the clock, but knowing precisely what time it was.

"What, I gotta tell you everything I do?"

"No, Frank, it's just... it would be helpful. I made dinner four hours ago."

"Oh I'm sorry... am I not being 'helpful?' I was doin' my JOB, Kate... ya know... work, you mighta heard of it?"

Kate knew the wave of rage was swelling, but on that night, for whatever reason, she did not step out of the way.

"I am perfectly aware of what you do, Frank, and of course I know what work is."

"Do ya?"

"Of course I do," she paused, and then continued timidly, "I work around the house every day."

"Oh my gawd, please, you change that little shit's diaper a couple times and maybe, maybe do some laundry. Ah you fuckin' kiddin' me?"

"It's a bit more than that."

"Oh, I'm sorry, let's see... after watching some TV, you feed the kid some Cheerios and maybe wander around the grocery store."

Frank knew how to push her buttons, and he wanted nothing more than to upset her. Kate was furious inside but knew remaining calm was her best defense. She turned the other cheek. She just wanted things to calm down.

"I'll heat up a plate for you," she said and went back into the kitchen.

"Bitch," he mumbled, and then walked into the bedroom.

Kate quickly microwaved the supper and was pulling out the steamy plate as Frank marched into the kitchen.

"What the fuck is that?"

"It's dinner," she replied, looking down at the meatloaf and mashed potatoes on the dish.

"Well, it looks like shit on a plate."

"It's meatloaf, Frank… I don't know what to say."

"Ummm… I guess you could say, 'Sorry for making you a plate of shit after you worked all day.'"

Frank looked over at Kate, waiting for a reaction, but there was none.

"I lost the fuckin' Warner development bid today, can you say something about that? No, you can't, but you got no problem jumpin all over me like a cunt."

At that, Kate said nothing, but released the plate from her hand, dropping the dish on the hardwood floor with a crash, the hot food splattering onto Frank's legs.

"Oops," she said, knowing the rage wave was about to hit shore, but unaware how hard.

Frank moved to her faster than anything she'd ever seen. Like a wild animal, he sprung and snatched her hair, wrenching her neck and thrusting her backward. He'd thrown things at her and even punched the wall next to her, but he had never grabbed her. Kate stumbled, falling into the wall, and then it happened: Frank's open hand hauled back and violently slapped across her face. She felt a sting of pain as her skin lit hot and her eyes blinked to darkness. The momentum of the slap knocked her instantly to her right. She crashed to the floor and knocked a cabinet open as she collapsed in a daze. Kate's reality had been shattered in a way that could never be repaired. He had hit her.

6

Kate finished planting the bulbs and wiped her dirty hands off on her jeans, leaving dark smudges that made clear what she had just done. It was early October, and the yard was still awash with the faint purples and reds that dominated this season's painting.

She wore a thick, white-cotton shirt and red bandana that, with her blue jeans, matched the American flag that curled and occasionally snapped in a shifting breeze. The flag used to be her dad's and hung from a pole that jutted out from the porch pillar, as it had every summer since her mom gave it to her. She took it down every year when the first snowfall fell, folded it neatly and placed it in the trunk in the basement that also belonged to her father when he was in the navy. He used to call it a footlocker, and although its black-leather exterior was worn and torn in a spot, its brass rims and lock still glowed, and the blue- and white-striped interior looked brand-new. It was her place with her dad. Beside the flag, there were photos and a sort of yearbook from the naval ship he was assigned to, as well as a dark-blue wool blanket that smelled like mothballs. As she watched the slightly tattered and faded flag flutter, she knew she'd be bringing it to the basement soon.

As Kate walked slowly to the front gate and out to the mailbox, closely flanked by King, she paused, turning back towards the house she had spent the last thirteen years in with a son she loved dearly and a husband she feared deeply. A stoic colonial built in the 1800s, it was alleged to be a former ship captain's home, with a brick walkway that led straight up past the dense lawn to a wide porch flanked with two soaring pillars on either side that held the large, triangle-shaped dormer with a lead-glass half-moon window in its center. When facing the house from the sidewalk, the front door was off center to the right third, and beyond the porch to the right was a driveway leading to the detached garage and backyard. To the left of the front door stretched a twenty-six-foot-high and thirty-foot-long curved, white-shingled wall with four large windows, each guarded by tall, black wood shutters. The lawn sloped back to a smaller porch, with a second, smaller door and a single pillar supporting the overhung roof two floors above. A black lantern hung from a long, iron chain in the vaulted cover of that second porch. Despite the size of the house, it was only a few feet from the neighbor's driveway to the left. If they ever used the side door, which they didn't, they could walk out of their house, hop the fence, and be in their neighbor's house in twelve paces.

Kate stood on the sidewalk looking back at the place they lived. As she opened the door of the mailbox and retrieved the letters, she marveled at the view. She loved her house… and hated her home.

Instead of returning to the front door, Kate walked with King along the sidewalk and turned at the end of the fence. She made her way up the cement driveway to the door on the right side of the house that was most commonly used, as it was closest to the garage where Frank parked his truck every night. She plopped the bundle of mail on the step and collected her gardening tools to put them away.

Leaves were already starting to flutter down from trees, and soon the smell of autumn brush-burning would permeate the neighborhood. Kate loved that smell, and so did her son Anthony, who would be fifteen that winter. She bent down, scooped up the tools, and placed them in the basket. Sometimes she wore gloves to protect from the thistles and thorns of the roses and weeds, but mostly she loved the feel of the plants and dirt in her hands and on her skin. The moist earth and textured plants were a visceral part of the experience. She looked down at the now barren rectangle of soil and murmured "you're going to be so great," and a smile spread across her face.

It was 4:52, and Anthony would be home soon from school. He had soccer practice and would walk the quarter-mile home each day from the late-bus drop-off. Frank thought soccer was a sissy sport, and he called Anthony "Tony." Frank didn't know much about soccer because he had never been to a single game, but Anthony was fairly good at soccer, and the sport was becoming more popular each year.

He was also a talented artist: it was his true passion, and he would spend hours drawing everything from comic-strip figures to sketching stills of his mother's flowers. At school, most people called it doodling, but his art teacher Ms. Devoy encouraged him, having recognized his talent. Anthony shared very little of the artwork with Kate and had never shown any of his work to his father. It was a passion he hid in the cracks of life to hide the evidence.

Seeing Anthony walk up the street on days like this was often the best part of Kate's day. He would carry his books in a worn leather and canvas bag that his uncle Patrick had sent him one Christmas. Frank called it a pocketbook. Anthony had inherited his dad's swarthy skin and had big, white teeth that shone brightly when he smiled. He had emerald-green eyes, a dimpled chin, and was handsome like his younger father. He was, however, a quiet boy who tended to his studies and was not particularly social. It was rare that anyone would see his handsome smile. He did not have a girlfriend or regularly hang out with any group of boys, and in reality, he had just one friend at school.

Unlike the neighborhoods that Kate and Frank had grown up in, this small area of South Boston was an older demographic, and there weren't many kids. The Brunos lived in an historic area of the town, so while they were close to Boston and very much in the city, these were older people with a certain level of affluence. It was an above-average

25

neighborhood, and everybody had a nice car and a summer place on the Cape, or at least vacationed regularly on Nantucket or Martha's Vineyard. These were very much the well-educated, left-leaning, and successful brand of Bostonians who read the *Globe* and not the *Herald*. Frank hated every last one of them, but wouldn't trade his house on the hill for anything.

7

Kate knew that if it was 4:52, Frank would be home in thirty-eight minutes, and she could set her clock to it. Frank would pull out of the driveway at 5:30 a.m. and in at 5:30 p.m. In actuality, it used to be 5:00 p.m., but a certain neighbor with a similar penchant for keeping a structured calendar walked his two Yorkies up and down the block looking for some neighborly conversation every single day at 5:00 p.m. sharp.

His name was Walter—"call me Wally"—Heaney and he had a tendency to catch Frank rolling into the driveway, and Wally would attempt to engage in some light banter. This was a fate worse than death for Frank Bruno, to have to sit and listen to someone and not be able to control the situation. When confronted with a potential conversation with Heaney, Frank would streak up the driveway and into the garage to avoid it. But the stretch from the garage to the side door was an opening, and nine times out of ten, Wally would be just at the end of the driveway poised to shout out a "hello," make small talk, or ask for advice on building something.

Frank complained about Heaney constantly.

"I swea-ya I am gonna run that fuckin' jerk-off down some night," he would tell Kate. "Him and those useless dogs in their queer little jackets," he continued.

27

"C'mon Frank, he's harmless. At least Mr. Heaney means well," she replied trying to diffuse the situation. "He is our neighborhood watch," she joked, trying to lighten the mood. "He saved Mrs. Thomas last year!"

"Yeah, and she'll probably drop dead this winter because she never takes her diabetic shots. Next time that creep won't be hidin' in the bushes," he said, walking away.

"Never a nice word," Kate thought to herself.

Eventually Frank got so sick of Heaney that he parked down the street for a couple days and timed Wally's walks. Heaney and his Yorkies wrapped things up, conversation or not, in roughly twenty-five minutes each day and disappeared back into his big, red home up the street. By shifting to a 5:30 arrival, Frank could avoid running into the pesky neighbor. The extra thirty minutes did mean that Frank had to alter his schedule and move some kind of home activity to work, so he began to do some of the bills at the office.

Wally Heaney didn't bother Kate at all, and she would often chat with him when he strolled by on his morning walk, which kicked off at 10:00 a.m. sharp.

"How are the kids?" Kate would joke to Wally.

"Just livin' the dream, Katie," he'd say with a smile, often wandering over to chat.

She felt he was harmless and probably just bored. He seemed to know something about everyone in the neighborhood, and almost always started a sentence with "Well, I heard…." To Kate, he was just part of the neighborhood's mosaic, and her commitment to Wally was pretty undemanding.

Her wristwatch read 4:57, and as expected, Anthony ambled up the driveway and flashed a smile to his mom as she closed the garage's side door and grabbed the mail off the step.

"Hi, Sweetie," she said.

"Hi, Mom," he replied, with a bit of a sigh.

"How was school?"

"It was what it always is," he said with a wry smile and looked down at the evidence of gardening on her hands and jeans. "You finish planting?"

"Almost," she said, grinning back at him.

"Are you doing more perennials or annuals this year?" he asked.

"Yeah… ah…Well, it will be a good mix," Kate revealed, "but I am really excited about what the spring will look like. This may be my best arrangement yet."

"That's cool… I'm happy for you, Ma!" he said honestly, but trailed off into an awkward silence as Kate looked long and hard at her only child.

Anthony seemed to sink swiftly into another place.

"What's going on up there, kiddo?" she said, pointing to his head.

"Nothing, why?" he asked, perking up and slightly defensive.

He shifted his book bag to the opposite shoulder and brushed back his hair with his hand.

"Doesn't seem to be 'nothing,'" she pressed a bit.

"Yeah well… you're not Columbo, Ma, even if you think you are!" said Anthony, who slipped past her, raising his voice slightly as he disappeared inside.

"You see, Mrs. Bruno, there is one thing that doesn't make sense," said Anthony, from the mud room, in his best Columbo impersonation.

Kate did like the TV character Columbo. She also read Agatha Christie novels and loved to watch *The Rockford Files* and *Ellery Queen* as a young girl. There was just something about trying to solve the mystery before the rest of the audience. In fact, one of her only real friends in the world was an elderly woman named Vida Mudgett, a novelist who lived five houses up.

Vida Mudgett wrote the Daisy McQueen series about a young female private investigator with a dizzying intellect, who cracked all the unsolved cases the cops were flabbergasted by. Mudgett was an eighty-two-year-old, eccentric bird, and while her books weren't best sellers, she had a real following and wrote the most creative stories Kate had ever read. In fact, she had read every book Vida Mudgett published in the Daisy McQueen series. Anthony's mention of Columbo made Kate think of Vida, and she felt another grin coming as she glanced at her wristwatch… Twenty-eight minutes, she thought, as the grin promptly retreated.

"Better get to dinner," she whispered to herself.

29

8

At five-thirty on the nose, Frank's hefty truck streaked up the driveway and pulled into the garage. After the usual opening and closing of doors, in he came. He was his gruff, typical self.

"What's for suppa?"

"I am just getting started, but I have the roast from Sunday to reheat."

"Yeah that's great," he said, opening the refrigerator and leaning in. "I love leftovers after I work twelve hours."

Kate thought to defend that she had good corn and red potatoes as well, but Frank jumped back in before she could slip a word in edgewise. He seemed particularly irritable.

"What is it you do all day?" he asked with a consciously demeaning tone as he flipped through the day's mail that Kate had left on the counter. He would open each letter, sort them by perceived importance, remove the bill portion, and fold it inside the return envelope. She didn't need to watch; he did it every day, and even the sound of the crinkling paper made her head hurt.

Kate said nothing but glared at the reflection of them both in the window over the sink, her hands scrubbing the potatoes with a wire brush. She did not respond to this verbal grenade, despite it being one of the most knowingly harmful in his arsenal. Calling her an idiot or bitch was fairly standard flack, but it tended to glance off because it was baseless, but "what do you do all day?" indicated that she was aimless and frivolous. It reminded her that in the scheme of things, she probably hadn't done that much, and she certainly hadn't done all she wished she had.

Some couples have hot and cold relationships: they argue explosively then make up as the pendulum swings. Others seemed to have a general dislike for each other, but co-exist, having capitulated to their places in life. Still others seem generally to care for one another, and though the romance may have dimmed, the respect and love remains. Kate and Frank had arguably migrated through the first two, and definitely never landed in the third. They instead fell into a category of complete disdain, so that even the presence of the child whose DNA they shared could not inoculate the venom. As she picked up the potato peeler, he continued on.

"Well, I guess I gotta wait for at least another hour to eat, so I will go starve in the basement. Long days out there Kate… long days," he said, pausing at the staircase at the corner of the kitchen that led to the basement.

Frank's words assailed her as he went on, doing all he could to make her feel less of herself. The skin of the potato flinging off the peeler and clinging to the walls of the white kitchen sink. She was only peeling them because Frank didn't like the skin and insisted they be peeled and either steamed, baked, or mashed. With each word he said and each peel she stroked, she pushed the metallic tool with more force, slicing deeper into the fleshy white potato and flicking off thicker slabs. He didn't like the black spots of the potatoes either, so she would stop and take the sharper-curved tip of the tool and jab it in, carving deftly around the brown-black blot that was called an eye but was really a sprig of growth from what was essentially a seed or placenta. She flicked the blemished patch in amongst the peels.

"I don't just sit around in the yard diggin' shit up and moving it around. I actually do work."

"Yeah I know… Frank."

"Oh you know? OK, well it's Tuesday… you know that?"

Kate did know that. She knew the Tuesday night ritual was beginning as scheduled.

"I'll be downstairs," he said as his boots clomped down the wooden stairs to the basement.

Frank had mentioned it was Tuesday, and this was not insignificant. Each day and night had its purpose; Monday evenings were spent in the study crunching the numbers for work and organizing the week. Frank generally went to bed before 9:00 p.m. and rose before 5:00 a.m., so two hours of work after consuming a meal, and he was off to sleep.

On Tuesdays, he indulged in a personal pursuit when he descended to the basement to spend time with his collection of firearms. According to Frank, they were all registered and legal and, outside of the compact .22 he carried in a fanny pack to jobsites, they never left the house. He wasn't a hunter, and instead referred to himself as a collector. He was a secretive man, so it was not like his hobby would come up at cocktail parties, should they ever actually attend one. It was just something he spent time on every Tuesday evening.

Kate was not too sure what he actually did with the guns every Tuesday, but Anthony had once sat in and reported that: "He just took them apart, wiped them with a diaper, oiled a couple things, and put all the pieces back together."

Anthony dared to pick up the chrome-plated .45 that Frank claimed was a collector's edition and worth several thousand dollars. He promptly made Anthony feel like an idiot for touching it and emasculated him with a barrage of insults.

"Be careful will ya, and don't put your grimy hands on things you don't understand… I don't need someone accidently getting shot!"

Anthony had enough after one go-round and never joined his father again for Tuesday night.

Wednesday night was just like Monday night because payroll was completed that day, but Thursday evolved over the years from bowling or softball night into "I'm just goin' out" night. Friday nights were always out with the guys. Saturday night he stayed in and watched some TV or a movie, and this was the night Kate got to "enjoy" Frank's company. At least, that was the way he viewed it. On a very rare occasion, they would head out for a movie or dinner.

Kate suspected that within the last two or three years, Thursday and Friday nights weren't with the guys at all. In fact, there were no guys. On occasion, Frank would have drinks with his boss or other tradespeople if he was angling a deal, and on even rarer occasions, he would hit the town with one or both of his younger brothers. Leo was divorced, and Lenny liked to brag that he had never been caught. Kate had suspected there was another woman, and even considered leaving Frank. She knew he was not a good husband and it didn't take Columbo to sort out the clues.

Franks Routines Become

OCD

Then So Rigid.

He wasn't Human

9

Anthony often sat in his room alone and was nearly always drawing or sketching something. He was only fourteen years old and already soured on life. In his mind, his father was a stranger, and his school was a bland mix of people he did not wish to be... or be around. He had no siblings and no close friends to speak of. Even his extended family was dreadful to him. His dad's brothers were knuckle draggers who worked dead-end jobs, were disrespectful to women, and giggled like children at racist or gay jokes. His aunts had married even more devolved versions of his uncles, and they liked to sit around and get fat every Sunday while they fawned over each other and condescended to everyone else on the planet. Worst of all, his grandma and grandpa just ignored him.

Most of his mom's family was dead, and her only brother Patrick, who he liked the times he had seen him, had moved to New York City a long time ago and became some "big shot" in the fashion world. Uncle Pat always sent really cool gifts for his birthday and Christmas, and they exchanged letters now and again, but he never seemed to visit. There was his mother, of course, and he loved her with all his heart. But if he was sour on life... he figured she should be bitter.

a frame for flowers

Anthony looked ahead to a time when he could be away from his father. He didn't know where or even when, perhaps not until college, but he could sense that place perfectly. A place not so much filled with joy per se, but absent of misery.

10

Frank and Kate belonged to the two factions that dominated the Greater Boston area for decades. Frank was Italian, and Kate was Irish. The Italians owned the North End, and the Irish owned Southie. Italians had delicious restaurants and bakeries, and the Irish had fun-loving pubs. There was the straight-up Cosa Nostra mob that controlled Rhode Island and much of Boston, and then there was the Whitey Bulger-style Irish mob that controlled a lot of neighborhoods around Boston and owned the streets of Southie. It is not to say either or both of these cultures had a penchant for criminal activity: to the contrary, these were mostly hardworking folks who were busy carving out their slice of the American dream, but both the Irish and Italians had a distinct criminal element who any street-wise Bostonian could differentiate on sight. The entire eco-system for these heritages ran deep in the communities in and around Boston. They made up a huge, blue-collar workforce that included the fire and police departments, and they were an esoteric band dominated by males. These two teams were willing to coexist and even at times coalesce because, for the most part, they were all Catholics.

Kate's dad Teddy Kelley was a good cop, and although he never discharged his weapon in the line of duty, he put a lot of bad guys behind bars.

"That's justice!" he used to tell his kids. "The bad guys always get it in the end!"

He died of a heart attack on the beat when she was just eleven years old, and from then on, the word *justice* rang hollow. A lifelong smoker, her mom passed away from cancer six days after her eighteenth birthday. Both of these events were devastating to Kate and Patrick. Teddy and Moira Kelley were old-school Irish with Gaelic sayings and blessings pinned up throughout their humble one-floor, three-bedroom home. A brass letter sign hung above the thick oak door that read: *Cead me Failte*—or a hundred thousand welcomes, and their door knocker was the omnipresent two hands clasping a heart surmounted with a crown symbol, known as a Claddagh.

The Irish held up to many of the stereotypes: hardworking, hard-drinking, salt-of-the-earth folk who were fiercely loyal and prone to martyrdom. They lived by perhaps paradoxical tenets: often gregarious and joyful, yet just as likely to be pensive and surreptitious. Don't be a bother to people, but if you bother us, look out.

The Italians were much different. I love you unless I don't know you, and then I'm not too sure about you. They ate more, and they drank less. They fought just as much and were tough and strong, often more athletic than their Irish counterparts, but they could be Momma's boys and vain. Italians were music, and Irish were dance. Italians were meals, and Irish were libations. Italians were gifts, and Irish were toasts. Hard-grinding America where the good was celebrated and the bad was repressed, where the guilt of knowing you were not living in God's image was what made you restless and angry… or drove you to the drink.

11

The following day was Wednesday, so Frank left at 5:30 a.m. and got home at 5:30 p.m., but Anthony didn't get home until nearly 6:00 p.m. That day was different for Anthony. For no apparent reason that he could understand, a school punk named Mark Angus had challenged him to a fight. He had been in gym class with the kid, but had never spoken a word to him, good or bad. They accidently collided in the hall, and that quickly, like being stricken with a disease, he had to deal with it. Angus challenged him to fight.

As the day was nearing its end, Anthony meandered down the cinder-block halls of school, his eyes locked on the gray floor. Square, square, square, rectangle: the pattern slowing with his gait. Black scuff marks from Anthony's work boots interrupted the floor's pattern with statement. If there was to be a fight, he knew all of the stoners and outcasts would be there. Sometimes they talked to Anthony because he was a loner, and there is a loose bond amongst the outliers.

The bell rang with disappointing accuracy, and Anthony's stomach began to twitch as the sound found his ears. A fight was a big deal, and throughout the day, kids in the hall had turned to whisper, while others spoke right at him. Still others shouted encouragement or jabs, the words bounding off the hollow, concrete walls.

a frame for flowers

"You betta show up, Bruno!"

"Don't be a pussy," they taunted.

School fights were an event, a gladiator-match-at-the-forum. These were rather puny gladiators, but school fights were a thrill, and every one provided a chance for greatness. Sometimes a kid's popularity could shift in an instant. When someone proves to be strong or tough in a way they were not considered to be before, it can change their life. Peter Miller was the only friend Anthony had. Miller was a scraggly kid who was picked on because he was smart and slight of frame… and because it was easy. Peter met him at the outer door as he often did where he encouraged Anthony to leave and go home, or at least tell a teacher.

"You don't have to fight, Anthony. Mark Angus is a bully and in trouble with the cops all the time. Let him pick a fight with someone else." Peter went on, nervously clutching his textbooks as he scurried to keep up with Anthony, who walked with conviction.

"This is just dumb is all. Fighting is dumb, makes no sense, and people always get hurt. Nobody wins a fight, you know, that's what my dad says… nobody really wins. Just go to the principal or Mr. Roberts, and they'll put a stop to this!"

Anthony didn't acknowledge Peter and steered through the migrating crowd like an ambulance. *Let's just get it over with,* he thought to himself as the saliva in his mouth vanished.

The quicker the better, win or lose. Let's just get it over with. I can beat this guy. Let's just get it over with, he told himself.

"Are you even listening to me? You don't have to do this, Anthony," Peter implored, as it seemed apparent he was marching right towards the conflict. "You don't have to fight!"

The asphalt turned to grass, which turned to dirt, as he trudged across the parking lot behind the V.F.W. that stood dilapidated and adjacent to the junior high. Dirt filled the air with each step as the forming mob of excited teenagers kicked up puffs of dust. There was a short climb up the hill, then a hundred feet of woods to the logs, to the spot. Everyone fought at the Logs. There were long-ago cut-down

39

trees laid out like walls of a makeshift arena cleared for combat. The thick trunks looked like benches, but people rarely sat. These events were standing-room only. Anthony had been to a fight as a spectator once but had never gotten very close to the action. He swallowed hard and looked up the hill as Peter tried one last gasp.

"Anthony, please… you're going to get hurt."

And with those words, Anthony stopped, turned to Peter, and finally spoke.

"Hurt? Fighting doesn't hurt. Getting punched doesn't hurt. You know what hurts?" he asked, drilling into Peter with his eyes.

"Being a coward hurts. Being invisible hurts. Not standing up for yourself… hurts. You can watch or run and tell or just go home, Peter, but don't tell me about being hurt."

Peter stopped as Anthony marched on, the dust swirling up and around his skinny schoolmate. "You don't have to do this, Anthony," Peter called from behind.

Anthony smiled slightly, looking back as Peter disappeared in the dust. "Sometimes you do," he said softly in return.

The sounds of those around him, salivating for the impending violence, became suddenly muffled. The dust in his nose settled down his throat to his tongue, and the taste of dirt became irrelevant. The sights, swatches of color, faces, fall jackets, all became a blurred canvas and the trees that loomed above obscured the autumn sun. His heart raced and squeezed up into his neck, swollen and constricting. His hands clenched, knuckles whitening. He would become conscious of it and release. Clench, think and release. His teeth clamped down, grinding dust into the enamel.

Although he did not know why, Mark Angus was the enemy. "He started this," Anthony told himself.

It may have been a fight-or-flight instinct, but suddenly Anthony realized he was going to miss (or at least be late) for soccer practice. He didn't play that much, and no one would likely notice his absence, but at that moment he was almost convinced he needed to turn back. Like sitting on the table awaiting an operation and thinking, *I could die. This isn't worth it, and I can live with the alternative.* But somehow he pressed forward.

Angus was there and looking confident. There were lots of eighth-graders, and one of them who Anthony recognized as a popular stoner nicknamed Chewy became the self-appointed emcee of the event. Chewy was a bit of a legend, and he quickly took charge of the anxious crowd. Chewy explained the rules: no biting, no scratching, and *no* quitting. Chewy was an experienced "hood" who knew the time constraints. The principal—if not police—response time was twenty to twenty-five minutes, so Chewy hustled the combatants into position. It was happening before Anthony had time to reconsider. At that moment in time, the world didn't just slow down, it stopped.

All he could see was Mark's thin face and awkward teeth, and he noticed for the first time the boy's blue eyes beneath his short-cropped dishwater hair. Mark's clothes were faded and unclean. His skin was oily from puberty, and his fingernails were dirty. Behind his eyes was a rage, but that didn't frighten Anthony; he'd faced that before.

Chewy gave the word, and against all expectations, Anthony struck first, lunging headlong into the boy's midsection. The thrust of the impact shot Angus back on his heels, toppling them both to the ground. Angus reached back to break his fall and was met with a pointed tree stump that sliced into his hand. He yelped in pain, and the sound frightened Anthony, who immediately released and backed off, despite the no-quitting rule. Chewy oddly called for a time-out and allowed Angus to check his wound and regroup. Impressively, the boy, wincing in pain and bleeding from his hand, regained composure and signaled he was ready to continue.

With a moment to think, Anthony once more considered flight as an option, but in a blink the fight was happening again. This time it was Angus barreling into Anthony. The attack was swift, but Anthony was quick on his feet and buffeted the advance with stiff arms, dropping Angus to his knees. The boy appeared confused as he climbed to his feet and backed away, but just like that, he tilted his head and charged again. This time Anthony countered his charge with a sidestep that sent Angus stumbling past and flailing to the dirt. The boy whipped around with a blue-eyed glare and nostrils flared. He dropped into a stance and charged once more. Anthony again stepped sideways, and this time took the opportunity to shoot a punch to the back of the other boy's head, which caused Angus to stumble and fall face-first into the soil.

This is easy, thought Anthony.

A now-enraged Mark Angus scrambled forward until he clutched and climbed Anthony, who fired off several punches that landed flush with Mark's reddened cheeks. He felt his knuckles impacting cheekbones, eyes, and teeth, culminating with a crack shot to the bridge of Mark's nose that burst red on contact. Upon that, Chewy quickly intervened. This was in no way what they had expected, and although the crowd roared with excitement at the sight of blood, one-sided fights were boring. Angus was once more granted a time-out.

The sun was back, and Anthony could suddenly breathe clear. The taste of dirt was rotten, but the taste of victory was intoxicating. He felt the blood flowing into his hands and fingers.

This is what it's like to win, he thought to himself, but as he was savoring the moment, the battle was called back on.

Angus looked unfazed and again approached fists up and poised, his nose streaming blood that gathered in the cracks of his lips and mixed with dust. It seemed Chewy had provided some tips in an effort to sway the tide. A comeback is the best kind of match. However, it wasn't to be.

Anthony continued to dominate the fight, despite Chewy seemingly stretching the rules to favor Angus. He was confused and elated all at once. When was it over? He anticipated it to be broken up by authorities, but no principal or policeman materialized. It appeared to Anthony that despite being bloodied and beaten, Angus would never quit, and the battle went on for nearly thirty minutes. Anthony found himself hoping someone would have the sense to break it up, yet no one did. Exhausted and tired of punching his enemy, Anthony announced: "I'm done… it's over," and turned and walked down the hill as quickly as he'd scaled it.

He left feeling good about the fight, that he had been vindicated and beat up the kid who started it. He left confident that an upgrade in social status had occurred.

It would not be the case.

The next day he appeared more of a pariah than ever. Anthony had broken the no-quitting rule, and it would turn out to trump beating the crap out of your opponent. To his astonishment, he was dubbed a chicken, and in the halls, he heard again and again that he had "wimped out" and "went home crying." It wasn't true, but it didn't matter. He was on the outside and was destined to stay there. Peter's warning had proven true: nobody wins a fight.

None of it mattered though, because Anthony now knew something that trumped it all. He was tough enough to fight back.

12

Kate had first met Vida Mudgett about ten or so years before, although she only started helping her seven years back after Vida broke her hip at the ripe age of seventy-five. She fell down trying to shovel her driveway and wasn't as mobile afterward. Although her mind remained as sharp as a bee sting, her ability to get around had become painful and restricted. Mrs. Mudgett hadn't taken well to the nurses she had hired and had chased a half dozen of them off. It was a slow evolution, but eventually Kate's help here and there turned into a quiet agreement. She looked after Vida a couple of hours, most days of the week.

Vida owned the oldest, nicest, and biggest house on the hill, and Kate—along with everyone else—knew it. It was obscenely oversized for an eighty-two-year-old widow, but to know Vida was to understand.

"It's my house, and I ain't leavin'."

Vida was a big fan of Kate's landscape creations and often took the labored walk over to ask for advice on how to plant tulips or alter the color of chrysanthemum blooms. They developed a real rapport, and Kate found her fascinating.

Before Vida began her writing career, she had been married to successful businessman. He had been a rag-to-riches story, and she had

44

ridden shotgun the whole way. Vida was a creative woman and had helped Hank Mudgett turn a small hardware business into a booming tool and dye company over their forty-two years of marriage. She had considerable money and assets before she had ever taken pen to paper and stowed away more wealth in the twenty-one years of writing the Daisy McQueen series since Hank had left her. No one but Vida, her lawyer, and her accountant knew exactly how much money she had, but everyone knew it was a lot. Frank had been trying to suck up to Vida for years because he knew she had lots of money. He had no idea how deep the relationship between his wife and Ms. Mudgett ran, and that was fortunate, because he certainly would have sought to manipulate it. Vida didn't tell Kate in so many words… but she found Frank to be repugnant.

Vida hadn't even begun writing until she found herself alone in the world. She and Hank had no children, and he had been her life. They had been very active in the community and gave large sums of money to charities.

When she was alone in her spacious house, her imagination would wander through it, and she filled the empty rooms with characters both good and evil. She was angry that Hank had left her. She was probably angrier at God that she had so greatly outlived her beloved husband, but she'd never muttered a word about it. Instead she wove it through the twisted mysteries that Daisy McQueen could somehow always solve.

13

The nights of fall repeated themselves like the reruns on TV56, stumbling aimlessly but relentlessly towards winter. At the Bruno house, each night there were the timed arrivals, the predicted schedules, a slightly varied hot meal, and a noticeably colder Atlantic wind that tested the white shingles. Kate's backyard oasis got less colorful as plants retreated to the soil and trees to branches, the thick sod becoming thinner and harder with every passing day. Each winter, the bark of the trees seemed to shrivel in the icy wind that tapped at drafty windows and made her house groan.

As the days grew shorter and the temperatures slipped, Anthony became more withdrawn, the pale sky ebbing with his summer skin. Each night he seemed more alone, and Kate made a promise most days that she would talk to him or be more engaged.

"Come here a minute," she called to Anthony after supper as he was washing off his plate and placing it into the dishwasher.

"What?" he inquired.

"Nothing… just come sit with me for a minute," she begged.

"Mom, I got homework,"

"It'll wait… and besides. You're not actually rushing off to do homework!" She laughed out loud, and his smile acknowledged he was guilty as charged.

"Yeah, I know."

"Don't leave me alone with King and his bad gas… sit with me, will ya?"

"Yeah ma… sorry. What's up?" he asked, as she realized she didn't know what to say. She just knew that she wanted him next to her. There were actually so many things she wanted to say to him, to explain. But instead she sat there running her fingers through his hair as if he were a child. After a minute or two, he fidgeted.

"Okay, good talkin' to you, Ma," he said and rose quickly from the table.

He stopped just at the doorway of the kitchen… "I love you, Mom." And she was suddenly whole.

A parent-teacher night at school was coming in two weeks. That would make a good opportunity for interaction, she thought, as she watched him slough away from the dinner table to drift upstairs. She rose from the kitchen table slowly, with the faint sounds below of Frank cursing at his Tuesday night gun fondling or Wednesday night paperwork or whatever day it actually was.

She walked over to the pantry, its smell reminding her of being a girl and of the tasty sandwiches her grandmother would make. She stopped just inside… leaving the light off and turning around to face outward. She stood in front of a calendar that had pictures of different kinds of power tools being held by some different pretty girl each month. It hung from a painter's nail just inside the entrance to the pantry, and there was a thin pencil tied to a string that dangled beside it. Frank used it to keep track of certain things. There was another calendar in his office, and still another in the basement workshop, and each had some sort of role in his organization that she couldn't comprehend. This was the only one she was allowed to utilize. She snatched up the pencil and circled the date of the school event on the calendar.

"I am going to make that a special night," she whispered.

Kate cleared the table, gathering the silverware as she brushed crumbs onto the dirty, stacked plates. Dinner appeared to have been

47

acceptable: a peppered steak done medium well, green beans, and mashed potatoes. There was just a little meat left, and after a quick look around, Kate threw it to King, who promptly took it to the other room. There were only smatterings of green beans left, so she funneled them down the disposal and began to wash the plates.

Kate could see the driveway from the kitchen sink and some of the backyard from the pantry. Perhaps influenced by Frank or just an attempt to feel purpose, Kate had created some of her own rituals. They were more like small games. One such game was the way she tried to prepare dinner faster night after night. She would move swiftly from spot to spot, trying to execute her steps quicker; sink, stove, pantry, and table. It was like the spaces on a Monopoly board, or perhaps more appropriately the game Life. The clock on the wall was her scoreboard that ticked down to Frank's arrival each night. In her mind, it was more like prayer than a game. It became the repeated process to remind her of life and duty, the life she endured for her son.

She could drift off in the pantry but for a moment... imagining the flowers, or reliving images of her young boy, joyously searching for Easter eggs in and amongst the colors. But then she scooted across the hardwood floor to steal a glance out the kitchen sink window, anxiously timing his arrival. Quick then to the table to place the forks, then back to the pantry, pause by the stove, stir, quick to the window (nothing to wash), and then she scurried back to the pantry for nothing forgotten.

It was a small window in the pantry, but one with a view, and even in the winter it brought solace. From the sink again, Kate looked out the larger window to see light flakes of snow floating down, and it was the first they'd seen. Tomorrow I will take down dad's flag, she thought to herself, checking each pot for progress. She had never told Frank about the importance of the flag; it was her own secret.

14

As Kate stared at the white flakes cast against the black of night, she felt a chill. It was not from the cold air, but from a chilling memory. Lots of people have secrets. In fact, pretty much everyone does. It is just a question of how dark those secrets are. Frank Bruno had a real dark secret: he had killed someone.

15

From the porch steps of his red Victorian, Walter Heaney could see Frank pulling into the driveway. He knew only too well what type of man Frank Bruno was, with his bellicose nature and his obvious effort to avoid interaction. He also knew how he treated his wife and son. Guys like Frank had never associated with Wally, and though Wally would never turn down the chance to try and converse with someone, he wasn't fooled by Frank's shift in schedule.

Walter Heaney had grown up in a nondescript town just north of New Hampshire's most populated city, Manchester. He was the smartest kid in his albeit small graduating class, and although he took some razzing, he had won the state science fair three times and was a bit of a celebrity in those parts. When Walter was a boy, he didn't want to be an astronaut, he wanted to be one of the guys with the short-sleeve white shirts and thin, black ties with matching black rim glasses. They all wore headphones curled over their crew cuts and seemed to smoke a lot of cigarettes. They also seemed to be intellectual: well-versed in physics and engineering. Walter told his parents for years he wanted to be an engineer, and as graduation drew closer, the Massachusetts Institute of Technology seemed like the right place for him. He had read as much as he could about NASA engineers, and it seemed like they all went to MIT. He had perfect grades and a near-perfect SAT score, so MIT happily opened its gates and let young Walter Heaney in. He showed up on the first day like he was reporting to a desk at NASA, minus the cigarettes.

Walter found the work to be challenging and interesting but felt a complete lack of camaraderie with his fellow students. It seemed to him that the NASA guys were buddies taking on the world, but MIT felt like an ocean of individuals vying for the top grade. What he had read failed to mention that the work necessary to achieve such a career was terrifically hard and chronically tedious. It wasn't like the work was over his head. Walter was one of the brightest students at MIT, and his understanding of quantum physics impressed even the faculty. The truth was... he was bored.

Walter spent his downtime (which was generally the short span after studying and before sleep) walking around the dorms trying to talk to people. He quickly realized this was not exactly a gregarious crowd, so he began to interview people, telling them it was for a story in the MIT school newspaper, *The Tech*. This tactic got them to open up, and he learned all kinds of fascinating things about these tremendously bright people. Not just how smart they were, but where they grew up and what it was like there. What kind of people their parents were and how their educations had impacted their development. He learned bits of different languages, was exposed to new art and music, and practiced foreign dialects to perfection. More than anything, Walter frequently got his fellow student to relax—and sometimes even laugh.

Eventually people started to get suspicious when no stories actually materialized, so Walter did the only thing he felt prudent: he joined *The Tech* staff as a cub reporter. He wrote for the campus paper every year he was there and was granted his own column in his junior year under the byline "Wally the Wonk". Walter Heaney was known as Wally from then on.

After graduating from MIT, he did not become a NASA engineer as the race to the moon peaked right after his graduation and slowly lost steam. Instead, Wally spent the majority of his thirty-five-year working life as a successful newspaper reporter and then editor. He later went on to spend several years as a professor, teaching younger folks how to get to the story. He was a very keen observer.

Wally knew Frank Bruno loved to dodge him, and it was a running joke between him and his Yorkies. "Here he comes... watch this. Will you two stop sniffing the ground for a second and watch this? I am like human repellant to this guy."

He giggled as he scurried toward the white fence that bordered the Brunos' gorgeous yard. He would wave frantically like someone floating on a raft that had finally been located by the Coast Guard.

"There he goes speeding into driveway... Someday he is going to do himself in on that fence," Wally said to the Yorkies.

Wally had noted some months ago that Bruno's familiar truck was parked just out of reach down the block from his typical turnaround spot. He had chuckled to himself, knowing full well what that time-obsessed, angry, and petty man was up to.

He told the dogs, "We got a tail, kids. The moron is on a stakeout!"

Wally knew Frank was trying to figure out how he could avoid running into him, and he had even thought about shifting his dog-walking time as well, just to annoy the bellicose man.... But why bother?

Wally named his dogs Byron and Shelley, but unlike the authors themselves, the Yorkies were a boy and girl. He thought it was funny, although few seemed to understand the humor. He would've preferred to have gotten a larger breed, but they could have been too much to handle with his duties and the little Yorkies just seemed practical. His wife Grace had grown increasingly ill with Parkinson's disease over the last five years, and Wally spent much of his day tending to her or quietly reading. They didn't own a TV, and the twice-a-day walks with Byron and Shelley allowed him to not only get a break from the home and exercise the Yorkies, but also to take in the seemingly endless soap opera in the neighborhood. You see, Wally didn't need a TV. This was reality TV, long before the concept existed.

From the loud conversations drifting out through screen doors on warm summer days to the silhouettes that filled the windows on winter evenings, Wally took it all in. While many viewed him as a nosy neighbor, he thought of himself as the central repository of information and purveyor of insight for the drama and challenges of their community. He would only pick up snippets, but enjoyed taping together the storylines by extrapolating the missing pieces. He was careful who to share what with, as some folks just couldn't seem to contain anything.

The neighborhood had its moods that seemed to hinge on the seasons or economic climate, as well as the political cycle. Certain evenings there was an operatic harmony, as perhaps a Red Sox game cascaded out from successive homes, and Wally could catch an entire inning walking up and down the blocks. It was like walking back from the concessions at an old-style drive-in theater with the volume of dialogue rising and falling with each passing speaker.

Some evenings, he would traipse across a real nugget of conversation or argument, and have to pretend the dogs were stopped to do their business so he could take it all in. There were clashes unfolding in living rooms and kitchens ranging from financial strife to infidelity, from falling grades to failing marriages, from lost jobs to big promotions, from elation to despair. He, of course, was not invisible, so most of the neighborhood was cautious not to air the laundry too vocally, in the proximity of open doors and windows. At times, he was privy to noisy lovemaking or people in various states of undress, but the fact was Wally derived no increased thrill from any such observation. To him it was just part of the story. He was a reporter, and this was his beat.

The previous winter, Wally assisted a woman who was having a diabetic episode in her car in the driveway, and he likely saved her life. In addition, some three years back he helped authorities nab a cat burglar who had broken into several of the neighborhood homes, so that bought him some breathing room. Even to his biggest detractors, Wally had his moments.

16

Kate made her way across town to Dr. Marchand for a standard check-up. She stayed in shape, ate healthy, and would jog regularly when the weather was tolerable. She had been going to Dr. Marchand since high school and had to drive a bit out of the way to his office, but he was comfortable and familiar, so she stayed with him. Kate drove a gray, older-model Volvo station wagon. It was very reliable and handled well in the snow, so she just kept driving it. Frank called it a tree hugger's car.

Dr. Marchand's office was a first-floor office, accessed via a parking lot behind the building. It was a very basic office. The waiting room was wood-paneled with a small, framed opening that led back to an office area. There was a sharp contrast between the dull brown walls of the waiting room and the nearly translucent white walls beyond a sliding-glass pane that made the opening appear like a window. A sliding-glass pane that had likely never been closed. The central focal point of the room was a glowing aquarium with neon-blue gravel and a few goldfish. There was a bland mustard couch with stiff, square cushions and a series of similarly blasé orange chairs. Kate could recall her brother Patrick pretending to stick his fingers down his throat and vomit while pointing to the very same furniture many years earlier.

a frame for flowers

Behind the sliding-glass opening sat a couple of ladies who dressed like nurses but were actually just office clerks. Dr. Marchand shared the office with another doctor who Kate had to see once when she had strep throat and Dr. Marchand was on vacation. She couldn't recall his name.

Despite having visited dozens of times over the years, Kate filled out a similar clipboard with a long series of nos. She did, however, report some unusual things. Although she felt it was probably nothing, Kate had been experiencing some soreness on and around her nipples and even noticed a strange discharge, as if she were lactating. She was pretty darn sure she wasn't pregnant. She and Frank had not had sex in quite some time, and she was on the pill, even if they had. She jotted down "soreness around the nipples" on the chart.

Dr. Marchand was a lifelong New Englander. He grew up in Western Massachusetts, went to college, med school, and did his residency all in Boston. He had briefly considered being a surgeon, but his grades, timing, and the cost of school just found him more suited as a general practitioner. Thomas Marchand, M.D. was a gentle soul who lived a fairly simple life, but he had many people he called friends and had built up a good client base, as well as a referral network to specialists that paid him pretty well. He had a nice brick house in Brookline, a solid nest egg, and his kids were getting a good education, so he was content with his place in life. Dr. Marchand's father was also a general practice physician, although he had long since retired. Marchand Senior had been Kate's mom's family doctor.

A woman in scrubs called Kate's name, and she made her way to the door adjacent to the sliding-glass window. The woman said hello, but never made eye contact as she led Kate back down the bland hallway. The stopped at a scale where the assistant proceeded to take Kate's weight and check her height.

"Weight is good, a few pounds lighter actually... so good for you skinny-minny!" said the woman with half of a smile.

Kate was pleasantly surprised, as she felt like she had been slacking off on exercising lately.

They walked a bit further and into one of the three observation rooms that all looked the same. She asked Kate to slip into a robe, then turned and walked out. Kate slowly undressed, removing her shirt over her head and knocking her hair out of the makeshift ponytail she had thrown in that morning, her blonde locks falling down just short of firm and muscled shoulders.

She glanced at the door as she unclasped her bra and removed it, quickly pulling on the thin, light-blue cloak that provided neither warmth nor privacy. She reached back and tied one of the twin strings that closed up the garment, removed her jeans, and sat at the edge of the examining table. With her feet dangling below, she noticed she had left her socks on and thought about taking them off, then decided it was of no consequence.

The examining table was cold with its shiny, fake leather cover and thin, antiseptic-white paper draped over it that was dispensed from a large reel resembling a gift wrapping station at the mall. On the wall were diagrams and pictures of the inner ear or digestive tract, as well as the balanced-diet pyramid she remembered from high school.

"I guess that hasn't changed," she whispered to herself.

Kate sat at the foot of the examining table facing a rack of strange black-and-silver instruments, which included one of those odd rubber triangle mallets used to test reflexes. Kate had always wanted to pull it off the wall and try it on herself, but never had the nerve. The room smelled like a hospital, with hints of human and cleanser. She waited quietly, eying the reflex mallet, as invariably it would be an additional ten to twelve minutes before the doctor would materialize. She stared at the mallet, deciding several times to pick it up and play with it, but the doctor arrived before she could commit.

When Dr. Marchand came in, he looked the same, if perhaps tired, but it was nine-forty in the morning, so it was probably more mental than physical fatigue. He looked up to confirm it was the Kate he saw on the file and slowly assembled a friendly smile.

"Good morning, Kate."

"Hi, Dr. Marchand," Kate said.

"How have you been feeling, Kate?"

"Good."

"Any headaches, anxiety, general discomfort, or… trouble sleeping?" he asked as he plucked one of the tools from the wall and selected a wooden tongue depressor from a huge glass jar. He peered into her ears, mouth, and throat. Dr. Marchand briefly dimmed the lights in the small square room and clicked on the little bulb in the strange tool. He moved in uncomfortably close, and she could feel the heat of his face and hear his soft breathing. She noted he had thick, black, coiling hair sprouting from his eyebrows and ears that appeared to have been trimmed at some point, but were now filling back in. His breath was remarkably odorless.

"Just relax," he said as he peered into her eyes, hovering just inches away. She tried her best not to blink.

"So how have you been feeling?" he inquired once again, as if dissatisfied with the initial response.

"I'm good"—she paused then continued—"I have been a little extra tired lately. I don't know why… probably just the winter coming on. I have been crazy busy in the yard getting all my things in order, so I'm sure that's probably it."

The doctor said nothing and kept probing and squinting, so Kate continued.

"Oh… and I think I might be getting arthritis or something in my hands. They are definitely sore after I work in the yard. My knuckles and joints kind of ache when I sleep, is that normal at thirty-seven?"

He nodded in affirmation that he was listening, but didn't answer her and wrapped the familiar blood pressure cuff around her arm, twice stopping to readjust the Velcro seal like a baseball player adjusting his batting gloves. His delicate hands rapidly pumped the small, rubber bubble that inflates the black band, cinching it tighter around her arm. Just as it approached the level of discomforted, he released it. Kate could feel the rhythmic pumping of the blood moving through her arm. It was there all the time, but feeling its pulsing thump, she was suddenly aware.

"Okay… so some aching and you're extra tired. Would you say that it's related to inadequate sleep, or you are just feeling uncharacteristic fatigue?"

"I seem to be sleeping… ummm you know adequate… adequately." She stammered a bit, thinking about how Frank slept in the guest room most nights. "I mean, I sleep through the night. I don't have insomnia or anything. It's more like fatigue. I wake up tired. I feel like I went for a real long run the day before, even though I didn't. I guess this is getting older, huh?"

"Thirty-seven is not generally described as older, Kate. And you have the body of someone ten years your junior."

It was clearly a compliment to her body, which she kept fit. Coming from anyone else, this might have been uncomfortably flirtatious, but from Dr. Marchand, it was just a doctor talking to his patient, so it was okay. It made Kate feel good.

Throughout the examination, the doctor kept jotting down notes on the clipboard and flipping from one page to the next, then back again. It was as if he was reading the same thing again and again.

"Okay… so I see you are experiencing some redness or soreness with your breast or breasts. Can you tell me about that?"

"Well yeah, I mean, it's again like I was out running with a crappy bra… not that I have too much to bounce around," she said with a forced laugh, "but it's like I have rubbed them raw, and to add to that… they're also ahhh… leaking something? Dripping… you know… some liquid… but it's not milk and I am not pregnant!" she added assuredly.

"Are you confident of that?" he asked, raising his eyes up over the clipboard with an authoritative but comforting look.

"Unless I am giving birth to Jesus… I am pretty sure."

The doctor cocked his head and furrowed his brow a bit as though confused, but quickly recognized the reference.

Kate assumed her attempt at humor had zoomed right over the doctor's head, and before he had the chance to ask awkward questions, she just threw it out there.

"I haven't had sex in nearly six months, Dr. Marchand, so if there's a baby in me, either it's not growing very fast or it's the work of God."

"Right… that's fine, I understand that," he said. "We'll give you a pregnancy test, just to be sure, and ah … I am going to go ahead and run a few other tests as well. We're going to need to take some vials of blood. Are you OK with that?"

"Yes, of course."

"Okay… so back to the soreness, did we do a breast exam on your last visit?"

"I don't recall," she said.

"Well, we're going to do that right now."

17

Patrick Kelley designed clothing under the name Christian Harford, and he had done quite well in the years since graduating NYU and achieving a secondary fashion degree at Parsons The New School for Design, known colloquially as just "Parsons." Lots of influential designers came out of Parsons, and although Christian Harford was hardly being featured on runways in Milan, he was gaining acclaim around the Village in lower Manhattan and had sold designs to some of the bigger houses. He was being courted to join a couple of renowned brands, and although he would work as a grunt at first (and again), joining a team like that was a fast track to real success. Patrick had an excellent sense of style and could mesh very common themes in new ways that stunned and impressed those that mattered. His real niche was that his designs appealed to a yet-realized segment of the fashion market, the "everyman"—a massive group with huge spending power, but the least likely demographic linked to high fashion.

Patrick found that a whole new world existed when he moved to New York City and began his freshman studies at NYU in lower Manhattan. He had never actually spent any significant time with a black person, did not know well any Jewish people, and had certainly not hung around Hindus or Muslims, but New York's Village was a global potpourri that he found exhilarating. There were an estimated 150 languages spoken in New York City and a different indigenous restaurant on every block. Every day represented a new experience with all five senses explored and tested. Patrick had also never spoken to an openly gay person before, and he could not believe how normal they were. It made him ashamed to have assumed the worst.

Losing his parents young was hard on Patrick, but it also made him independent. He knew how to take care of himself, and he had proven that on the streets of Allston as well as the hockey rink. In New York, however, there was a whole new brand of toughness that existed from the street vendor to the little old ladies walking their dogs in Washington Square Park near the school's campus. They walked quickly and with a purpose; they confronted inequality and felt there was a God-given right to negotiate anything. Unlike Bostonians who seem to fit into convenient little buckets, Patrick felt New Yorkers provided endless contradictions: He found them insightful, erudite, and urbane while simultaneously myopic, monolithic, and insular. In his experiences they could vacillate from brash and blunt to open-minded and conscientious. He could not decide if they were irrationally fickle or deliciously adventurous.

Patrick found it to be the perfect place to explore his artistic realm, and he studied hard. He had to in order to maintain his scholarship. His parents had wisely left behind a small trust with college tuition in mind, but coming from a police officer's pension, there was not an abundance of funds. Had his sister Kate not given up her part of the inheritance by selling their parent's house, Patrick would not likely have been able to attend NYU. He was forever grateful to Kate for that. He felt indebted to her because she sacrificed her own education, attending a small associate's college so he could fulfill his dream. He also felt guilty for moving away, and for the fact that he was somehow incapable of visiting with any regularity. The reality was that he'd visited Boston only five times in the last nine years. New York was his home now.

Next to a legion of actors, musicians, dancers, artists, and opera singers, Patrick had worked through school in Manhattan eateries. He had a good gig as a bartender at a couple of well-established restaurants in mid-town, and the tip money was adequate to sustain his student life. Most students at NYU and pretty much everybody at Parsons wouldn't dream of heading north of the village. That worked perfectly for Patrick; he could ride uptown on the red line and make money in a part of the world where he would never need to interface with his fashion peers, at least not the ones still in school.

The irony was that the closer Patrick got to success and what it seemed he had been tirelessly pursuing for so many years, the less important it felt. He had been thinking about Kate quite a bit. She seemed to have grown numb, or even hollow, over the years. He also thought about his nephew Anthony, with whom he felt a strong connection despite not really spending much quality time with at any point in his life. One evening it just hit him that he had to make a change. That the family he had distanced himself from, or the city he had long since abandoned, still had an important place in his life. He made a commitment to himself that he was going to reconnect with his sister Kate, despite her bad choice in husband, and get to know his nephew better. He decided to head to Boston for a visit around the holidays.

18

Vida Mudgett was working on a new Daisy McQueen mystery, *The Twin Pepper Murders*. It would be the twentieth book in the series, and her publisher was making a pretty big deal about the release. No single title had ever been a best seller, and even the most popular scarcely approached forty thousand units sold, but year in and year out, people bought the books and got sucked into the entire series, so she enjoyed steady sales and equally steady royalties.

Vida's books were popular with two groups: women aged forty-five to seventy, and girls, thirteen to nineteen. The teenage girls seemed to relate to young Daisy McQueen, who traveled with her grandmother unraveling the twists and turns of sordid love triangles and vengeful murderers. The older fans seemed to relate to the sage grandmother who quietly provided invaluable insights. She appeared ostensibly to be a forgetful, old, self-appointed sidekick who seemed more a burden than anything, but to the fan, the grandmother most often provided the observation or hypothesis that led Daisy to the truth. She was the secret weapon.

Her most popular title of all time was *The Fractured Doll Mystery*, which was the seventh book in the series. It told the story of a man who had been assumedly murdered by his wife. The case seemed air-tight as the forensic evidence and timelines aligned with the apparent guilt of a jilted spouse. The prosecutor was relentless, and the burden had shifted to the defense, who to date put forth no reasonable explanation or plausible alternative. There were many who hated Leonard LeBlanc, and would perhaps wish him dead, including his wife Lucy, but all the evidence supported that she was the only person capable of committing the murder in such a way and at such a time.

At twenty-five years old, Daisy McQueen was not a lawyer, but rather a private detective. She was spunky with auburn curls and pretty green eyes that she most often kept behind glasses. Daisy had been blessed with incredibly sharp skills of observation, and she could interrogate anyone into bewilderment, often coaxing a confession from the murderer themselves, and at times with the criminal unaware they had just betrayed themselves. She was loved by the police and loathed by the lawyers.

Daisy took on the case of the doomed Mrs. Lucy LeBlanc after reading about her likely conviction and the death penalty in the newspaper. She traveled by train with her grandmother to New Orleans where the crime had occurred. After extensive private interviews with the accused wife, Daisy shockingly proclaimed in a dramatic speech to the police: "Lucy Leblanc is innocent!"

This proclamation came after the author described a conversation with Daisy's grandmother that was kept private to the reader. The mysterious content of the conversation sucked everyone in.

New readers and avid fans alike searched for the clues to solve the crime. They also marveled at the intuition that led Daisy to fly in the face of the seemingly insurmountable evidence. "Who was the real murderer?" they wondered, turning page after page, as Daisy McQueen eliminated suspects one by one. As she slowly reached the end of the list of suspects, readers found themselves perplexed. Had Daisy been wrong? Could the wunderkind have missed something? Even Daisy herself seemed to be questioning her own conviction that Mrs. LeBlanc had not committed the heinous crime that left her husband Victor LeBlanc's head crushed beneath the marble statue as he sat in the great room.

a frame for flowers

"I just can't put my finger on it, Grandma… yet I know it is there."

"You'll figure it out; you always do."

"I suspect I will, but I am running out of options… and time."

"Sometimes, Daisy, the solution is right before our eyes, but it just isn't obvious until we see it."

This type of seemingly obvious statement made some believe the grandmother was not all there. Yet so often this type of simple statement would trigger the answer in Daisy's mind.

As Daisy went back through her notes, recounting all her interactions, she recalled a brief encounter with the young daughter of the housemaid who lived in the servant's quarters adjacent to LeBlanc's estate, the same conversation her grandmother had told her she found "quite interesting." Daisy had questioned the maid, who seemed unhappy perhaps, but in no way a murderer. And besides, she had a tight alibi, having been out for the evening on a date in a public place. She recalled further the odd girl who loomed sheepishly in the corner as the local police detective on the case took Daisy through the crime scene.

It finally dawned on Daisy that the conversation was not what her grandmother found interesting, but instead the woman's young child who hovered nearby. She had originally thought little of the girl, except that she appeared unusually pale and that her stringy, brown hair and shabby dress indicated a difficult life. Later, however, she recalled the white-faced china doll that the twelve-year-old clutched tightly the entire time, as well as one other compelling fact: the china doll's head was cracked, a long fissure extending out of her hairline and across her smooth, white face. She rang the local detective and asked to speak to the maid once more.

Daisy also asked him to be sure the young daughter could join her mother during the interview. This is what made the *The Fractured Doll Mystery* such a hit. No one had suspected the young girl. In every other book, there were usually a few potential suspects, and often she led the reader to believe that one was guilty then surprised her audience with the less-likely murderer, but this pattern was pretty recognizable after a few titles.

This had been the first real jolt to the system for Daisy McQueen fans, and they loved it! After a riveting scene in which Daisy appears to be pinning down the mother for the murder, the daughter burst open and confessed. Victor LeBlanc had been raping the poor woman, and the daughter knew everything. By attacking the one person the young girl had sought to protect, Daisy got her to admit that it was she who toppled the marble bust off the balcony perch and killed Victor LeBlanc on the living room couch below. The young girl admitted she'd tested out the plan on her poor china doll and created the telltale fracture. The policeman stood stunned as the girl confessed, and Mrs. LeBlanc had been exonerated. Daisy McQueen had done it again.

Vida Mudgett had a way of drawing in readers, who often shared their delight with her in fan-mail. It was a gift Vida had: she could direct readers with her words.

19

Kate hurried in from the garage with two of the five brown paper bags from her Volvo. She had placed the bags with the eggs and coldest items furthest back in the car so they would be the first removed and spend the least time out of refrigeration. Kate was always conscious of things getting spoiled. There was a small, family-run grocery store at the end of their street that had the freshest fruit and vegetables, as well as a solid deli. Most of the people in the neighborhood patronized that grocery store and so did Kate, but when it came to doing a full grocery run, Kate would drive over to Stop & Shop. They were far friendlier at the local store, but Stop & Shop was more economical and Frank watched the budget pretty closely. That is to say he complained about the bills constantly.

"Kate, what ah you buyin' at the store… cavi-ah? It's three of us for Gawd's sake… How do you manage to blow a fortune every frickin week?"

King came bounding up as Kate walked across the kitchen floor with her arms full; his brown eyes were bright, his feathered brown and black fur shiny, and his tail knocked happily into the kitchen table chairs. He was always happy to see Kate, and the clicking of his toenails on the wood or tile followed closely as she moved through the house. It was exactly 11:00 a.m., and the clock in the living room that sat atop the fireplace began to chime, slowly marking the hour that had passed.

The chill outside had been creeping in where it could, and now Kate had left the side door open because her hands were tied up with the grocery bags. The frigid air barged its way into the kitchen making itself at home, so Kate paced back to the door and closed it, then paused as she realized she needed to go back outside to retrieve the rest of the grocery bags. Just then she noticed the blinking red light on the answering machine.

There was one message, a call from Dr. Marchand's office. The recording from one of his assistants was cryptic, alluding to some additional tests that were needed and advising Kate to phone back as soon as possible. The tone of the call struck Kate as odd and alarming. She finished putting away all the groceries, tossed King a treat, then sat down at the kitchen table to phone the doctor's office. They picked up in three rings.

One of the assistants answered, and after Kate introduced herself, there was a discernible change in the woman's demeanor. She introduced herself as Phyllis and spoke to Kate as if they were suddenly friends.

"Hi, Kate dear, thank you for calling us back so quick. I am going to ask that you stand by while I track down Dr. Marchand. Is that okay with you?" she asked Kate.

"Yes, of course."

Kate was taken a bit off-guard. The assistants had always been fairly cordial, and Dr. Marchand certainly had been friendly over the many years, but this was somehow different. Had she reached some sort of customer milestone? Had she forgotten something? It never dawned on Kate how the conversation went next; it just never occurred to her as an option.

"Hello Kate, this is Dr. Marchand. How are you feeling?" He asked, and now she felt he too had an unfamiliar tone to his voice.

"I'm better, I think. Good energy today!" she said, feeling suddenly defensive.

68

"So we have some irregularities with a couple of the blood screens we ran, which we will not only run again, but ah… we will take another sample and run some other tests as well."

Kate felt her chest tighten and breath shorten as she listened to the doctor's words, her fingers now nervously twisting the coiled phone cord as she stood up from the kitchen table and walked toward the pantry.

"What does this mean? What's an irregularity? Are you saying something is wrong with me? Am I sick?"

"Well, it is difficult to say at this time, Kate, and I think you should come in so we can discuss it in person." Dr. Marchand was doing his best to sound reassuring and calm.

"I will be right over," she said as her pulse quickened and her flesh prickled. After a long silence, she managed to swallow. "Doctor? Are you there?"

He exhaled slowly. "Yes, Kate. Sure, come on over now."

20

At the pub Ted Kelley used to frequent on Fridays after a long week of keeping the peace in downtown Boston, some of the old-timers or newly arrived Dubs would throw around Gaelic phrases and vernacular to demonstrate credibility. There were always lots of cops from the Emerald Society mixed in with working-class craftsmen of every shape and size, throwing back some beers and laughing off another paycheck's toil. The bar was warm, the beer was cold, and the people were kind.

It was more or less a male event, although some of the wives would stop by. The younger gals would pop in around seven o'clock to pick up their guys and head out for a date. Sometimes that would result in the ladies hanging around for the rest of the evening, and sometimes the guys would slip away for a Friday with their "future." Still other times it could become contentious, and the relationship would be played out for everyone to observe and judge. Moira Kelley would only appear a couple of Fridays a year for a drink. She had no issue with Teddy unwinding on a Friday; he was a good man.

The regulars commonly spoke of *Gael-Mheiriceánaigh*—prominent Irish-Americans—as beer-spiced conversations would wander from sports to politics to the evening news and back again. They would reference anyone famous who was Irish with disproportionate attention.

"It's just a fact that F. Scott Fitzgerald told the American story better than anyone," someone would say.

"Walt Disney is really the best business success story you can tell," another would proclaim. "Gene Kelley had the best moves hands-down!" they would chorus.

Jack Dempsey's boxing and Ben Hogan's golfing… even John McEnroe's tennis were worth a mention. The Irish were happy to take credit for at least fifteen presidents and countless more successful, if not controversial, politicians. The mayors of Boston in Ted's years were Kerrigan, Curley, Hynes, Collins, White, and Flynn. It was also a common position that John F. Kennedy and Bobby Kennedy had died martyrs.

"They made the ultimate sacrifice fighting for life, liberty, and the pursuit of happiness," someone would announce, as pints rose around the bar.

The younger men were eager to absorb the proud rhetoric and feel a part of what bound these people together. They mostly made note of the positive stories, but on occasion they would lament a man gone bad.

"That apple fell fah from the caht, and I'll tell ya. He's nothing like his old man, that boy just cahn't get off the drink!"

It's not like the whole bar was Irish; anyone who could pay was welcome. In between the boys who came from Dorchester, Lawrence, or Milton with names like Murph, Sully, Jonesy, Mac, Doones, OB (O'Brien), Higgins, Moore, and Connors, were two of Ted Kelley's better friends on the force: Lou Bertucci and Peter Hacek.

Lou Bertucci was a hulk of a man with thick muscles and a five o'clock shadow at 10:00 a.m., and he was as Italian as they came. He was funny as the day was long and could very likely take any guy in the joint. Peter called himself eastern European, which just meant he wasn't Irish. Peter was pretty reserved, but could drink like a fish and whip anyone in darts. Both would regularly join the crew at O'Hara's, and even though they weren't bandying around Irish limericks, they would raise a glass with everyone else. They were friends, brother of the thin blue line, and this pub is where they spent their Fridays.

71

Peter Hacek had retired and gone to Florida six years ago. Lou Bertucci had also retired some years back, but his son Joe had followed his footsteps into the police force, and he was a good cop. He had made homicide detective like his father, but at a much younger age. Joe was good friends with Patrick Kelley and knew Kate as well, from the years growing up around each other. He ran into Kate every once and a while around town, but had lost touch with Patrick a few years after he moved to New York. Joe had not found the right woman and had yet to settle down. Joe always had a crush on the pretty Katie Kelley when they were young.

21

Kate did not like having so many guns in the house, even though most were locked up in the basement. She always felt no good could come of it, especially with a child. She had been frightened for years that Anthony would get his hands on one and think it was a toy. More recently she had joked with Vida that he might use one on Frank. She apologized for the poor attempt at humor, but the words lingered with both of them. Frank had instructed her on how to handle a gun many years ago. She didn't have the heart to tell him that her dad had showed her how to use his service revolver many years earlier, and she knew her way around a pistol. She could fill a clip, pop the safety, aim, and squeeze. In fact, Kate had demonstrated she was pretty handy with a gun—so much so that her accuracy at the range had irritated Frank.

But she hated guns. It had always made her nervous to hold the weapon in her hands, the weight of it making it all too real. To be so close to something that could kill a person seemed like a scenario she should avoid, and so she kept the gun time to a minimum, just enough to appease Frank. The way Kate saw it, a handgun was good for one thing; killing someone.

22

Kate could hardly focus as she tore across town towards Dr. Marchand's office. What could it be? Both of her parents had died pretty young, but at thirty-seven? "Are you kidding me?" she thought aloud, her hands gripping the worn steering wheel.

"Maybe I have diabetes," she thought. "That's why I'm losing weight."

Her hands were moist with sweat, but her mouth felt dry. The tightness in her chest persisted as she swerved through midday traffic, the now-brown leaves of fall leaping out of the way as she sped down the potholed side streets that led to Dr. Marchand's office. As she reached a stoplight, her head felt thick, as though a pillow was being slowly wrapped around her head, smothering the air and muffling the sounds of the world around her.

Her eyes drifted to a small, laminated picture of the Virgin Mary that sat just in front of the steering wheel, tucked into the crease between the dials and the dash. It was a memorial inscription from her mother's funeral. Below her name, Moira Ann Powers Kelley, was a short prayer. Kate softly murmured the words of the passage to herself at the stoplight, and her chest eased as the oxygen gently re-entered her lungs. Outside a mother and small child made their way past the front of the car, the mother with her head down, leaning forward into the day, while the child, tucked behind and oblivious to the thoughts in both of the mothers' minds, smiled dreamily at Kate.

"Be strong," she whispered to herself.

When she arrived at the office, her tires squealed on the asphalt in the parking lot as she angled into a yellow-lined space. Her hand nervously searched for the car handle she had opened countless times before. The air felt prickly as she stepped in the parking lot and made her way across to the door; on it, etched in the glass, it read Dr. Peter Marchand, M.D., as well as Dr. Lawrence Wargrave, M.D. She had never noticed that before.

When Kate slipped in the door to the familiar wood-panel waiting room, one of the assistants glanced up, looked down, and then quickly looked up again before whispering to the woman next to her. Kate watched the whole thing as the woman sprang from her chair and walked around and out through the door that led back to the patient rooms. She was a shorter, heavier woman, and today her scrubs looked more gray than blue.

"Hi, Mrs. Bruno," she said with a forced smile. "Have a seat quick, and I will tell Dr. Marchand that you are here."

"OK," said Kate, as she made her way over to one of the ugly orange chairs as the woman disappeared back through the door as quickly as she had emerged.

Within a few minutes, Dr. Marchand appeared, exiting the door completely to meet her in the waiting room.

"Come on back, Kate," he said softly, and he turned and walked assertively back through the door, stopping abruptly upon entering the white area and inviting her in and ushering her past.

Kate didn't say a word, although she was thinking of saying different things in her mind, but nothing came out. They made their way, not back to an examining room, but instead to an office she had never been to: a left turn at the end of the hall instead of the standard right she was accustomed to. The doctor still said nothing, but again stopped and motioned her into a room. It appeared to be his personal office, and immediately the feeling of a smothering pillow descended once more. The doctor pointed to one of the two red leather chairs that sat at the front of a large oak desk and said simply, "Please sit."

Kate used her hands to grasp the armrests and lower herself into the comfortable chair as her eyes panned the new room. Her hands were damp in the creases, sliding up and down the armrest from wood to leather and across the bumpy rivets that held it together. The doctor made his way around behind the desk to sit in a large, black leather chair that looked rather worn. On the wall were several certificates, honors, and degrees, as well as a picture of Dr. Marchand's family. She never knew he had a daughter as well as two sons. She noted that his wife was very plain, but her smile seemed sincere.

"I am glad you could come over so we could talk face to face."

She nodded and tried to smile in response.

"I don't want you to be frightened, but I am pretty concerned about these test results, especially when combined with the symptoms you've been experiencing."

"I feel a lot better, much more energetic," Kate said, once again feeling suddenly defensive. "I think it is just the weather. I am always stretched thin trying to get the yard squared away for the winter and school and the dog and Frank's business and all…"

"Kate," said the doctor, trying to interject, but she continued on nervously.

"I know I should be exercising more; it's obvious. I am losing weight because I am losing muscle."

"Kate," he said a bit firmer and raised his hand like a traffic cop motioning her to stop, which she did.

"Kate, this could be nothing, okay? We have to eliminate the possibilities, and we will do that by taking more blood today and rerunning the tests, as well as running a few more."

He was so serious and devoid of emotion that Kate was suddenly petrified. She felt herself about to cry, but quickly fought back the urge and instead spoke calmly.

"What do you think it is, Dr. Marchand? Please be honest and, and, and even give me the worst scenario."

"Well," said the doctor, as he leaned back and brought his hands together, the tips of his fingers lingering just below his mouth as if to catch any cruel or unintended words before they could slip out. "Your white blood cell count is high, and that means your body is fighting or rejecting something." He went on. "We need to run additional blood markers and tests to determine what we are dealing with, as well as do a mammogram as soon as possible. During your exam, I felt some small nodules in your breasts that could be tumors."

"Oh my God," she gasped. "Am I gonna die?"

"Now hold on Kate, again, we need to understand this, understand what precisely we are dealing with before we can fully diagnose it and then start fighting it."

Kate sat dumbfounded by the words that confronted her, and what stunned her most was that when she asked if she was going to die, he did not flatly say no.

"I understand," she said, and again she felt her eyes welling with tears.

"I suspect it could be something like Paget's disease or some other form of breast cancer. The mammogram will help us get a better look, so we need to schedule it right away. I also think we should take a biopsy right away to get a closer look at the tissue. At this time, Kate, I am going to have to refer you to some specialists, so we can have true experts focus on your health. I will remain involved, and I have relationships with the best in the business at Mass General, Beth Israel, and specifically the Dana Farber Institute. They do some of the premier work on cancer."

The rest of the appointment was a blur as the doctor explained to Kate the science behind the situation. He was reassuring, but all she could think of was Anthony. While she strained to listen, her brain tugged her to the images of her son flipping through her mind like a magazine on a windy beach.

They scheduled the mammogram and biopsy for the following morning, and when Kate finally got back into her car to head home, the reality overwhelmed her and tears streamed down her face.

23

Fashion week in New York City generally fell in February. Much like an accountant heading towards mid-April, those who earned a living in the fashion business worked at a torrid pace through the holidays. Patrick Kelley (a.k.a. Christian Harford) had been thoroughly immersed in this pursuit for roughly a decade, and this was largely the reason that traveling during the holidays was never feasible. Of course, it was feasible, but that had been his excuse for not making it back to Boston.

Coincidentally, Patrick had phoned the house while Kate was at the doctor's and left a long message, trying to apologize for being so distant and sounding excited about his intention to visit, while simultaneously trying to sound indifferent should Frank somehow retrieve the message before his sister.

"Hi Kate, it's your brother. It's Pat. I have been thinking, it's been a real long time since I've been back to Boston, and I'm thinking about a visit. If you are around and not too busy for the holidays, I am thinking I might make my way up there for a whole week. It would be nice to see some old friends, and... you know... some sights and go to the cemetery and stuff. Maybe even do a skate around at the rink. And of course it would be nice to see you, and I haven't seen Anthony since he was, well whatever. Smaller? Shorter? Anyhow, it would be nice."

There was a long pause as he considered hanging up.

"I don't need to stay with you or anything, but if you're around, it would just be nice to be together around Christmas for a change. Like old times." Again he paused, as if someone might respond.

"Right, well, call me back whenever is convenient. You have my number, I think. It's 212.865.6102 in case you can't find it. All right, talk to you soon."

After he hung up the phone, Patrick turned slightly to look out the partially opened window at the street two floors below. His windows were part of a huge, nearly thirty-foot wall of small opaque square panes as seen in an old factory; at the bottom were smaller, metal-framed sections with green metal handles that could be turned and pulled to tilt the window inward and open. The faint red-painted logo of some textile company from yesteryear was still visible, although faded and in reverse, from his perspective. There was no fire escape on that side, and the windows were twenty-five feet up from the sidewalk, so Patrick kept them cracked open most of the time. The brisk air of fall was mingling near the openings, but the building was heated by iron-cast radiators. There was little in the way of temperature control. The building and loft would often get so hot, even in the dead of winter, that folks would often need to crack a window to negotiate a comfortable setting.

He leaned his forehead into the cool glass pane and wished he could call back or somehow erase the message and start again. Regard-less, he was glad he called and looked ahead to a chance to visit with Kate and see his nephew. He missed Boston, even though he struggled to envision calling it home again.

Patrick's loft was on the edge of Tribeca, a multi-decade gentrifica-tion project transforming a heavy industrial area of the city into an artistic Bauhaus neighborhood and eventually a super high-rent dis-trict that was home to several of New York City's A-list celebrities. In the seventies, the population for this triangle neighborhood plunged to under four hundred people, but by the time Patrick got in, there were some eight thousand residents and throngs of eager artists (and entrepreneurs interested in supporting them) migrating to the area each week. Patrick had gotten in early so the rent was reasonable for him and a group of friends and schoolmates. Over the years, he slowly shed roommates and squirreled away cash until the entire loft was his. Eight years ago, he bought into the place. He was now 55 percent owner of 3,500 square feet of loft space in a heavily sought after area. Despite living pretty lean, it was probably worth quite a sum.

Tribeca was an acronym for TRI-angle BE-low CA-nal. The neighborhood had timeless architecture, and the artists created a new brand of working and living spaces that were both comfortable and unique, with sprawling, open layouts that meshed the creative worlds with the living space, serving as an environment for new and creative forms of art. It also led to some of the coolest loft apartments ever seen. Many of the restaurants and shops maintained the feel of the former industrial tenants, which made for a unique experience. Despite the fact that the huge loft sometimes felt lonely, Patrick loved being there.

To him, Manhattan was a brother who had gone away to get a college education and done well for himself; Boston was the older brother who was well-liked, loyal to the end, and could still take him in a fight. Both brothers seemed content with that.

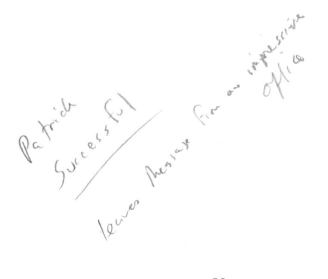

24

Frank Bruno was just four hours into his twenty-first birthday when he crossed paths with seventy-year-old Marine veteran, Edward Charles Stuber.

One night after several beers Frank had casually reported the memory to Kate in brief headlines:

"I went out for a work thing, and then stopped by a house pa-hty for a couple drinks in Southie. I couldn't believe the bad luck that night. There were lots of accidents. It was cold, snowy, and still real dark when I hit Stuber's cars. The old-timer must have been trying to beat the weather and traffic by heading out of town before traffic. At least that's what the reporter in the news said. I guess the guy was a Marine, but just wasn't strong enough to survive the crash. No point stickin around for the pap-ah work, the guy was dead. It sucks, but it happens. It was a tough night, ha-hd to forget. He probably shouldn't have been out drivin. To be honest, they shouldn't let people that old drive at all. It's not safe."

Frank had recanted his version of the story one night to Kate. They were freshly married and still trusted each other. He spoke uncharacteristically softly to her, as perhaps a parishioner would to a priest, explaining the tragic tale, yet she sensed no remorse in his voice as he delivered an invocation for understanding instead of a confession of guilt. She sensed it ate at him, that he knew how wrong it was to leave the scene and that the man had died, but that was something Frank would never say.

Frank Bruno had worked to establish himself as a skilled framer, building houses with a regular crew and working his way up in the trades' community. He wanted to move up in the workers' pecking order, so he took every chance to demonstrate he could do more than work: to prove he should manage people. Often it meant being friendly to folks he didn't care about. That part was hard, but he was up for it, because the payoff was good.

He had begun that fateful night joining some of the influential local Union members out for beers in downtown Boston. He didn't set out for a big evening, but the Union boys liked to drink hard. He found himself half cut by 10:00 p.m. and raring to go. Frank knew he couldn't risk staying in Boston proper liquored up, so he slipped away without a word to his colleagues and headed back behind the walls of Southie to continue the party in safer confines. The snow fell lightly at first, but grew heavier as Frank proved he could outlast the energy of the evening, churning forward until the quiet of next day's morning would nudge its way in.

When he and Kate started out, they had a small apartment in Southie. They had since moved slightly south into a nicer area, but Frank knew Southie well. He knew exactly where he could locate a safe haven with booze and some local girls who, by that time of night, might be up for screwing around with little effort. As expected, Frank found a bustling spot stoked by familiar townies at the house of John Paul Fallon, a local, low-level pot dealer who threw parties like it was his job. Frank considered Fallon a loser, and he had no interest in drugs, but there were always ladies looking for a good time at his place. It was safe, cheap, and open late.

Frank positioned his truck along the tree line, gliding in front first and slamming it into park, then stepping out into the cold of the night, warmed only by the mild haze of earlier cocktails. He popped a couple of Tic Tacs, which he rattled around in his mouth then chewed impatiently, as he ran his rough fingers through his hair and strode to the house. The bass of the thumping music was vibrating through the front porch from the basement below as Frank marched to the entrance. He didn't knock or ring the bell; he just turned the brass knob and pushed his way through the thick, black door into the starkly furnished house that reeked of marijuana and cigarettes. A thin veil of smoke lurked in the upper reaches of a vaulted ceiling in the old Dorchester Heights home. In spots, paint curled in thick, white chips. It was a beautiful place in a good neighborhood that Fallon had done his absolute best to ruin.

Frank knew John Paul Fallon paid the local cops to leave him alone, but he could not believe how stupid the guy was: a bunch of young kids drinking, music blasting, and clouds of pot smoke, and yet he left his door left unlocked. More confusing to Frank was the oversized gorilla, who stood watch at the first-floor door that led down to the cellar, as if there were any logic to protecting the entrance to the basement when you could walk right in the front door.

"I wouldn't run my operation like this," Frank said to himself.

The gorilla's name was Damon Coughlin, a former football standout at Catholic Memorial who got injured then busted for boosting a car with some friends. He blew his athletic career and devolved into a local thug and part-time muscle for petty chumps like J.P. Fallon. Coughlin claimed to do some odd jobs for the Winter Hill gang, but no one could confirm it. He was tough and strong, but Frank didn't sweat him. They had seen each other fight and were mutually disinterested. He and Frank acknowledged each other as Damon waved him into the basement. He was instantly embraced by the warmth and energy of the homespun speakeasy, affectionately called "the Pit."

Frank was an infrequent drinker, but he was capable of knocking them back when he felt like it. He got even more aggressive than his normal persona when he drank and was generally considered poor company. No one ever really went out with Frank; they more or less accompanied him. He was either dragging out someone he had influence over, like a girlfriend, younger brother, or subordinate worker, or he was with others out of some necessity. On that night, he kept things in check with the Union guys to make a good impression, but now he was revved up and dead-set on a good time. He navigated straight to the well-constructed bar in the dim corner of Fallon's fully finished basement for a drink. The music was loud and the air thick with a variety of indulgent smells. Another of J.P.'s minions was tending bar and recognized Frank immediately.

"Frankie Bruno… what's up?" said the crew cut kid through a crooked toothed grin.

Frank had no idea who the skinny kid in the white and green Adidas track suit was, but he had the booze so Frank nodded his head with a smile.

"Hey bud, how ah things?"

"Tip top… business is good brotha!" he said pulling a thick rolled wad of cash out of his sweat pants to show Frank.

"Nice… gimme a gin with just two ice cubes, will ya?"

"Yeah, sure thing, Frank," he replied. "J.P.'s upstairs tending to some business, but he'll be done soon."

"Yeah… cool," said Frank, laughing on the inside at the notion that John Paul Fallon was tending to some business. He was selling dope to some local shithead, and everybody knew it.

The place was bumping though. Frank counted twenty-three partiers, and there were at least a couple girls Frank had made some measure of progress with in the past, and another one he didn't recognize, but would like to take a run at. One of them, whom he had slept with some months earlier, crept up on Frank like a pigeon in Franklin Park.

"Hey, Frank. What brings you out on a cold school night?"

"I'm just out," Frank responded, wagging his head indifferently.

"Oh, I guess he's out slummin', lucky us," she said with a wink to her friend and a flirtatious flip of her brassy blonde hair.

Frank couldn't recall Lisa's last name, but he knew her from years of traveling in the same circles in South Boston. She was a town mattress, but very attractive with the shapely body years of hard living had yet to dismantle. He had connected with her over the years on evenings when their worlds collided and there was no better option.

"Shut the fuck up, Lisa," he said with half a laugh through his white smile.

"I'm just bustin' ya balls, Frank," she said, with a coquettish grin.

"So… Shelly, this is Frank," Lisa continued, introducing the girl he did not know.

"Yeah, I see his name on his shirt," she said with a seductive smile.

Shelly was an attractive redhead from New Hampshire, in town visiting relatives or, as Frank quickly assessed in his head: "She'd be hot-ah if she wasn't a ging-ah, but she does have a tight body and nice rack."

"You wanna buy us a drink?" the strange girl asked in her Nampsha twang.

Frank had no idea the drinks cost money because he had never paid. Fallon treated Frank with respect because they were both considered locals. The reality was the drinks were dirt cheap, but Fallon charged most revelers a couple bucks a pop to "cover costs," so Frank begrudgingly peeled off some bills and bought the ladies a cocktail.

The night pushed on, but deteriorated. With a steady flow of drinks, the venue slipped deeper into an alcohol-fueled buzz, the patrons grooving to the music, smoking, and drinking. The girls were grinding and hanging on the attractive construction worker, drawn to his dark complexion and pocketful of cash. With each round of drinks, the three wound tighter as their brains stumbled to a hazy state.

J.P. Fallon materialized for a spell and greeted Frank with a familiar "'sup," then proclaimed loudly, "Round of drinks on the house!"

By then Frank was quite intoxicated and fixated on the two girls he was taking turns kissing. He didn't pay Fallon much mind.

By 3:00 a.m., the air was getting stale in the basement bar, and they were trying to disappear into the darkest corner, seemingly oblivious to the others who partied on. Intertwined in each other and in various stages of dress, Frank was having his way with the two, but the evening became suddenly long and he grew weary of their presence. Frank sensed the circumstances restricted the trio from taking things further, so he was instantly uninterested. He decided it was time to go home.

Frank announced abruptly to the two wide-eyed girls, "I gotta piss," and he bolted towards the stairs.

Without another word or a second thought, he started to leave. He had seen enough and his night was over.

"What no time fa' me, Bruno?" said a sullen Fallon from the darkened corner adjacent to the stairs.

"What the fuck, J.P.? Shit... I didn't even see you there," said Frank.

"You leavin'?" said Fallon, emerging from the corner and stepping into the light.

"Yeah... I'm done here," Frank said with a wry smile and a glance back to the ladies he left behind. Fallon bristled at the response.

"I see... so ah.... I'm good for a free round at the bah, but you got no time to visit with me, huh?" he said like some movie gangster.

"Visit with you? Whateva," said Frank, taking the first step upstairs and out, but pausing to look back to see the drawn face on J.P. Fallon.

With an exaggerated laugh, Frank continued up the stairs.

"Fuck you then," barked Fallon, stiffening and planting his feet instinctively. At those words, Frank spun around quickly.

"What the fuck did you say?"

"Do I stutt-ah?" said Fallon with dramatic antagonism, aware that much of the room was already watching the exchange.

Frank stood rigid on the stairs as his fists curled slowly to a clench, fingertips pressing down firmly on their palms assuming the familiar position, his icy glare connecting with Fallon's equally serious gaze. The music halted and the conversation instantly dimmed to a murmur as the two faced off, shifting the evening's tenor on a stark pivot.

"Be careful, Fallon," growled Frank in a condescending tone, as the door from above creaked open and big Damon Coughlin appeared at the landing.

The room stood still for nearly ten seconds.

Frank could hear his own breath drawing deeper into his lungs and sending his pulse faster. He slowly craned up at Coughlin, then back

down to Fallon, scanning the room in between ،
was not in his best interest. Frank's mind worked tha،
be very logical when it was in his best interest. He slowly .
fists and again began to ascend the stairs.

"Good night," he said in his best effort to promote peace.

He was nearly two-thirds of the way up when Fallon again flippeo
off. "Fuckin Guinea pussy!" muttered Fallon.

The words pierced Frank's ears as he reversed direction in a flash,
rapidly descending the stairs, his feet on every other step and his
right arm extending out like a coiled snake springing for its prey. His
calloused mitt snapped forth to Fallon's throat, instantly gripping
the muscled flesh. He was on top of him so quick that J.P. could not
defend himself, and his thin frame fluttered in Frank's control.

Frank could hear Coughlin lumbering down the stairs from the
rear and turned to see the young track-suited buck springing forward,
having snatched up a baseball bat from behind the bar. This was going
to go bad quick. Frank spun out of position using his momentum
and cranking Fallon's arm up behind his back and using Fallon's
body to shield himself from the impending goons. In a fluid motion,
he flicked the latch on the leather holster at his side and drew out a
wood-handled buck knife, his thumb flipping the shiny, four-inch
blade and springing it from its fold.

"Back the fuck off!" Frank bellowed as loud as he could, his voice
cracking for punctuation. Fallon threw up an open hand signaling
the two men to halt.

"I don't want any trouble here boys," Frank said, his knuckles whit-
ened by the grip on the knife he held dangerously close to a pulsing
vein in J.P. Fallon's neck.

Everyone in the room stood staring and panting like wolves. Frank
knew the only way out was to cool things down as quick as it had
erupted, and he also knew that at least two of these guys had a gun
somewhere. His buck knife was not going to carry him very far.

"Look, I lost my cool. Okay, J.P.? I'm gonna put this down okay?"

Silence.

"Everybody's just a bit drunk here fellas... nobody needs ta get killed. Okay, J.P.? I'm askin ya to let this settle."

Silence.

"Alright, Frank... alright," said Fallon, nodding his head and again motioning his guys to back away and create space.

Frank slowly withdrew, holding his hands out for all to see as he slowly folded the knife and attempted to settle things back down. Damon leaned back against the stairwell, happy he wouldn't have to work for the moment.

"You're a crazy fuck, Bruno," Fallon said, wagging a finger and nervously laughing.

"A crazy fuck. You need to work out your fuckin issues there, Charlie Manson," he went on, pacing back and forth at the bottom of the stairs.

"Shit. You are fuckin' nuts pullin' a knife on me in my fuckin' house."

Frank stood expressionless, his arms to his side to signal his calm. These guys were losers and Frank knew it, but they were also criminals and they had something to prove every day they were alive. Frank wasn't interested in becoming a character in a prison story.

"No use Southie getting in a donnybrook here, I'm just gonna leave," said Frank, as he tested the willingness of Coughlin to let him pass by on the stairs.

The room was dumbfounded to silence, and the girls Frank had left in the back cowered in the corner. Whether horrified, impressed, or turned on, they were frozen.

"Yeah, go home," said Fallon, "and don't come back you wop faggot."

Frank bit down hard on his lip, aware of the price he would pay for a response—a price he seriously considered.

"You Italians never get it, this is our city. Southie is Irish, Bruno, you hear me?" Frank clomped to the top of the stairs and paused for one more look back. "Irish, you got that?" Fallon mocked as their eyes remained locked.

As Frank exited the door, he heard one last insult hurled by J.P. Fallon;

"Ya lucky, Bruno. You thought yer old man used ta beat ya? You almost gawt schooled on how the Irish deal with a disrespectful guinea."

As Frank exited to the first floor, he considered burning the house down.

88

25

Frank slipped out into the silence of pre-dawn. He took several deep breaths as his rage surged. There would be time to get Fallon, but for now he needed to get out of there. He was now an awake drunk, and it was just enough to instill confidence in his ability to handle the drive home.

"A short ride to bed," he thought to himself. It was, instead, a short ride to fate.

The cab of the truck was cold, and his steamy breath billowed and obscured the window. With each exhale, a snowflake-shaped etching sprawled on the cold glass. He pulled out of his spot aggressively and sensed the road's lack of traction, but having grown up in Boston's winter weather, was not deterred.

About halfway home, there was a four-way stop Frank had been at a hundred times. Yet on this approach he came in a bit faster than normal. It was nearly 4:00 a.m., and he assumed he was the only person on the road. By the time Frank registered the other vehicle emerging perpendicular from the right, the outcome was inevitable. He slammed down hard on the brake pedal, but careened straight into the intersection, rear wheels locked, hurdling forward at some twenty miles an hour. Edward Charles Stuber never saw him coming.

The collision occurred with a deep, crunching thud as the grill of Frank's hulking truck sunk cruelly into the driver's side door of Stuber's Cadillac. It was over in a second as Frank's body lurched forward, his hands and forehead striking the windshield like a deep corner hockey check. The ice crystal patterns morphed into a small spider web of cracked glass, yet there was little damage to Frank's truck, and he realized he was not badly hurt.

Edward Charles Stuber's neck was broken, but he was alive. He was wearing a seatbelt, but the impact had snapped him back and forth violently. He lay slumped, hanging partially out of the shattered driver's side window. The night was still, and after the noise of the crash, the neighborhood again fell silent.

Frank scrambled out of his truck and made his way towards the car he'd hit. He looked around anxiously as he approached and saw an elderly man in the crumpled vehicle. Remarkably, no one seemed to hear, or at least no one came to help, and he found himself alone, standing above the critically injured man with the hiss of his stalled engine, the only sound.

As Frank drew close, he could see the man was bleeding from his ear and mouth, his breathing shallow and deliberate. His eyes were open and followed Frank's every move. He did not appear able to speak.

"Hey," Frank whispered as he scanned the block for movement.

"Hey, you alright?" he asked, reaching out to touch the man, but then retracting his hand.

Again he looked around to see if anyone was responding, but the eerie quiet remained. When Frank looked back, the man's eyes rolled up into his head as he lost consciousness.

"Hey, old man, wake up," he said more audibly, but there was no response and the man released a fading exhale followed by a short, gasping intake.

"Fuck," Frank said to himself, realizing his situation was dire.

He'd had a lot of drinks and would likely fail a breathalyzer. He knew if the cops came, he would be in a world of trouble, but the guy was still breathing and might survive. Frank didn't know what to do. He wondered if the man had seen him well enough to recognize his face or his name on his company shirt. He panicked.

"Fuck," he repeated, and once more scanned for signs of a witness.

Then Frank stared at the man, an old man, who was probably dying right in front of him. He quickly rattled through his options and assessed the outcomes. He looked down at his hands, then back at his truck, both revealing little evidence of the event.

"This is bad. This is really bad," he said to himself.

He looked around one last time, then did the unthinkable. Frank reached out slowly and put his hand over the man's open mouth, pushing his palm upward until the side of his hand pressed flush with the man's nostrils, obscuring the air passages. Immediately the man twitched, and his eyes popped open to stare at Frank. Charles Edward Stuber released a guttural moan as the oxygen waned in his brain. His eyes glazed and slowly closed. It was over in less than a minute, and Frank pulled his hand away as the man's body went limp. His mouth fell back open, but he was no longer breathing. Frank quickly leaned in and wiped his hands clean on the old man's shirt, then turned and hurried back to his truck, leaving Stuber alone in the early morning cold. Frank knew the man's whole name because it was in the news.

"Edward Charles Stuber, seventy-year-old Marine, born in Worcester, Massachusetts, served our country bravely and was killed in a hit-and-run car accident in the early dawn."

Frank repeated the report to Kate as he justified the outcome.

"He was a dead man for shu-ah, and the-ya was nothin I could do," he explained matter-of-factly.

"I tried to help, but nobody was around. I mean, it was fo-ah in the moa-nin! I got no idea what the old guy was doin drivin in that shit weatha," Frank explained, looking at Kate's eyes.

He could tell she was horrified.

"Can you imagine? Ice is everywhe-ya… Okay, I'm tryin to defrost the frickin truck…. I can still see my breath in the cab and all a sudden this big boat of a Caddy is slidin out in front of me. You know, I slammed the brakes, but of coahse it's too late. The truck was just too high up, you know, the fend-ah slammed right into him, and it was over in a second. It's just a shame. You know, it is … it's just a shame.

The way he explained the crash made it sound like Mr. Stuber had somehow deserved to be hit and was killed due to his own negligence. That it was his fault he was out in those conditions, and Frank was merely a victim of the elderly man's ineptitude. In Frank's mind, the situation was unavoidable, and while perhaps tragic, it was how life goes, and there was no point in laboring over it.

Frank's explanation was vague enough to not reveal the full extent of what he'd done, but Kate knew that a man had died and that Frank had left the scene of the accident. She knew it was a crime considered homicide.

In Kate's mind, she believed his eyes betrayed him. She held on to the notion that deep down, Frank had remorse for what had happened. This was something she had clung to in the early years of their marriage, the belief that beneath his hardened exterior there was a good person. That her husband and the father of her child did not mean it, that it had been an accident.

Edward Charles Stuber had survived D-Day in Europe as a young staff sergeant in the Allied forces, but he could not survive a run-in with Frank Bruno.

26

Vida felt she knew why Kate had never left Frank. It was easy to disagree with the decision from the stands, but to live a life and cling to a family, a home, and the dream that it will get better, is something most folks can understand. Kate had thought of leaving a hundred times and had every intention of getting out when Anthony went to college or moved out. This was still frowned upon in Boston and for sure in the church. Better to ignore the pain than acknowledge it.

27

When Kate got back from Dr. Marchand's office, she was numb and could not recall driving home. She parked her gray Volvo in her spot in the garage, pulling the windshield up to the tennis ball that hung from a string tied to the rafter above. It was a trick her dad had taught her when she was learning to drive and had served her well.

The garage was as aged as the house and was actually referred to as "the carriage house" in the official deed. It stretched wide, white like the house, and both her car and Frank's truck fit in it. The floor was a giant slab of concrete that had several ugly cracks as the ground had shifted and heaved due to the frost of so many cold winters. The doors of the garage had been retrofitted with automatic door openers, but when the doors were down it resembled an old stable. Atop the gray slate roof sat a cupola with a tilted weathervane.

Kate turned the key and pushed open the side door of the house that she always kept locked. She paced around the first floor, nervously wondering what had just happened. King trailed her as if she had a steak in her pocket, but seemed to sense that something was wrong as he nudged his cold nose into her hand. Kate wanted to talk

a frame for flowers

to someone. She looked over to the phone and noted the familiar blinking red light on the answering machine. She wondered if it was the doctor with new information. She hurried over and pushed the button to listen.

28

The voice message from her brother Patrick passed through her like radiant heat, his words wrapping a quilt of comfort around her. He was exactly who she needed to talk to, and once she had listened to his entire message, she lifted the receiver to dial the number she already knew. Patrick had been the only person she had confided in the first time Frank ever hit her. She had since kept those incidents to herself, but her brother knew enough. He wanted so desperately to exact revenge on Frank, make him understand what it feels like when someone hits back. Patrick had no idea the extent of the abuse or that it carried over to his nephew Anthony as well.

She dialed the number in Frank's New York City loft, and it rang several times before his answering machine beeped and came on.

"I just need to talk to somebody," she said to herself.

Kate hung up and looked down at King, his head cocked slightly to the side as if to say, "What, did I miss something?"

Kate realized that she had not finished putting away all the groceries from hours earlier and that several of the bags still sat atop the counter by the sink. She began to remove the items from the stiff paper bags and group them by where they would be put away. Cans of soup and beans together, fresh fruit and veggies, dry goods, each in sections. Even with the shocking call earlier, she had taken care to put away everything frozen or refrigerated including the meat as well as the eggs, cheese, and milk. She gently placed the apples and green pears in the wicker basket on the counter to the right of the sink, then gathered two cereal boxes, Saltines, and a loaf of bread. She carried them over to the pantry at the back of the kitchen.

The pantry went straight back exactly seven feet with four even shelves on either side. Kate walked in and pulled the long, thin string that stretched up to the single bulb in a ceramic fixture on the high ceiling. She began to place the boxes in their locations, placing Frank's Corn Flakes apart from Anthony's Cheerios. Then going back to the left where the Saltines belonged, she was suddenly startled as King leapt from her side toward the small window in the back, letting out a short, sharp bark. Kate's eyes darted out the window into the backyard where she caught a glimpse of a person moving to the left towards her garden. She walked straight to the window to see who it was.

"Oh King, stop your barking," Kate said with a hint of a smile. "It's just Vida."

She directed King back toward the kitchen with a swirl of her finger and called out to Vida, who had spotted her in the pantry from the backyard.

"I'll be right out, hold on a sec," Kate said, for a brief moment forgetting her life.

Kate walked out of the side door through the small mud room, pulling on a light parka and hanging a quick left into the backyard. The entire area was closed in by the fence, but Vida had let herself in through the gate. Kate had extended the open invitation long ago to Vida and the octogenarian never thought twice about appearing unannounced.

"I hope I didn't startle you, Kate," said Vida with a giggle, knowing full well she had. "Ha… I finally nabbed the tulip bulb thief!" snapped Kate with a sarcastic finger wag.

"It's getting colder quick," mused Vida as she looked down at the rectangular plot of freshly turned soil. "Even King is choosing to hang inside! But looks like you got the babies in their cribs for the winter's nap. What should we expect for next spring?"

Kate heard her but did not answer. It dawned on her at that moment that she was very likely sick, and she had no idea what the next year would bring. She thought suddenly of all the pictures of the bald children from the cancer society, thin and pale from the chemo-therapy. She caught herself and responded. "Why don't you come in for a cup of hot tea and we can talk about it," said Kate, forcing a smile.

"I can do that," said Vida.

"Besides, he is not due home for three hours and twenty-seven minutes," she chided.

It was actually three hours and twelve minutes, thought Kate, embarrassed that Vida even knew to make reference to the Frank countdown.

The two ladies headed inside, Vida stopping to remove the tall, green rubber boots she wore most days when she walked down to Kate's garden. Her house was just up the street, and it only took a few minutes to walk over. It often became impossible to make that short trek in the heart of the winter, so Vida usually increased her visits in the fall to fill up for the winter. Her hip was painful, but two Tylenol and an occasional spot of whiskey in her tea made the trip bearable. Stairs were the big issue, and she tried to limit herself to up for bed and down for the day.

"The ground is already getting harder," said Vida, as she sat on the white bench in the mud room and pulled off her boots.

"It sure is," replied Kate, "but I think I got everything in place just in time!"

Kate slid the gray teapot over to the right rear burner and turned it on, the familiar clicking of the spark sounding like repeatedly pulling the trigger of a gun with no bullets. Vida teetered over to the kitchen table and sat in a familiar chair. Knitted cushions tied to the back of the oak chairs were new from last year, a gift from Vida to Kate.

"Did you ever tell him about these cushions?" Vida inquired. "Or should I ask: did he ever notice?"

"He notices everything and thought they were ugly, until I said they were free."

"Ah yes, when it comes to a cheapskate… free trumps ugly," she said, shaking her head.

Within a couple minutes, the whistle of the teapot's steam filled the room, and Kate slid the kettle off, easing back the trigger of the pot to make the piercing noise stop. She poured water into the two cups and let the tea briefly steep, then carried the cups over. On the table was a round, rotating plate that held the salt and pepper, along with a butter dish. There was also a plastic squeeze jar of honey in the shape of a bear, and Vida reached across for it.

"A little dab will do ya!" she said, struggling to squeeze the honey out of the small spout at the top. Kate leaned over to help and placed her hands around Vida's for an extra push.

"Thank you. Gotta have some sweet in your life," she said, but stopped abruptly as she saw the single tear drop slip off Kate's eyelash and splash to the table.

"What's wrong, Katie?" she asked, reversing her hands to instead grip Kate's.

"I think I'm sick," she said as the tears burst forth. "I have these irregularities with my blood, and the doctor's running more tests, but I'm losing weight and I have these lumps…"

Her sentence veered as the tears welled and dripped.

"Slow down, honey," Vida urged, as she continued to hold Kate's hand. "Tell me exactly what your situation is."

Vida said these words with such conviction and in such a soothing tone that Kate's body calmed, and she took a deep breath. She gathered her thoughts and told Vida everything she knew.

29

Frank had three homes to close up before the weather got really bad. Once a house was buttoned up, he could keep guys working indoors. He needed to visit all three of the sites that day and was driving around frenetically. Frank did not generally drink coffee, like so many of the workers. He drank water out of gallon jugs he had his wife buy at Stop and Shop. He used to keep a jug on the passenger side floor until the time one toppled and spilled, soaking through the floorboard. Frank was so pissed, he punched the windshield leaving a small crack that eventually spread. After that he used the passenger side seatbelt to secure his water.

Charlie Hess was at the third house on Frank's schedule. The gable had been removed, and once the crane finally showed up, they installed the safe with little hassle. It was heavy as a tank, but Charlie directed his team like a pro, and they got it tucked in perfectly. The owners had stopped by, and the man was very pleased about the safe.

"I bet that was a bitch, eh?" the well-styled man asked Charlie with a nudge and a smile.

"It was pretty heavy, but not too bad, Mr. Owens!" he said respectfully to a man years his junior.

"You can never be too sure in this world, and I like to know I have some things close by and safe when I lay down to sleep. Keeping a pistol is just part of our way of life you know," he said, pointing his finger in the air and towards Charlie, as his spouse wandered into the garage and out of earshot.

Charlie nodded in affirmation despite not agreeing to the notion.

"That was very important to my wife, and so I thank you," he said, holding forth a small wad of cash discreetly for Charlie to take.

"I'm sorry, I can't take that, sir," Charlie said sheepishly.

He wasn't just being polite, it could end Charlie's employment if Frank caught wind. The man held it out briefly then retracted the money back into his pocket.

"I understand, buddy. The thank you stands, though, okay?" he said with a soft punch to Charlie's shoulder. The man turned and walked away briskly, joining his wife in the garage, his voice gently fading away as he launched into another topic with his attractive spouse. Charlie turned around just in time to see Frank bounding out of his truck and marching directly towards him. Charlie bit his lip and felt the muscles in his thin body contract as Frank drew within a few feet.

"Do something," Frank mumbled as he shot past Charlie to the garage.

"Tom, Leslie. She's looking great, isn't she?" Frank bellowed as he waved his hands like a game show host. "Gonna keep you and the little ones nice and cozy on the cold nights!"

Charlie headed around back and left the three in the garage. He felt a chill and knew they had likely closed this house up just in time.

30

Vida had listened as Kate described her fear of the diagnosis and anxiety over what it could mean. Vida was eighty-two and had dodged death a couple times in her life, including a bout with meningitis that nearly killed her as a young girl. She had been without her beloved Hank since 1983 and watched friends and family members wither and die around her for more than twenty years. Death was every bit as much a part of her life as living. She found solace in writing and could vent her demons and frustration through fictional characters in her Daisy McQueen mysteries.

Vida knew that a single woman nearing death possesses great clarity, an ability to view things logically. She was fortunate to still have all her faculties and could remember most of her life as well as what she had for breakfast. Vida knew that was a gift from God. She felt obliged to entertain her readers, but also to try and enlighten people with what life had revealed to her over eight decades.

Vida did not like Frank Bruno. Actually, she hated him. She watched a bully terrorize his wife and her friend for many years and a young boy grow confused and angry under a shroud of indifference. Some men hit their children but claim to love them. Some try to ignore that they even exist. Still others simply nag and jab a child into resentment. Frank did it all, and she detested him for it.

Vida, of course, had never admitted this, but she thought of Frank more than once when she planned a murder. She had written thirteen mysteries in the time the Brunos had lived five houses away, and Frank had inspired her to shoot, stab, drown, and strangle multiple victims. Of the twenty-nine people that had perished in those thirteen Daisy McQueen novels, twenty-four were men.

Vida had stayed long after the tea got cold and comforted Kate, telling her that everything would turn out fine. The darkness of a shorter day loomed, and with Frank due home shortly, she left Kate to prepare dinner and gather herself. It was 5:02 by the kitchen clock when she pulled on her green boots and hobbled down the driveway, leaving Kate staring out the kitchen window as she cleaned the teacups in the sink.

Vida turned right at the end of the driveway and followed the fence along and past Kate's pretty lawn. The flag was down for the season, and Vida knew the cold of winter would kill off most of Kate's beautiful creation, but she smiled knowing that the plan for spring's return was already in the ground, waiting.

Four houses down from Kate's and one from her own, Vida ran into her neighbor, Walter Heaney. He was out for his regular dog walk, and although she didn't recognize it, he was running a bit late.

"Days are getting shorter, eh, Ms. Mudgett?" he asked with a grin.

"They are indeed, Mr. Heaney," she said, bowing slightly to say hello to Byron and Shelley.

"Are you ok to walk home?" he asked.

"Well I'm 90 percent of the way there now, Mr. Heaney," she said, "but thank you nonetheless." She followed promptly, realizing her tone was perhaps impolite.

"How is the latest mystery coming?" Heaney inquired.

Vida knew only too well that this could turn into a lengthy conversation with Wally Heaney, so she parsed her words carefully.

"I would tell you, Walter, but then it won't be a mystery!" she quipped with a chuckle, then leaned in with a whisper.

"I will get you an advanced copy though, so perhaps you can give me your two cents!"

This was perfectly played. Walter got all the conversation he needed, and Vida got to slip away with a smile in her wake.

31

Wally Heaney realized that he was now several minutes behind schedule and picked up the pace. With the colder air, windows and doors would be latched and bolted, so tonight's neighborhood soap opera was likely to be more a silent film or painting. He made his way down the block, eyes scanning for movement as darkness settled in. Just then, he noticed the hulking truck of Frank Bruno a hundred feet ahead, curving into his driveway and barreling towards the garage. He was early.

Frank had not spotted him, so he slowed his pace as the vehicle slipped into its spot, the heavy garage door closing down behind it. He moved ahead briskly to the corner of the Brunos's lot, but ducked around a large maple on the tree belt that had probably lived there longer than he. Its roots had pushed the cement sections of the sidewalk up into a peak. Anthony Bruno jumped his bike over the bump in the summer.

Wally heard the familiar sound of doors opening and closing from the truck to the garage to the side door of the house. As Heaney moved slowly forward, he made out the face of Kate Bruno in the kitchen window and could hear muffled voices. Wally inched forward, moving closer to the driveway until he nearly pressed against the short, white picket fence that corralled the front yard, separating it from the concrete walkway. The conversation inside seemed instantly heated, but Kate never turned from her position at the sink, yelling at whatever it was that sat in the sink before her. He could only see an occasional shadow behind Kate, but the acerbic tone of Frank Bruno carried much more clearly.

Walter, lost in the moment, craned forward to discern any of the exchange, but was startled as young voice spoke from behind him.

"It's really not that interesting," said Anthony Bruno as he shuffled nonchalantly by, head hung low with a book bag slung over his shoulder. "The nine o'clock show is always better," he said without a laugh as he turned the end of the fence and headed up the driveway.

Walter was so nailed, so obviously caught, that he didn't even pretend he wasn't snooping. He simply tugged at the leashes of the Yorkies and toddled down the block on his route without a word.

32

Kate had suspected Frank was regularly stepping out on her with another woman for the last twelve months and that he had been a cheater for many years. Their sex life had ground to a virtual halt in the last four or five years, except for an evening here or there when he came home half in the bag and would try and cajole her into sex. She found it difficult to recall the last time they had actually made love. She had never caught him in the act, but the telltale clues were everywhere.

33

Tricia McAllen was twenty-six years old and had worked at Star Builders for two-and-a-half years. She tolerated the job because the work was easy and she was sleeping with the guy she believed would eventually own the company. Tricia grew up in Revere, a half mile from the dog track and not too far from Revere Beach, which is north of Boston Harbor and a part of Massachusetts Bay. Tricia had lived there her whole life and had always gotten attention for her looks. As a Mick, she had the rare combination of black hair, tan skin (which is to say it got tan and not freckled in the summer), and deep blue eyes. She had the eyes of her mother, who told her she had a darker complexion because she was 'black Irish.' Her dad joked that she was a product of the milkman. Her sister, with red hair and freckles, told her she was lucky, and pretty much everyone else told her how attractive she was on a regular basis. This fact had conditioned Tricia to do as little as possible to get by in life.

Tricia's father was Darren McAllen, a union electrician who generally worked commercial jobs in the city. Now that his daughter had "hooked up with a good earner," he would do some gigs on the side for Star. Frank would throw him some off-book work for extra cash as long as he remained competitive and could work on call. Darren helped him skate by some inspections in the past by flashing his union card, so Frank liked having him in his pocket.

Darren McAllen would say that he didn't mind 'the Guinea,' although he didn't know Frank was married because he never wore a wedding ring. In actuality, McAllen figured Bruno was a potential future son-in-law. After Tricia told her folks that Frank made 'tons of dough,' the relationship was blessed by both of them. Darren's wife had left him eight years ago, but they lived near each other and were able to co-exist without too much friction. Both of her parents drank pretty heavily, and Darren smoked like it was his job. They both looked a lot older than their fifty-five-some-odd years.

Jim Star had no idea that Frank was carrying on with the "nice gal" from the office. He thought Frank's wife Kate was a sweetheart and that Frank was a good hard-working father and husband. Jim had two daughters of his own, both married and living out of state. He had no son to pass the business on to, and Frank had earned the position in his eyes. Jim found Frank to be a bit rough, close-minded at times and even ignorant on more worldly issues, but the guy worked hard and delivered good work so he didn't look far beneath the surface. Jim owned a nice place in Falmouth, down the Cape, and counted the days when he could hang aimlessly at the beach in his flip-flops and watch the boats sail by.

Tricia knew perfectly well Frank was married, but she also believed he was in transition and that a separation was pending. She had held on pretty long though, and the two of them had begun to argue about the fact that he was still married. She couldn't understand how he could daily complain about his horrible "prison sentence of a life," yet still live with his family.

"It's just ha-hd to stomach Frank, you still going home to that bitch every night. How would you feel?" she'd asked him.

"You spend a lawt a money supportin those two, and the kid dudnt even caya!"

It was a common chorus for Tricia. She felt it was an injustice that Frank was still paying for the kid who treated his own father like he didn't exist. She obviously had no idea what she was talking about, but Frank never let that stop her.

34

On a standard Sunday at Frank's parent's house, the women were all in the kitchen where Kate would quietly cut vegetables or prepare garlic bread while Frank's mom Theresa and his sisters would endlessly stir bubbling pots of sauce and chew about people in the neighborhood. Kate always felt like a piece of furniture, or at best, the hired help.

Frank's brothers had driven down to the football game at Foxboro stadium, and just he and his father sat in the two comfortable chairs in the living room watching the same game on TV. They sat silently for some thirty minutes, Frank's dad, Emilio, sipping on a cream soda, his thick fingers scooping small handfuls of peanuts from a china dish that sat on a tin TV tray. He would roll them in his fingertips then pop them in his mouth in bunches. He and Theresa had matching chairs and TV trays and would settle in to watch their shows most nights of the week. Similar to his son, Emilio was a creature of habit, so when the TV was off, the TV trays were folded and placed in the closet.

It was the beginning of the second quarter in the football game, and the station cut away to commercial.

"Things ahn't workin out, Pop," said Frank.

a frame for flowers

"That's cuz the defense can't play for shit," said Emilio, his eyes still fixed on the TV.

"Not the Pats, Dad," continued Frank, his father now turning to look at him.

"I don't love her anymore," Frank said with a stone face.

There was a long silence as Emilio looked over his shoulder at the doorway to the kitchen. He could hear the ladies talking fifteen to twenty feet away and recognized that the coast was clear for a conversation.

"What you talkin bout, Frankie?

"You know what I'm talkin about, Pop… It's Kate. I don't love her no more." Again Emilio paused to look back towards the kitchen.

"So what?" he asked with a shrug.

"So I don't want to do it. I can't pretend no more," said Frank, trying to seem the victim.

"Frankie, fa Christ sakes… you got a family," said his father with a suddenly serious tone. "You think it never got tough with your ma and me?"

Frank pondered for a moment at his father's comment, his eyes squinting slightly.

"We went through rough patches, ya know? That's how it goes, son."

"It's not like that, Pop. It's not like some bump in the road that you roll past. We had enough of those," he said, swallowing hard for effect.

"Che cosa può fare un ragazzo," said Frank in his limited Italian with increased volume.

Emilio motioned for him to keep his voice down, then leaned in.

"If you are getting something on the side, Frankie, it's none of my business, you know? Till death do us part? It's a… it's a long time," he snorted. "But the fact is you're a family, and that means something. Besides, a divorce is half of everything you got. You understand that? Half of everything you built."

"Yeah, of course I get that, Pop, which is why I gotta move now before I take over Star Builders and lose half of that!" snapped Frank with surprising volume.

111

So much so that Emilio stood up quickly from his lounger and marched for the kitchen, all the way while leering back at Frank. He peered into the kitchen with a smile and then softly marched right back to his chair plopping down, now completely uninterested in the football game.

"Look, son, I'm tellin ya…. You need to think this through. What about Anthony? He is your son, you know!"

"He's her son, dad. He don't like me, and honestly, I don't like him. He's a brat and we have never been close at all. Lately he doesn't even look like me. He likes anything I don't and totally disrespects me as his father."

"I understand it's tough, Frankie, but you gotta think this through," repeated Emilio with a somber look. There was a beat, then Frank clenched his fists and fired back in a screaming whisper:

"I have thought this through. You think I came up with this today? That I am watching the, the, the Patriots and suddenly felt… Hey, I think I wanna leave my wife and get a divorce. You think I didn't think this through? That I don't think through every fuckin thing I ever do? I am not an idiot, Pop… I have thought it through."

A quiet fell as the game's announcers once again took over the room's conversation. There followed a long silence, Frank and his father staring at each other, contemplating their next words, each of them looking to get the upper hand.

35 T-BIRD

It was an excruciating three days of waiting before the results of the biopsy and mammogram were available to review. Dr. Marchand met Kate in the lobby of the Dana Farber Cancer Institute, which was less than a mile away from Fenway Park. There were two large buildings, one brick and the other cement, with banners hanging from the walls: "Pioneering cancer research for over 50 years" and "Home of the Jimmy Fund." Kate had seen the Jimmy Fund ads a thousand times and had dropped a good amount of change into those collection tins over the years. She never dreamed she was funding her own research.

Dr. Marchand smiled awkwardly and gave Kate a half hug as she walked up to him in the lobby. She had told no one outside of Vida about her medical situation, and absolutely no one, outside of present company, knew she was at the cancer institute that day. She hadn't shared an inkling with Frank and hadn't the strength to tell Anthony.

Dr. Marchand had explained on the walk up that he would be introducing Kate to cancer doctors he referred to as oncologists, one of whom specialized in breast cancer. Dr. Lynch was probably sixty, but had a full head of sprout-white hair, a pointed face with thin lips, and a soft voice. He seemed to never make eye contact, but Dr. Marchand claimed that Lynch was the best in Boston. This was comforting to Kate.

113

Dr. Amrita Johnson was a dark-skinned woman with jet-black hair pulled back messily into a bun, her face largely obscured by dull, brown-framed glasses. Kate wasn't sure what she was, but maybe an Indian who'd married some Boston guy named Johnson. She was not particularly attractive, but appeared to have a thin, shapely body beneath her white jacket. Dr. Johnson smiled at Kate as she shook her hand. She had a soothing confidence that made Kate feel more comfortable. Dr. Marchand had also mentioned how she was recognized as an authority on breast cancer, explaining that Dr. Johnson had worked tirelessly since the mid-seventies to draw the disease out of the medical journals it had been relegated to and into public awareness that would help diagnose the deadly affliction earlier in patients.

Dr. Marchand pulled a chair up to the glowing wall and invited her to sit, then he moved to the back of the room, leaving the floor to the two cancer doctors. Kate's breathing became deeper and more pronounced, the sound of her lungs inhaling and exhaling audible in her ears. Dr. Lynch began by explaining the biopsy and the presence of "malignant neoplasm" or "invasive cancer cells.."

"Do you understand what that means, Mrs. Bruno?" Before she could answer, she added, in the event Kate didn't understand, "It means you have a viral cancer in your body."

Kate nodded to the affirmative, but remained silent, her breathing heavy and steady.

He told Kate how the cells mutate and how the body attempts to fight off the disease. Using as simple language as he could muster, he explained that the cells were destructive and could multiply quickly, making them particularly onerous. Kate sat stunned, thinking to herself how normal she felt.

Dr. Johnson interjected, pointing to the image on the glowing wall of Kate's breasts and circling with a pointer the darkened areas that represented lumps or tumors in the tissue. They may have spoken for thirty seconds or thirty minutes… she could not be sure. The two handed off the conversation to one another about treatments and how they would "aggressively combat the cancer." They explained the side effects of chemotherapy, the disruption to virtually every bodily function, and the potential for the cells to spread or "metastasize."

Kate felt helpless, angry, afraid, and physically sick to her stomach. Her life was being explained in strange medical terms by charts, percentages, and blurry photos of her insides. Her life was now defined by some internal battle of cells she could not see, yet was raging in her flesh at that moment as her body fought to return to its normal state, a battle she could lose. She began to shiver.

"I need to know if I'm going to die, and if so, how soon?" she asked, her throat strangling around each jagged word as they eked out one by one.

"We can't be sure of anything quite yet, Mrs. Bruno," said Dr. Johnson.

"Please... will you please call me, Kate," she said, her voice quaking. "Of course I will, Kate," said Dr. Johnson.

She went on to explain to Kate that putting a time stamp on someone's life is not generally something a doctor wants to do because so often forecasts like that are incorrect. She also suggested they re-test everything and that she should consider attaining additional opinions, but added they were quite sure the current situation had been diagnosed properly.

"Kate," said Dr. Johnson, taking her hand. "It is our job to be realistic, but also to encourage hope in patients."

The doctor shared, "Many patients, when faced with a daunting health crisis, experience a sense of hopelessness and fear of abandonment. Some have shared a concern that after a difficult diagnosis has been delivered, that the doctors feel there is nothing they can do. The patients suspect them of walking out and heading down the hall to a patient they can save."

"I can assure you, we will not do that," said Dr. Lynch, who was back looking at the X-ray. He turned and finally looked directly at Kate with the face of a man who had been through this before. "We would never abandon a patient."

And with those words Kate was overwhelmed. "My little boy," she cried uncontrollably, sobbing into her hands.

36

After Dr. Marchand helped Kate collect herself and walked her down to the lobby, they spoke. "Are you ok?" he asked.

"Peter," she said, firmly calling him by his first name for the first time. "I'm thirty-seven years old. I am in a loveless marriage, my son hates his father and I can't seem to help him with that, my only friend is an eighty-year-old woman, my in-laws detest me and my own parents are dead, my only family is my brother who I never see, although he did just tell me he'd come for Christmas," she said with a nervous laugh and sniffle, wiping away the tears with the Kleenex Dr. Marchand had given her. "And now it looks like I may be really sick and may very well die. Am I okay? I don't think so."

"Kate," the Doctor began, but she interrupted.

"I accept this if it's my fate, but it's crap, okay? My husband has lied, cheated, disrespected, and killed everything he can in this world, and I'm the one who gets to die? That's bullshit!" she proclaimed, eyes swollen and red, the veins on her forehead bulging.

"Kate," he began again, but a meager "I'm sorry" was all he could muster.

Kate took a deep breath and patted each eye dry. She leaned forward and kissed the doctor she'd known for twenty-five years on the cheek, then turned away and walked out the revolving door into the winter's air. Doctor Marchand wanted to run after her, wanted to tell her they could beat this thing, but instead he stood helpless in the lobby of the one place where she might be saved and watched her disappear around the corner.

He watches her walk away, wanting to help, but frozen.

37

After the tense exchange with Kate in the lobby, Dr. Marchand retraced his steps and caught Doctors Johnson and Lynch exiting the same room. He was a bit out of breath when he reached them.

"How's she doing?" asked Dr. Lynch.

"She's sad," Dr. Marchand said, revealing in his face the similar emotion, but not quite sure how to articulate their exchange minutes before. "She seems to have accepted it, though."

"Well, I'll be," responded Dr. Lynch. "You know that is the exact thing both Dr. Johnson and I found so unusual." The two looked at each other, and then she chimed in.

"Had you suggested to Mrs. Bruno previous to our meeting that she could be terminal?" asked Dr. Johnson

"No," Dr. Marchand stiffly denied. "I'm not qualified to diagnose that. In fact, I didn't even allude to the seriousness of the test results," he emphasized.

Both Doctors Johnson and Lynch expressed to Dr. Marchand how Kate seemed to instantly transcend the first four stages of the Kübler-Ross model of grieving, denial, anger, bargaining, and depression, and arrive at acceptance.

"I have seen people skip steps or rearrange them, but never just land at acceptance," said Dr. Lynch.

Dr. Johnson went on. "I would estimate that in my tenure I have had this discussion with more than a hundred patients, and I too found it peculiar that she just took it at face value. I don't recall ever experiencing such an acute level of acceptance of one's own mortality. Really quite remarkable."

Dr. Lynch then continued. "It would appear that once Mrs. Bruno has what she believes to be the facts, she is able to remove the emotion and deal with it in pure logic."

"You got all that in twenty-five minutes?" asked Dr. Marchand, feeling somehow like a lowly resident once again. "I got it in ten minutes," replied Dr. Lynch without a flinch, while Dr. Johnson just stared dismissively as if to say:

"Of course, I recognize it was a first and brief meeting, but we wouldn't have said anything if we hadn't 'gotten it.'"

The doctors excused themselves and headed down the hall. Doctor Marchand didn't bother telling them that he saw a good dose of the anger stage down in the lobby. He did recognize that Kate seemed to process the news and reach acceptance very rapidly, but chalked it up to her being in shock.

38

Days went by, each seemingly the same. The temperature ticked slightly lower as the morning's darkness lingered longer and the light faded faster. Kate kept busy cleaning the house and winterizing the last of the windows, but it was difficult to stay focused. King followed her everywhere she went as if he knew something was wrong.

Anthony would trudge off to school then wander home each day seemingly more distant. Kate tried to talk to him, and she hugged him so hard sometimes that certainly he must have suspected something was afoot. Frank predictably stuck to following his well-worn trails: Monday nights, paperwork; Tuesday nights, fiddling with the guns; Wednesday night, payroll; Thursday, out (no longer referred to as bowling night with any conviction); Friday, out (no longer clear with whom); next, the dreaded Saturday; followed by the exhausting Sunday with the in laws.

When it finally came, Kate quickly erased the message from Dr. Lynch and phoned back. After several misses, she caught up with the doctor, six days after they had first met. Dr. Lynch outlined how they had run the tests again and consulted additional colleagues. He expressed that it was their "professional opinion that she had a locally advanced or stage three breast cancer, and immediate and aggressive

120

steps were necessary to treat the disease and mitigate the spread of the dangerous cancer cells."

He spoke calmly and slowly, asking Kate throughout if she would like him to explain something further or repeat a portion of the dialogue. Kate got it all, and it confirmed what she had expected. It was very grave and she feared it would cut her life short, leaving her limited time to get things done. With each passing word and moment she began to plan the end. This frequently made her cry simple tears at times, but more often with deep sobs.

On Saturday night, Kate and Frank would sit in different rooms, like siblings sharing a bunk on vacation, pushed to the opposite ends as far as possible. He would watch TV, and she would read or do a crossword puzzle from one of the many books she had, some filled with the most challenging versions available that she could tackle handily. No night felt right to share with Frank what any wife would have likely shared immediately, so each day passed with his irritability or indifference allowing Kate to defer the conversation she so dreaded.

How could she fear telling him about her terminal illness? She asked herself this over and over. In some ways it was the fear that he would react indifferently, that his obvious lack of love would be made so instantly tangible, cementing the notion that her chosen partner in life didn't really care if she lived or died. Perhaps he would respond differently and quite the opposite. Perhaps he would apologize and seek to rekindle the relationship, realizing the error of his ways and the breadth and depth of his abuse and neglect. Perhaps it would be a seminal moment where he would accept his shortcomings and commit to a better life. Perhaps her mortality would provide him an opportunity for redemption.

All of this gave her angst for several reasons; she didn't want redemption for him. She had long since abandoned the very concept of love with this man. Moreover she did not want him redeemed and therefore capable of enjoying a fuller life as a better man after she was laid to rest. Also, it was so implausible that he was redeemable at all, and that even a temporary correction would likely lead to a reversion back to the person he truly was: abusive, self-absorbed, and cruel. All of which would leave Anthony damned.

And so the winter's days and nights passed in quiet anxiety. She knew the chemotherapy would take its toll not only on her body and mind, and—more concerning to her—the loss of her hair was both inevitable and impossible to conceal. She had to tell them both and could not reconcile which would be harder. If only there were a way to make this right. She was not asking God to save her life as she believed that if death was her fate, then it was certainly God who'd picked this time for her to go. Rather it was a desire to create the softest landing, to leave a legacy, and to die with peace. She asked God for the answers each day.

39

Patrick was set to arrive for a holiday visit on the twentieth of December, a Monday. He planned to take the short flight up from LaGuardia and would land at Logan at 3:16 in the afternoon. He and Kate had been talking regularly in a way they had not in ten-plus years. It felt so good to hear her voice. Kate offered to pick him up, but Patrick said he would take a cab.

Kate also had insisted he stay at the house, but it was going to be six nights, and Frank's grumblings coupled with Patrick's insistence on getting a hotel led to a compromise: He would stay the first four nights in a hotel, and then come to the house for the weekend starting on Christmas Eve Friday.

He booked a room downtown near Faneuil Hall, more commonly known as Quincy Market. The name Quincy was not like the old TV show with Jack Klugman; it was pronounced Kwin-zee. No one in Boston could tell you why, but if a tourist asked for directions to KwinSee market instead of KwinZee Mahket, a Bostonian would likely send them off in the wrong direction. Patrick was already talking about reciprocating on the hospitality and wanted to lock up some spring dates for Kate to come down to New York City for a visit.

"You can take the Amtrak down," he said with energy, bursting through the phone. "I have a great big place with lots of room, and you have to promise to bring Anthony. I can take him to see all the touristy things in the City and take you to the hip, cool bistros and fashion crap that I do." He went on like a kid talking about summer camp. "It would be such a great trip for you two! Tell me you will do it," he persisted.

Kate had never mentioned a word about her sickness. She planned to tell Patrick in person. She was afraid of ruining Christmas, but felt it was the right thing to do. She told him she would love to visit and agreed it would be great for Anthony.

"He is so into his drawing, but at his school it's called doodling and is seen as the hallmark of a kid bored with their studies or incapable of keeping up."

"What a joke," said Patrick in reply. "It's a shame you don't live here. There's a school on the Lower East Side that combines art and music into the curriculum. It's not like a Juilliard, but more of a progressive learning environment that encourages younger people to pursue the things that most interest them as opposed to following a regimented textbook-style model. They don't even have classes or periods per se, I mean they have to complete certain tests and curriculum, but for the most part they study what they like. Isn't that cool?" he barreled on before Kate had a chance to respond, but in her mind she could see Anthony in a place like that.

Patrick paused then continued, "Someday if I have a kid, I would want them to go there. It just seems like the kind of place that would have catapulted me ahead in my career. Heck, I spent the first ten years out of high school pretending I didn't do what I did and wasn't who I was. What a waste."

It sounded so like Patrick. His excitement always invigorated Kate. He had always served as an example that you can do anything you want if you are willing to sacrifice to get it. He made her believe that anything was possible or that anything could be achieved. Even if you faced a dilemma that most people would run from, that if you are willing to go through some pain and suffering, you can and will achieve great outcomes.

40

It was true that Thursday nights were not bowling nights. Frank took his co-worker and girlfriend Tricia McAllen out on Thursday nights and nearly every Friday night, as well. He was pretty brazen about it, taking her out to dinner or dancing at any venue in town, seemingly never concerned about getting caught. He knew Kate had no family to speak of in town, and her only real friend was the crazy old bat up the street. He was far more concerned about other guys checking out Tricia when they were out. He did think now and then to cover his tracks, hiding the scent of Tricia's heartily applied perfume, destroying an incriminating expense or removing a long, black hair left in the cab of his truck. The thing he had to remind himself about most, though, was inadvertently calling Kate, "Tricia."

Frank had started out by just having sex with Tricia. He found her very attractive, and she was flirtatious from the first day Jim Star introduced her as "the new office gal." For months they played a coy game of schoolyard crush with innuendo and calculated brushes in the tight quarter of the Star Construction office.

The flirtations gathered momentum over the months. The stares lingered and the conversation often turned to sexual innuendo. It reached a crescendo and crossed the threshold to a physical relation-

125

ship one Thursday night after some post-work drinks at a bar in town. Tricia was beside herself when he pulled her in close and kissed her. Frank had thought about her a lot and had begun to not just want her, but like her as well. Tricia was smitten by the ruggedly handsome and successful man. The slow boil had begun.

Previously the office work and scheduling had been done by Jim Star's younger daughter Denise, but when she got married and moved to Connecticut with her husband, who was "rich as fuck" in Frank's words, Jim placed an ad in the paper. Tricia McAllen was the first to interview. Frank had actually messed around with Star's daughter as well on a few opportunities, so the new girl being attractive appeared to be a company benefit and another reason to stay at Star Builders.

"You have to keep your workers happy," Jim Star would say. Frank couldn't have agreed more, laughing to himself at the irony. Jim Star had no idea about his daughter's dalliances with Frank and remained equally oblivious to Frank and Tricia's relationship.

41

When Vida would write her novels, she would sit down and rattle off 100,000 to 150,000 words in a torrent of typing. She took, on average, four months to complete a mystery, which is to say the time when she would sit and actually type out the words. However, the story may have been in her head for years.

Vida would often test out concepts on people, unbeknownst to them, and gauge their reactions. She would also undertake often elaborate experiments to test human intuition or tendencies. She loved to understand the human psyche and felt it vital to writing a truly suspenseful mystery. If one were to ask, Vida would describe herself as a psychological thriller novelist. Though some would view her books as a Nancy Drew-style series, certain literary critics made note throughout her career of the in-depth psychological undertones in her writing. Why do people commit murder? What could drive an otherwise normal person to commit such a serious offense? When could a murder be justified? Is guilt the unavoidable, silent killer? Could the reader kill someone? These were all the questions Vida Mudgett made her readers consider.

Vida was also a fan of science and believed it critical to create a story that was, if not realistic, then at least plausible. She read biology and medical textbooks, as well as journals and papers from psychologists and psychiatrists. The more obscure, the better. Early in her career, she spent endless hours at the public libraries as well as slipping into the university libraries with the help of some friends. She had an insatiable thirst for information and fact. The smallest of experiments or oddest of anomalies could be the centerpiece for her next mystery. In recent years, she had begun to rely on Kate to retrieve books for her. Kate would go to the library with some simple guidelines like 'poisonous plants of South America' or 'bipolar disorder in twins'.

Vida liked to weave scientific facts into her tomes, providing explanations to scenarios that seemed impossible and small pieces of evidence that could unravel an otherwise well-crafted murder plot.

"No matter how well you cover your tracks, you will leave something somewhere that points to your guilt." —Daisy McQueen.

42

It was a bitter cold day, and Kate wrapped her black wool scarf around her neck one more time before hopping out of the Volvo to feed the meter. She expected to park in the hospital garage, but as she pulled up she noticed the open parking spot right out front. She looked around to ensure that no one else was already eying the convenient spot and slipped into it. The air nipped at her thin fingers as she slid her coins into the machine. "Forty-five minutes should be enough," she said softly to herself, smiling at a deliveryman scurrying up the sidewalk.

Kate had gone to the cancer institute to meet with Doctors Johnson and Lynch. The purpose was to explain to Kate the specifics of how they intended to treat her cancer. She felt hollow as she made her way up to the doctor's office. When she stepped into the elevator and clicked the round button for floor four, it illuminated and the doors began to close. She looked up in time to notice someone reaching to grab the elevator, and she instinctively thrust her hand between the closing doors that clamped down slightly before springing back open. There stood a nurse in pink scrubs alongside a young girl who was obviously a patient. The girl's head was hairless, her skin sallow and pale, and her cheeks sunken, yet she smiled ear to ear and thanked Kate for holding the elevator. Kate felt a lump in her throat.

"Thought we weren't gonna catch that one," said the girl joking with the nurse, the two seemingly sharing some kinship.

"Yeah, thanks," said the nurse.

Kate could not take her eyes off of the young girl's perfectly sheer skull.

"No problem," said Kate, and the two turned to face forward, watching the floors click off. Kate figured the girl to be perhaps fourteen and thought to herself, "That is so unfair."

When they reached the fourth floor, Kate excused herself, exited the elevator, and headed left as she had been instructed. "Third door on the left, room 422," she whispered, mimicking the directions she had been given by Dr. Johnson.

"420... 422!" she counted out loud as she reached her destination. Kate took a deep breath and stepped into a waiting room. She removed her warm hat and her healthy, blonde locks fell freely about her shoulders. She then unwound her scarf and removed her thick ski jacket, placing them all on a chair in the room. There were four offices inside, and she could hear Dr. Lynch's voice as he apparently spoke on the phone in the room furthest to the left. The room was empty. So she stood for a moment, then took a few steps towards Dr. Lynch's voice, then stopped, turned around, and walked back to her coat and sat down. She was a few minutes early.

There was a round, red clock on the wall, several chairs, and a coffee table with magazines, as well a small table with a lamp just next to the chair that held her outer garments. On the table was a plastic bowl with those little lollipops called Dum-Dums. She thought about having one when she saw her favorite flavor Butterscotch sitting atop the pile, but was still thinking it over when Dr. Amrita Johnson came in the front door.

"Hello, Kate," she said in her usual soothing tone.

"Hi, Doctor," Kate replied.

"Give me just a moment, and we can meet in my office," said Dr. Johnson. "I'm sure Dr. Lynch will be wrapping up his call here shortly." She spoke loud enough for Dr. Lynch to hear.

a frame for flowers

Kate had stood up when the doctor entered, but slowly sat back down.

"Sure, of course," said Kate as Dr. Johnson strode into her office and briefly out of sight.

As she predicted, Dr. Lynch finished his call just as the clock ticked to 9:00 a.m., and moments later he strode out into the common room. He had an apple in his hand, still chomping on the first bite.

"Good morning, Mrs. Bruno," he said, mopping his lips with the back of his hand as he swallowed. "How are you feeling today?"

"I don't feel like I have cancer," she said with a sardonic grin.

"Mmm, yes," he said awkwardly as Dr. Johnson leaned out from her office and motioned the two to come in.

"Well then, you feel okay?" he continued, leading the way toward his colleague's office.

"Yes, Doctor, thank you. I guess I'm just scared," she said, suddenly serious. She fell into an uncomfortable silence as the two of them filed into Dr. Johnson's office.

The tight office was crammed. There were file cabinets, a desk and chairs, a small round table with still more chairs, pictures including degrees from universities Kate had never heard of as well as photos of the doctor alongside some local celebrities: Red Sox and Celtics players mostly. There was also an abundance of art pieces, many of which seemed to be from India, including several drawings, sculptures and figurines of elephants. Kate had read once that elephants are sacred to Indian people, but she had no idea why. Most notable to Kate were the numerous, lush plants including a Boston Fern, a gorgeous Peace Lily, and a large Sansevieria that is commonly referred to as a mother-in-law's tongue.

"I love your plants, Dr. Johnson," said Kate, suddenly brightening.

"Thanks... they're my babies!" she said with a glimmer as Kate looked each of them over. "I do think I am killing the Ficus though," said the doctor, making a twisted face.

"It's a weeping fig actually, which is a Ficus," said Kate reassuringly. "You may wish to move it back a bit further so the window's light can

131

bounce off that white wall instead of hitting it directly. They really like bright light, but it is best to be indirect."

Dr. Johnson was taken aback, but impressed by Kate's rapid diagnosis. "I'll do that, thank you!"

The doctors had outlined a multipronged approach to attacking the cancer and would use both local and systemic therapies.

"It will be a three-phase attack," said Dr. Lynch, stiffly raising three fingers in front of his face.

The doctors went on explaining that they would do surgery to remove the tumors in her breasts, and in the case of her left breast, they would give her a full mastectomy. Then the doctors would use targeted radiation to kill the remaining cancer cells in the impacted areas. Lastly, the doctors would use chemotherapy, basically toxic chemicals, to stop the rapid cell division of the cancer. Dr. Johnson described it as more or less starving the cancer cells to death. It sounded to Kate like a strategy for war, and in reality, it was.

Kate sat with both doctors for nearly three hours, going over what to expect over the following months. Kate paid close attention, but at times found it so overwhelming that she would retreat back to a place in her head where the doctor's words became muted. They kept talking and she kept nodding. Kate noted that Dr. Johnson's hair was neater today, tucked into a bun with a bright-red band holding it close and tight to her head. She had removed her glasses, revealing pretty, almond-shaped, brown eyes. The doctor wore very little makeup, but the thin black eyeliner looked good on her.

Kate sat nervously shifting in the soft brown chair as Dr. Johnson and Dr. Lynch took turns explaining different elements of the treatment. With each topic, they handed her relative pamphlets with titles like: "Radiation Therapy Side Effects" and "Coping with Cancer."

The doctors also explained that the toll on Kate's body would be tremendous: loss of weight and appetite, as well as her hair—and not just on her head, but everywhere.

"The drugs and radiation can be pretty devastating, Kate," said Dr. Johnson.

"You are going to feel rundown and will need a lot of help from friends and family to get around for the weeks following the surgery," she continued. Realizing suddenly that she had no one to help her, Kate thought she could figure out something.

"Most patients experience a loss of appetite, but it is critical to eat and do your best to give your body nutrients. You're also likely to experience regular bouts of nausea, vomiting, and diarrhea. "

"Great… what else do I have to look forward to?" asked Kate, trying to inject some levity into the somber setting.

"I realize this is very difficult to comprehend, Kate, but it is vitally important that you are prepared for the war you are going to wage with this cancer." A common theme was war and the battles needed to take back her body from this evil interloper.

Dr. Lynch put his hand on Kate's forearm and spoke to her more directly than he ever had. "We will be here to help you every step of the way and can provide you with information on just about anything, but you need to do and learn everything you can about how to beat this."

Kate was used to going to the library to gather research items for Vida, but now it would be for herself, and the research had never been so important. Kate would read everything she could find on the subjects of cancer, mastectomies, chemotherapy, and radiation. The way she saw it, the chemicals and radiation essentially kill you with the concept being: it will kill the bad you and allow for the good you to survive, if just barely. And hopefully then you can regrow into a whole new good you.

Dr. Lynch was going to perform a modified radical mastectomy on Kate's left breast, removing the entire organ to include the sentinel lymph node which the doctors described as an important gateway to her body that needed to be closed. There were multiple areas of cancer in the left breast, and the doctors felt it prudent to remove it in its entirety. He had used both diagrams of the anatomy, as well as photos of actual patients to demonstrate the procedure.

It seemed horrible to Kate: her womanhood carved right out of her chest. The photos showed women with a single breast or no breasts at all. The ugliness of their absence was palpable. Craters were left behind, and in many cases, the nipple or nipples were gone. They looked like a sunken cake. The faces of the patients were never visible in the photos, but the slope of the shoulders indicated the sadness of the mysterious women, a sadness she suspected lay beneath the surface for her.

Kate was to begin her chemotherapy in exactly a week, and she knew it was now unavoidable; she would have to sit Anthony down and tell him. It was Friday, so Frank would be out that evening, and it was a good chance to have the conversation in peace. Once she told Anthony, Kate believed the rest would fall into place. She would tell Frank, and they could begin to plan for the potential outcome. The issue of insurance was going to have to be dealt with as well, and while Kate was sure they had some level of insurance through Frank's work, she was not aware how much of the cancer treatment it would cover.

The doctors would periodically pause the meeting to ask Kate if she had questions. She could only think of one: "What are my chances of survival?"

This question had come up in various formats since the very first meeting with the Doctors and each time they answered slowly and vaguely, with this time being no different.

"It is a complex operation and we remove a significant amount of tissue," began Dr. Lynch. "There are always risks associated with an extraction of this magnitude, from the anesthesia, to the loss of blood, to the exposure to infection, but this is an operation we have done many, many times and have had a very high success rate with. The key is to stay strong and focused, because the operation is just the first phase. Once the healing of the tissue begins, we are going to promptly attack the area further with elements that are contrary to human life."

That statement struck Kate as quite shocking. It made sense as they had explained the toxicity of the chemicals and radiation, but it was made so vivid by Dr. Lynch's words; "contrary to human life."

What Kate heard was: we are going to kill part of you.

"We need to view the totality of the treatment," said Dr. Johnson, stepping in. She seemed to sense Dr. Lynch's factual portrayal of the situation may have seemed stark, if not insensitive to Kate.

"What Dr. Lynch is saying is that we are very confident in our ability to eradicate the tumors and infected areas," said Dr. Johnson, rising from the chair behind her desk to speak.

"This gives us an advantage in the battle. The tricky part is that cells are so small, and the cancer cells are so aggressive that it is always a possibility that some can be missed. That is the danger," she continued as she walked over to one of the plants and plucked a dead leaf from an otherwise green tendril and dropped it into the wastebasket.

"I don't know if you are asking us for a percentage number or something like that, but that is counterproductive in our opinion," she said, looking at Dr. Lynch for affirmation, who nodded as if to agree.

"Let's say this: we will have a better idea after the surgery of the potential long-term prognosis. Is that fair?"

Kate didn't feel any of this was fair, but nodded in agreement.

43

The air outside was just as cold as when she entered, but the sun crept out from behind spotted clouds to provide a bit more comfort. The sun's position in the sky made her realize that she had been in the cancer institute way longer than the forty-five minutes she'd put in the meter. As she hurried across the street, she could see the familiar, bright-orange glow of a parking ticket hugged tightly by her windshield wiper.

"Son of a gun," she mumbled aloud, looking heavenward.

She pulled the ticket off the windshield and climbed into the car. She slid the ticket down between the seat and the console and turned the key, the car rumbling to a start. Kate could still see her breath in the car as she adjusted the rearview mirror and glanced at herself for a moment. The lines around her eyes seemed more distinct today, and she noted her eye shadow seemed a bit unbalanced with too much on the right or perhaps too little on the left.

She looked deep into her own eyes and thought about dying. What happens? Would she float into the light as is often suggested, or do the lights just click off? Will she see or sense her parents when she goes? Will she be able to watch over Anthony from beyond? Does she need to answer to God for her life? Will it hurt? All of these thoughts swirled in Kate's head as she pulled her hat down tighter. The recently familiar tears again slid down and off her face, landing on her black scarf and sinking in or falling further to her jacket, beading up and rolling off the material callously.

Kate pulled out of the parking spot and drove slowly away. She was heading north over to the Boston Public Library on Boylston Street downtown. She made her way down familiar streets with the hum of the engine the only sound. As she took the overpass above the speeding cars on the Massachusetts Turnpike, she imagined swiftly veering off the edge to a crash below that was sure to be quick and painless. For a moment, she believed that a quick and painless exit would be better than a long, drawn-out suffering through cancer. Her mind drifted, though, to the young bald girl on the elevator and her smile of hope. And she thought instead of Anthony and seeing him in the future a grown man smiling. By the time she knew it, she had cleared the overpass.

44

Kate had rehearsed the conversation in her mind again and again, but it wasn't getting clearer. At the library, she'd collected several medical books on cancer with the help of a kind librarian and was headed home to read them. Her mind kept searching for the proper words to tell her son she was ill, but each time she began the speech in her head, it fell flat.

Heading south on backroads to their neighborhood, Kate passed one of the many large, stone churches that dotted the landscape in Boston. Upon seeing the enormous stone building with its towers pointing to the heavens, she stopped without hesitation. This time there were no parking meters to contend with, and she once more pulled into an available spot along the red brick sidewalk that surrounded the huge cathedral. There were several people milling about, but all seemed engrossed in their day as she made her way to the front of the church.

As if she were late for mass, Kate headed quickly up the twelve stairs to the massive wooden doors of a parish she knew nothing about. She was not sure the doors would even open, but they did, quite easily considering their size. It was warm and silent inside as she crept softly up the center aisle to the rear of the pews. The place was massive, and there were several votive stations with the candles burning in the familiar red glasses lining the rear-most wall. There was a wide, open foyer lit by a large, round stained-glass window whose colors shone down on the smooth, hard floor. There were dozens of dark wooden pews stretching long and wide, flanked by tall white pillars that rose to the ceiling some fifty feet above.

Along the outer wall were large, raised etchings of the Stations of the Cross depicting the final hours of Jesus—or as Frank's mom would say, "the passion of the Christ." It was common for the devout to pray the Stations of the Cross, stopping at each of the fourteen stations that tracked the trials of Jesus from being condemned to death to being laid to rest in his tomb. She had seen them many times before, but this time Kate walked from frame to frame and viewed each scene depicted. She remembered from her upbringing and confirmation classes how he suffered through those hours. Three of the fourteen pictures showed him falling: once, again, and then a third time, each time pulling himself up to continue. She wept as she made her way around the entire cathedral. She was remarkably all alone. Just beyond the last station in the cathedral was a plaque that briefly summarized the stations:

1. Jesus in the Garden.
2. Jesus is betrayed.
3. Jesus is condemned.
4. Jesus is denied.
5. Jesus is judged.
6. Jesus is scourged and crowned with thorns.
7. Jesus takes up His cross.
8. Jesus is helped to carry His cross.
9. Jesus meets the women of Jerusalem.
10. Jesus is crucified.
11. Jesus promises His kingdom to the repentant thief.
12. Jesus entrusts Mary and John to each other.
13. Jesus dies on the cross.
14. Jesus is laid in the tomb.

After making her way completely around, Kate stopped at the votive station in the back and knelt before the candles. She recited the Hail Mary to herself. She slid a folded dollar into the offering can, took the stick from the sand tray, lighting it with an existing candle, lit her own candle, and then quietly left the church.

Back in the car, Kate sat for a minute as the car warmed and thought about what she had just seen. Each of the pictures made vivid the trials Jesus suffered, and they impacted her deeply. Oddly, she couldn't relate to the one promising his kingdom to a thief. As a girl she had questioned the thief's motives, and for some reason, she couldn't get past it even now. She just felt like the thief would bargain for anything at that moment, but how could he have fooled Jesus? It never made sense.

45

When it came to church—and for that matter religion—Kate wasn't sure where she stood. Her parents had always belonged to a parish, and they attended Catholic mass every Sunday when she was growing up. But outside church on Sundays, there was little talk about God or religion in the Kelley home. When Kate's dad died, they had a funeral at the church, and around that time, their mother, Moira Kelley, frequently alluded to Ted going to see God or going home to heaven. There were references to the Lord in the Irish blessings that hung on the walls in the modest home, and Kate would always remember the final words from Father Dwyer at her mother's burial: "May god hold you in the palm of his hand."

Both Kate and Patrick had received first communion and when they were about fourteen years old, confirmation. However in the time between her mother's death and her marriage to Frank, Kate rarely if ever had attended church outside of Christmas mass. She talked to God now and again, but could not make a connection to the church or its ritualistic Sunday mass.

Frank wasn't religious: he didn't give two shits about God or the church. He slipped as little as possible into the offering plate every week, but sat pious and stone-faced through every mass. Frank's mother liked to sit up front, and this was the rare occasion that he would break rank and do his own thing in her presence. He always sat in the back of the church, and it was not by accident. He would bide his time, scanning the pews for attractive women, watching them stand and sit, sit and kneel. It was so obvious to Kate, that she felt embarrassed for him.

From the first Sunday after they were engaged, Kate and Frank attended mass every week at Frank's parent's parish in the North End. Each Sunday morning, they would make their way crosstown to the church and then spend the afternoon at Emilio and Theresa's house where they would remain until supper, which was served around 4:00 p.m. Unless a football game was still on, they would leave shortly after coffee and dessert. There was always coffee and dessert, and in fact, part of the Sunday tradition was stopping by one of the many excellent bakeries in the North End to pick up cannolis or some other pastry, cake, or cookie. As a young boy, this was Anthony's favorite part.

About two years ago, Anthony had stopped making the trip and only came now and then, usually for holidays when Frank insisted. Anthony had expressed a lack of interest for so long and had asked if he could skip on numerous Sundays, to which Frank had always responded with a flat no, usually accompanied by some childish insult. When the straightforward approach didn't work, Anthony resorted to moping around. He did so with such consistency that Frank finally exploded one day driving home, tearing into Anthony, who sat wedged in the small seat behind the passenger side in the truck. Despite the lack of room, they always drove in the truck.

The verbal attacks always started slow, as if Frank were trying to control himself, but to Anthony it felt more like the way a cat likes to knock around its prey for a while—then eat it.

His father was predictable to him. The irritation manifested itself in the same fashion every time. It started with heavier breathing and shifting back and forth, the short sniffs through his nostrils like a bull taunted by the color red. His father would grip and twist at the steering wheel with his strong hands, twitching until the words spewed out.

"So anotha tough Sunday at ya grandparents, huh, Tony?" said

Frank, trying to make eye contact through the rearview mirror at his son. Anthony didn't respond.

"I'm talkin to you they-ah, buddy," he said, nodding in affirmation to himself, his eyes now glaring at the mirror then turning over his shoulder to stare directly at the boy.

"Anotha tough Sunday of home-cooked food and ah warm roof ova ya head? It's a real bitch, huh?" said Frank, still nodding.

Still, Anthony said nothing, though his eyes lilted knowing this wave signaled the flood. It was a solid half-hour ride back to the house and that was without traffic. This beating had just begun.

Kate had worn out her welcome as a mediator and given up trying to deflect Frank's vitriol once it began. She found it better to let him get it out, to tire himself and vent his frustrations. She wanted to protect her son, but too often in the past her attempts to put a salve on things led to greater fits of rage. Two of the worst beatings Frank ever gave her was in response to her defending the boy. Equally frustrating to Frank, though, was Anthony's silence, which he viewed as further disrespect and a lack of courage by his son. The silence served only to raise the stakes. Anthony knew it perfectly well, but watching the veins rise on his father's neck and the saliva spew meant he was gaining the upper hand, so silence was the best course.

"You know what you ah, Tony? A fuckin ingrate!" snapped Frank, his voice booming throughout the cab of the truck as Anthony bowed his head in anticipation of the blow. "A fahhh-kin ingrate!" he repeated with greater staccato for emphasis.

"My motha and sistas work so hahd cookin a good family meal on Gawd's Sunday and you sit theya like ya dawg just died. What the fuck is wrong wit you?" And still no response from Anthony.

Frank was now seething with anger as the initial onslaught of insults appeared to bounce harmlessly off of Anthony, who had pushed himself back into the corner of the cab with nearly inhuman capacity. Frank's left hand, clenched tightly in a fist, began pounding on the dashboard and steering wheel as the lava-filled words belched and boiled from his gaping mouth.

"You don't deserve my motha's cookin," he said, now pointing a menacing finger back at Anthony. "Ya hear me? You fuck! From now awn, you can sit ya pathetic, skinny ass at home every Sunday by ya-self and chew on fuckin left ovas!

Frank had delivered the judgment. Anthony was not going to be allowed to join the family for the traditional Sunday meal from there forth. Upon sentencing, Frank looked back once more over his right shoulder, expecting to see a cowering if not weeping child. Instead he saw Anthony, expressionless, staring right back at him. Frank detected a smile desperate to break from beneath the boy's blank stares. Anthony knew right there he had pushed the skirmish to a dangerous place. Frank fell silent for the remainder of the drive, but Anthony knew it was far from over. He knew that at some point after arriving home he was going to meet his father again in a regretful way. Whenever Anthony pushed his father to the level of silence, it meant violence.

Kate was unaware what had happened and assumed it would cool off and blow over, but after ten or more Sundays when Anthony remained absent from the gathering, she began to lose hope. She was also unaware that Frank had beaten Anthony mercilessly that night when he told the boy to take out the trash then followed him to the garage. He was sadistic and minded to not strike the boy in the face where it would be obvious. Instead, he left cruel welts on Anthony's back and legs. Anthony never cried or even wailed out in pain. He quietly took his punishment, and quieter still, he begged God to kill the man.

That evening upstairs, Kate sat at the end of the bed, slowly removing her shoes and stockings as Frank spoke calmly from the bathroom as he washed his hands.

"I don't know who that kid is or how he comes off treatin my parents with such disrespect. To be honest, I'm glad he'll be sitting at home by himself on Sunday from he-ya on. I'm serious. I don't get how that kid is my blood," he said, emerging from the bathroom shirtless. "He's nothing like me."

"Frank, he's your son," said Kate, trying to appeal to any shred of decency in the man.

"I don't think so," he said curtly and made his way down the hall to the guest room.

46

The trees of fall begin to turn in the northern region of New England sometime in September, and by mid-October, the change drifts steadily south as the leaves burst with color in a kaleidoscope of yellow, orange, and red. From Maine to Rhode Island, the landscape of rolling hills and mountains extend away from the northern reaches of the Appalachian Trail, spilling a bold canvas of color that stretches as far as the eye can see, imbued with a hue that is uniquely New England foliage.

It was sweater weather, and people flocked to Boston and the surrounding areas to pick crisp apples from the trees and carve bulging, orange pumpkins. Countless farmstands lined the country roads, and the folks who worked them step out of the past with their kindness. The yards were filled with children playing football and parents raking leaves into big, fluffy piles. As kids, the Kelleys didn't have much of a yard, but when leaves fell, they would pile them high and jump on them as if they were soft mattresses. It was a great time to play outside in the fleeting vestiges of tolerable weather.

If New England was lucky, baseball would carry on until the fall. If not, it meant weekends would once more be filled with college and professional football games. It also meant Thanksgiving was not far off, and that was a hop, skip, and a jump from Christmas, which made every kid smile right through their chapped lips.

Fall was a passage into the winter that would invariable test New Englanders but make them strong. It was the time to prepare for the long, dark cold and Fall would ease them into the challenge that lay ahead. It was also the time that people tucked away the thoughts of summer's hope and focus on the future that perhaps now lay a bit further out. Winter was about getting through it.

47

Frank had already told Tricia McAllen that he was leaving his wife. He had explained it would be a long and complicated process from the beginning, dating back to a time when he wasn't very serious about the prospect of actually leaving Kate for Tricia. Over time, however, the bond with Tricia grew stronger, and he began to plan for a future without Kate and Anthony.

"We're better off not togetha," Frank told his brother Lenny over lunch at a deli downtown. "All we do is fight, and she's been wantin to leave me fa yee-as,"

"What, is she messin around, Frankie?" said his youngest brother, wiping away a gob of mayonnaise from his mouth and leaning across the small, red table.

"I don't know," he said, coyly shaking his head as to suggest he could perhaps be a victim. "But I doubt it. She don't like sex. I'm serious. Like she does not like to be touched no mo-ah."

Lenny's eyes widened at this sordid detail. "Come on?"

"No, fa real. She used to like to do it, you know, when we were younga, but like... I'm talkin for yee-as now, she just is as cold as a dead fish."

"But you don't think she's screwin around?" Lenny asked, again interested in the angle.

"No bro,please. I woulda caught her. You know her, Len. She is a pathetic ly-ah. That broad cahn't even pretend she like's some new food or something. She can't hide nothing," he went on, now glaring a bit at his younger brother who continued to look unconvinced.

"She isn't cheatin on me, okay? So let's try and forget about that," said Frank to his brother who got the hint that Frank didn't want to discuss it.

Lenny did know Kate, and unlike most of his family, he had always kind of liked her. He also knew it was true that she was terrible at lying. She couldn't keep a secret to save her life. Anything like a surprise party or a Christmas gift, if you pressured her at all, she would crumble.

"Ya... of co-ase," said his brother assuredly as he plunged into another bite of his chicken salad sandwich. Frank sat blankly staring and scarcely touching his sandwich. He was drawing his young, muscular, and not-so-bright brother right in.

"It's just hard," said Frank with a dip of his head, and there was a long pause between them.

"Life's too short, Frankie... you know... to be unhappy. You gotta do what you gotta do."

"I know," said Frank, appearing introspective.

"No, I'm serious. Let me be yo-ah voice of reason. Sometimes you gotta te-ya the band-aid off, and it hurts a bit at first, but then It's ov-ah."

"It just hahd."

"Of course it is," said Lenny, trying to provide comfort. "It's hahd to break up the family, you know?"

"Well that paht is true," said Lenny with a chuckle. "Mom is going to be very upset and dad's gonna give you a lotta shit about this."

"I already talked to dad. So just shut the fuck up on that," said Frank, briefly unable to maintain his melancholy charade. "I mean, you ahh right about our motha. She aint gonna like it."

"It's your life though, bro. You cahnt stay in a prison cell and suffa. You know? Life's too sho-aht to be locked up in ya own home, Frankie."

148

a frame for flowers

"I know yo-ah right, Lenny. I guess sometimes you just gotta take matt-ahs into ya own hands, you know what I mean?" Frank asked his brother.

Lenny nodded in accordance, but thought to himself, "That's how the mob talks when they're gonna whack somebody." For a split second, he asked himself if his brother would off his own wife, but he quickly dismissed the question as silly.

Frank was the kind of person who, if he needed to get something done, he would tell people he did it. It wasn't lying to him; it was assuring that it would get done. If he told Jim Star the house on Fisher Street was done, then he would have to go and make sure it was done. To him, this was a great way to force the conclusion.

Lenny says to someone else?

48

K ate leaned her way up the street towards Vida's house into a
biting wind that was whipping through the trees and knocking off the remaining leaves that had refused to fall. She had a pair of
jeans on with a warm flannel shirt tucked in and cinched tight with
a belt. She wore knee-high, brown leather boots that resembled the
type an equestrian would wear, and her hair was concealed beneath
a wool-knit ski hat. Her body was wrapped in her familiar ski jacket.

Under her arm was tucked a book for Vida who had asked to see
some literature about justifiable homicide. Kate had picked it up along
with her medical books at the Boston Public Library. There were lots
of books on the subject of justifiable homicide, and some dated back
hundreds of years, indicating that this topic had been under scrutiny
for eons and perhaps still remained an unresolved issue.

Vida had clarified to Kate that she was working on a new mystery
in which a woman killed a man in self-defense. The plot thickened
as the woman in question was a defense attorney who understood
the law and was familiar with the court's diversion from society's
convention. In the woman's experience as a lawyer, she noted a disproportionate tendency to still prosecute an allegation of self-defense
as a murder nonetheless. Even if the charges were lowered to man-

slaughter, the verdict was guilty and the person was sentenced.

Kate reached the large, front steps of Vida's house and climbed the five wooden steps to her spacious, covered porch quickly. Vida never used the front door herself, mostly due to the stairs, but it was the fastest route from Kate's house as opposed to walking around back to the door Vida preferred. She rang the bell that echoed inside the large Victorian home, and after a minute or so, Vida appeared at the door with a smile. She was wrapped tight in a black-and-gold, oriental robe that she was fond of, with a pencil tucked behind her ear. It was clear Vida had been writing, as she always kept the pencil behind her ear when she was. She used an old-fashioned typewriter that she would not part with, and the pencil was needed for the eraser at its opposite end; the typewriter ink could be erased.

"Oh my gosh. You come in quick from that horrible cold!" said Vida with a giggle.

She was tough as nails and was being sarcastic about the temperature. She loved to tease people who couldn't handle the elements.

"What a lily," she would say if someone whined about frigid air.

"I've just made some tea," said Vida, pointing anxiously toward the book she spotted under Kate's arm.

"Is that the book? Was there only one? Is it about a lady killing a man?" she asked in rapid succession as Kate peeled off her layers. Vida was obviously excited.

"Actually, there were lots of books, so I wasn't sure which one or how many to get, but this one seemed interesting," said Kate.

On the inside flap it read: "The author explores the legal and societal reasons why women have historically been denied the right to act in self-defense."

"The librarian explained that it cites lots of actual cases along with the ruling, so I thought if your character was a lawyer, it might be a good fit."

"We shall see!" said Vida wryly as she tottered over to the kitchen with Kate in tow.

Kate sat at the old wood table in Vida's kitchen, a familiar spot

where they had shared countless conversations about virtually everything. The table was nicked up and likely dated back to when Hank
was still around. It had leafs that folded under, changing the table
from large and round into a more manageable square that would
accommodate pretty much anyone Vida might entertain. She had
distant relatives, but like Kate, they were all dead.

Kate would have gotten up to help Vida carry the tea across the
kitchen, which at times seemed challenging for her. But you can only
be scolded so many times before you accept at face value that she
didn't want assistance. Vida placed the teacups on multi-colored potholders that were likely as old as the table, sat down, and folded her
hands to talk.

"There's a real twist to this one Katie!" she said with a grin, her still
straight but tea-stained teeth pushing through her thin lips that had
a fresh, yet discreet coat of ruby-red lipstick.

"Not even my editor knows this," she said, building the suspense
in the precise way she did for her adoring fans. "Daisy knows the
woman is guilty, and there is no scandal to that—heck, she always
knows who's guilty," she said, leaning back and smiling into a slight
laugh, yet not revealing the scene-stopper quite yet. Vida paused and
took a long draw on her steaming tea.

"What?" asked Kate, now fully engaged and totally intrigued.
"Daisy knows she's guilty, and lets her get away with it?"

Kate had read every McQueen book, so as a fan, this was a shocker.
Daisy was a precocious sleuth whose moral compass was immovable.
There had been many cases where there was empathy for the murderer
and/or disdain for the victim, but no one ever got away with it. That
was the whole point. Daisy would outsmart even the most cunning of
plots and vindicate the victim by righteously placing the blame where
it belonged: on the guilty party.

Vida went on to share more details of the plot, and Kate smiled
wide as she listened to her friend. Vida seemed very excited about
this latest mystery in a way Kate had never witnessed. They talked
for about an hour, long past the heat of the tea.

a frame for flowers

Eventually Kate had to get going and tend to the house before her evening life began. She got up and began to reassemble her cold-weather wear.

"I'm officially sick, Vida," she said suddenly.

"How sick, honey?" asked Vida, immediately shifting to concern.

"I am real sick. I have cancer, and it's serious," she said as her jaw clenched a bit.

"Who told you this?" Vida asked suspiciously.

"Several doctors, Vida. It's for real."

"Well, what are they going to do to stop it?" she asked insistently.

"Lots of things, actually, but it's crazy and scary. They are going to do an operation for breast cancer and remove a lot of me."

"Remove? Is that what they call it?"

"No, no. Those are my words. It's a mastectomy: they remove a breast. I have lots of tumors."

"Oh my lord," gasped Vida, her hand knotted and held before her mouth. "When did you find this out, Kate?"

"I just did. It happened so quick; I went from a regular checkup with Dr. Marchand to talking to these experts in a couple weeks. It's bad, too. I need chemotherapy, radiation, and the operation. They are afraid it is spreading."

Vida reached for her chair, feeling faint. "Oh my lord," she repeated. "And here I am going on and on about some silly book. Oh forgive me, Kate," she said, edging closer to embrace her young friend. "What are you going to do?" Vida asked, and then went on, "What are we going to do?"

49

Thursday evening was the event at Anthony's school when parents would tour the classrooms to see the projects, view art work in the gymnasium, and get a snapshot of the progress their kids were making in their curriculum. Kate would meet with his teachers and get some feedback on how things were going, but that wasn't really on her mind. It was also the night she planned on telling her only son that she was very sick—perhaps deathly sick. She was not sure how it would go or what she would say, but the operation to remove her left breast was set to take place in eight days, and she had delayed long enough.

Kate made her way over to the smaller family-run grocery store to get a cut of meat. She wanted to make a nice dinner for Anthony. Frank would be out, and although he would stop home to throw back a meal, she planned to make him one thing and then prepare a real dinner for her son. The school event started at 6:00 p.m., so she would have to leave by 5:40 p.m. to get a parking spot. That meant she would only see Frank for a few minutes. She calculated her schedule to minimize contact. She was standing in front of the butcher case when a voice came from behind.

"Katie?" she heard in a faintly familiar, deep voice. She turned slightly to see a handsome man who looked to be about her age. Her eyes darted quickly to the brown-leather holster on his hip with a thick, black pistol tucked in tight. He wore well-fitting jeans and dark boots with a leather jacket that was unzipped to the waist. A shiny, familiar badge hung from a lariat around his neck. He was obviously a cop.

"Kate Kelley. I mean, I'm sorry… Bruno?" he inquired further.

"Yes!" she said, only fairly confident she knew who he was, but he smiled through a handsome face and a flicker of the past lit his name in her memory. "Joey Bertucci? Hi! Oh my God, it's been forever. How are you?"

He puffed up a bit, pleased that she remembered. "I'm good, real good. Made detective last year, so I'm still working C-6 and C-11 collaring dirtbags, but now I do it in street clothes… and I get paid a bit more," he said, cupping his hand to the side of his mouth to pretend he was sharing a secret.

"Good for you," she said, nervously shifting.

Kate always thought Joey was handsome, but their dads were such good friends that he always felt more like a brother than a guy she could ever date. Lou Bertucci was one of Ted Kelley's best friends, and Kate would always remember watching as the terrifically tough man cried at her dad's funeral.

"How's Patrick?" he asked. Joey and her brother had skated together at the local rink a bunch growing up and were pretty good friends. "Last I heard, he was a photographer or something in New York."

"Yeah… or something," she said. "He works with photographers all the time, but he is a designer now." Kate said nervously, not sure how Joey would react to that revelation. "He makes people's clothes, or I should say he comes up with the ideas. A couple of celebrities wear his stuff."

"Oh yeah?" said Joey, seemingly interested.

"Ya. Not like Robert De Niro or someone, but yeah, he's doin good. He's doin real good."

"That's awesome," said Joe, not sure how to respond, but fixated on Kate's big, blue eyes.

"Hey," she said as though a lightbulb had just appeared above her head. "Hey, ahh, Pat's coming up for a visit at Christmas and said he's gonna hang for a whole week. He might even skate while he's here. Will you be around?"

"Yeah, for sure," Joe said with a smirk, as if to say, where else would I go?

"My dad and mom are actually flying home as well. So, yeah... I'm here for sure."

"I should have him call you."

"For sure. Let me give you my cell phone number."

"Perfect," said Kate, nodding and fumbling with her purse to dig out a pen and scrap paper. "Okay, go ahead."

Joey rattled off his number, double checking to make sure she had written it down correctly. He stared at her as she focused on the number, and he thought how pretty she still looked.

"You haven't aged a day," he said, half by accident.

"Ha!" she chirped. "That's a looong day."

"No, I'm serious. You look great, Katie."

She smiled back at Joey and realized this was the first time she'd felt attractive in years. "It's really good to see you," she said and turned back to her shopping.

50

Nathaniel Bourne High School was not very far from the Bruno house, about a mile and a quarter, and most days Anthony took the standard yellow bus that dropped him off down the street. He would hoof it the last hundred yards or so home. It took about four minutes in the car.

It was the last week of soccer until spring, and Anthony did not play a winter sport. With the event that evening, all sports practices were cancelled, so Anthony would be home early that day. The average day at Nathaniel Bourne High School ran from 7:45-2:45, so he would catch the bus and be home by 3:10—maybe 3:15. On soccer days, it was more like 4:45, and he would get dropped off further away and walk a quarter mile to the house.

When Kate returned from the store, she started preparing the supper, even though it was barely noon. She thought about Joey Bertucci as she moved around the kitchen.

Anthony walked in the side door at 3:12, but Kate had not seen him coming up the driveway. She had been sitting at the kitchen table reading about the chemicals they would use to attack the bad cells in her body. She had felt a bit lightheaded lately, and her weight had continued to slip slightly. The description of the chemicals and how they worked to kill off the cells scared her, but she knew they would help and that she would have to overcome her fear and use whatever weapon necessary to make things right. The book had lots of warnings and bad news, but it had just as many success stories. One of the doctors or scientists who wrote the book offered this advice to a reader who may be stricken:

"You can win this, but you have to be strong, brave, and do things that scare you."

Anthony grabbed a few chips from the pantry then headed upstairs. He gave his mother a hug in greeting that she held a bit before she let him go.

"Lay out something nice to wear, okay, hon?" chimed Kate from the kitchen as he clomped up the stairs.

"Yeah, ma."

"I'm serious…"

"Yeah, mom," he repeated and thought a bit about what he could wear to make his mom happy, yet draw minimum flak from fellow students who would be on hand.

"We need to leave right as your father gets home," said Kate.

"Fine with me," Anthony replied from atop the stairs as Kate went back to preparing Frank's food and Anthony's dinner.

51

The activity in the house picked up speed as Frank's truck rumbled up the driveway at 5:33 and his arrival made its familiar noises. Kate listened to each noisy step that brought him closer. Garage door up, garage door down, car door open, car door close, garage side door open, garage side door close, house side door open, house side door close... and he stood in the kitchen.

"What's for suppa? I gotta hustle," breathed Frank.

"Be ready in a minute," Kate mumbled, not even looking his direction.

"Anthony and I need to leave here in a few to head over to Bourne for parent-teacher night," she announced, but turned to notice Frank had already scrambled out of the room to head upstairs and get dressed for his Thursday night.

"Good talkin to ya," she said to herself, wagging her head.

Kate left Frank a plate of hot dogs and baked beans on the counter and walked out to the front hall. She had gotten dressed an hour earlier and looked stunning in a pair of cream slacks and tight, black turtleneck. She checked herself in the long mirror in the soaring hallway as she called up to Anthony.

"Three minutes, sweetie"—the word sweetie assuring Frank would know she did not mean him.

Kate did a short half-turn in the mirror, as she imagined her brother Patrick's fashion models would do, and examined her body in her reflection. She looked thin, and the bra she wore even made her look busty in the black material that clung tightly to her curved torso. She held her hands, cupping her breasts and pushing them up and together a bit.

"Enjoy one of your last nights out, girls," she said with a melancholy laugh.

"How pathetic that our last night out is parent-teacher night at Nathaniel Bourne High School," she said aloud to the mirror.

Anthony came down the stairs slowly, and to Kate's surprise he was dressed sharply in pressed, black dress pants with a blue-collared Oxford shirt. His hair even appeared to be combed, parted lightly to one side. He had a black belt with a silver buckle and his Sunday shoes on. He acted sheepish, as if it was all quite normal, but Kate was thrilled. He looked so handsome, but she made no mention of his attire.

"Good timing," she said "We need to get going."

Frank was still knocking around upstairs as they slid softly out the side door, climbed in the Volvo, and backed out of the driveway. Although she could not see him because of the reflection, Kate could sense Frank was watching from the window above. She could also sense he had no remorse for going out on the town instead of attending a parent-teacher night. In every year of Anthony's schooling, Frank had never attended a single event. If he was watching, it was to make sure they were gone.

Vida alone: How can I help Kate?
Startst writing

52

Parent Teacher Night

As they pulled into the high school, there were cars buzzing around as frantic parents navigated the parking lot, searching for their spot. There appeared to be more than one tense family on hand, and as they glided into a space, the car next to them found a family in a heated exchange. The mother was blasting away from the passenger side of the family minivan as the father sat quietly behind the wheel and a young girl slumped in the back with her hands over her eyes.

"Yikes," whispered Kate to herself just as Anthony spoke.

"I want to go to college in California," he said abruptly.

"California? Why? And what college?" she asked, immediately thinking of her high school love who had left her to do the same.

"I don't know. What I mean is outta state," he clarified.

"Okay. Do you have an idea where?"

"Nope… just not here."

"Yeah, well, I guess it depends on where you get in. You are still just a sophomore, so we have a little time."

"My grades are good."

"I know, sweetie, for sure. And the sports help too!" she said to encourage him. "But the big thing is your SATs, or at least that's what I understand."

"Yeah, I'll crush those," he responded confidently. "I took the PSAT already and scored in the 92nd percentile in verbal."

"And in math?" she quipped.

"Ma, you know I didn't do as well in the math part, so why are you asking?" he said, smiling because he knew his mother was not being mean.

"I'm just saying they look at both, right? I mean that makes sense," she said, smiling into her son's eyes.

"I just don't find it very interesting, and let's be honest, ma, it is pretty much useless in life."

Kate couldn't disagree, but still gave him a discerning look.

"I'll study the next couple years and get math figured out."

"You'll solve the problem?" she said with a laugh.

"I will solve it in less than a year, I promise!" he proclaimed, smiling at his mother's humor.

"I know you will," Kate said softly, wondering if she would be there to see it.

She knew he was right. Math didn't matter and following his interests would almost certainly provide a happier life. She thought math was useless and couldn't believe she heard herself defending it as important. "I guess for good or for bad, we just become our parents eventually," she thought to herself.

"Okay? You ready to go inside?" he asked.

"Yes," said Kate, turning off the car. "Let's go get em!"

53

The school was humming with people as they made their way over the cement walkway and through the glass and metal doorways that opened into a long hallway. There were families of all kinds: single moms with sons or daughters, single dads in shirts and tie being led by their children, and whole families with little brothers and sisters in tow. Even some grandparents seemed to have joined.

"This is a madhouse," said Kate lightly.

"That's one word for it," Anthony replied as he waved awkwardly to a gentleman passing by.

"Who was that?" asked Kate curiously.

"Huh? Oh… just Mr. Roberts."

"Okay, but who is he?"

"He's a coach."

"That wasn't Kyle," she said skeptically.

"Not soccer, mom. He's the cross country coach and shop teacher. He's a cool guy, one of the only cool teachers here," he said, and then interrupted himself.

"It's right down here on the left. I think you know my homeroom teacher is Mrs. Devoy. She's kinda an older lady? Well, she's also the school's art teacher, so I have her for a class, too."

"I recognize the name, but I don't think I've ever seen her."

"Well, now you have!" he said as they turned into the classroom with a slender, silver-haired woman standing by the windows and speaking with two parents. The room was filled with artwork, and unlike the other classrooms they had passed on the way up the hall, there weren't rows of desks, but rather workbenches with four chairs pulled up to each.

"This is kind of a weird homeroom," said Kate in almost a question.

"Yeah, well, we sit here for like ten minutes every day and listen to the morning announcements, then head off to first period. It's more of a lobby than anything else."

"But she is your art teacher as well?" asked his mother, eyeing Mrs. Devoy over his shoulder as the teacher finished with the other couple and made her way right at them with a brimming smile.

"Yup," he responded.

"Well, I hope you're getting an A, cause here she comes," Kate murmured, trying not to move her lips. Mrs. Devoy was fifty-six years old, but she looked ten years younger. If she dyed her hair, Kate was thinking she might look closer to her own age. Pamela Devoy was the kind of physically fit person you could detect in a snowsuit. Her face was drawn tight, her skin pure yet flushed with color. She had steel-gray eyes with accents of blue that were highlighted by her white eyebrows plucked thin to perfect crescents. She wore a gray pantsuit that seemed out of place on an art teacher and a silk, crimson shirt whose buttons seemed dangerously open.

"You must be Anthony's mom," said Mrs. Devoy, extending her hand.

"I am," said Kate, not really knowing what else to say.

"He is a wonderful student," began Mrs. Devoy as Anthony quickly recused himself from the conversation, pretending to be distracted by some painting in the corner.

"That is so nice to hear!" said Kate, feeling the firm grip of the attractive woman.

"I would imagine you're already a big fan of his work, perhaps the

164

biggest," she said with a laugh. "But I, too, find it to be so amazing!"

Kate was stunned. She really had no idea what this woman was alluding to. She had seen his drawings on schoolbook covers and in his room a few times, but what was she talking about?

"After he won the Nathaniel Award, we sent Anthony's pieces up to the Kennedy Library for the big show!"

Kate must have betrayed herself with a blank stare or gaping chin drop, because the sharp Mrs. Devoy copped on instantly.

"Oh my heavens," she said suddenly sullen. "He hasn't told you anything, has he?" The two of them turned simultaneously to look at Anthony. He stood with his back to them looking out the school window, perhaps oblivious to the stare.

"Told me what?" asked Kate, feeling suddenly like she had learned too many secrets as of late.

Mrs. Devoy again took Kate's hand and the smile returned to her face. She recognized it was the boy's humility, not shame or arrogance, nor the lack of parental relationship that had concealed the story. Kate was flush with joy, actually.

"Your son, Mrs. Bruno, is so talented that he has been chosen out of every student here to represent our school in the Massachusetts art expo sponsored by the Kennedy Foundation."

Kate was floored and a little embarrassed that she had known nothing of this. She was also, for a moment, upset at Anthony, but Mrs. Devoy's observation rang true. He was neither arrogant nor evasive. She had never inquired, and he never felt fit to explain, but it now made sense why he had dressed so nicely for the evening. He knew the story would come out.

Kate spoke with Mrs. Devoy for several minutes longer as the two shared their affection for the young man. The well-versed art teacher pointed out the numerous pieces around the room that were his, calling them, "Bold expressions of color," and "Stark portraits of compelling characters." She mused that Anthony brought "powerful maturity, but often dark and even haunting imagery to his paintings." She said his work reminded her of an artist named Francis Bacon.

Kate thought she remembered Francis Bacon as a philosopher from a report she had done in college, but maybe he was a painter, too. She didn't dare inquire and simply nodded in affirmation.

Eventually, other parents wandered in, and the teacher had to excuse herself, but they smiled warmly to each other and exchanged pleasantries. Kate was overjoyed that Anthony had someone so special at school. She knew it had been tough at times at Nathaniel Bourne High School with bullies and fitting in. She also recognized it was no picnic at home. Just knowing Mrs. Devoy was in his life made things a little brighter.

54

After wandering the school a bit more and meeting with various teachers, the two headed home. Kate had said nothing about her exchange with Mrs. Devoy, and they both climbed into the Volvo. It was about forty degrees, and there was cold, misty rain as the darkness circled in. Browning leaves stuck to the windshield as the wipers fought to shoo them away, at times catching beneath the wiper and streaking back and forth in rhythm.

"So whatdya think, ma?" he asked as he fiddled with the button on the glove box.

"It was nice. It's a nice school. Mrs. Devoy and I had a very interesting conversation," she said dramatically but with a smile.

"Oh, yeah? She's a little crazy."

"About you!"

"Huh?" he said, looking puzzled, but certainly aware.

"What you mean, 'Huh'?" Kate continued. "Mrs. Devoy told me about your artwork getting picked for the Kennedy event."

"Mom, it's just being held at the library. It's not like I am flying out to their compound in Martha's Vineyard to meet with the Kennedy family!" said Anthony with a heavy dose of sarcasm.

"It's just awesome, is what it is, honey. I can't believe you never said anything. I mean, it's just so neat to be recognized over everyone else, and I'll tell you: Mrs. Devoy was beaming in her praise of your work. She compared you to a famous artist. It is just amazing."

Anthony said little on the short ride home, but he was feeling really happy. He loved to paint and draw, and he did appreciate the fact that people like Mrs. Devoy, Mr. Roberts, and Principal Carter all complimented him. The rest of the students just didn't get it, and so what, he thought. Lots of people are misunderstood. Lots of people don't know what they are capable of because they let others intimidate them into never finding out.

His mother looked happy, and that made him feel good. Anthony would do anything to make his mother happy, a trait he inherited from her.

55

When Kate and Anthony got back to the house, it was dark and quiet, the light rain and rhythmic wipers the only sound. But King quickly burst into barking as they pulled into the garage and kept it up until they got all the way into the kitchen. The German Shepherd quieted the moment he saw Kate and Anthony, but his fingernails clicked and tapped on the floor as he hopped up and down in excitement.

"We can always rely on King being happy to see us!" Kate said as she reached down to pet their furry friend. "You keeping the bad guys away?" she asked the dog.

"That's kinda hard when one owns the place," Anthony said under his breath as he headed for the front hallway.

"Hold on, there, I'm going to get dinner served shortly so don't vanish upstairs."

"I am just gonna change quick. We have no homework tonight because of the teacher thing. I'll be down in a minute"

"Okay," she said.

It was 7:38 by the kitchen clock, and Kate checked the roast she'd left in the stove. She slipped on her big, gray oven mitt and lifted the glass lid of the casserole to hear it sizzling away. Kate pushed the thermometer down into the meat, the long, steel pin sliding into the cut, and waited for it to register a temperature.

"Medium rare to almost medium," she said. "Just the way he likes it"

After firing up the green beans in a gray pot on the stove, she pulled a treat from the freezer. Steak fries were Anthony's favorite. She'd have preferred scalloped potatoes with the roast, but the fries were easy and tasty. She laid them out on a cookie sheet and slid them on to the rack above the meat. She turned the timer to eighteen minutes and began to set the table.

Kate cut a portion off of a loaf of freshly baked French bread and dropped it into the warmer sitting on the table. She also poured herself a small glass of wine. Dr. Lynch had instructed her to avoid alcohol, but Dr. Johnson later whispered to her that a small glass of red wine to calm the nerves was fine.She had spoken briefly to Vida about the discussion with Anthony. Vida suggested she come right out with it and treat him like an adult.

"It is hard to say how he will respond," Vida pondered. "He may cry instantly like the child he is or respond stoically like the young man he is, but if you treat him like an adult, he will most likely respond like one."

Kate believed it was good advice and had organized her thoughts and prepared her words. She did not want to scare Anthony unnecessarily, but she also did not want to act as her mother had so many years ago.

When Kate's father died, her mother didn't tell them for more than a day. Ted Kelley had a massive heart attack and was dead on arrival at the hospital, but Moira Kelley maintained to Patrick and Kate that their father was in intensive care. It was a slip by a neighbor that revealed the truth, and both she and Patrick were angered by their mother's withholding. A year later, their mother explained she had done it to 'protect' them.

"Protect us from what, Ma?" Patrick railed. "Did you expect the situation to somehow change? He was dead. What was gonna change?"

Kate's mother had sobbed uncontrollably at Patrick's confrontation and proved that sadness could not be suppressed; avoiding the truth was only a delay of the inevitable.

a frame for flowers

Kate never confronted her mother, and she passed away without a mention, but Kate felt their relationship had been damaged by her lie. Although she forgave her, Kate felt let down by her mother, and that always stayed with her.

The wine was tart, but eased her nerves and pushed the worries of the world to the darkened corners of her mind. King had been following her closely as she tended to things in the kitchen, but had taken up a spot by the table and waited, half asleep. She made a round and checked on each item, confirming they were sufficiently warm. Then she folded a napkin and placed the silverware on top. Without thinking, she poured a second glass of wine and placed it at Anthony's spot at the table. Moments later he walked in.

"Smells awesome!" he said in an upbeat voice as he took a seat at the table.

Kate was putting together the plates and walked over to put a trivet on the table. It was then that she noticed the wine, because Anthony was taking a sip.

"Oh my God, did I put that there?" she asked, half shocked.

"Wasn't me," he said with a wide smile that she hadn't seen in months… maybe longer. There was an extended pause as she thought of speaking.

"The roast will be done in a minute," she said and took a seat. Anthony reached into the bread warmer and began to break off a piece when Kate took his hand.

"I'll get it," she said and lifted the warm bread from the basket and placed it on her plate. She took the steak knife from the napkin and cut a thick chunk of the bread, handing it to Anthony then placing the remainder back in the warmer.

"I'm very sick," she said.

"You shouldn't be drinking then," said Anthony with a smile as he chewed on the bread. But her blank face shrank his smile, and he winced as he swallowed the instantly dry bread.

"I don't know how to tell you other than to just tell you, honey," she said as her voice began to crack. "I have cancer and it is serious."

"Since when?" he asked, lost for words.

"Since recently." She reached for him and drew her chair closer. "I am going to have an operation, and the doctors are going to remove the tumors. Then I need to do some treatments, and they'll be really hard on my body." The words became strained as she watched the fear wash over her son.

"I'm going to lose my hair and get real thin and ... it is going to be hard."

"Why?"

"What do you mean?"

"Why you? You don't smoke, you barely drink, and you go out jogging. Why?"

"I don't know. Sometimes it just happens," she said, not knowing how else to answer the question she had asked herself a hundred times.

Anthony sat there, and he could not cry. He was scared and sad, and his mother looked so frightened, but he could not cry. It wasn't like he held it back to be strong for her; he just felt the anger go deep below and no tears came.

"You need to talk to another doctor. Even doctors screw things up, Ma... all the time."

"I have, Anthony. I talked to lots of doctors." Which was true. Beside the numerous colleagues of Drs. Johnson and Lynch who had confirmed the findings, Kate had another oncologist from Providence, Rhode Island look at her results. It was his opinion the diagnosis was accurate.

"Well, they're wrong. You don't look sick at all."

"I don't feel sick, honey, but it's inside, and it's real."

"This is bullshit," he blurted, turning his head and clenching his teeth.

"Can't I donate blood or a kidney or something?" he asked, desperately bargaining with the situation. "Anthony," Kate said firmly as he grew more agitated. "It's breast cancer. It's real and we are gonna fight it, okay? You can't donate anything, although I appreciate you saying that. The doctors are going to do everything they can to help us win

172

this battle, but we have to accept it for what it is. This is happening."

His body slumped as his face fell into his hands. There were still no tears, but as he heard his mother's words and recognized them as firmer than he'd heard in ten years, he knew this was real. He knew that just as she had stated, this was happening. He looked at his mother.

"You were the prettiest mom there tonight," he said and then the tears came, swollen streams of tears from them both, and their eyes, so similar, flowing with the salty tears pushed from their wells by the smothering sadness.

56

Kate and Anthony ate the meal together, then lit a fire in the living room and huddled late into the wintery night. They talked about the cancer, but more about life and what the future would hold, which made Kate happy. She confirmed that his uncle Patrick would be there for Christmas and shared all the stories she had heard recently about his adventures, his cool apartment, and the creative school down the block. Anthony seemed very intrigued by the school.

"Is it a private prep school or a boarding school?" he inquired.

"I don't know, but Pat seemed to know all about it, so you can ask him when he's here."

"I'm glad he's coming. It's been a long time."

"Too long," agreed Kate.

Throughout the entire evening, they never discussed his father and what he knew and what he was doing in response to her illness. For a three-person household, that said a lot. They managed to get off to bed before Frank got home, but Kate heard him come in around 11:30 and did her best to fall asleep before he retired upstairs.

57

On Friday morning, Kate woke feeling surprisingly refreshed. Frank had already gone, and she could hear Anthony stirring about, getting ready for school. She pulled on her robe and headed downstairs. The house was cold, and the frosted windows indicated that last night's rain had likely frozen and things could be slippery outside. Somehow there were still a few birds chirping outside, but from the gray sky, it was clear that the warmth had left for good and the trudge to spring was on. She was scheduled to head up to Vida's in two hours and hoped the hint of sun would melt things, even just a bit.

Kate slid on the kettle to make a quick cup of tea and pulled out the cereal box from the pantry for Anthony. He was pretty good about having breakfast before school, and Kate had read it was the most important meal of the day so she tried to encourage it. She put a banana next to a bowl and spoon on the same table where they spoke the night before. As she stood over the place setting, some of the emotion came back up, but when Anthony strode into the kitchen, she smiled through it.

"How you feelin, ma?" he said, now with a different emphasis on this previously banal question.

"I'm good. Slept like a baby."

He ate his breakfast in a hushed tone, then packed his book bag and slipped on a jacket to make the bus.

"It's Friday!" said Kate with a smile.

"I'll see you right after school," he replied.

"Thanks, hon," she said back, surprised by her own words. She had meant to say goodbye, but thankful was how she felt. She relished the time they had spent together the night before.

Kate poured food into King's steel bowl and made a piece of toast, spreading a thin coat of margarine on it. She stood by the counter and nibbled, not very hungry but determined to eat. The doctors had warned that cancer cells can use up much of the body's energy supply, and it was "vitally important" that she sustain her strength. She had bought the heavy grain bread from Pepperidge Farms at the local grocery store that she assumed was a healthier option. The dizziness came and went, and anytime she stood up too quickly she felt like she would pass out. The rash around her nipples remained red and itchy, although the doctor had prescribed an ointment that had made it less so. She felt thin.

Kate finished most of the toast and then let King out on his runner. Frank hated the dog and called it "stupid," not as an insult but as a name. He did, however, build a runner that allowed Kate to open the side door and simply clip King in, so he could run around on the driveway as well as do his business on the strip of grass than ran up its far side and butted up to the neighbor's fence, which unlike theirs, was chain link. King could go in the backyard in the summer when Kate was at work, but she learned the hard way the damage a winter's worth of dog dump could do, and the runner was a good solution.

The neighbors to that side were older as well, but had an adopted daughter from some place in China who was about ten. The parents weren't visible much: the father was a banker and the mother spent a lot of time at a social club. Kate knew little else about them, but the young girl would play in the yard at times and loved to play with King. There was a nanny who would sit on the front porch and sneak cigarettes while the girl would play by herself in the yard. Kate always felt bad to watch the young girl interact with the dog through the chain link and had on countless occasions invited the girl around the fence to play with King up close. No matter how many times she invited her, though, the girl would never come over on her own.

Kate headed upstairs for a shower.

58

Kate felt clean and energized by her shower, and she pulled on a white sweater and comfortable corduroy pants. She still had an hour until she would head to Vida's, so she sat down and read more of her medical books from the library. The information in the texts continued to intimidate and even frighten her. The words were cold and factual and spoke of horrific bodily functions and reactions associated with fighting cancer. More specifically, the books explained the impact of the very weapons the doctors said they would use to fight the cancer.

She read about how the hair loss meant everything, not just the crop on your head. It described losing your eyebrows, which people contended with by penciling in fake ones, and it also went on to mention nose hair, which she had not considered. There were comments from patients who described a perpetual runny nose due to the absence of the previously unacknowledged nose hair.

"How horrible," Kate thought to herself, "to have to mop up your own snot all day."

Kate had just about enough of the cancer tribulations when the timer chimed alerting her it was time to head up the street. It was Friday, so she needed to take out the trash there at the house and when she got to Vida's. Kate let King in and gave him a treat. She pulled on her ski jacket and hat, as well as a pair of mittens, and King perked right back up thinking it was time for a walk.

"No, boy, that's why I just let you out. I will walk you later, I promise!" she said, giving his head a pat.

The air was as cold as expected as she stepped out into the side yard and made her way to the trash cans that sat against the garage. There was a glaze of ice on the barrels as she began to pull them down the driveway, and there was a bit of ice here and there on the cement as well. The overall icy conditions from first thing that morning had begun to melt off as she had hoped, the sun pushing through the gray cover to provide just enough warmth. Kate was breathing heavily and had to pause a couple times as she dragged the barrels across the surface. When she was done, she walked straight up to Vida's home.

This time Kate did not go to the front door, but instead walked the long way around and down Vida's driveway. She repeated a similar process of taking out the trash, but Vida had just one lightly filled can, so it was pretty easy, although she found she was still panting when she finished.

"Oh, Katie, I meant to get that. You shouldn't be pulling that heavy thing," called Vida from her back door. "Get in here! You make me nervous huffing and puffing out here in the cold!"

Kate gave her a wink and walked up the driveway to the back stairs sniffling.

"They say I will lose my nose hair, and my nose will run constantly," she exclaimed to Vida's surprise.

"Who says that?"

"It was in the book I am reading, where the patients who had gone through radiation and lost their hair explained losing the nose hair."

"Ha! Don't believe what you read in books," she said with the ironic snicker of an author.

"Nose hair is a menace anyways. So maybe that's a good thing!" she continued, trying to make light of it.

"Yeah, well, I can't say I've thought much about it before."

"Lots of new things to consider, Katie," said Vida. "And on that note, I made us hot chocolate today instead of tea!"

"Yum!" Kate cooed. "With marshmallows, I hope!"

"Nothing but the best," Vida replied.

The two sat down, and in typical Vida style, she just dive-bombed into a conversation. "Why have you never left that man?"

"What?" said Kate, her eyes darting about.

"Frank, why have you not divorced him?

Kate sat staring silently into her hot chocolate, a tuft of marshmallow floating on the top. Most people would perhaps apologize for being blunt or intrusive, but Vida just sat waiting for an answer.

"I don't know."

"What do you mean you don't know? You've never thought about it?"

"Of course I've thought about it," she said softly, now looking up but pausing to collect her thoughts.

Vida had blue eyes like Kate, but the years had drawn them back into her face, and their sharp contrast had faded with the passage of time. She had curled, white hair that was styled at the beauty shop every two weeks. She was on the shorter side and thin, although broad through the shoulders for a woman her age.

Kate continued, "I've thought about it a thousand times. I have thought about where we would go. I have thought about what kind of job I could find. I have also thought about how it would impact Anthony," she said, looking down again at her hands clutching and rubbing the hot mug. "It's just complicated."

"Katie, I know it is. I am not asking because I think you've missed something or insinuating you have made an error with your choices. That is not my place to say. What I am considering is how these new conditions will change things. How he will respond? And what should you perhaps be thinking, moving forward?" Vida pulled herself to the edge of her chair and reached over, placing her hand on Kate's forearm and continued.

"I am an old woman, and I have everything sorted out because I am eighty-two years old and surely closer to death than anything else.

Even if I find some way to hang on til I'm ninety-something, that's still just eight years down the road. So I have seen to it that if I go, be it tomorrow or eight years from now, things will be settled in my absence. Do you understand?"

Kate did understand the concept, of course, but her vacant look betrayed her. She wondered what Vida was getting at.

"I am telling you, Kate, that you need to think about every scenario. I believe you are going to beat this thing, but it's going to take a toll. You need to be sure you are squared away for any outcome, and I want to help."

"Thanks Vida," said Kate. "You're a friend."

"I am a friend, and you have been so good to me these years. I would be a crotchety old woman with my detestable house nurse if it weren't for you, so I am grateful, and I want you to know that."

— Vida Description:

181

59

Saturday night was upon her, and with six days until the operation, Kate knew that the time had come to confront Frank with her health crisis. On a normal Saturday, they would eat as a family in the dining room instead of the kitchen, as if the family unit were anchored by the ritual. The stark absence of conversation would assure the mundane act of simply eating in the presence of others would not transcend into bonding of a family unit.

Like most things in Frank Bruno's sphere of influence, certain days were associated with specific things and these included meals. Fortunately for Kate, it was really just four days that she needed to comply with: Mondays, Tuesdays, Wednesdays, and Saturdays. Saturdays were steak with mashed potatoes, but Frank hadn't picked this as much as he eliminated other options. Being they were headed to Emilio and Theresa's home the next day, all Italian food was off the table. Kate took the path of least resistance and cooked a steak or roast and made mashed potatoes every Saturday. It was Frank's favorite meal. Monday night was paperwork, and Frank needed "a good meal" so he could "focus." Kate would make a chicken dish, which most Mondays were chicken parmesan with a side of asparagus. Tuesdays she made fish.

Wednesday had its own story. When Kate and Frank were growing up. there was a commercial for Prince spaghetti that was on TV for more than ten years. It started with a mother leaning out of a brick-faced North End apartment window and calling to her son, Anthony Martignetti.

"Anthony! Anthony!"

The commercial featured a young Italian boy running home for supper. In the end it says, "In the North End of Boston, Wednesday is Prince spaghetti day."

It was brilliant marketing, because the Brunos, and undoubtedly many others, began to serve spaghetti on Wednesdays. This became one of the rituals that gave Frank comfort as a young man. Based on that ritual, every Wednesday Kate spent the afternoon making meatballs so that she could serve spaghetti that evening. Kate once joked to his family at a Sunday gathering that the commercial is why Frank insisted on naming his son Anthony. The in-laws laughed; he called her an idiot.

Anthony did come to the dinner table, but he was hardly running. He slipped in quietly from the front hallway entrance and then, just noticing his father, veered to the kitchen to join his mom. Kate had explained to Anthony that she planned to tell his dad about her condition that night. For a brief moment, he reveled that he knew something important his father did not know.

Kate was bustling about in the kitchen, nervously finishing the last turns of the steak to make certain it was cooked to specifications. The house was creaking a bit as the northeastern wind picked up outside. Their lot was inland somewhat, but sat atop a hill, and the Bay was less than two miles away. If the wind swept onshore, it carried the bitter cold straight down from Nova Scotia and crept in and around the white shingles that clung to the exterior like the scales of a snake. Frank had done a lot of work to improve the house over the years, but it was still over a hundred years old, and it would let out a groan now and again.

The smells of well-cooked steak wafted into the dining room where Frank sat waiting. Anthony helped his mom by bringing out the fluffy mashed potatoes that looked delicious with a thick slab of butter melting in the hot center, as well as a steaming white crock brimming with fresh cut green beans. He placed them on the potholders already sitting on the dining room table. He returned to the kitchen, poured himself a glass of milk, then went back in and reluctantly dropped into one of the dining table chairs.

"Are we almost ready to eat?" Frank asked, accentuated by a loud belch. Anthony stared at him and said nothing, but Kate responded from the kitchen, "One more minute."

Frank sat leafing through the newspaper, unaware of the activity around him. The living room was a battleship gray with a white chair rail and dark wood furniture. The table was old with etched carvings that adorned the corners. It matched a sideboard and hutch that sat pushed to the far wall away from the kitchen, which held the china set Kate and Frank had gotten when they were married. They used it only a few times a year.

There was an impressive silver set with a green, hard leather case and soft felt interior that Anthony used to play with. It reminded him of the story of Johnny Tremain and the silver spoons that he had read as a young boy in school. He would take out one of the felt pouches that held various pieces of silverware and fill it with silver spoons to pretend he was delivering them in secret to John Hancock and the Sons of Liberty from the Revolutionary War. He liked pretending he was them because it felt like those people had a mission, a purpose to their lives.

Kate walked in shortly and set the plate of steaks down in the center but closer to Frank. After a quick, obligatory grace, the meal was eaten as it always was, with Kate inquiring about Anthony's school week or Frank dictating the conversation based on his interest. On this evening, Frank was disengaged, so Kate and Anthony spoke softly amongst themselves as Frank gulped and slurped at his meal. It wasn't that Frank had particularly bad manners—his mother would not let him—but rather that he ate like a wild animal that had no concept of when its next meal might be. He always held one utensil in each hand

and gnashed at food with the smack of his lips echoing through the room. He never looked up and often leaned into his plate to shorten the distance to his gullet. Intermittently, he would slosh back a swig of wine or water—on this evening it was a cheap, red table wine. He wasn't the type to tuck the napkin into his shirt, but it was always close by, and he would use it to mop at his face every five bites or so. To Kate, his eating was repulsive.

When Anthony finished his supper, he asked to be excused, which Frank granted with a wave of his hand and without looking up. Kate began to clear the table and set the conversation.

"I need to talk to you before you settle in for TV."

"About what?" he said, leaning over to pick up the paper he had dropped by his chair.

"Something important," she said, stacking the dishes on her arm.

"Yeah, well, me too," he replied, sucking through his teeth at the small bits of steak that were wedged in between.

"I am just going to clean up quickly," she said, exiting the dining room and heading to the kitchen.

Her hands trembled a bit under the weight of the dishes and the greater weight of what lay ahead. She had worked up her strength, though, and this conversation was going to go down.

"I don't want to wait. Let's talk now," he said in a firm tone, calling after her into the kitchen.

"That's fine with me," she thought to herself.

"Okay," she said. Kate placed the dishes in the sink and began to wipe her hands as Anthony shuffled through the kitchen to grab a cookie from the pantry.

"I'm outta here," he said heading upstairs. "Are you okay to do this?"

"Yes, I'm ready."

"What do you think he'll do?" Anthony whispered.

"Who knows," she said. "I just gotta get it out. It's a family problem, and we are a family."

"Not much of a family," said Anthony without a hint of a smile.

"Perhaps, but that doesn't matter. We can sort out our differences later."

For now he needs to step up for this family and help us pull through."

"He will," said Anthony, seeming to question his conviction.

"We'll see," she said and blew Anthony a kiss.

"I love you, ma," he said as he disappeared.

"Who you talking to?" asked Frank who had appeared at the opposite entrance to the kitchen.

He knew full well she had been talking with Anthony, but like a child, he could not resist. Kate did not respond and turned on the faucet to rinse the dishes.

"So I have been thinking about things," began Frank, leaning against the doorframe and picking at his fingernails, but Kate realized he was launching into some trivial, other subject and ignoring the fact that she expressed the intent to discuss something important.

"No!" she yelled, spinning to face him.

"What the fuck?" he replied, shocked by her response.

"I am talking and you are listening," she said, mustering all her strength.

Frank rolled his eyes, turned and began to walk out of the room.

"No!" she cried out once more, and followed him quickly into the dining room where he was already retrieving the newspaper once more.

"You done crazy?" He asked with a disgusted look on his face.

There is a deafening silence as the house groaned under the wind's gale. "I have cancer, Frank," she said clearly, staring directly into his eyes.

"What?" was all he could gather, and for a moment, he was stopped in his tracks.

"I have breast cancer, and it is very bad. I am getting an operation on Friday, and they are removing the cancer tumors from me. I am very sick, and I could die from this."

Frank stood silent in a way that she had perhaps never seen before, and so she continued.

"I have been to several doctors, I have lots of opinions about my condition, and they're all the same. I have it, it's bad, and I gotta do this."

Still silent.

"I am going to have my breast cut off and then receive radiation that is gonna make me very sick. Lose my hair. Get super thin and be really sick, Frank. I don't know you even care anymore, but I need your help. Anthony needs your help. They think they can save me, but I gotta do this now, and it's gonna get real bad before I have a chance to get better."

Still silent…

"Do you understand what I'm telling you?"

Frank bowed his head and remained quiet as Kate took a step closer. "Do you understand?" she repeated.

He was not weeping nor even close, but Frank looked sad in a way she did not recognize. The two had been together since she was twenty, and that meant they had spent the better part of eighteen years sharing their lives—most of their lives, but she had never seen him look this way.

"Are they sure?" he asked, finally breaking the silence.

Kate nodded her head yes.

"They're gonna operate on Friday?" he asked to clarify.

"Yes," she said.

"Where's the operation?"

"In town, by Fenway. At the Cancer Institute."

"When did you find this out?"

"It just happened. I mean it took a month to figure out it was real, but I just found out. That's how serious this is, Frankie," she said, inexplicably using the affectionate name that she had abandoned years before.

"As soon as the other doctors agreed, it was like 'we gotta operate right away!' and that's where we are."

"Does the kid know?"

"Yes. Your son… he knows. I just told him," she said, proactively addressing Frank's inevitable inquiry as to how she could tell "the kid" before she told her husband.

"Okay," he said, turning into the pantry and yanking the light on. He grabbed at the pencil and began crossing things off the calendar and scribbling new things down.

"Okay, I will get things cov-ahd at work and make shuya to drive you to the hospital."

"Cancer Institute," she said.

"Yeah… Whateva," he said back. "This is fucked," he continued. "Why does Gawd do shit like this?" he asked.

"I don't know," she replied and felt tears welling once more. "I'm not sure he does."

Kate stood there crying and feeling frail while the sound of the wind howled outside. Frank walked over and placed his arms around her, his eyes looking skyward as he wondered how he should handle this.

60

When Katie Kelley was in fifth grade, she knew she wanted to be a mother. She didn't know what it meant to find a husband or what it would be like to be married. She had no idea how you gave birth or even exactly how babies were made, but she knew she wanted kids of her own someday. Katie loved her mom, dad, and her little brother Patrick. Holidays spent as a family were the happiest times of her life. As a young girl growing up just outside of Boston, the thoughts of someday preparing hearty Thanksgiving meals or placing carefully wrapped gifts beneath the tree filled her heart with joy and hope.

It was 1976 and the year of the bicentennial in Boston, Massachusetts, and that was a big deal. They had taken class trips to see re-enactments on the battlefields of Lexington and Concord (pronounced Cong-cud) and then down to the Harbor to see the battleship, "USS Constitution," nicknamed "Old Ironsides." The boys seemed to like the guns and soldiers, but Kate was drawn more to the heroines of the American Revolution, women like Molly Pitcher and Nancy Hart.

As a young girl, Kate was angelic. She had white-blonde hair and big, blue eyes, with freckles that spotted her pretty face in the summer and ivory-white teeth that came in straight from day one. She read the stories of the women who helped fight in the American Revolution, nearly all wives and mothers who served in unique ways yet were never recognized in the way their male counterparts were. She never felt that was unfair or anything, she just thought their stories were more interesting and that people should hear them.

The first time Kate read about the American Revolutionary heroine Nancy Hart, her skin bristled. "How could someone be so brave?" she asked herself.

When a couple of British Redcoats questioned Hart about coming to the aid of a Patriot soldier, she openly admitted to it. They took over her home and condescendingly forced her to cook them a meal, which she did. But in addition, she killed both of them. She didn't poison them with the food, she shot them with one of their own muskets. Kate did not think about the gore of the soldiers being shot at close range with a large gauge weapon like a musket, she thought about how rude they were and foolish to overlook and underestimate a known enemy. She thought about the revenge and the justification of the killing. This was war, she thought to herself, and they deserved it.

Another woman she read about was Mary Ludwig McCauley, also known as "Molly Pitcher." She served in her local militia, braving dangerous battle conditions to bring fresh pitchers of water to the weary soldiers. McCauley witnessed her husband, a brave soldier, get shot in the arm and despite the danger rushed to his side. Showing no fear, she took over his position at cannon, blasting the oncoming British forces. Her bravery and steady aim drew the respect of other soldiers, and they rallied with renewed strength, pushing the Redcoats into retreat. Kate was mesmerized by the pictures depicting Molly Pitcher as she stood stalwart in her full-length dress with ruffles and heels, packing the cannon amidst a storm of shrapnel.

"How could someone be so brave?" she asked her teacher.

Kate and her girlfriend Molly Coyne, who was there the night she met Frank, played softball together in high school. Molly was the team's star pitcher, and Kate called up the historical reference about her favorite Patriot, Molly Pitcher. She rallied the whole team behind

a frame for flowers

Molly's pitching, calling her "Molly Pitcher." No one really understood why, but the nickname stuck and the team went on to win the local championship. It was a good memory for Kate.

Molly was married to a nice guy, and she heard they had five kids and lived in Western Mass. They hadn't spoken in years.

61

Patrick was looking forward to his trip to Boston. It had been a long time, and while he was very happy in New York, he recognized that he had lost touch with his roots and was excited to get a bit of that back.

He booked a flight and hotel and reached out to some friends back in Boston who still lived in or near town. His buddies seemed genuinely excited to hear from him, and as men seem to, they spoke as if they had chatted just last week.

Kate informed Patrick she ran into an old buddy of his named Joe Bertucci, and she had left his cell phone number on the answering machine. Pat was hoping to get a good group of guys together for a pickup hockey game one or two nights Christmas week, and he remembered Joe was pretty quick on the ice.

Patrick had been pushing the envelope to get the final pieces of his clothing line finished and into the hands of the show people so that he could make the trip feeling comfortable about leaving things in order during his absence. He recognized he was likely flattering himself that his presence was quintessential to the success, but this was a big year for him and he wanted to do his best.

The show people were where the real glitz and glam of the industry came from. Most of the designers he knew were pretty reserved and sometimes antisocial. They definitely had insecurity issues. In that way, Patrick was an anomaly as he was bursting with confidence and very social. In the beginning of his career and for many years, actually, he was not well received. Those in the know found his clothes to be more rugged than expected, and they couldn't relate to his common masculinity. They really couldn't believe a New York City fashion designer played on a rugby team in Central Park.

Over time, though, several influential designers in the city began to recognize not just his individual style, but more importantly, the marketability. A new generation of men wanted to wear his clothes. There were a lot of upsides to the Christian Harford clothing line.

The sun was down and the radiators that heated the spacious Tribeca loft were banging and clanking as the hot water and steam pushed their way through the old pipes that lined its walls. The heat was blasting, and Patrick pulled the window open a hair more to let the evening's chilly air meld with the heavy, hanging heat. He picked up the phone and dialed Kate, but there was no answer and he hung up before the beep. He reached into his loose jeans pocket and pulled out the small scrap of paper that he had scribbled on during Kate's long-winded message. He unfolded it and tapped Joe Bertucci's number into the phone, then hopped over the couch and plopped down with a thud.

"Detective Bertucci," said the man on the line in a firm but comfortable voice.

"Tucc?" asked Patrick knowing it was him.

"Who's this?" he asked inquisitively.

"Hey, buddy, it's Pat Kelley. Katie gave me ya numba," he said, unwittingly slipping into a Boston twang.

"Holy crap, he's alive!" said Joe, smiling through the phone.

"I am indeed. How you doing, Tucc?"

"It's so funny: no one calls me that except the boys anymore. All my fellow policeman call me detective now!"

"Yeah, I heard that on Kate's message. Congrats, Joe. I'm sure you earned it," said Patrick sincerely.

"Thanks, man. Just trying to be like our pops."

"Thin, blue line. Better you than me, I guess!"

"Happy to do it. Just keepin the peace in Southie," he said, and they both laughed heartily. They knew their dads had gotten them out of a jam in South Boston a few times. It paid to have a friend on the force; it was a gift when it was your old man.

"So the reason I'm calling is that I'm coming home for Christmas and wanna catch up with everybody. I know I've been away, you know, a long time, and I feel like a shit not keeping up, but, well… that's what this is about."

"You're not 300 pounds are ya laughed Joe, half nervous that it was true.

"Heck no. I'm in wicked shape… smoke your ass on the pond," Patrick said with a chuckle. "No, it's nothing major. I miss Boston and seeing everybody, and I haven't seen Katie and my nephew in so long. It's just time."

"Well, that's awesome, and it was lucky I ran into your sister, who still looks great by the way."

"You would know, lady killer. But wait, aren't you married yet?!"

"No, haven't gotten around to it. Married to the work, I guess."

"Oh, so you're trying to pick up my sister at the grocery, eh?"

"Na. I just said she looked good, that's all. A little too thin maybe, but I guess that's the way women are these days!"

"Ha! Tell me about it. I work with fashion models, Tucc. They're like paperweights! They would make Katie feel fat!"

"Yeah, I wouldn't know!" he laughed. "How's ahhh her and her husband doing?" Joe asked, trying to sound like a detective.

"Who, Frank? He's a fuckin moron. I'm hoping to avoid him on the trip. I love my sister, but she married a douche bag."

"Yeah, how bout that." Joe sighed then quickly shifted gears. "Hey, I hate to do this and you are going to think I'm making this up, but I am actually staking out a suspect. He just came out of his apartment, so I gotta roll."

"No problem, good to hear your voice. I will send a message about skate times and look forward to seeing you for a drink or two when I get there."

"Bet on it," he said, then hung up quick.

Patrick loved New York City around Christmastime, and the buzz of Manhattan was undeniable. When the snow fell gently past the glowing, decorated windows of Macy's in Midtown, or you tuck into McSorely's out of the bitter cold for a beer by the piping hot potbelly stove, or you stand beneath the lights of the towering pine at Rockefeller Center and watch the skaters swirl, you can feel the holiday spirit. When the hardest city on the planet lets a little joy seep in, it is a great place to be and a great sight to see.

"Next year I will bring them here for Christmas," he said out loud to himself as he eased back on the couch and closed his eyes.

62

It was a restless night's sleep for Kate, but that Friday felt no different than most others, except that Frank was there when Kate woke up and was sitting at the kitchen table as she made her way down stairs. She had showered and slipped on loose clothing as suggested. She felt unattractive in the unforgiving bathroom mirror, having applied no make-up. She was not allowed to eat or drink anything, as it could have a negative reaction with the anesthesia, but she did not feel hungry. She felt strangely calm, but there was a looming fear that lurked just below the surface. It was not as if she was holding it back, but rather that it was waiting for the opportune moment to emerge. Frank looked uneasy as he pushed cereal around in a bowl. His thick, brown hair was perfectly combed through, and he was dressed sharply, as he would be on days he met new clients.

"Good morning," she said, breaking the silence.

Frank looked up from his breakfast then shuffled abruptly to his feet. Over the past several nights Frank had done the unthinkable… he had broken rituals. He did paperwork Monday, but he spoke with her later that evening. He did clean the guns on Tuesday, but he finished early and they watched TV together. On Wednesday the same, and on Thursday night, she was pleasantly surprised when he did not

196

go out. Instead, the two sat in the living room in a way they had only managed for certain holidays over the last several years. They discussed the details of the operation as well as the diagnosis and prognosis for recovery. Frank asked questions and listened to her explain what the doctors had told her over the past weeks. He was unemotional, but appeared interested in the information. He went through the insurance carefully to assure they were properly covered and comforted Kate that he would be there when she woke up. Frank had not told his parents or anyone else about Kate's condition.

"You doin okay?" he asked.

"Yes."

"We gotta go if we're gonna beat the traffic," he said. "Did you eat enough?" she asked.

"Huh? Yeah, I'm fine," he said.

"Okay," she said, heading out.

Kate walked all the way to the door and stalled suddenly. She turned and looked back, taking in the room with her eyes. The danger was not as much in the operation itself, but in what lay beyond. The doctors had given all kinds of disclaimers though, and knowing she was to be knocked out for hours, she could not help but wonder if she would even wake from the procedure. Her chest again tightened as she scanned the kitchen, the clock, her table, and the black-and-white photo that hung in the corner depicting her younger parents arm in arm in front of the first home they ever bought. She realized it was possible she would never see this room again. She had embraced Anthony for over an hour the night before as he fell to sleep, but she felt an emptiness at not hugging him as she walked out to face her fate. The fear was overwhelming, but she knew what she had to do.

"Let's go. It's cold," said Frank, holding the door.

63

The drive to the hospital was silent. Kate was in a trance as the places she had known all her life rolled by outside, the world going on with its day like any other. In her mind, her life's images were streaming by like a Super 8 film, choppy memories and flickered moments like a waterfall of snapshots sliding off a dumptruck. The fan from the heater was humming, but the truck's window was cold as she leaned her head against it. She could pace her breathing by the foggy cloud that swelled and retreated on the glass.

Frank flicked on the radio then turned it off. He started to get after a truck driver for weaving, and then reeled it in. He thumped at the steering wheel until he realized what he was doing, and stopped. But he said nothing.

When they arrived at the hospital, Frank pulled right to the front as an ambulance would. Kate had phoned ahead as instructed confirming their arrival, and there were nurses waiting outside. One of them, a man in typical scrubs and a white coat, approached Kate as though he knew her. Her heart quickened as she forced a smiled hello.

"Mrs. Bruno?" he inquired.

Kate nodded her head as she stood just outside the revolving door of the Farber, her breath smoking in the cold air as Frank lowered the passenger side window and yelled out.

"I'm gonna pahk. I'll be in, in a minute."

She said nothing, but lifted her hand in confirmation, then followed the nurse who had turned to go into the building. As she shuffled through the revolving door, with each passing moment, her situation became more vivid. "This is really happening."

Her inner self told her be strong, and she thought back to the Revolutionary heroines of her childhood. "Stand stalwart in the storm of shrapnel," she whispered herself.

"How are you doing, ma'am?" asked the man as they stepped into the heated lobby. She again smiled in response.

"Mrs. Bruno, I'm Dr. Lee," he said, "I am an intern working under Dr. Lynch, and I am going to help you with your operation prep today. Okay?"

"Yes. Hi, nice to meet you," she said with a suddenly dry throat. "I'm sorry I thought you were a nurse," she followed apologetically.

"That's okay, we both work for a living. Not much of a difference actually at this stage, but I am a doctor so you're in good hands!" he replied with a wink.

After a quick check-in at the front desk, they winded back into the hospital as massive beds with half-awake patients wheeled by and workers in scrubs scurried in every direction. The place had a familiar but unsettling smell that wavered between antiseptic and the results of bodily functions. Kate wondered how Frank would find her.

"Right in here, Mrs. Bruno," said Dr. Lee.

She followed him into a large, blindingly white room with six or eight beds, some of which had curtains pulled closed around them. Dr. Lee began to draw down the bed and arrange certain items that had been laid out in a plastic bin on the bed. Overall, it was pretty quiet, although she could see that other hospital staff like Dr. Lee were conferring with patients, and there were also people, probably family members, standing around the beds—some talking as well. The people not working seemed to be in all states of emotion. Most appeared to be attempting a light-hearted approach in an effort to make the patients feel more at ease. Others seemed more emotional than the patients themselves, and as a general rule, everyone seemed uncomfortable. Kate looked around at the different types of patients and wondered what each of them was there for. She hoped they would be all right.

"Right over here, Mrs. Bruno," said Dr. Lee, pointing to one of the gurneys. "This is your personal bed, nice and comfortable for you to take a nap on while the doctors work their magic."

"He seems nice," she thought. "He probably hasn't had a lot of patients die on him yet." Kate wasn't sure what an intern was, exactly, so she made small talk.

"What does it mean to be an intern? Do you get paid?" Kate asked, as Dr. Lee handed her a white medical gown with blue polka dots on it. He pulled the floor length solid curtain that hung off of metal beads that fit into a u-shaped track that encircled the bed. After the curtain was pulled completely around them, he answered.

"Why, are you thinking about a new career?" he asked with a snort, then went on "I am considered a physician in training, which means I've completed med school and received my medical degree, but I am not fully licensed to practice medicine unsupervised. So I go through a period of on-the-job training and practice under the watchful eye of doctors like Lynch and Johnson. Oh… and yes, I get paid."

"Yeah, I figured you must. Good for you, getting your degree," she said, still watching the others in the room.

"Should I put this on now?" Kate asked, holding up the flimsy gown.

"Yes. Just, ahh, fold up your clothes and put them in this plastic bin on the chair here. The hospital will have them put in a locker, so if you have anything valuable, don't be concerned about it, okay?

"Truthfully, Doctor, I'm a little more worried about the operation than I am about my stuff getting stolen," she said, offering forth a tepid smile. The smile on Dr. Lee's face in turn vanished.

"Yes, of course, Mrs. Bruno," he said, realizing he had allowed things to get a bit too casual considering the fact that she was headed in for a major surgery that was to remove the majority of her breasts, a surgery based on malignant tumors and rapidly metastasizing cancer that could easily kill her even if the operation went perfect. The young woman was facing a health crisis that could take her life and that she was likely terrified.

He quickly switched to a more professional tone. "I apologize. I like to keep things light to help patients feel as at ease as possible. If I can answer anything for you about the procedure you are about to have, Mrs. Bruno, please let me know," he said, nervously eying the wristwatch on his arm. "Dr. Johnson will be in shortly," he said, slipping his arm out through a slit in the curtain to create an exit.

"All right" Kate replied.

"I will leave you to get changed, then, Mrs. Bruno," he said, looking back and now quite serious. "Try not to worry. Your doctors are the best at what they do," he said.

"Thank you, and good luck with your career," said Kate as he walked out and the curtain flap closed.

Kate felt bad, as if she had just gotten him in trouble. A moment later, Kate peeked out of the curtain and called after Dr. Lee, realizing Frank had not found the room yet. However the doctor had left or was at least out of earshot. She hoped someone would help Frank find the room.

Kate began to undress behind the curtain feeling suddenly alone and cold. She folded the light-blue sweatpants and sweatshirt slowly and placed them in the plastic bin. She did not have any valuables, as her purse was in the truck and she had removed her jewelry as she had been advised. She had shaved her armpits that morning, and they felt cool in the air. Kate looked down at her breasts. She was never a busty girl, but they had been ample and firm all her years. She was happy with her body. She ran her hand over her left breast then pushed down on it and tried to envision it being gone. She had seen the pictures of other patients, and they seemed so peculiar... so ugly. The left nipple would be completely gone, and it seemed somehow unnatural that she could exist without it. The doctors hadn't dwelled on it, but had suggested a plastic surgeon who could rebuild the breast.

"Some patients say the new version is better!" they claimed.

Her skin seemed pale as she pulled on the thin gown and reached behind her back to try and tie it off for some privacy. She felt weak, but flexed her arms to feel the muscle and to try to increase her blood flow.

"Gotta stay strong," she thought to herself.

Kate could hear someone weeping nearby and the muffled voices of people talking. Once the gown was secured, she slipped off her underwear, placed it in the bin, and tucked it discreetly between her sweatpants and top. She climbed into the bed, pulling the sheet and blanket up towards her chest.

The bed was one of those adjustable beds like the ones on TV commercials, and the back was raised up so she could sit nearly upright. The sheets felt cold as she slipped in, her feet sliding down into the depths. She felt instantly alone and overwhelmed, and the impulse to get up and leave stormed into her head.

"Maybe we should delay this," she thought. "Maybe I really should talk to more doctors. What if they are wrong? What if this is it, and I die on the table, in this cold bed with this horrible robe on?"

She began to breath heavier and felt the tension like a vice grip clamping down on her temples.

"I don't have to do this today," was her fleeting thought as the curtain whooshed open and Dr. Johnson stepped in, her almond-brown eyes connecting immediately with Kate's.

"Hello, Kate," she said, bringing stillness to the moment.

"Oh, Doctor Johnson, I'm feeling really scared all of a sudden," Kate admitted.

"It's very normal, Kate. Try and just breath, okay?" she said, then turned her head sharply. "Can I get a warm blanket here!" she barked out to no one in particular, but within thirty seconds someone hurried over with a blanket. "Are you cold?"

"Yes, but I think I am shivering in fear. It feels like my blood has stopped flowing!" she said with her voice inflecting at a higher pitch and her throat bone dry.

When the doctor said "warm blanket," Kate had assumed she meant an extra blanket that would eventually make her warm. Instead, she was startled by a blanket that felt it had been plucked from a toasty dryer just moments before.

"We use a big oven to heat them up," Dr. Johnson said with a smile that equaled the blanket's warmth. "Take a sip of water," said the doctor, having poured a cup from a small, plastic decanter that sat on a small table in between her bed and the next patient's.

Kate did, but the doctor warned to take just a sip and not drink the water. So she did just as she was told, and the water dampened her mouth enough to relieve her arid throat. The doctor was constantly moving as she talked.

"Is your ride here?" asked Dr. Johnson as she rolled up the sleeve of Kate's robe and began to swab the inside of her elbow joint with iodine.

"He's parking the car," said Kate, "but it's been awhile and I am wondering if he can't find me."

"It's your husband?" she asked almost skeptically.

"Yes."

"Okay. We'll have someone track Mr. Bruno down, but we need to stay on schedule okay?"

"Sure, of course."

Kate had really never spoken about her husband, nor had he attended any of the numerous appointments with any of the doctors, but Dr. Johnson did not inquire further.

"We are going to put in an I.V., okay? So I will be inserting a needle, and it may burn a little as it goes in, but it will go away quickly."

"Okay," said Kate, biting down on the inside of her cheek in anticipation.

The doctor moved swiftly, removing packaging and opening up the intravenous kit. She nimbly wrapped rubber tubing around her arm, strung a bag onto a hangar, and sorted out the tubes and needle. She appeared to struggle to find a strong vein in Kate's arm, but with a tightening of the rubber and some massaging, she spotted the bulge and within seconds slid the long, steel hypodermic up into the thin, blue vein on Kate's arm. Kate's adrenaline was surging, and she barely felt it go in, but bit into her cheek to offset the burn the doctor had warned of.

"Are you and your husband still together?" asked the doctor.

The question shocked Kate. "Why is she asking this now?" she thought, but in Kate's mind she justified the inquiry as important. She also figured the doctor was highly intelligent and would likely see through an insincere answer.

"Kate, you with me still?" asked the doctor as Kate had stared blankly in response to her question.

"Yes."

"Yes, you're with me, or yes, you and your husband are still together?"

Kate glanced down at her hand as if to say I am wearing a ring aren't I, but eerily the ring was gone. She had of course removed it with her other jewelry, and her stark finger displayed only the pale indent of the ring.

"Frank and I are still married."

"Okay."

Just then Dr. Lynch walked in. He was dressed in heavy scrubs that included booties and a blue hood that enclosed most of his head. He had a mask on, but it was pulled down to his chin. His face looked handsome, and he appeared confident in his surgical gear.

"How are you feeling, Mrs. Bruno?" he asked, as he always did.

"She's got some pre-show jitters," interjected Dr. Johnson.

"Yeah, I'm a little nervous, but the warm blanket is helping," said Kate.

"Aren't those great? I wish I had them at home," said Dr. Lynch blithely.

"It helps," she repeated.

"So Kate, we have gone over this, but I am going to summarize what we are going to accomplish here today. Are you good with that?" asked Dr. Johnson.

"Yes."

"Dr. Nasrimi, our anesthesiologist, will put you under about ten minutes before we head to the O.R., okay? It's real easy, needle's already in, and he will administer the medicine through this tube. The doctor will have you count backwards, but you won't get very far before you go to sleep."

Kate had never seen Dr. Nasrimi, but there was a stout, swarthy man who had just wheeled up a small cart to the end of the bed and began to arrange some small bottles. No one made an introduction or even spoke to the man, but Kate assumed this must be the person who Dr. Johnson was referring to.

"I hope he knows what he's doing," Kate thought to herself.

"Once you're under, we will bring you into the operating room. Both Dr. Lynch and I will be scrubbing in for the procedure, and we will be joined by Dr. Nasrimi and Dr. Lee as well as our operating crew, so it will be a busy room. And we are all there for you, Kate," she said reassuringly.

"And I won't remember anything?" asked Kate.

"Not likely. Some people don't even remember this part or the recovery room later, so all the hard stuff is while you sleep."

"Well, that's good, I guess."

"Once you are on the operating table, we are going to begin by removing the bad stuff in the right breast. Once we get it all out, we will move to the more complex part of the operation on your left side. You will be getting some blood during the operation, and there can be side effects associated with that: fever, hives, and in rare occasions, more serious reactions, but it is not a major concern. The whole operation will take us several hours, and it will be very shocking to your body. As we have spoken, we are performing a radical modified mastectomy and will be removing quite a bit of muscle and fatty tissue. This is shocking to your body."

Kate heard the words, but it was difficult to process the magnitude of the situation. She didn't really understand why he was telling her all the details. She would have been happy with "We are going to put you to sleep and fix you," but she appreciated them talking to her. She was confident in the doctors, but the gripping fear would not subside.

"Has Frank shown up yet?" she interrupted.

"Ahhh, I don't think so," said Dr. Johnson hurriedly. "But I have someone tracking him down. If he is not here by the start, I will have to talk to him after we are done. It will be fine."

"Sure, thanks," said Kate.

"Once we remove all the cancerous tissue from the left side, we will close you back up and bandage the area." Dr. Johnson paused briefly and reached over to pull away some hair from Kate's face, then let her hand linger on her forehead.

"When you wake up, you will still be on some serious meds and will not feel any pain. We expect you to mostly sleep for the subsequent twenty-four hours. You can have visitors, but you may not be much of a conversationalist. We will let you heal for about three days, then you can go home for the remainder of your recovery. After about ten days, we will run some tests and take some pictures to see that we got everything. I know it's a lot to process, but we are almost done. Are you doing alright?"

"I think so."

Dr. Lynch had been leafing through papers on a clipboard and conferring with Dr. Nasrimi at the end of the bed as Dr. Johnson spoke. He tucked the clipboard under his arm and stepped forward. The doctor asked Kate to sit up and pull down the front of her gown. She did so, untying the back of the gown and draping it open, exposing her chest.

"You can lean back," he said, as he took a black marker from his clipboard and began to draw on her skin. "This is where we are going to make the incision," said Dr. Lynch calmly as Kate's heart began to flutter and accelerate, thinking of a scalpel slicing into her chest where she had always known her heart was.

He drew some lines beneath and over her left breast, and she was suddenly overwhelmed. "This is really happening," she thought. "Why is this happening?"

After a minute of drawing, the doctor tucked her gown back up, but told her not to re-tie it. He pulled the blanket back up and looked at her assuredly.

"Mrs. Bruno. I am going to go get scrubbed in for the procedure. Do you have any questions for me?"

"Is this going to work?"

"We believe it will," he said, then turned and walked away.

64

Frank had still not shown up by the time Dr. Johnson needed to leave to prep as well. The warm blanket had lost its radiance, and Kate was feeling chilled again. Dr. Nasrimi ambled up to her and introduced himself. He had a strange accent. His face was chubby and his eyebrows were thick and bushy.

"How you are doing?"

"I'm ready for the sleeping part," she said with an exhale.

"That's goot," he said with a grin. "I am the Sandman."

The doctor took one of the small bottles and drew the clear liquid into a syringe. He looked at Kate and said, "It's counting time. We do it together from ten down, ready?"

"I'm ready."

He pressed the plunger of the syringe, and the liquid pushed its way into the tube that led to her arm.

She felt nothing and began to count from ten backward as Dr. Nasrimi suggested. Kate glanced around to look for Frank, but he was not there.

"Ten, nine, eight..."

Black.

65

Vida was very concerned about her friend Kate. The reality was that now that she had fired her day nurse, Kate was in essence her sole provider, outside of a handyman who looked after the house. Now that Kate needed help, Vida realized just how much her younger friend did to make her life more comfortable. Vida wanted to be there for Kate, but she could not arrange to be at the hospital for the operation, and only immediate family could spend time visiting her for the initial recovery. She had offered to take Anthony for a few days if it would make things easier, but Kate could not impose. Besides, as much as Anthony didn't like living under his father's rule, it was unlikely he would consider bunking with an elderly woman an upgrade. Anthony thought Mrs. Mudgett was a trip, but probably not as a roommate.

Instead, Vida wrapped herself in her work and typed furiously, edging forward to the completion of the latest mystery. As she tapped away at the round keys of her old-school typewriter, the type hammers slapped at the page. She was compelled forward by this twist in Daisy McQueen's journey. It was how she viewed the stories, not just as entertainment, but also as didactic. She wanted her readers to learn something from the moral dilemmas of her characters and to reflect on their own choices in life. This new twist, though, seemed to throw it all on its ear. If Daisy has solved the murder, yet conceals her findings to protect the perpetrator, then she has either lost her moralistic true north or she feels the crime was somehow justified and the victims—or in this case victim—has gotten what they deserved. Is it possible that the penance, and perhaps even exoneration for the murder itself, was the suffering that led to it?

For the first decade plus, Vida did all her writing upstairs in a sewing room she had converted into an office, but seven years ago she relocated the office to the sitting room on the first floor with the help of her handyman, Mike O'Rielly. She remembered O'Rielly and another man lumbered the big oak desk she used down the winding staircase in her sizable home.

"This may be the heaviest desk in the world, Mrs. Mudgett!" chuckled O'Rielly after they lowered it into the position it sat in ten years later; the sweat beads forming on his and his young assistant's foreheads.

"Handcrafted oak. Isn't she a beauty? Hank bought that for us about fifty years ago," she said, admiring the desk and its new location. "I guess they made wood heavier back in the day!" she said with a typical Vida quip, and neither O'Rielly nor the young man seemed to sniff the sarcasm.

"This will be a nice office for you. Good light in here."

"I think you're right, Mike," she said, agreeing. "At least I will use it, and use this room. Who has a sitting room anyways? So silly."

"Yeah, I converted my sitting room, too," he said laughing and mopping away the sweat with his sleeve as he walked out.

"I am going to let Kate be the first to read this," Vida said out loud, staring at the page she had just written. "I will bring it to her to read as she rests up."

66

Anthony sat at his desk, heart-heavy and totally disengaged. He knew his mother was in an operating room and that it was very serious. As soon as the final bell rang he knew he could leave and take the T over to the hospital, but the minutes were dragging like an anchor behind a bicycle. He had told no one at school, which was not unusual. When he met Peter in the hall, the boy had his usual happy-go-lucky stride, and it never dawned on Anthony to share his plight with him.

Moping through class was hardly standout behavior for any kid in high school, so he went about his day unnoticed. However, when he returned to his homeroom for art class, Mrs. Devoy picked up on Anthony's vibe right away.

"We're going to try and finish our charcoal series today. So let's get right to it," she said to the class but while looking directly at Anthony.

The class had been doing charcoal sketches on paper. Anthony liked the simplicity of black on white. The reduced variables demanded that more texture and shape be uncovered with less. He had drawn a series of pictures using a fisherman as the central character. There were ten or so sketches that highlighted the fisherman's sea-beaten face and work worn hands and cataloged him performing various challenging tasks of his life: negotiating with the vendors, hauling in the ropes and hoisting his craft, carrying his nets on his shoulders up the hill to his home, and standing in the sun handing out fish to all in need. The man was rough but stoic, and Anthony had drawn him with such detail that his character spilled off the pages. Mrs. Devoy was moved by the work.

"It's a tough life," she said, standing over Anthony's shoulder as he half-heartedly touched up shadows in one of the sketches.

He looked up at her a bit surprised as he had not seen her approach. "The life of a fisherman has always been a tough one," she went on.

"I wouldn't know," he replied.

"My two uncles were fisherman up in Gloucester for years. They were my dad's brothers... younger brothers! But they looked ten years older."

"That doesn't seem fair," said Anthony, looking up with half a smile.

"They liked it. They were happy and said they felt most alive when they were out to sea," she said, crouching to take a close look at his work.

"Your fisherman looks worn but resolved. What made you draw him that way?"

"I don't know."

"Okay. Well, what's his name?"

"Jacob."

"Is he married? Any kids?" she asked, half-joking. "Yes... he's married with two kids, both boys."

"Ah... a family man," she said, playing along.

"He doesn't want them to be like him... a fisherman, so he works very hard to save money. He is trying to educate them to be the businessmen who own the boats and buy and sell the fish."

"You see all that?" asked Mrs. Devoy, taken aback by his swift response and specific detail.

"You see this?" he asked, thumbing through the sheets and withdrawing one of the sketches, then smoothing it out on the work bench in front of him.

"This is number three. If you notice in the back you can see his two sons."

Mrs. Devoy was mesmerized. She was originally just trying to get him to talk because he seemed to be in a bad mood, but she was instantly drawn in. Sure enough the third picture depicted two young boys and they were playing in the background. She could not believe it. The two boys were small and blended in with the rest of the environment, not immediately noticeable, and nothing would indicate that they were related to the fisherman. They were dressed in nicer clothing, but upon further scrutiny you could see they were in uniform like that of a private school, and although they were smiling and playing, they were still very neat, with their shirts tucked and their ties pulled tight and straight.

"He knows he can give them a better life, so he sacrifices every day to build their future." Mrs. Devoy was speechless.

67

Kate's next memories were blurred and seem to fade in and out like movie scenes. She was conscious of people around her but was most interested in not moving. She felt little pain, but as she first came to everything around her body felt damp, as opposed to her mouth, which was beyond dry—the unfamiliar taste of chemicals strong, as though they were baked to her throat and mouth. She could hear herself breathing through her teeth as she again drifted out.

Each time she resurfaced to consciousness she felt more aware. There were people around, but nobody she recognized. They asked if she wanted food; she tried to answer but could scarcely do so. She remembered the food came, and the nurse raised her Craftmatic bed up so she could eat, but she didn't remember eating. When she resurfaced once more, she could finally muster some words to the nurse who was changing out her bedding.

"What happened to the food?"

"What's that sugar?" said the nurse.

"I was so excited to eat," said Kate.

"Honey… we took your food outta here two hours ago after it sat there getting cold for a loooong time!" she said, laughing. "Happens all the time though, so don't you feel bad. You hungry now?" she asked kindly.

"I am… is that alright?"

"Of course… you're the patient," she said, like that was the employee manual's proper response. "You like ham and eggs?"

It seemed like a strange question to Kate. She looked to her right, out the windows that had a light scrim pulled across them. For the first time she noticed that she was alone in this room, with no other patients, and it was much smaller. There was a TV hanging in the corner at the opposite side of the bed. She noted that it was light out, even though she had been thinking it was the night after the surgery and her instincts were to have dinner. The TV was on and she was one-quarter upright in her adjustable bed.

"What time is it?" Kate asked.

"It's just past eight in the morning."

"What day is it?"

"It's Saturday, honey…. The cartoons are on!" said the nurse, pointing to the TV.

"I've been asleep for a whole day?"

"I see people sleep for three days," she said. "You fine," she continued, folding and gathering the dirty linens.

"Okay, ham and eggs it is," Kate answered, unsure whether she already had.

"They pretty good, you know… you want some orange juice?" asked the nurse with a glowing smile.

"Yes please," she said politely.

"I will get that in for ya and you just rest… it will be here before you know it."

"Thank you," said Kate, as the kind woman gathered the bedding and began to walk out. "Is my husband… is Mr. Bruno here?"

"I don't see ya husband, but there is a boy sleeping outside who said he's yours. You want me to wake him up?"

"How long has he been here?"

"Well, don't tell anyone," she said, shuffling back into the room with her arms hugging the blankets tight. "But he's been here all night waitin' on you. We made him sleep out in the lobby because ain't nobody supposed to be in these rooms after 9:00 pm."

"Oh God yes, can you get him?"

"Sure, sure," she said, then slipped out the door.

Kate was increasingly aware of her surroundings. The reality of why she was there leapt quickly back into her mind.

"I guess I survived."

She looked down at the wadded bandages across her chest and realized also that her left arm was strapped down tight with her forearm crossing her rib cage. She dared not move anything, but there was remarkably little pain. She could sense a difference in herself, though, and her heart felt somehow deeper in her chest, in addition to her left shoulder seeming closer than she recalled.

She still had an intravenous, but it had been moved to the back of her right hand, which made her not want to move it for fear of painfully ripping out the needle. So she sat still and looked up at the TV.

"I wonder if they got it all," she said out loud to herself.

"Hi ma!"

When Kate heard Anthony's voice, she was elated. He walked in, looking as he did so many mornings in their lives, half-asleep, hair tousled, and handsome as ever.

"Hi, baby," Kate said, choking back emotion. "Are you feeling ok?"

"Yeah… it's crazy. I feel fine."

"Where are the doctors?" he asked.

"Where is your father?" she replied.

"I haven't seen him."

"What? What do you mean?"

"I never saw him. I got here after school as quick as I could on the T, but he wasn't here?"

"What time did you get here?" she asked, now perplexed and trying to sit up a bit in her bed. She felt the first sharp pain, as she had shifted her shoulder trying to shuffle up the bed's angle to be more upright.

"Just move the bed mom. Hold on—I'll do it," said Anthony, moving over to grab the remote control that sat right on the mattress near her right hand.

He pressed the button and the bed craned upward, raising her up.

"What time did you get here?" she repeated.

215

"Um… it took like an hour so… I don't know exactly, but I would say 4:00?"

"That doesn't make sense…. And you haven't seen him since?" she continued, pressing her voice coarse and scratchy.

"No."

"But you've been here all night?" she asked, before realizing the 3rd degree she was giving her son. "Come here honey."

Anthony approached the bed nervously. His mother looked gaunt and pale, almost not like herself at all. Her flaxen hair was listless and matted. There were marks on her forehead, like someone had left tape and brown smudges of iodine that he thought might be blood, left stains beyond the monstrous bandages that jutted from her chest. Her arm was pinned across her in such a way that it looked like she was in a straitjacket. He wanted to be strong so he kept a blank face, but her condition made him sad and angry. He felt useless.

"I love you," she said abruptly, and it nearly stirred the tears in Anthony.

"I love you, too, Mom," he said, then leaned in to kiss her.

Just then the nurse came back in.

"Alright sunshine. We got ya breakfast, hot and tasty!"

"I see you joined us, sleepy head," she said, eying Anthony as she placed the red plastic tray onto an adjustable table and rolled it over to Kate.

The plate was covered with Saran Wrap, and the heat from the food had steamed it, inflating it like a clear balloon. On the side were a small blue-and-white carton of milk and a round, ribbed, plastic orange juice container with a tinfoil top.

"What a good kid," she whispered to Kate, although Anthony heard. "I got six of 'em… God bless. Wish I could say they were all this loyal."

Loyal… a strange descriptive, Kate thought to herself. "Where is Frank?"

"Well, he is my one and only… so we just have each other," Kate whispered back.

The nurse removed the Saran Wrap, releasing a puff of steam, and opened up the enclosed packet of plastic white silverware and a napkin.

"You think you can eat?" asked the nurse sympathetically.

"I can help her," said Anthony, stepping closer.

"All right then… what a good young man, I will let you to ya break-fast… enjoy. You can always press my button on the remote if you need me. I am the red button with the little white cross."

"Thank you so much, Nurse…" Kate squinted to read her name tag.

"My name is Odna, "she said. "Just remember Odd Name: Od Na," she repeated casually, as though she told everyone the same thing.

"Thank you, Odna" said Kate.

"Yeah… thanks," echoed Anthony.

And off she went, leaving Kate and Anthony alone. "Are you even hungry?" he asked.

"I think so." Kate rasped, eyeing up the meal. "Can you open the juice? I do know I'm thirsty."

"Yeah," he said, grasping the container and peeling back the foil lid.

Kate slowly lifted her right hand—complete with tubes and tape—and clutched the cup. It felt strange in her hand and she again felt a jolt of pain in her chest as she tried to raise the juice. The pain was evident in her face as the shocks of pain intensified. She put it back down and lowered her arm.

"I'm sorry. Can you do it for me honey?"

"Of course, mom, I told you I would be here for you. I can do any-thing." He lifted the cup to her lips, sounding more like a man than she had ever noticed.

"Where the hell is Frank?" her mind repeated again and again.

68

Frank dropped Kate off and drove into the parking structure... but after driving around and around for ten minutes, he left. Frank had not told anybody about Kate. All he told his parents was that Kate was feeling really sick and they might not make it Sunday for dinner. He told Jim Star that Kate was having a small procedure to get something removed. Mr. Star assumed it was a mole or something minor considering Frank's nonchalance. He had told his youngest brother that Kate was sick with "something", but made no attempt to convey the magnitude of it. He did, however, tell Tricia McAllen a few days before the operation, because this provided a great distraction that might get her off his back about moving in together.

"She's sick and I mean real sick. She's got canc-ah and has to get on operation," Frank told Tricia as they ate a burger and fries at a local diner.

"Is she gonna die?" she asked, not even looking up from her plate of food.

"I don't know... it's serious, though, and I mean fuckin' real serious. It's breast canc-ah and they ah cuttin them off."

"Ahr you serious... Cuttin' em off?"

"Ya... only one actually, but she's got tum-ahs all ova."

"That sucks…" said Tricia, dragging a French fry through a puddle of ketchup and jamming it in her mouth. She spoke with her mouth full.

"What's her Docta say's gonna happen?"

"I don't know… I haven't talked to 'im."

"That sucks."

"Ya… it's hah-sh."

"What ah you gonna do?" she asked, her head cocked slightly to the side. "I'll figure it out afta the operation. It's this Friday."

"You betta," she warned. He looked right through her.

"Shut the fuck up." He said sternly then motioned to the waiter for the bill.

69

Frank drove away from the hospital and straight to a jobsite as if it were any other day. He justified to himself that he needed to work to pay for all of the medical bills. Most of the morning commute was out of the way so the roads weren't too bad.

"If I don't work, we're gonna go broke… It's that simple," he recited to himself in the truck.

"Who's gonna take care of the bills or keep the lights on, if I can't be makin' money?" he mumbled as his shoulders twitched and the familiar short snorts of breath through his nose set in.

He was accelerating down the Jamaicaway toward a new home site in the suburbs. The radio was off and the sound of the churning engine filled the cab as he continued to argue with himself.

"I'll go back to get her before she wakes up… for Christ sakes, she said she's gonna sleep for a whole day. What the fuck am I gonna do—sit there and do nothing… lose money?"

He was getting increasingly agitated, as if his silent conscience were winning the argument. The tree line of the road was slowly blurring as he picked up speed, tearing down the asphalt stretch. The Parkway had four lanes, and people drove at a good clip, but Frank was cooking along at nearly 70. He was lost in an argument with himself, to justify leaving his cancer-stricken wife alone at the hospital.

"If I stop workin', all these sites stop, all these guys lose the-ya jobs, Jim Stah loses his money and everything's a mess. It's a fuckin' mess."

His knuckles drew white as he clamped down on the steering wheel, his body now rocking front to back slowly as the anger simmered and bubbled up in his throat.

"This life is bullshit, and I waited too damn long. God fuckin' dammit," he shouted, now clenching all available muscles.

"You wait too long and this is what you get.…. This is what you fuckin' get!"

Just then Frank recognized he was screaming toward a red light, and although there was no one stopped in front of him, his mind fired with adrenaline. He quickly slammed on the brakes and the truck lurched and pitched to a slight angle as the momentum of the heavy rear axle pushed forward. The world slowed as the vehicle skidded dangerously through the red light and into the intersection. Frank gripped for impact… but there was none, and the truck rattled to a stop. The smell of burnt rubber seeped into the cab as Frank took account of his self, recognizing he was not hurt and that the truck suffered little damage. He was all right… but somehow furious.

The truck's engine stalled, and there was remarkably no one around as an eerie quiet settled. Frank panned the horizon, his eyes stopping at a playground just off the road, drawn to the noise of children. There he saw a group of young boys chasing each other and running wild, as boys will do, each of them smiling widely. He thought of a time when Tony was that age, and he was lost for a moment.

"That was before she turned him on me," he said. "Life was perfect then."

70

As Saturday evening approached and the darkness of a cold evening crept into her cramped hospital room, Kate knew that Frank was not coming. The hospital was quiet now; Odna had finished her long shift and left for the night. Kate had wanted Anthony to catch the train home to get back before it was too dark, but she couldn't find it in herself to tell him to leave. No one had come to visit: most noticeably, the man she was married to was still totally absent. The pain was consistent now, and the button that released the medicine seemed to have lost its power. Her chest was tight and intensely sore, the pain extending throughout her torso. She recognized that they had pulled her open, taken some of her out, and then sewed her back together. All of that led to discomfort. Kate felt wilted, like a lily in the blazing sun.

Kate was aimlessly flipping through the channels on the small square TV when Dr. Johnson walked in with Dr. Lee.

"Good evening, Mrs. Bruno. You look remarkable," said Dr. Lee, with his standard wink and a smile. "Hi, Kate," said Dr. Johnson.

"Hey, doctors, I'm glad you're here." Kate said as she shimmied up a bit in her bed that lay nearly flat, but was angled enough to view the TV.

"Oh yeah? We don't hear that much," said Dr. Lee. "What is it, Kate?" inquired Dr. Johnson, cutting him off.

"Well, it's a few things," she began timidly. "My husband has yet to show up. He dropped me off for the operation, and I have not seen him since."

"I don't understand… you have not seen him since he let you out of the truck yesterday morning?" asked Dr. Lee.

"Has he called?" asked Dr. Johnson.

"No… nothing, and my son is here, and I don't even know if Frank is home or at work or if he skipped town."

"Okay… we will have Administration try and locate him, it's really bizarre. We scoured the hospital during the operation and couldn't find him, but figured something must have come up. He never picked up the phone number you left at check-in and now it is all looking so devious."

"It never occurred to me that he would leave during this," Kate muttered looking right at Dr. Johnson.

"Do you think he's okay?" Dr. Lee asked.

"Okay?" Kate retorted indignantly. "I would guess he's just fine… quite good even!" she went on, with more than a hint of irritation in her voice.

At that point Dr. Lee made himself busy checking Kate's bandages and her vitals' monitor, which could report recent body temperature, heart rate, blood pressure, etc. He peeked gingerly under the bandages and looked into Kate's eyes and mouth as she continued speaking with Dr. Johnson. He had, however, checked out of the conversation.

"I don't know what to say Kate… I've never seen this before. We will try and track him down," Dr. Johnson stated calmly. "Do you want me to contact anyone else for Anthony's sake?"

Kate thought about it. Who could she call? She couldn't really call Vida—she had no transportation. She could reach out to his grandparents of course, but if Frank had just disappeared then it is unlikely he had even told them. Calling them and explaining everything would crush Frank. It was pretty tempting to do it at that moment and if she had had a great relationship with her in-laws—if she cared about them—she might. Somehow, though, she could envision them blaming her for the cancer and finding a way to sympathize with a husband whose wife may leave him all alone with a son to raise on his own. The mere roleplay in her mind ruled out calling them.

"There is no one to call," Kate said.

Now Dr. Johnson began to inspect the wounds as well. She peeled back the entire bandage from the bottom near her stomach, folding it inward toward the center and looked beneath. Kate could only see the upper left portion, but could see the deep red line and thick black sutures that held the gash together. There was a small clear tube perhaps a quarter inch in diameter coming right out of her flesh and yellowy puss and blood seemed to be draining out of it. Kate found the sight shocking and frightening. Her chest was sunken with skin appearing to no longer have a proper fit, stretching tight up by her shoulder then rippled and folded by her armpit and below. She could tell immediately: her entire breast was no longer a part of her.

"This looks good," said Dr. Johnson.

"Not to me…" Kate replied.

"No, seriously, Dr. Lynch did a phenomenal job here."

"Did he get everything?"

"Well it looks really good, but of course we won't know for sure until we take pictures and run the test… But, Kate, this looks real clean."

"It looks rough right now, but beneath the surface we have saved the area and created a healthy environment in which to re-grow healthy tissue. You have to try and envision this as it can look and will look and try and get past how it looks now."

"A garden starts as an empty patch of dirt," Kate said, half to herself.

"Yes… just like that," Dr. Johnson replied.

71

As Frank pulled away from the near accident, the smell of burnt rubber and oil quickly dissipated, but the reality of life outside settled back in. He tried to refocus himself and began to run through the checklist he needed to accomplish for the jobsite to keep on track. Yet as he ran through the list in his mind, he could not escape the nagging thoughts.

"What are people going to say?" he confronted himself, slowly unraveling an inner dialogue:

"What am I supposed to do? I cahn't talk to anyone about this…. ah marriage has been a joke fa ten yee-as, but have I stopped providing? No! I provide a nice life, a very nice life, a good roof ova the-ya heads, and money to do whatever. I don't make her work… compayed to lots of otha people. She spends her time weedin' the gah-den every day while I do the fuckin' work. Are you kiddin' me? She gets herself pregnant and I get life sentence for it!"

Frank railed on, bellowing aloud to himself in the truck, yet in his mind all he could see was Kate, weakened and frightened, walking into the hospital. He could hear himself telling her he would be right back… that he would be there.

"This thing is just bad timing. That's where I screwed up. It's the timing… it's not having done this sooner like I should. We would be happy with otha people. By now she'd be with someone else... some los-ah. Wouldn't be my problem and it shouldn't be. We shouldn't have done this and now we're stuck"

Frank rubbed his coarse hand up and down on his face, closing his eyes and opening his mouth.

Of course that ain't what society says. Oh Gawd no! How are people gonna see it? Phhff... that's a joke. My family will understand... my mother will... they will understand... they've seen it... they know. You cahn't stay miserable. It's not like I just up and quit... ten years... c'mon and I provided a lot over these years. What are you supposed to do? You gotta do what's best even if it ain't right... is that what Gawd wants? he asked himself, continuing the cross-examination as the truck rolled closer to the destination.

"What ah you supposed to do if you don't feel anything anymo-ah? How long do you have to live a lie and not live your life? It was a wrong choice... so sue me... I gotta pay for it foreva? The truth is she'd be happier too. I can pay for all this crap, but we cahn't get the days back. I gotta be strong and stick to it. Once she gets a bett-ah... I can fig-yah this out. I'll set her and the kid up for a new life just fine."

Frank paused, as though perhaps he'd figured it out. Get a divorce and move on.

"Half of everything is bullshit though... good luck getting that. They gotta find it to get it!" he thought, feeling instantly defiant... before shifting again.

"I better go to the hospital... at least call. Maybe I should go the-ya now. I need to go to this house though and finish the list.... That's best... gotta make the money, gotta keep the money running or we're all screwed. I will finish the house list, then go to the hospital and clean this up," he said, looking at himself in the rear view.

"She's probably still sleeping. The-yas nothing I can do if she's sleepin'. She said they told ha like 24 owas of sleep. I probably did the right thing stayin' away and letting ha get betta. I'll head the-ya right afta. That makes sense."

"Shit!" he yelled at no one... "Now you made me miss my Gawd damn turn."

72

I t's being Saturday, the site was lightly staffed: only Charlie and one other guy were working. Frank was uncharacteristically nice.

"Hey, Charlie," he said, hopping out of the truck in the driveway of the house, "how we doin' today?" Charlie stood up from where he was installing an outlet in the garage and walked out to meet Frank. He was unsure how to respond to the jovial greeting.

"It's looking good... you guys have made some solid progress," Frank continued.

"I think we're doin' some good work," replied Charlie cautiously. "Rick over there's finishing the major electrical, and we are reading for the flooring people early next week."

"You mean Monday?"

"Yeah... Monday." Charlie qualified.

"That's good news," Frank said as he walked past Charlie and into the garage, looking up and down.

"I have the punch list to run through so get your pencil ready, Charlie. I only want to do this once."

"I ahhh... I'm ready when you are boss."

After tending to the checklist with the Charlie with limited ridicule, Frank headed back toward to the hospital. As he drew closer to the city he got a call on his cell Phone. It was Tricia. "Hey there," she said in a coy voice.

"What's up?"

"Jees… grouchy guy."

"I'm busy, Trish… what's up?"

"That guy Barry Holcomb called again and said he's got a good one, but you need to move fast. He wants you to call him right away."

"Who?"

"Barry… The real-estate guy."

Frank had been looking at places for several months and had been thinking about moving out of his house for over a year. Tricia was very excited about the prospect and had been talking about it incessantly.

Barry Holcomb was a real estate agent Frank had worked with in the past, and he had hooked up some deal to access new construction projects that were in distress. Barry was kind of a slippery guy, but someone Frank could easily handle. Holcomb had somehow gained access to confidential information about buyers or builders whose cash fell through in the 11th hour and whose properties were quickly in jeopardy. Holcomb had a couple days head start to align Frank as a buyer, as the banks were generally anxious to deal.

Frank figured it was best to buy a place, because he couldn't "waste money on rent." He knew if he left Kate he would need a place so he had been poking around for a while, but nothing perfect had popped up. He hadn't given up on keeping the house, but he needed a back-up plan if things got heated. Frank was able to use a lot of cash to make the transaction. Collapsed financing and quick cash was a good formula.

Frank had been siphoning money into a secret safety deposit box for years and he was sitting on $117,650 in cash. He didn't steal the money per se, but he had taken payments in cash and supplemented his income with bonuses using cash from the company till. Star was aware of the bonuses, but did not realize the money was transacted in cash. Frank also got kickbacks from vendors and contractors; he considered those to be side deals negotiated solely by him and not Star Builders deals.

a frame for flowers

"Oh yeah right...Barry Bonehead," he said sarcastically, "give me his numba... I'll call him right now," said Frank. He knew the time frame was short so he wanted to get in before anyone else.

"6-1-7... 5-4-3-... 8-1-0-2..." she recited slowly. "Call him right now, baby." She cooed.

"Did I not just say I was gonna call him right now?" he snapped back and she fell silent.

Frank repeated the number back to Tricia to confirm, then quickly exited the call, telling her he would call her later. He was rolling back up the Jamaicaway as he dialed Barry's number.

"This is Barry," he answered.

"Holcomb... it's Frank Bruno... whatta ya got for me."

"Oh...it's juicy, Frank. Get this—a great stand-alone in a sweet part of Brookline just imploded and the buyer's totally out. The Jews at the bank are freaked about it. The buy price was set, the units totally done... but these folks bailed... paid frickin' nothing... and the bank's in to the builder now. They are freakin' out! I think we could close this at a sick price right now."

"How much?"

"Well we gotta move quick and l if we consider how much the bank's in."

"HOW MUCH Barry!" Frank barked into the cell.

"350?"

"How little can I put down?"

"Gonna need 20%, but this is a 180 grand discount and there will be others willing to pay that... it's an awesome price. I think you go in above 25%.... hundred large... and lock it right up."

"Give me the address... when can you meet me there?"

"Today... this afternoon... in like an hour," Barry said, sounding like a kid negotiating a trip to an amusement park.

There was a long pause from Frank as he calculated his situation. This was a time-sensitive deal and really necessary to work this out for everyone... he could hold off going to the hospital until that night...

"Give me the address and I'll meet you there in an hour."

73

Joe Bertucci was looking forward to seeing Patrick Kelley and excited to get back on the ice for some hockey. He had clocked a little skate time with some beat cops at the station who belonged to a pickup league in town. They weren't very good skaters, but it was just nice to lace up and slap the puck around. He could feel the energy coming back a bit, but his thighs burned after even a short shift, and he knew he had better tighten up his game before the puck dropped with his old gang. He had not heard from Patrick since they spoke, so he phoned him to solidify the plans. He caught Patrick at about the same time of evening they had spoken previously.

"Patty... hey its Tucc."

"Tuuuucc! How's it goin bud?"

"Good! I wanted to touch base about skating."

"Don't even think about backing out... I don't want to hear how you sprained your man bone doing laundry or some bull shit!" They both laughed into the phone and it felt like they were twenty again.

"Not a chance... I've been skatin' and everything... you can bet I'll be there... I'll be the one checking your melon into the glass! No seriously... I have been skating with some guys from work and getting ice time can be tough... I wanted to see if you worked something out or if I can help from this end."

"Shit—I'm glad you called. I touched base with a few guys and have a half-hearted commitment from Dougie Francona, but I've been crazy busy and need to get on it. You know, actually… If you can help me it would be huge."

"Of course…. I'm pretty jammed myself, but yeah I can call Dougie Fresh and ask him to lock it up."

"Well, if you're busy, bro," said Patrick sarcastically.

"Yeah fuck you…. it's not all donut shops for us," he retorted and again they laughed.

Joe explained he was working a suspected homicide case of a man who appeared to have killed his business partner. The guy claimed to have found the dead body of his associate after he committed suicide, but the pieces were not coming together. He sensed something was missing.

"It may not be exactly like TV, but forensics is huge these days and when people leave clues… we tend to find them. Sometimes it's just the threat of the science that helps solve the crime."

"What do you mean?" asked Patrick, now very curious.

"Well… you tell someone you have evidence back in the day… you know like a finger print, but the suspect knows they wore gloves and any finger print would be more likely to get 'im off rather than convict them. Then it's not very powerful. You bluff under those scientific terms and it can actually back fire letting the suspect know you've got nothing. But you tell 'im you have their DNA, and explain the science of how it can be retrieved off any of a dozen resources like skin, hair, saliva…"

"…man butter…" chimed in Patrick, laughing.

"No, seriously… we nail more people with semen than I care to admit!"

"Nail them with semen… is that scientific jargon, Joe?" giggled Patrick.

"Ha-ha… At any rate… we catch a lot of people like that and we get even more to confess when they are convinced we already have them."

"That's some crazy stuff."

"That's detective work… and it does keep us busy."

"Sounds like it," Patrick responded.

"I'll take care of booking some ice time though. It's going to be fun."

74

Anthony watched his mother drift in and out of sleep from a comfortable-but-ugly chair in the corner of the compact hospital room. She looked so thin now, and her bandages obviously concealed an operation that had ravaged her. She smiled at him—but through grayer teeth and pale lips. She just didn't look like herself, and it made him so sad to see. It was hard to understand why God would do this.

He sat watching her sleep and thought about her dying. What would it be like without her, the person who had cared for him his entire life? Without his mother, who taught him to tie his shoes, or pushed him on his bicycle, up and down the street until he pedaled on his own. The person who never ridiculed him, never taunted him for being different, and loved him unconditionally. How could he possibly go on without her, left to face the world, stranded with a father like his—a man who abandoned his wife in her hour of need.

After his mom settled into a deeper sleep Saturday, Anthony slipped out to head home. With Odna not around he recognized that sleeping at the hospital was a one-time gig; besides, he hadn't changed his clothes or showered in more than a day. The air was bitingly cold when he pushed out through the revolving doors and it pinched at his

232

cheeks and sliced through his thin jacket as he made his way into the night. It was a short distance over to the Green Line T station, and Anthony covered the ground quickly. He would take the subway up into the heart of the city, then head south on the Red line. He could get pretty close to the house and run the rest of the way. They lived in a nice neighborhood, but after dark in South Boston, you didn't want to stray too far from your hood.

Anthony and his mom did not speak about Frank. He figured she had too much to contend with. She figured he was largely unaware. Anthony was furious and didn't know what to expect when he got home. He figured he might see his dad at home eating a potpie in front of the TV like nothing had happened... or he might have moved out. It was hard to say and he didn't really care except he wanted more than anything to punch him in the face. He knew it would bring down a world of pain upon himself... but to just get one clean shot in would make it worth it.

His dad had been beating him for years, and at this point he was numb to the abuse. The verbal jabs were more exhausting than anything else, as they extended the sophomoric bullying from school, spilling over into his only refuge. He really couldn't care less about the endless parade of "morons" and "idiots"—it meant nothing coming from him. He had abandoned him as a father ages ago and was at peace with it. Frank Bruno was now just a landlord who happened to share his last name.

Anthony sat alone on the subway car, the train rocking back and forth and clacking along, in and out of shadows, over trestles, and into tunnels winding towards home, the lights of the city slowly revealing the holiday season that seemed to come sooner every year. It was hard to leave his mother's side, but he knew she was strong and he believed the nurses and doctors would make her whole again. When they did he knew he would make things different. Make them better. He hoped his father would move out. Just go on with his life and leave them alone.

Across town a few hours earlier... Frank was planning that very thing.

75

Dr. Johnson phoned Dr. Lynch shortly after she visited Kate to give him an update.

"How was the patient?" asked Dr. Lynch.

"She looked about as worn down as expected, but the sutures look good."

"How is the swelling?"

"Remarkably controlled on the left and modest on the right, I think you did a real nice job in there, Doctor."

"Well, thanks… we all know it doesn't matter much if just a bit of it escapes us… but I agree it went well and it is the best first assault we can provide. I will be over there Monday to check in myself and we should be able to start testing by mid-week."

"She is a strong woman," said Dr. Johnson.

"She is strong period." corrected Dr. Lynch.

76

When the train rolled into his station and the familiar chime sprung open the doors, Anthony vaulted up the steps from the subway station and out to the street. The train went underground in his neighborhood so it truly was a subway.

In Boston, the subway is affectionately known as the "T". A lot of people assume they called it that as an abbreviation for Train, but Vida Mudgett explained to Anthony the real story. A year or so earlier, his mom needed to take Vida down to city hall to sign some legal documents and Anthony went to help carry the files. Vida insisted they take the subway and not drive.

"It's more scenic," she explained which made no real sense, but Kate and Anthony were fine taking the T. "When's the first time you rode the T, Mrs. Mudgett?" asked Anthony with a curious smile.

"Back before it was called the T... that's for sure!" she replied grinning at the boy. "Seriously?" he asked.

"Oh certainly, it used to be the MTA before it was the "T"... you know like that song "Charlie on the MTA?"

"I don't think I know that song," he replied with a slight smirk.

"Well at any rate... they changed it from the Metropolitan Transit Authority to the Massachusetts Bay Transit Authority that it is today… but the kept the logo… the big "T" with a circle around it" she explained. "Local folks have been calling it the T ever since."

"Did you know that, ma?" Anthony asked.

"I did not… but I know that song and you should, too… your uncle Pat would sing it when he played his guitar."

Kate began to sing the locally popular Kingston Trio song that told the tale of an unfortunate poor man who got stuck on a ride and could never get off.

'Well did he ever return? No he never returned, and his fate is still unlearned (what a pity) He may ride forever 'neath the streets of Boston. He's the man who never returned!'

The air bore a deeper chill close to home and nearer to the water, and Anthony was in a full sprint as he turned the corner and darted into his driveway. There was a key hidden near the garbage cans under a rock, but Anthony wasn't sure if he would need it. The lights were on inside, but he couldn't tell if his dad's truck was in the garage. When he stopped at the house he was breathing hard and thick steam jets expelled from his strong lungs as he reached out for the door. His heartbeat was strong in his chest as he turned the knob and found the door open… his father was there.

77

The way Anthony saw it… there were two ways that a hero enters a fight in a movie. They walk in slow and the verbal exchange escalates into a fight… or they charge in guns blazing. It seemed to him that if you're the underdog the best way to enter are guns blazing, but in the movies… a slow approach always produced the best one-liners. He already knew he was the underdog so rushing in guns blazing only to lose, didn't seem appealing… why not walk and get the words in first.

He opened the door and crept cautiously into the kitchen, avoiding the creak at the edge of the doormat. The house was dead quiet, but after one step into the kitchen, King heard him and came bounding up the stairs from the basement as he barked out a warning. This meant his father was downstairs… where the guns were kept.

Anthony knew there was one other gun hidden up in his parent's bedroom, locked in a tan metal box and tucked in the closet. He hadn't been snooping; his mom had revealed it to him a few months earlier, when they were awakened by the sounds of a potential intruder downstairs. Their eyes had met in the hallway in silence as they huddled listening to the heavy footsteps below. Unsure of how to react, they froze in fear of the unknown.

King was barking, but Kate knew that was about the extent of the German shepherd's offense... so she felt it was important to act. Snapping to action Kate had grabbed Anthony's hand and pulled him swiftly and quietly into the closet, her finger pressed to her lips. She knelt nimbly and deftly retrieved a metallic snub nose .38 from the tan metal box and moved fluidly out of the closet and back toward the hallway. The weapon shimmered in the dark as it reflected the moonlight that streamed in through the bedroom window.

Anthony's heart felt like it stopped dead in his chest when King suddenly ceased barking, but his mother relaxed lowering the weapon to her side. She turned back toward him, shaking her head. Anthony was very confused and also very impressed by the way his mother had so rapidly assumed the role of protector when faced with the potential intruder. He had never seen her take on a role like that, a protector.

When King had stopped barking, Kate realized it must have been Frank getting in particularly late that Thursday. King would not have stopped for a stranger and shortly after, she heard Frank call the dog "stupid," assuring it was not a robber. She peered into the third bedroom and quickly realized he was indeed not in yet. As quick as she had retrieved the weapon, she replaced it and motioned Anthony back to bed. Neither of them ever said another thing about that night.

For a split second, Anthony contemplated getting the weapon before confronting his father... but logic prevailed.

Anthony knelt briefly and petted King. "You're a good boy," he said, then walked directly to the basement door and began down the staircase. He was halfway down when Frank appeared at the base of the stairs leering broodingly up at him. The basement was dark, and Frank's image sent an icy shiver to the base of his skull. Anthony felt his breath shorten and fingers curl up... then they spoke.

"Hey... I was wondering where you were," said Frank in a calm and deliberate voice as if they had been briefly separated at a mall.

"Where I was? The question is, Where were you?"

"Watch it... I dropped your mom off and ahhh... went to take care of work. Someone has to pay for all this stuff you know? You can't just ahhh draw pictures or plant tulips to pay for all this," said Frank thrusting his arms in the air, his agitation meter swiftly flirting with the red zone.

"Mom's been out of the operation for more than a day... where were you? Don't you even want to know if she's alright?"

"I've been talking with the Doctors," said Frank in a stone-cold lie.

"Really, and what did they say?" Anthony inquired skeptically.

"Ah... look—it's complicated, and your mom's going through a tough time."

"A tough time... my God, you don't even know do you?" Anthony said digging his heels, his jaw jutting to the side as his upper lip tightened.

Frank seemed at an uncharacteristic loss for words. The truth was he didn't know, and now wondered if there was something he should know about Kate's condition. His indecision had him locked. Anthony wanted desperately to hit him and standing a step or two above his father on the stairs gave him position and confidence. However, he knew from experience his father was quick and strong and that this was an unwise plan. He sensed a better approach was to see if he could actually pry emotion from the man, if he could actually evoke the one thing that may damage him: guilt.

"Well, to me... mom looks like she dying... and I couldn't do anything about it. I lay there all night near her, listening to her breath and praying to God it didn't stop... she is so thin and weak and she looks like she might die... but she sat up and tried to eat her meal and be strong for me. She was worried about the nurse for God's sake... and most of all... she protected you. She knew that you didn't come, but she said nothing. I knew you didn't come, the damn nurse even knew you didn't come!" He said now his voice rising steadily as he stood on the stairs.

Anthony struggled, fighting back the ball of emotion that swelled in his throat, pressing at his neck and popping his eardrums.

"What is wrong with you... how can you be so cruel?" he yelled as his anger swelled.

"That's enough out of you," Frank warned, as he squared his shoulders and set his feet.

Anthony could tell his words had cut deep. Without lifting a hand he had slapped his father hard across the face. He knew he was running out of time, but kept up the assault.

"No, it isn't," Anthony screamed, but his father fired back.

"It's complicated… we've gone through a lot, yer mum and I, so you can show some respect and shut your Gawd damned mouth. I….. ahhh… we… agreed that I would just drop her off! Fa-get it… yo-ah too young to unda-stand."

"Understand what? That you don't love her? That you don't love us and probably never did? That you are more interested in your work and guns and friends to even notice us, to notice how sick she is or how much pain she is in."

"Enough!" belted Frank jutting his thick finger into Anthony's face and leaving it… hovering an inch from his eye.

"Not enough! He snapped in return, leaning into the finger defiantly.

And then it happened as he knew it would, and yet he never saw it. Frank in his rage unleashed a right hook that struck Anthony flush in his temple, shocking his skull, a blue spark cracking in his mind. Anthony's young body, dropped like the condemned at the gallows, crumpling at the bottom of the basement staircase

Frank stepped over him and marched upstairs.

78

When Anthony came to he was all alone in a dead silent house and for a moment he did not know how he had gotten there. He had no idea how long he had lain there knocked out, but King had laid himself down beside him on the cold cement floor and waited patiently for the young man to regain consciousness. He wondered if it was all a bad dream, but inside he knew it was real.

79

A few days had passed since Kate's operation and Vida had still not spoken with her. She had buried herself in the manuscript and although the book was far from being ready to publish, the story was complete and she was excited to share it with Kate. Anthony had stopped by around dusk on Tuesday after school to get a message to Vida from Kate. He climbed the stairs to her front porch and rang the bell. A minute later Vida appeared. She wore a nice, if perhaps old-fashioned, dress, and her hair looked freshly done.

"Hi, Mrs. Mudgett."

"Hello, Anthony, how are you holding up?"

"I'm good… I can't go to the hospital tonight, but my mom is supposed to come home tomorrow or the next day so I'm happy about that," he said.

"Come on in dear. I just got out some cookies and made some tea."

Anthony was not particularly interested in tea, but the cookies sounded ok and he wanted to be respectful. He knew that Mrs. Mudgett was an important person in his mom's life and so it meant a lot to him to have a connection with her. She was really old, but he struggled with his grandparents, Emilio and Theresa, and always felt awkward or out of place around them. With Vida there was such an ease, a comfort.

a frame for flowers

It was hard to explain for Anthony, but he trusted her in a way that he didn't trust many. He thought Vida was genuine and kind, but most of all… Anthony found her to be unique, and that to him was a badge of honor. She was a real individual. He found it amazing that she wrote books and was pretty much famous, but lived in obscurity. He had read a couple of the Daisy McQueen books himself and although he found them a bit predictable, he recognized the creativity and always appreciated the inventive nature of the plots. She had a way of developing complex stories that were bizarre and even preposterous at times, but somehow plausible. She also created characters he liked—people you could envision in your mind. In fact, he had imagined Daisy McQueen as an attractive young woman with impressive intelligence and an athletic body. He liked her character.

He followed Vida into the house and back to the kitchen where he sat at a small wood table. "How do you think your mom is doing inside?"

"What do you mean?"

"Well she's good at putting up a strong exterior, but she told me all about what this operation would do and that's got to be tough on a person," Vida said as she brought over a small plate filled with homemade chocolate-chip cookies.

"Do you want some milk?"

"If it's not any trouble," he said.

"Only trouble is eating a good cookie with no milk!" she replied.

"I guess she's doing ok with everything. She just looks so skinny. It hurts to see her like that, and I feel like I can't help… I can't do anything."

"Well, you mustn't feel that way… foolish Catholic guilt's all that is."

Anthony hid his smile by slipping a bite of cookie on past its flash. Vida poured him a very small glass of cold milk and placed the glass gently next to the plate of cookies along with a folded paper towel. She then wobbled back across the kitchen to her waiting tea.

"Your mom is strong, but she needs you… she needs your love, and that is something we both know you can do for her. It's gonna get harder too… and you both know it," she said as she lifted her tea to her lips, taking a draw of the warming liquid.

"A whole heck of a lot harder… and I don't suspect you can rely on that man to be pitching in," she said, craning her eyes furtively above the teacup that hovered just before her rounded face. She was watching for a reaction.

"Huh… yeah… that's yeah… that's obvious, huh?" Anthony replied, half-asking, half-telling. "I think he's movin' out…" he said as his eyes drifted out.

"Yes, well, never you mind that either. You two are taken care of. Do you understand me, Anthony?"

"Huh…" he said, refocusing. "Yes, of course."

"No," she followed, "look at me."

Anthony swallowed and placed the half eaten cookie back down on the plate, brushed off his hand into the paper towel and focused his eyes on this small, serious, and steadfast woman who stood before him. She took a step towards the young man and asked him again.

"Do you understand me?"

He was silent and she further clarified.

"Anthony… you and your mother are going to be taken care of… do you understand what I'm saying? That you don't need to worry about your father or how any of this goes. What you must do… is stand by your mother no matter what happens, and understand that she loves you more than life itself."

Anthony believed he understood. Maybe that she could take care of the house payments or something. He wasn't precisely sure, but he knew it felt good to hear someone saying something comforting. He knew his mother loved him but Vida's reassurance felt good.

"Thank you, Mrs. Mudgett…. My mom loves you, too."

"And I love her very much," she said, averting her eyes and biting down on her lip just a bit.

80

The doctors ended up keeping Kate for four days to allow her extra time to gain strength, and by all accounts she was recovering remarkably. Frank had yet to even call.

The color was slowly returning to her face, and Odna kept her well fed by talking up the entirely mediocre hospital food with such exuberance that Kate actually looked forward to her next meal. Dr. Johnson stopped by every day as well as Dr. Lee, and they tended to her bandages and checked her drainage and biometrics. It was good to see Dr. Johnson, as she was a good listener and always upbeat.

"How are your plants doing, Doctor?" Kate asked.

"They are really flourishing Kate, thanks," she said taking her glasses off... her face lighting up. "I added the egg shells to the water like you suggested and I think they are really responding."

"Is your Weeping Fig doing any better?"

"Well, that's the best part... she was on life support until you suggested the reflected light trick and now new leaves are sprouting every day; in fact, there is a second shoot coming up from the soil!"

"That so great... they can grow real big, though, so you may need a relocation plan if it lives a long time."

"Well, I think the patient is going to make it!" she said, and they both felt a brief moment of kindred happiness as Dr. Johnson began to swab at the edges of the massive wounds that were slowly healing.

When Dr. Johnson changed the bandage, she pushed the door shut and removed all the cotton dressing revealing for the first time Kate's bare chest. She could finally see all that wasn't there. She had seen glimpses of the left side already, but the swelling had decreased and the divot in her chest was deep and unnatural. The scars were sunken pink, red, and black zippers that ran like train tracks beneath where her breast once was and up into her armpit. The image was that of a female Frankenstein, and it was far more frightening then the movie monster ever was.

On the right side her breast was partially held down by a plastic film and what looked like a round white decal with the center missing like a donut. In the middle was her nipple, which looked red and distorted. The exposed portion of her right breast was lumpy and seemingly lopsided, while beneath the plastic her flesh was a pale color that resembled tapioca pudding under cellophane. The sight made tears pool in her eyes.

"It gets better, Kate," said Dr. Johnson, noticing her tears.

She had been there before many times with patients and she knew the psychological impact of losing your breast or breasts. The metaphorical loss of womanhood made instantly real.

"Surgery can be done to rebuild the breasts with implants, and the scars will fade considerably. Some women have full breast work done subsequent to healing."

"Oh yeah," Kate said, with only her eyes crying.

"It's just too hard to believe it's really happened. I think people always say that… I never thought it would be me. Somehow they knew they'd win the lottery… but no one ever suspected they would be the one to get sick or die… that's for someone else right?"

Dr. Johnson stopped and replied.

"The percentage of people stricken with cancer is small… it is an outlier. You are an outlier to have gone through this. In my experience… 100% were shocked it happened to them. I have to be honest

246

though… you were the first patient that either Dr. Lynch or I have ever seen who accepted their fate so quickly. You seemed to deal with it without much drama or self-pity… how is that?"

"Because life happens to you no matter what, and there is not much you can do but deal with it the best you can. No matter what it is… you deal with it. Sometimes you have to redefine what it is that you believe your life to be… sometimes you have to dig deep. This is what life gave me so I calculated the best possible outcome. Be strong, fight it, and get through it. No pity," she said looking up at the doctor with honest eyes.

"It helps me get through the tough times and has proven to me that I can do things I didn't know I was capable of. This is real and this is happening. That's what I tell myself, and once that sets in… I can take anything."

Dr. Johnson had never heard something so powerful.

81

Anthony had not told his mother about how Frank had hit him, and he had not seen his father for two days after. Anthony knew his mom was set to come home that evening after being released from the hospital. He was to go there after school; they planned to take a taxi back home together. Anthony had been taking care of himself and King. He had no choice. He fed the dog, choked down a bowl of cereal, and went to pitch the bowl in the sink when he saw his father's truck pulling into the driveway. His first instinct was to run and hide.

He felt instantly vulnerable in the huge house and wondered if his father had seen him in the kitchen window. His eyes darted to the door, which he was sure he could reach and lock, but he remained still at the sink simply staring at the entrance. Within ten seconds the door burst open and in he strode.

"Don't you have school?" he asked incredulously.

"I'm leaving in a second."

"Your mom and I have talked things through," started Frank.

"We feel its best with my busy work and her needing to rest a lot that I move out for a bit to create a good quiet place for her."

Anthony suspected that they had not actually spoken, but he went along with it as casually as his father did.

"That's probably the best idea."

"Yeah… it is." Frank said trying to appear somber and logical. "So you got school then?"

"Yeah… I'm leaving."

"You know the other night is just a bad night, right?"

"Huh?"

"It's been stressful for all of us and I had a bad night."

"Well that makes two of us… I woke up on the floor in the basement."

"I said I was sorry… you might want to appreciate that. If I did that as a kid I would still be knocked out." Of course Anthony was not going to correct his father by pointing out that factually he had not said he was sorry, but simply stated that he had a bad night.

"My parents are splitting," he thought to himself… "good."

"I'll be at the hospital when mom gets out this afternoon."

"Huh… yeah right… um what time you getting there?" asked Frank fishing for the info.

"I gotta take the T, but I will be there before 4:00."

Frank appeared to ponder on that information and scratched with his fingernails just beneath his chin.

"Hey you know what? I'll pick you up and bring you over so we can give yer mom a ride home in comfort."

It dawned on Anthony that his father: one—had no idea she was even getting out today. And two—considered it to be a luxury for him to be picking up his wife of 15 years after major cancer surgery! And three—that he may not actually show to pick him up that afternoon, but again he played along.

"Ok, I can be out front of the school at 3:15. Pick me up by the tennis courts to avoid all the buses," Anthony instructed.

"OK… I gotta leave a job so wait fa me if I am running behind… lots goin on with wintah comin'!"

"Yeah of course… see you after school, then, by the tennis courts."

"Yeah, yeah… I got it."

Anthony scooped his books into his bag, pet King good-bye, and slipped silently past his father, who was rummaging through the fridge, and out the door. It was the Wednesday before Halloween weekend and the younger guy directly across the street must have been playing hooky from work. He was hanging a ghost from a rope on his front porch where he had set up several Halloween decorations, pumpkins and even some fake tombstones in the yard. The kids would be trick-or-treating that Friday night. Anthony hurried to the bus stop.

82

Frank drove to the hospital to find out what was going on and make sure he could pick Kate up that afternoon like he had planned. He had assumed Kate would be there for at least a week and was taken off guard when Anthony mentioned she was being released that day.

Frank had checked into the health insurance for this ordeal and they were pretty well covered so it shouldn't be too much out of pocket. It only got harsh when they exceeded like $65,000 or so. He had also called up the guy who held their life insurance policies. Frank was insured for a million bucks, but he was a bit disappointed when the insurance guy, Tom Morley, informed him he had only purchased $200,000 on Kate.

"You see, Mr. Bruno, when we discussed this many years back, we felt this was adequate coverage considering your wife's age and health and desire to keep the premiums low... Now we can certainly increase the levels if you'd like." stated Tom Morley in his vanilla tone.

"Yeah, well, how much is it to do that?"

"Well it depends on what you want to raise the level of the policy up to, so for instance, one million, or two million? Of course, this all has to coincide with new and full medical examinations, and we will..."

"Oh," Frank interrupted, "Oh Jesus... we gotta go through all the medical exams again?"

"Yes."

"But we already got a policy and we've nev-ah missed a payment—what's the difference?"

"Well, there can be changes to people health condition, Mr. Bruno, and these policies were written almost ten years ago. Most definitely the insurance companies are going to want to feel comfortable with their levels of risk."

"Fuckin' crooks," Frank sniped.

"Well… he-he… that may be true…" said Tom, forcing out a laugh.

So that wasn't an option for Frank.

"It's not like I'm wishing she die or anything," he thought to himself, as he pulled into a Dunkin' Donuts drive-thru for a quick coffee.

"I mean, that's what you get insurance for right? It's to pay for the stuff that person can't do if they die…it's why we frickin' pay for it!" he rationalized.

He couldn't help thinking that 200 large would help him buy out Jim Star faster, but he fought back those thoughts. "That's just wrong," he reminded himself.

"I want out of this mistake, but I would never wish someone dead," he further rationalized. He felt that was an honorable position.

Frank had spent two hours packing up a couple suitcases of clothing and personal belongings. He would have to stay in a hotel for a while.

Holcomb came through big-time on the condo in Brookline. The place was killer, and Frank was gonna make a move on it right away. Tricia was ecstatic, but he had to tell her to shut up and calm down repeatedly. The downside was it would take several weeks if not months to get into the place, but he knew he just couldn't stay with Kate anymore. The getting-sick thing was bad timing, but life needs to move forward. He would give her some space to recover and then file for divorce once she was back up and running. In some ways the sick thing was a blessing. It helped him realize they were both wasting their lives in a loveless marriage.

"It's weird how things work out," he thought to himself as he took a belt of his large regular Dunkin's coffee…

83

Kate really wanted to go home. She felt modestly better, but the pain was often intense and at times the tightness in her chest made it very hard to breath. The struggle to breathe only served to make her anxious, which in turn tightened her chest more. She was feeling stronger, though, and she could move and sit up on her own now. She really felt optimistic that brighter days lay ahead and that she could rebuild.

She was leaving in five hours though and feeling a bit tense. She was worried about Anthony's being able to handle all this. Frank's perfidy was not necessarily shocking, but she had not expected him to be a complete non-factor. He did not even appear to have made any of her in-laws aware. They had never surfaced or contacted her, and it is not as if they would be worried about her per se... but the opportunity for the drama that surrounded an operation like this would have been irresistible for Theresa and Frank's sisters... they would have surely made this their cause. It was really hard to believe that she had just endured a life-threatening operation to remove cancerous tumors... and only one person had come to see her.

Some of that was her fault of course... she had only one friend who was eighty-two years old and not very mobile... and she had not told her only sibling a word about it. Kate never doubted she would survive the operation, but had nonetheless explained it all in a note to Patrick, a sort of back up to her will which Frank and she had both completed with a lawyer years earlier. The note was tucked into her personal belongings at the house where it would have been easily found. She had mentioned it to Vida to cover herself in the worst scenario.

Seeing Odna usually made her relax. She took her for walks up and down the hallway, helped her with her food, and in general kept her company.

"Hey, you, did Maury or Jerry Springer come on yet?" Odna asked with her unique cackle of a laugh.

"I hope to not watch TV for the next month!" Kate replied. "I am so tired of watching these depressing people... I just feel so bad for them."

"I love it... silly folks all worried about nothing!"

"I'll say."

"So you goin' home girl.... You ready?"

"I think so... It will be nice to sleep in my bed and see my dog and just be around Anthony every day."

"You all done?" Odna asked about the partially eaten breakfast that sat on the tray in front of Kate.

"You didn't like today's stack of flapjacks and bacon? Me and the girls call it the lumberjack! You don't feel like choppin down no trees today?"

"I am more of a gardener's breakfast kind of gal!" Kate said as Odna place a napkin over the top of the tray and removed it.

"Yeah... you like the yogurt-and-granola kind of stuff... I know, I know," she said, smiling.

Odna tidied up around the room and loaded the tray onto a big metal cabinet on wheels in the hall. Another worker carted off the empties. She gave Kate a little wave as she headed forward on her rounds and walked out. Kate sat in her room as the morning sunrays eased across her blankets, warming her legs. It was hard to get the image of her sunken chest and scars out of her mind, but she tried to think about the things Dr. Johnson had said, as well as some of the before-and-after pictures of women who had gone through reconstruction after the surgery. Many of them looked perfect and in some cases Kate thought they looked a bit better.

"A long way to go to hide a boob job from your friends and family," she said to herself with a giggle.

Some of the woman in the photos had tattoos done in place of their breasts, putting designs over the now flat flesh of their chests. None of that was really of interest to Kate, but the thought of looking normal again appealed to her. She also had to consider that, based on her husband's behavior, she may be single again. Kate was lost in thought when Odna popped her head back in the door and pinned it shut against herself as if to keep someone out.

"You gotta visitor" she said in an uncharacteristically serious and somber tone.

"Who?" asked Kate, calculating that Anthony should certainly be in school at that time. "I think it's your husband."

84

Kate felt flush and grasped at the sheets gathering the bedding to pull it up around her. She brushed at her hair pushing her fingertip lightly across her scalp. She had met Frank Bruno seventeen years earlier when she was just twenty and had his baby two years later in 1988. He had been with her half of her life. He was Anthony's father. Yet when he stood in the doorway of the generic hospital room he was somehow unfamiliar. She did not feel safe around him or secure the way she had those years before. She felt a cold stranger stood in her midst using up her air.

Frank was dressed for work with jeans and a dress shirt covered by a bulky, navy-blue Star Builders jacket. His arms were crossed in defense of shame as he stepped forward into the room and closed the door, leering suspiciously back at Odna, who peered past him to catch Kate's eyes. The door clicked shut and they were all alone.

"How you doin', Kate?" he asked, channeling his younger self.

"I'm okay," she answered reluctantly.

"Doctors say you can go home, huh? That's good."

"Yeah… we think so," she said curtly with an austere face.

"I know this has been tough Kate… we've been goin' through a tough time for a while he-ya," he began.

"Tough? Are you out of your mind?" Kate said sitting up without the aid of the bed. "I have cancer Frank… it's a bit more than tough and it's me… not we."

"I know you have canc-ah for Christ's sake…?"

"Oh yeah… and when did that finally occur to you, huh, because I have been in this hospital for five days Frank, lying in this bed, begging for the pain to stop, with a couple of pounds of my flesh missing! So when did you suddenly figure out what was going on? When is it exactly that you had this epiphany?"

"Don't start with me and… and don't start using… college words Kate… you know… I don't know what that fuckin' word means…. I'm here trying to make things right and help us move forward."

"Forward? Ohhh….Okay… Okay…. What is your plan to ah… move things forward, Frank?"

"Well, obviously look at this… we don't get along… we haven't been a good married couple in the eyes of Gawd for a real long time."

"In the 'eyes of God'? Oh… I can only hope the Lord is watching this," she said in disgust.

"Look—I want to drive you to the house today and get you settled in and, you know, get you comfortable. Maybe we can get a nurse or something to look after you, or I can call one of my sisters… but we can get you outta here today and that's a good thing.

"Anthony is coming to get me this afternoon."

"I know… I talked to him," he said, gloating.

"Ok then you can come back at four o'clock when he gets here and… you can drive us to the house."

"I'm movin' out, Kate," he blurted.

"Yeah… fine. I figured that might be coming."

"I figure the best thing is…. I think we should get a divorce."

Those words burrowed right into Kate's brain as she rifled through the meaning and impact. She was instantly at odds with a head full of emotions swimming and diving around her… each stating their case. Yet she remained silent.

"Did you hear me?"

"Yes… I heard you," she stated blankly.

"Well, do you have nuthin' to say?"

"Yeah… I do." She replied but again paused in silence. Kate looked down at herself and did her best to square up her shoulder and lift her chin.

"Well?" he insisted.

"Get a good lawyer."

85

Odna helped Kate prepare to leave the hospital. She assisted her getting her sweats on and tying her white tennis sneakers. Odna had brought in a little makeup kit and held up a small round mirror as Kate applied a touch of eye shadow and blush, bringing shape and color back to her face.

"How'd it go with your man, if you don't mind me askin'?" Odna said, gently sliding the sneaker onto Kate's foot but never making eye contact.

"It went as expected. He's a bad guy, Odna..."

"Sometimes I think they all bad," she replied.

"I really don't know about that, I hope not... but I do know this man," she said with fixed eyes, "any good there was... is gone."

"Well, then... it sounds you might be better off without."

"You're probably right," said Kate, fixing her hair with her hand, "I could just imagine me doing this to him... he gets sick and is in the hospital, and I walk in and ask him for a divorce... ha!... I could only imagine."

"I'll say... how you think he would handle that, eh?" said Odna, giggling sarcastically. "Oh... he'd kill me." Kate said with a laugh.

"Throw you out the window huh?"

259

"No…oh no, that would be too quick… he'd probably strangle me so I would suffer."

"Yikes," said Odna.

"Yeah… yikes." Kate said blankly.

Odna knelt before Kate, who sat on the ugly, donkey brown chair in the corner of the small hospital room. Once she had tied the second sneaker Odna held Kate's feet in her hands pressing them together softly as if she were hugging them. Kate reached out her hand and touched the woman's face gingerly with the back of her fingers. Odna's skin was radiant and her cherubim cheeks were naturally graced with a hue of rouge. Her eyes were big and brown, her skin as soft as flower petals. Her smile was effusive.

"I'm pretty sure how this story ends, Odna, but we all have our crosses to bear."

The two sat for a moment and just looked at each other without a word. It was as if they both believed they knew what the future would hold, but did not wish to burden one another with it.

86

Frank had left in a huff and Kate was not sure if he would even return as he had stated, but at 4:00 P.M. sharp he waltzed in the door with Anthony in tow, as though nothing was wrong. Kate sat still and watched. Anthony signaled to her from behind Frank, shrugging his shoulder and raising his hands as if to say, "I don't know why he's here."

"You ready?" Frank asked casually. Odna rose, and pushed pass him.

"I get a wheelchair for you, honey. Be back here in a spell, but don't go nowhere. All the paper works gotta be done and right before we can actually release you. Okay?"

"Sure... no problem," said Kate.

"Hi, Odna," said Anthony. She winked him a grin as she shuffled out the door.

"She full of herself, eh?" said Frank to no audience. "I'm stahving, so I hope they don't drag this out forevah. You must be hungry?" he said to Kate.

"I just ate," she replied.

"This ain't food though, am I right?" he asked Kate but looked at Anthony.

"It's fine... I'm not hungry." Kate responded, and then turned to Anthony. "You want to eat, honey?"

"No, ma… I'm fine."

Frank grew gradually more impatient as the time passed and Odna didn't return. "Take your time, fatty," he mumbled.

Kate didn't care enough to scorn him.

Odna and Dr. Lee reappeared about fifteen minutes later. Odna was pushing a wheelchair.

"Going-home day," said Dr. Lee to Kate, then turning to Frank, "You must be Mr. Bruno; it's a pleasure to meet you."

"Thanks for taking care of her, Doc. You guys do some miracles here," said Frank extending a firm handshake.

"She is tough as can be," the doctor said back to Frank, with a quick glance over to Kate for recognition.

Odna rolled over to Kate and reached out to help her stand, then turn, and finally sit in the wheelchair. She flipped the footrests out and helped her get settled in.

"You know, I think I can walk, Odna," Kate said. "Hospital rules, honey… gotta use the chair."

Anthony stood at the ready to help his mom with the chair and scooped up her overnight bag.

"We can discuss the paperwork on the way down," said Dr. Lee, "and handle the John Hancocks in the lobby. Does that work for everybody?"

"Whatever you need from us," injected Frank as Kate nodded her head. They exited the room with little fanfare as Kate took a mental snapshot.

"Hope to never see you again," she thought to herself, and then they were out in the hall.

A patient was being wheeled by as a doctor and several nurses hovered over, walking and attending to a variety of things at the same time. They seemed to be moving with a profound sense of urgency.

"Heartbeat is fading, forty over twenty," reported one of the masked nurses. "We're losing her."

The doctor then barked out orders in rapid succession: 20 cc of some drug… with a something-push and shouts to start pumping.

"Get us in there" he ordered, and then they were past.

"Poor woman," Kate thought to herself, as they watched the group disappear down the hall.

"That shit's crazy, huh?" said Frank to Anthony with a smile.

"Yeah, you can hardly imagine it happening to someone you know," Anthony replied. Frank got the reference and said nothing else.

87

The car drive home was quiet, with barely a word spoken, but as they pulled into the driveway, Frank began.

"I know everyone thinks I'm the bad guy he-ya, and I do feel bad for not be-in at the hospital. I unda-stand the silent treatment, ok... I've been living with it for ye-ahs. You and this house, it's my house, but I am gonna move out and give you what you want. I get it, I'm the bad guy, and nobody wants me he-ya so fine... I'm getting out."

"You're moving out?" asked Anthony, shocked by the casual reference.

Frank pulled the truck all the way into the garage despite the fact that it would have been easier to stop and unload Kate in the driveway and make the straight shot into the side door. He left the garage door open and the truck running.

"Frank, I don't know why you're getting into this now... and by the way, nobody is kicking you out."

"Where you gonna go?" asked Anthony, but Frank ignored him.

"Yeah, well... I packed my stuff and it's in the bed of the truck. You two can enjoy this big expensive house to ya-selves. I will just keep workin' to pay for the frickin' thing."

Kate was in the passenger seat and had to exit first and wait for Anthony to climb out of the pinched position in the back. She felt wobbly, but stable enough as she stood on the cement floor in the garage, pleased to feel her feet beneath her. The air was musty, but it was a familiar and she welcomed it. Everything felt a little numb and tingled like a sleeping limb. Frank kept talking from the driver's seat.

"Anthony!" he shouted.

"Yeah?"

"You got this?"

"Got what?"

"Got ya motha, stupid!... I'm not wanted he-ya."

"Oh my word with the drama!" Kate railed, rolling her eyes.

"Ummmm yeah sure... I got it." Anthony slung Kate's slight bag over his shoulder and put his arm around her waist. The two walked carefully back out of the garage towards the house. Just then a holler came from the street. "My gosh, Kate, what happened?"

It was Walter Heaney and sure enough he was right on schedule with the Yorkies. He tottered up the driveway and let the dogs go to join Anthony in helping his mother.

"Are you fuckin' kidding me..." Frank groaned as he slapped his hand down on the steering wheel. "What is with this guy?" Reluctantly he climbed from the truck as if he intended to the whole time. "We got it, Heaney, okay?"

"Oh, hello, Frank... sorry I didn't see you.... What the blazes is going on? Katie, you look like you've been through a war!" Walter rattled nervously, but empathetically.

Having watched his Grace struggle so many times he knew how to help and it was in his nature to do so. "I said we got this Heaney..." Frank reiterated, noting one of the dogs peeing on the driveway.

"Sure thing, Frank... just trying to help," he said backing away from Kate. "Ya? Well help your dog find a different bathroom!"

"I had an operation Walter." Kate interrupted to the poor man. "I am a bit shaken up, but on the mend. Thank you so much for lending a hand... we're all set... don't worry okay? Thank you!"

"Thanks, Mr. Heaney," echoed Anthony

"Goodbye, Heaney," Frank said.

They eventually shuffled everyone inside, and in the kitchen Frank turned immediately back. "I'm leavin'. I will be at a hotel for a while," he said. "I'll call tomorrow."

And that quickly he was gone: out the door, into the garage, into the truck, back down the driveway and gone.

88

Anthony helped his mother sit down at the kitchen table, and the two collected themselves. Outside, the evening seemed to darken at a sprint. King took up residence beside Kate immediately. Anthony instinctively put on some hot water and noticed the small stash of dirty plates that had accumulated over the previous days. He turned on the faucet and ran the water until steam started to creep off. He got the bottle of detergent out from beneath the sink and squirted large gobs of it onto the yellow and green sponge before turning the spigot to begin filling a bowl with the water.

"Ow," he yelled as the steaming water scalded his hand. "What am I doing?"

He turned to his mother who sat there looking at him and petting the dog... her eyes looked sad. "What are we gonna do, mom?"

"What, sweetie?" she asked, slowed by a recent dose of pain medicine.

"What are we gonna do... how am I supposed to take care of you when you still take care of me? How are we gonna get by?"

"We're gonna live."

"What?" He exclaimed... confused by the answer.

"We are going to live Anthony... and that is something I understand vividly now. I..." she paused, "... we have not been living for years. We have not been talking… for years. We have let that horrible, wretched person dictate everything for most of our lives and we are done with it. Do you understand me? We are going to start to live, and it begins now. I may be weak, but I will get strong again and we will rebuild."

Anthony turned and shut off the water, then walked over and sat with her at the kitchen table. "I hate him, mom," he said solemnly.

"I know it's been hard," she said.

"No… I hate him, mom, I really hate his guts and I have for a long time…. I know it is wrong, but I can't help it. It's not just the bullying or hitting… it's so much…. It's the cruelty. He is mean like a sick person or some rotten enemy, like some Nazi in a movie… he is so cruel to us. Why is he so cruel to us?"

"I don't know… I'm sorry, honey… I haven't protected you from him… I know… But this is over and we are going to start living today… and every day."

Anthony wrapped his arms around his mother. She felt so small in his embrace, but the warmth of his mother's love burned strong and he filled with joy. After several deep breaths he withdrew.

"I know you told him you weren't… but for real you must be hungry…"

"I'm starved," she said, grinning.

"I will make us grilled cheese sandwiches," he offered. Kate loved him so much.

89

Anthony wanted to skip school the next day but Kate convinced him that he ought to go. She had called Vida to see if she could spend time with her and she was more than happy to walk down for a visit.

"I'll be down at 7:30 sharp!" Vida said with a notable pitch of excitement in her voice. They hadn't spoken for days and she was talking a million miles an hour on the phone.

"That way Anthony can see me and know you got company before he leaves for school. He's been so good through all this... its tough on a boy when his dad doesn't set a good example. My word... I can't believe that scallywag of a husband left you alone and never came to the hospital... good Jesus, they're warming a seat in hell for him."

"It is hard to believe Vida... it really is. I've known him for 18 years... and he's done some creepy things and even some downright rotten things... But this is just hard to fathom."

"It's just so selfish." Vida said in response.

"That's the proper word for it, but hey... we can talk all about it tomorrow. You get some rest and I will see you in the morning."

"You're the one who needs to focus on rest, my dear, and we will make sure you get it... good rest in your own bed—and I can keep you fed and entertained.. I've got just the ticket, you know. The new mystery is ready to read and I am so looking forward to your feedback. I am bringing a copy of it tomorrow."

It dawned on Kate at that moment that Vida would not be able to get up and down the stairs very easily. It did not appear that Vida had thought about it. She rarely ventured upstairs in her own house, how was she going to be hoofing it up and down the big staircase in Kate's house? Kate was going to have to figure out a way for it to work.

90

In a follow-up call regarding the now fully hyped hockey reunion, Joe Bertucci told Patrick that he was closing in on the guilty man in his homicide case. He said the suspect probably had no idea how much he had on him. Joe would never discuss a case with anyone outside law enforcement, but he did tell Patrick he thought he was going to nail the "perp" pretty soon.

What he didn't tell Patrick were the specifics of the case. The victim's business partner had a huge motive to kill him. The two men were principals in a wealth-management business, and they did estate planning for wealthy clients. The suspect had been using funds inappropriately and had tried to conceal the missing money by making risky bets on long shots in the stock market. When those bets didn't pan out, it exacerbated the losses and he was increasingly under water. He continued this cycle until they were essentially insolvent. The business they had built over fifteen years was suddenly in debt and collapsing from the inside out.

It turned out that the two business partners had invested in a "first-to-die" insurance policy many years earlier. Just like many other business partners, the two men had reasoned that the business would struggle and could fail if either of them were to die and leave the other to run the business on their own. They each handled vastly different parts of the business and possessed different skill sets that, when coupled, were what made them a tremendous partnership. One was a sales guy who handled the customers and the other was a numbers guy who handled the investments and finances. The suspect probably believed it was the only way out for him. He would kill his partner and conceal his role in the losses then collect the million-dollar payout on the policy.

"So why don't you go arrest the guy if you got the evidence on him," asked Patrick, fascinated by the intrigue of his friend's investigation.

"It's not that easy... Sometimes we have everything on someone and still can't arrest 'im. It really boils down to either a confession or overwhelming evidence. If you can't get them to confess, and you rarely can, then you need significant physical evidence to prosecute it. You get one shot to prove them guilty, so you better have a real strong case... shit, you can't even get a trial if it's not a real strong case."

"But you think you got this guy?"

"Yeah... he made some mistakes and was sloppy."

"I know it's sick, because someone's dead... but it is pretty cool."

"It will be if we get a conviction."

"You think you will?"

"I hope so... the evidence is there, so we should be able to get him to confess or prove it out in court."

"Well, if you kill someone, you deserve to pay for it."

"That is generally the case—not always, but generally. In this case, if we put this guy away forever, he will get exactly what he deserves!"

91

Frank was struggling to close the deal with Barry Holcomb. The bank was dragging its feet. It looked like he'd get the place, but it was going to take longer than expected. Frank was staying at a hotel and was pissed for having moved out too early. He was considering moving in with Tricia, but with his rituals already in major turmoil he couldn't imagine it. Besides, his story was that he got kicked out and the hotel supported that. He would have to suck it up for now.

92

Anthony was up early to make breakfast, before his mother made her way downstairs. There was not the usual selection of fresh fruit in the kitchen as Kate had not been shopping for a while, but there were oranges on the windowsill, so Anthony made some scrambled eggs and placed sections of an orange on the plate. He also made a mess brewing some coffee, unaware that Kate was advised to steer clear of caffeine with her medications. It felt good to make his mother breakfast.

Kate had been able to make it upstairs the previous night, although the climb was painful. Anthony had tried to help, but she asked him to let her try it on her own. She was getting a little stronger but the sutures were still very sore and her insides periodically shot spikes of pain as a reminder of the mayhem endured. She still had a lot of painkillers, though, so she would just need to plan the timing of the journey up and down to coincide with a dose.

Vida arrived just in time to see Anthony off to school. It took her a bit longer to walk down then she had expected. The air was cold, and small patches of ice made it a challenge to navigate, but her excitement to see Kate spurned her forward. Vida's lawyer had been to the house to visit days earlier, and she had given him the newly finished mystery to deliver to the editor and, more importantly, to make copies, assuring she'd have an extra for Kate. The lawyer had dropped by the evening before to deliver the copies to Vida and to tend to some additional business. She had packed a little bag and tucked Kate's copy of the mystery in it.

Vida tidied up around the kitchen as Anthony finished getting set for school. She peeked into the living room where Kate was dozed on the couch under a couple of blankets. Anthony scurried into the kitchen as he tried to find the second sleeve of his jacket and adjust his book bag at the same time.

"I will be home right after school, Mrs. Mudgett... do you know where everything is?"

"Oh I can find it, Anthony... don't you worry about the old lady!"

"Okay, Mrs. Mudgett—thanks. I will see you when I get back." And off he went with Vida trailing him to the door.

"Have a good day at school, and don't worry about your mom," said Vida, leaning out the kitchen door after him.

"Thanks, Mrs. Mudgett. I set mom up on the couch in the living room... it's what she said she wanted. I put lots of extra pillows and blankets with her to make her comfortable. She said it would be easier for you not having to go up and down the stairs."

"That's your mom... always looking out for others!" she said with a matronly smile. "Now scoot before you're late!"

"Okay," he said, then took off down the driveway. "I will be home right after school!"

Vida drew back into the kitchen, where the warm air of the house calmed her. She finished cleaning up, rinsing off the plates and placing them in the dishwasher before running a sponge over the counter where a seemingly endless supply of coffee grains was strewn. After twenty minutes or so, she made her way back to the living room again. Kate was, as Anthony had explained, propped up with pillows on the couch in the living room, and was now awake. She looked tired and momentarily confused by Vida's presence. Vida had been through hard times herself, starting with being a young girl during the Great

Depression. She knew what it felt like to suffer, but she also knew that the magnitude of Kate's trials, all compounding at once, was worse than any she had ever endured.

Kate had done her best to style her hair and apply some make up before heading down stairs to set up in the living room, but she still looked pale and skinny in the mirror. Once she got her bearings… Kate was happy to see Vida, who dragged a chair over closer to the couch and plopped down.

"So here we are," said Vida.

"Yeah… look at me—some caretaker I am!"

"It's my turn, sweetie… you've looked after me for some time now. The truth is I don't really need anyone, Kate… it's why I always sent those nurses away. All I need is a friend and that's what you are," she said.

She reached over to brush Kate's bangs aside.

"So I am here as a friend to help you get past this."

"Thanks Vida," said Kate.

"So let's focus on the good things!"

"Well… there's Anthony… and you of course….but not much else at the moment."

"Fiddlesticks!" snapped Vida. "Maybe all you need is that boy… but you have other things too. What about your brother?"

"Did I tell you Patrick is coming for Christmas?" a smile exploding on her face.

"Yes, Katie, about five times!"

"Geez… of course, what is with me? I think they may have removed some of my brains along with my boobs. I can't seem to remember anything."

"Yeah… well, wait 'til you're eighty!"

"Anyways… yes, he is great, and I am so excited to see him. That is a blessing and you are right… a good thing in my life."

"You see! Anthony, Patrick and… and… well… you got this great house… and that beautiful garden! I'll tell you what… we're gonna make sure you enjoy it."

"That's true. I do think I can get the house from Frank."

"What do you mean?" asked Vida, confused by the statement.

"He moved out. We're gonna get a divorce, Vida."

"Are you serious, Kate?"

"Dead serious… he dropped that gem on me at the hospital when he finally showed up after four days. That bastard… he realized I was still alive and then decides it's an opportune time to evaluate our relationship," she explained, shaking her head. "Low and behold he comes to the conclusion that we are in a 'loveless marriage in the eyes of God'."

"What the hell?" Vida said with wide eyes.

"He said that? Can you believe that one! He said that our marriage had been bad in the 'eyes of God'… the nerve. It's totally crazy. He sounds just like his mother—eyes of God. How ridiculously pious!"

"Do you think he's serious about this?"

"Absolutely I do. Frank thinks through everything," said Kate as she propped herself up on the pillows Anthony had thoughtfully positioned on the couch.

"It's true that there has been no love in our relationship for many years. I'm sure he calculates the upside of our marriage no longer exists, and he is simply moving on. To him the cancer is just bad timing… in fact, he said exactly that."

"I just can't imagine!" said Vida.

"It's worse then you even know, Vida," said Kate, locking on her eyes. "What do you mean?"

"Just the way he's treated us."

"More than the stuff you've told me?"

"A lot more. He's been abusive for a long time now."

"I know he's hit Anthony and has been wretched to you verbally, but are you saying there is more… worse stuff? Has he hit you as well?"

"Many times."

"That's abominable, just abominable! How a man could hit a woman… oh! It is just wretched. He is an angry person and so capable of cruelty. It makes me shake just talking about it."

Vida sat staring at Kate as her mind raced. All she could think of was giving her the manuscript. Suddenly it was like it wrote itself: a story of an abused spouse who kills their significant other and gets away with it. It suddenly made sense to her why she was inspired to have Daisy McQueen go against all her better judgment and turn a blind eye to the truth. She was sending a message... She couldn't believe her thoughts, but this was exactly what she was thinking. Despite every moral imperative to the contrary, Vida believed something drastic needed to be done. Although she honestly feared she might be veering into senility.... The thought was clear in her mind. The world needed to get rid of this evil man.

How to
Bring this out?

93

Dr. Johnson called Kate at the house to set a follow-up appointment. The doctors had explained at the hospital they would not be removing the stitches for ten to fourteen days after the operation, but the drainage tube could be taken out after a few days, at which point they could get some images of the operation as well as a tissue sample. So Kate had been expecting the call.

"How are you doing, Kate?" she asked.

"I am feeling better every day," she replied. "Are you doing the exercises we went over?"

"Yup, hurts like crazy, but I have done them every day!"

"Yes, the pain will lessen and in reality it is a good sign. The pain is the stretching of the muscle and tendons and nerve endings that are recovering. Hopefully the pain medicine has been able to dull that somewhat."

"They have helped. I feel almost nothing for about an hour or so after I take them so if I time it right, it works."

"Are you all set to come in tomorrow for our follow-up? Dr. Lynch and I will both be there."

"Yes. I have to take a cab over there, but my good friend is joining me so I have company."

"Ok…umm… you couldn't get someone to give you a lift? Where is your husband?"

"He is not a factor, Doctor."

"Oh… um okay. I'm sorry."

"Don't be: we're getting a divorce."

"Now, was this planned?"

"No he just kind of sprang it on me after he did nothing to help us get through the operation."

"Can you two not agree to sort of co-exist until you get through this?"

"Yeah, I don't think so. And let me tell you doctor this was totally of his doing. I was surprised by his news and more so by his timing, but it is what it is. I guess I am just not as attractive without my boobs," she said with a laugh.

There was silence on the other end.

"You know, Kate, this is hard on the patient. Lots of women, and please don't take this the wrong way, but a lot of women suffer from varying degrees of depression after an operation of this nature. It can be morally and mentally debilitating. I am not making any assumptions here, but if your husband has chosen this terrifically inappropriate time to leave you, well, you just might be vulnerable to depression. I guess that is what I am trying to say."

"I appreciate your concern, Doctor, and I am in no way offended, but I just don't feel depressed about this… any of this. There are other words, adjectives, that may apply, but it's not depressed. This has been difficult, no doubt, and you're right about my husband, but you don't know the half of why he qualifies as a creep. I gotta be honest: I am just not depressed. I want to move on and get healthy. That's it."

"Again, you amaze me," said Dr. Johnson.

"We will see you tomorrow Kate. Get plenty of sleep!"

94

Scenes of them working together

Getting into cab

Talking with Doctors

Anthony and Vida got into a groove, working like a good team to help Kate get stronger. Vida would walk down each morning before school and Anthony would walk her home when he got back. Halloween came and went, the three of them handing out candy to the few kids in the neighborhood who ventured to the door. They had made it through the toughest days.

Kate was increasingly up, walking around on her own, and gaining back some weight. She was set to go to the appointment with Vida on Tuesday to get chest x-rays as well as taking tissue samples in her breast and in the left armpit where they had removed several lymph nodes. Vida was amazing to both Kate and Anthony, showing tremendous energy for an eighty-two-year-old. She seemed to be leading the team.

After Anthony had left for school Kate called a cab that picked them up out front and took them across town to the Farber Institute. The cabbie was a nice fellow from some other country, and upon seeing an old woman and a seemingly unwell younger woman, he hopped out of his taxi to help them get in.

"Good morning, ladies… the name is Bruno, yes?"

"That's us… we are going over to Binney Street."

"Ok, right... Please watch the danger," he said. "I will get that door it can stick a bit in the cold."

"Thank you," said Kate as they climbed into the cab and drove off.

It took about twenty minutes to get there.

The doctors greeted Kate in the lobby before taking her back to an examining room they had not been to previously.

"It appears the first wave of attack was successful," announced Dr. Lynch, as he examined the incisions and withdrew the drainage tube.

"So far your body is reacting well and the external portion has healed up quite nicely," he continued speaking directly to the wounds; then, looking up, he addressed Kate: "This looks pretty good, Mrs. Bruno... how do you think you are doing?"

It seemed like a strange question to Kate, but she did her best to answer.

"I guess I'm doing well," she said, "I mean I am in pain frequently and I am buzzed on pain killers the rest of the time, but I feel better today than yesterday and that has pretty much been the trend since the operation. Does that... Is that what you're asking?"

"Well... yes. It is the one thing we can't ascertain, and often the most critical to recovery. Does the patient believe they are getting healthier? It is important to us to understand," clarified Dr. Lynch.

Kate was only there for about two hours; the nurses took blood and positioned her on a table for several X-rays of her torso. It was Dr. Johnson who inserted the very long needle and extracted some blood or liquid from the areas that had been operated on. Kate was not exactly sure what she was doing, but felt her fingers run along the groove of the new scars. Vida sat out in the lobby and chatted with some strangers.

"You're doing great," Dr. Johnson affirmed.

In another week Kate was scheduled to begin chemotherapy and possibly the radiation treatments based on how things looked. Kate knew this would provide new challenges, but she was feeling resilient and up to the task.

Kate wondered if Odna was around, but they were in a different area of the hospital from recovery… so she thought it unlikely they would run into her. Kate knew Vida would get a kick out of Odna—two funny ladies with two funny names. She had told Vida about Odna's line:—'Odd Name: Od-Na'—and Vida thought it was catchy.

"I should have come up with something like that ages ago… but I guess it doesn't work as well with Vida… maybe Vibrant Dame… Vi-Da."

After bringing Kate back to Vida in the lobby, the two doctors disappeared for a bit, resurfacing after twenty minutes or so to speak to her. Kate rose to her feet as they approached.

"Well, Mrs. Bruno, we took a preliminary look at the images and we are going to need to look at everything closer, but we see some areas that will need attention," began Dr. Lynch.

"It's nothing to be immediately alarmed by… we have always intended to use combined modality chemotherapy and we will proceed as planned. Do you understand?"

"I guess you mean… we are going to do the chemo like we talked about, right?"

"Yes, that's right, Kate," continued Dr. Johnson, "what Dr. Lynch is confirming is that the operation was a success and removed the primary areas for concern, but we suspect we need to attack the cells now to keep them from reconstituting. The chemicals we use in the chemotherapy technique attack at the cellular level and are more precise. Does that make sense?"

"Yeah… it does… I mean you both explained in detail before, so I think I got it as much as I am going to."

"Okay. Well, then you understand it will be about a six-hour session, give-or-take, and we will do injections every fifteen minutes or so. The process is fairly painless although you will feel cold as your body temperature could drop a bit," Dr. Lynch explained.

"We will keep you insulated, though, and it's only temporary," Dr. Johnson added.

"So it doesn't hurt at all?"

"Well, a lot of patients report discomfort twenty-four to thirty-six hours after the procedure, but it is predominately fatigue and not pain per se."

"Oh… okay."

"It will be fine; you'll do great."

The last statement from Dr. Lynch seemed to ring hollow in Kate's mind, and she wondered suddenly what had just happened.

"Did I just get bad news and… I'm… I'm just not catching on?"

"It's all just news Kate until we beat this thing. It's hard to call it good or bad."

"It's only an update of information," Dr. Johnson re-affirmed, "try not to read into it too much."

The doctors confirmed the appointment and discussed the ongoing exercise regimen and recommended diet. When they departed, Dr. Johnson gave Kate a small hug. Vida asked how it went as they left the hospital.

"Sometimes I think I am just a passenger in my life and would follow anyone who was willing to take the lead. It is time for me to step up, and you inspire me to do that. Thanks for coming."

95

After the first week, Vida did not come down every day. Kate was pretty sure she could drive herself to the chemotherapy appointment, but Vida insisted they do the first session together to see how it went. Kate was worried about her sitting in the hospital for six hours, but Vida claimed she was looking forward to it. She knew Kate was not at full strength and had a lot of distractions. She also knew she had not started the new mystery she had given her yet... so Vida brought the manuscript to the first chemo session, where she read it to Kate.

A nurse administered the chemical shots to Kate every fifteen minutes, and just as Dr. Johnson had warned, it made her cold. The nurse gave her a blanket and some mittens to wear. Vida sat in a chair nearby and began reading the story, slowly unfolding the latest plot for Daisy McQueen. Kate was mesmerized and instantly drawn in. She couldn't remember the last time she had been read to. With each page Vida drew her in deeper, introducing new characters and unraveling the mystery.

Kate felt no pain, but her mind raced, knowing the chemicals in her body were sent to kill her—or at least part of her. The drugs targeted rapid growth cells, and that is why the hair follicle was affected as it shared that characteristic with tumor growing cancer cells. She had stared into the mirror the evening before and tried to imagine herself without her hair. It was an ugly thought.

96

Frank carried on his life as normal. He was living at a hotel, which drove him crazy. He could not follow his rituals and it was so unsettling that he left a voice message to Kate telling her he planned on coming by the house the following Tuesday night to work on his guns. However, everything else was as normal. He had not told Jim Star anything about the situation with Kate, and he remained focused on staying on schedule with the homes under construction.

He had been seeing more of Tricia, and although he was always carefree about it, he felt less guilt now that he was to be divorced. He felt like it justified their relationship. Barry Holcomb was busy at work trying to iron out the deal with the bank and get Frank settled into the place in Brookline; Tricia was already picking out furniture. She began to talk about their life together once the divorce was final. Although he never expressed it, Frank had no interest in having her move in.

Frank also told his family about it when he showed up alone for the regular Sunday ritual. He waited until after church where he sat restlessly on his own in the back row. He had simply told his mother that Kate couldn't make it and that was enough for her. She did ask him to sit up front with her, but he declined. After mass he made his regular visit to the bakery and picked up some pastry. He was feeling a little anxious about telling his family. Based on his father's initial reaction to the option of divorce... he couldn't be sure how they would react.

When Frank walked in to his parent's home, the Sunday meal was already in full swing. The smell of homemade red sauce with oversized meatballs and a bubbling pot of sweet sausage, filled the air, and he was instantly hungry. His mother and sisters were busy in the kitchen stirring pots, taking samples and chatting away. Frank's mom was discussing the priest's homily and doing her best to recall the Bible passage from which it was derived. Frank's brothers Leo and Lenny were visible through the doorway leading into the family room. They were standing just behind the recliner, and Frank was relatively sure his father, Emilio, was parked in the chair in front of them. The three ladies in the kitchen stopped talking and looked at him as he walked in. Before they could great him, he spoke.

"I need to tell you all some news and I need ya to come in here and sit down for this... it's serious."

At this command the whole family gathered, with Frank's sisters following him into the living room to join Emilio, who was, as predicted, plopped down in his recliner. Theresa lowered the pots to simmer and removed an oven mitt as she was the last to file into the room.

"What's all this, Frank?" she said wiping her hands on her apron.

"Frank's comin' outta the closet!" said Leo guffawing over his one-liner.

"Shut up, Leo, you frickin' jackass," Frank snapped, "Kate and I aah splittin' up... ok... is that funny?"

"Oh my god, Frankie..." gasped his mother.

"Did she step out on ya, Frank?" chirped his sister.

"Please..." he sighed, dismissing his sister's comment.

"This has been comin' for a while now," chimed Lenny as the living room quickly rattled with moans and murmurs.

"All of you, shut yer mouths and let the man talk!" yelled Emilio, slamming down his hand on the arm of his chair before standing up.

"Frank... tell us what's going on," he continued, knowing full well.

"It's over... and Lenny's right... it has been comin' for a long time," he said as he sat slowly on the couch, his siblings closing rank around him.

"I just couldn't keep pretending... you know? Plus she's been sick lately."

"Sick how, Frank... whatya mean?" asked his mother, the back of her hand pressed to her forehead. "She's having emotional problems?"

"No, I mean, well... she's been depressed and shit fer years, but now she's sick, too... real sick with some lumps in ha chest that had to get taken out."

"Lumps," aped his mother.

"Like canc-ah, Frankie?" asked his youngest sister.

"When did all this start?" his mother asked, pushing his sister aside to get closer. "How in heavens have we not heard anything about this, Frank... Have you just been suffering on an island by yourself, dealing with this?"

"I don't know, wait... which part?"

"Her being sick?"

"Give him a break here, Theresa," injected Emilio with a glare.

"No it's alright pop... It just happened recently... although she was keeping it from me. I had to..." He paused, then started again, quickly recognizing how preposterous his next statement was going to be.

"She went in for an operation about a week ago... you know we got her back home now, settled in and recovering, but it is serious. She's pretty messed up."

"Wait—so I don't get it..." asks Lenny. "She gets sick and then tells you she wants to split? That's retarded!"

"No... you see... it's been goin' on for a while. It just all came apaht at the same time. We just... it all came out at the same time.... That's all."

"Sounds crazy to me," added Leo.

"It is crazy," echoed his older sister.

"Frankie, are you sure," asked his mother, "people go through things... Everybody faces hard times."

"This is already a done deal, ma. I moved out."

"Oh God and Jesus." She moaned, covering her eyes with the rag in her hand.

"Say goodbye to that house, then, bro," pops Leo, his mother swatting at him.

"Shut up," says his sister.

"Yeah, shut up," Frank echoes. "This is just what's happening, and it's not good or bad… and it's not a maybe—it's happening and I need to move forward. I can get another house!"

"Oooo money bags," says his youngest sister with a mocking gesture, as both of the girls laugh.

Frank's father remained fairly quiet though the look on his face was not one of pleasure. Frank read that to be disappointment and he could only guess what his father was thinking.

"I told you about this. You work through it, get some on the side if you need, but you have a family."

In the end Frank had never continued the conversation with his dad and just made the decision. As a grown man he didn't give a shit what his father suggested, because it was his issue, but he knew his father would be insulted and he didn't want that. Frank knew he would need to patch this up later.

"What about Anthony?" asked Leo.

"The guy never gets custody," said Lenny to Leo. There is a pause as Frank dips his head.

"What is gonna happen with that, Frank?" asks his father.

"I don't know for sure, Pop. I gotta get a lawyer, but she's gonna have one too. It's hard to say, I just feel bad for the kid. I'm gonna try and get something worked out… you know, so I can see him."

"That bitch," his sister mumbled under her breath.

97

Patrick was thrilled to be back in regular communication with Kate; he regretted having let it lapse so greatly over the recent years. He had been a bit concerned when he was unable to reach anyone at the house lately. He had tried a dozen times in the previous weeks and gotten no one, and the voice mail had been changed to an automated voice saying, "Leave a message... beep."

Although Kate had called back a couple times—so he knew she was alright—he still felt something was amiss. He neither liked nor trusted Frank and just had a strange intuition about things. He called Joe about it.

"Detective Bertucci."

"Hey, bud."

"Patrick?"

"Yeah... hey, you got a minute?"

"Sure... what's up?"

"It's nothing really... but can you do me a favor?"

"Of course, Patty... what do you need?"

"Do you mind stopping in or doing a drive by Kate's house? I've had trouble reaching her and their voice mail is different... I know as a detective you must be laughing, but I just have a weird feeling you know?"

"What do you thinks going on?"

"Nothing… I mean nothing concrete… this is just a hunch," said Patrick, pausing a moment to think about what he was asking.

"You know what… forget it, I sound like an idiot."

"Not at all, bro… I'll look in on it. I can cruise by in the unmarked tonight and have a look. Do you want me to stop by the house?"

"Could you?"

"Yeah… of course, not a problem."

"Just tell Kate… you know… some bullshit about hockey or whatever. You deal with crooks all the time I am sure you've learned how to make up some lame excuse on the fly!"

"Ha… yeah we do learn some things from the bad guys that come in handy now and then!"

"Alright cool… well, thanks, Tucc, I appreciate it."

"Anytime, buddy."

98

After the first chemo session, things had happened just as Dr. Johnson had described. Kate felt just fine, no real impact, and she believed she could have easily driven home. In fact, after twenty-four hours, she began to think she would be somehow unscathed.

However, as the first hours of the third day fell upon her, Kate felt the impact of the poison in every cell in her body. She felt as if she'd been dipped in lead and stuck hip deep in mud; no rest could replenish her energy. Food tasted like styrofoam, and what she did eat came back up thirty minutes later. She also developed a skull-crunching headache. At its worst, she reasoned she might be dying. Kate had heard and read droves on what to expect, but nothing truly prepared her to experience what introducing your body to destructive chemicals would feel like.

The doctors assured her it was very normal, but she wondered.

"What if they got the dose wrong and I got too much? Could this stuff not kill me right along with the cancer?"

Kate was scheduled for six-hour cycles every week for four weeks, meaning she would finish around Thanksgiving. By the second chemo session, she had already lost clumps of hair. She sat in the bathroom feeling sullen. The hair loss began with loosened strands here and there, then one morning she woke with a large cluster of hair on her pillow, and the attempts to brush it over only served to dislodge whole swaths of her golden locks. As she scratched at her dry eyebrows, her fingers erased the thin lines, as short spikes of hair sprinkled down to the porcelain, a cruel reminder that it was everywhere and she would not be spared. As reported, the hair in her nose fell out as well, leaving a clear conduit for an incessant nasal drip. It was every bit as annoying as the patient's testimonials had reported.

Kate fixed a bandana on her head and obscured the remaining hair that looked patchy, frayed, and listless in the vanity. She typically adorned this look to spend time in the garden, and the sight of her bandana usually coincided with the joy of spending time in the soil amidst her arrangements. Undeterred, she brushed her teeth and applied her makeup. She walked downstairs with her face freshly made and chin held high beneath her red cloth top.

Vida waited for her in the kitchen. Vida had offered to come along as a backup. She was excited to continue reading to Kate. They had churned through nearly half the new mystery during the first six-hour cycle. Kate begged her to surrender the manuscript so she could finish it, but Vida insisted it needed some tweaks and told Kate she would need to wait. The reality was that she made no changes at all, but instead rehearsed reading the story aloud. She was committed to finishing it during this second six-hour session.

"You look as pretty as ever!" said Vida to Kate.

"Thanks, but I don't feel that way. This bandana just doesn't feel right, but my hats all looked worse, and I cannot bring myself to wear a wig."

"You wear that with pride, Katie," insisted Vida, stone-faced. "You're a warrior, and everyone should know it!"

It was true that the people she had run into at the chemotherapy center felt and looked like they were warriors, just like Dr. Lynch had always described. Kate recognized with each moment of this treatment that she was in a battle to save her life. She also knew a positive attitude was a good weapon, and it appeared that the other patients had gotten the same memo. They also seemed to look at each other with an understanding, as if to whisper to one another:

"These other folks have no idea what we are going through. They've no concept of the pain and discomfort or, worst of all, the humiliation. Our bodies' dirty habits and capabilities are openly revealed, and nevermind the ever looming fear that death is still a viable outcome."

Yes, they all said the same thing with their eyes, and whether they were externally full of smiles or overtly moribund, they all felt it.

99

The second chemo session proved easier as the nurse inserted the catheter into the bend of her arm and began the first push of chemicals into her veins. She had less fear of the short term pain or discomfort, but Kate realized with that first injection in this latest session that the clock started ticking on the misery that lay some twenty-four to thirty hours ahead.

"I will do my best to enjoy the calm before the storm," she thought to herself.

Kate was one of the "smilers," and when a nurse came in or another patient shuffled by, she would always muster a grin, which Vida recognized as genuine.

"Some of the other patients seem to fake their smiles," whispered Vida, taking a break from reading to Kate.

"What's that?" asked Kate.

"The other patients... some of them seem to force a smile when you meet them, perhaps to give the impression that this is not bothering them."

"Oh God, am I doing that?" asked Kate.

"No, not at all. That's why I can recognize it in them. I can't say I understand how you are actually smiling, but I know you, and that is the same grin you give me when you are in the garden or around your son." Sure enough, that triggered a blooming smile from Kate.

"How is it that you are smiling?"

"I don't know for sure, but I guess, what else am I going to do? I am not going to spend what time I have left on earth moping. Besides, I believe it will get better, and that better things lay ahead. So we will smile through it. Don't mistake it for happy. I am not happy about any of this. I have just come to grips with the reality and will choose to enjoy what I can and stay optimistic."

The nurse returned promptly after fifteen minutes to push in the next batch of chemicals: not medicine, but rather chemicals that would kill the cells in Kate's body.

"It seems like a crazy way to cure a disease: let's pour some anti-freeze into you and hope it kills the bad guys," said Vida.

She saw the smile on Kate's face waiver as the nurse depressed the plunger on the syringe. She knew that Kate could see the next wave coming.

"It is difficult to comprehend, but I figure it to be like certain plants and flowers. Sometimes you have to cut them back to help them grow."

"This is true," added Vida with a suddenly truculent stare, "but you also have to make sure there is fresh water, fertile soil, and healthy sunlight around before they can really flourish."

"This is true, very true," Kate responded as the chemical push surged into her body.

100

As the true cold of winter settled in across Massachusetts, the trees became bare, and Anthony adapted to his conditions. School had gotten back into a routine, and he was coming to grips with life's arrangement. It was just four weeks after the operation, but their lives felt totally different.

It was now a huge house for a single parent and single child at home, but selfishly, he was happier. His dad rarely appeared, and when he did, he acted like a service person that came in, did his thing, and then left. No big talk between them, no reconciliation, nothing. It was as if someone had told his father, "Sorry, Mr. Bruno. We made a mistake at the hospital, and this is not actually your child."

He was amazed how this man could simply walk away. As much as he had experienced hatred for his father over the years, he always suspected there must be a good person in there somewhere. He gripped tightly to the notion that his father surely possessed some redeemable qualities that had simply failed to surface. Yet nothing, not an inkling of humanity from the man he had shared a home with his entire life. Frank Bruno was just another person on the planet now.

He suffered quietly, accompanying his mother's battle through the chemotherapy. He felt horrible watching her hair fall out, her body beaten down by the war she endured. He was proud of her, though, as she adjusted to her new reality, appearance, and wardrobe. It upset him to see the way people seemed to readily recognize her as a victim. Whether they had been through something similar, knew someone who had, read about it, saw it in a movie, or simply imagined what it would be like to battle cancer, they all noticed. The telltale loss of hair was the watermark, unconvincingly concealed beneath a scarf, hat, or bandana. Her appearance continually drew curious glimpses, furtive glances, and flat-out stares from people at the market or post office, and it made Anthony want to cry out: "Yes! She has cancer, she's sick, we're sad. It sucks and maybe you can relate. It's serious, and we appreciate that it evokes sympathy, but will you please just let her be?"

Yet his mother remained stalwart and never let it bother her. She held her head high, and encouraged by Vida, she wore the overt effects of the disease with the pride of a warrior. She never felt sorry for herself and seemed instead to have a heightened focus on him, which filled his heart. He had always loved his mother. He always assumed she was a great person. She made him and raised him. But now he saw with great clarity how the Lord had blessed her. How she, like Christ, could carry the cross selflessly. It shook him to the core and made him swear to a better life, a life with purpose and one worth living. It strengthened his conviction and passions, and the petty things melted away. It helped him believe that he could find his place in the world, and though life could be cruel, happiness could exist. It came in the simplest gestures, the way he caught her looking when she picked him up from school with her bandana and smile, rolling down the window in the cold to see him clearer. Her love was palpable.

Mrs. Mudgett had also been amazing, and she felt like a grand-mother to him. He knew it was hard for her to make the walk back and forth to the house, but she too never complained and brought a positive energy to every day. Anthony did not know his Grandma Kelley; she had died long ago. Grandma Bruno could be nice, but there was a price with her. He always felt like a second-class citizen around her. It was hard to explain, but it was like he didn't qualify.

101

Anthony stood in art class thinking about it all as he finished a new painting, his brush effortlessly sweeping the deep blue oil across the blank canvas. He was one week from the big art exhibit and was already feeling like his new work was better than the stuff being honored at the Kennedy Library. His mother's war was inspiring his work, or at least that is what Mrs. Devoy thought. She was the only person Anthony had told at school.

Outside was ominous, a dark storm lurking like sharp teeth behind lips. The gray of the sky thickened and pressed further down to loom just above everything, but the room was warm. After the bell, the class fell silent as the students each toiled and hovered above their individual projects. Everyone, including the popular couple in the back who were habitually cooing and cuddling, was immersed in his or her work.

Art class was amazing, and Mrs. Devoy had created a great environment. Once the door closed and the creativity began, the walls of high school melted away. It were as if a new society emerged in the classroom where everyone was suddenly equal. It took a while, but all of the students bought into her class, because Mrs. Devoy was subtly cool. She spoke to the students like adults, and if perhaps you slipped with a curse word, no big deal. She invited everyone to participate, and her positive encouragement spurred them to do their best, or explore, or at least try. The Jocks, Stoners, Gear heads, Gamers, and Goths all suspended the pretenses of high school and just got creative. It was wild to Anthony because once the bell rang and school resumed, so too did the subdivisions that high school demanded.

"That is really amazing," said a voice from behind that Anthony assumed was Mrs. Devoy.

"Thanks. I guess I'm going through a blue phase." He said with a chuckle, but when there was no response, he turned, wondering why the art humor was lost on his art teacher. Anthony was speechless when he saw who it was. He also realized why his Picasso reference was lost.

"Yeah, the blue looks really good," she said through perfect lips.

The girl's name was Nicole, and her long spirals of blond hair had inspired Anthony's art—as well as a fantasy or two. She was popular and the one generally snuggling with the athlete in the back of the room. Anthony gave her a quick look now and again in class, but they had never spoken.

"What's it going to be?"

"I don't know yet."

"Really? Like you just paint whatever?"

"I tend to just make shapes on the canvas, until it just kind of emerges."

"Your stuff is wicked awesome… the best at Nat, for sure." Nat was what the kids called Nathaniel Bourne High School for short.

"You really think so?"

"Yeah, for sure. I mean, you're going to New York for the big thing, aren't you?"

"Huh, no, um…. you mean the art exhibit at the Kennedy place? That's here in Boston."

"Yeah, but if you get picked out of that thing, they take the best stuff to New York City for like a huge thing!"

"Really? I didn't know that."

"Mrs. Devoy said you will make it for sure."

"She did?"

"Yeah. Where you been?" she giggled.

Anthony wasn't sure where he'd been or how he hadn't heard that or how the prettiest girl knew and he didn't! He looked up at her and tripped into her green eyes. Her face was a perfect oval wrapped in flawless skin that contoured and surrounded her thick lips. When she spoke, her mouth lingered open and her tongue slipped across a row of white tile teeth.

"My mom has cancer," he blurted out awkwardly, suddenly overcome by her presence.

"What did you say?"

"My mom… she has cancer, so I've been distracted."

"I'm so sorry, Anthony," she said with an empathetic look. He was stunned she knew his name. "Is she gonna be okay?"

"I think so. I don't know. I hope so."

"I hope so, too," she said, her voice swimming in his ears.

And then she was gone. She turned and walked back to her life. The bell would ring soon, and this moment would be forgotten, but not by him. As he gathered his things to leave, he looked up several times to see if Nicole was looking, but she was not. He did meet eyes with Mrs. Devoy though, and she was smiling like his mother. She'd seen the whole thing.

102

Vida didn't quite finish the entire book during the second chemo session, but neither of them could wait. Kate drove home anxiously, leaving the icy chemo session behind as Vida, strapped into the passenger seat, continued reading. Daisy seemed to have solved the crime, and the standard big confrontation scene with the murderer was coming soon. Kate felt sympathy for the woman who had killed the man, but she knew she was nailed. Little bits of evidence overlooked by the police were found by Daisy, and surely she had pieced together the mystery.

"Are you ready for the final chapter?" asked Vida, exhilarated by Kate's urging to continue.

"Oh my God, yes! I have to say, though, I feel bad for the lady?"

"What lady? The wife?" she asked coyly.

"Well, yeah. I know it's wrong, but I mean, she knows the guy killed the kid, and even if it wasn't on purpose, he covered it up. Then he took the money!"

"He's a real peach, huh?"

"Yeah, but he would have gotten his someday."

"Really, how?"

"I don't know. God, I guess."

"Could be, but he was going to walk free, and don't forget he had raped her as well. The guy was pure evil," said Vida, pushing and probing.

"See, you think so too! I was happy when she poisoned him. He deserved it."

"He sure did!"

"It's just too convenient, though, that an intruder killed the guy. I mean, Daisy is going to sort it out."

"Well, let's find out," said Vida, touching her finger to her tongue, then slowly turning over the page to the final chapter.

Kate felt a shiver and gripped down on the steering wheel, listening to every word that dramatically crept out of Vida's mouth.

"This is a bestseller," she thought to herself. She had no idea how intense it would get.

103

Frank visited a lawyer that Barry Holcomb had recommended to discuss his separation from Kate. The lawyer they had used for over a decade was very friendly with Kate, so he needed a new one. He got a quote to draw up the divorce papers, and cited irreconcilable differences.

"Is it true they get half?"

"Well, Mr. Bruno, it depends, case by case. It is often challenging to determine just what half is."

"You mean like if they can't find certain things?"

"I'm…. I'm not exactly sure what you mean?" asked the lawyer, removing his glasses and wiping them with a cloth.

"Nev-ah mind. Okay, so they basically count up everything, divide by two, and then you pick the stuff you want?"

"Sort of. That's a bit of an over-simplification, but essentially, yes. It usually boils down to large-ticket items like the house, retirement savings, and second homes. Stuff like that."

"Alright, so who counts the stuff? You?" Frank probed.

"There will be a mediator who will qualify the assets. Both attorneys will assist."

"Wait, a-h you saying I gotta pay some third asshole lawy-a to

304

make sure the two other assholes lawy-as count right? You gotta be shittin me."

The lawyer was silent as Frank rambled on.

"The house is the biggest thing, and I paid it down to almost nothin. Look what I get for that," said Frank, staring past the man.

"How do you split a house, cuz we don't got a second home? We-ah not like some of these rich pricks you seem to deal with. Can we sell it and split the money?

"Not unless she agrees."

"That'll nev-ah happen. She spends every waking minute workin on it—on the ya-ad anyway. She'll die in that house."

"Well you should ask, and if not, we will work on getting you a fair package with everything else."

"Yeah, well, maybe she won't be around long enough."

"What's that?"

Frank realized how it sounded and quickly set the record straight.

"I mean, she's sick, you know, canc-ah. It's bad. She might not be around for long. It's a… it sucks."

The attorney did not respond and contemplated referring Frank elsewhere.

104

Kate went to the local grocery store to get some food to make supper for Anthony. She had been going to the smaller local grocer almost exclusively since Frank moved out. She just didn't need as much food, so the shopping was easier—and she was secretly hoping to run into Joe Bertucci again.

It was all pretty innocent, and she knew she was not looking exactly attractive. She had begun the paperwork to divorce Frank, but she felt amazingly liberated. Seeing Joe had made her feel good, feel young again. She was amazed he wasn't married. She felt a twinge of guilt about thinking of another man while being married, but she couldn't help it. Thanksgiving was next week, so she would probably go back to the Stop & Shop to get a turkey, but she wasn't sure who would be eating it, outside of a cancer patient, a teenager, and an octogenarian.

"Poor Anthony will be eating turkey for a month!" she murmured to herself.

Kate did not see Joe at the store, but thought a bit more about him on the drive home. Patrick had mentioned that Joe was going to skate with him when he came back. She wondered to herself if he had plans for Christmas, and if perhaps Patrick might invite him over. It was a guilty pleasure.

a frame for flowers

"I could never," she thought to herself as she pulled into the driveway to see Frank's lunk of a truck obscuring a clean passage to the garage.

She clicked the door opener and veered around the truck and nearly onto the grass to slip her Volvo past him and into her spot. She shut the door behind her, climbed out in the chilly garage, gathered her plastic grocery bags, and marched in. Apparently he had let himself in.

"I guess I need to change the locks," she stated aloud as she shuffled into the kitchen, straining to hold the three heavy bags that stretched the plastic from their weight.

The house was quiet, but within seconds she heard the familiar clomp of Frank's feet lumbering up the stairs from the basement. As he pushed open the cellar door and strode into the kitchen, his arms were filled with a huge box. Two soft rifle cases were slung over his shoulder.

"Oh shit. I didn't hear you. What are you sneaking around?"

"Yes, Frank, I am sneaking around my own kitchen trying to surprise you. I think the question is, what are you doing here?"

"I'm just gettin my shit. What do you ca-ah?"

"Because I am going to change the locks. You can't just come and go as you wish. There has to be consequences, some price for your actions."

"Some price?" He snarled, instantly irritated. "I went to the lawyer, Kate. I am paying a huge price, and we both know it."

"You believe that?"

"What's the-ya to believe? It's true. Yo-ah gonna get most of the stuff I have earned over the ye-ahs. It is ridiculous. The man always gets screwed in a divo-ss, everyone knows it."

"It was your idea, and by the way, Anthony and I are fine, thanks for asking."

"Don't play that game."

"Is that how you see it? This is a game? Do you think we are enjoying this? Wait, no, let me tell you, we are enjoying it. We are enjoying a life with modest freedoms again. "

"Fuck you."

"You know what? Get out, and take all of those rancid guns with you. I have always hated having them around."

This sentence seemed to somehow impact Frank who stopped and looked like he was about to get emotional. He walked to the door and exited to his truck in the driveway. Kate watched him from the door as he loaded his weapons into the truck.

"You just hate everything about me. I get it," he yelled into the night air.

"No, Frank. I don't think you do."

"Fine. I'm leaving," he said, as if it were his idea.

"My lawyer will be serving you papers shortly!" he said.

"I figured as much, Frank."

"They're gonna count up everything and split it in half, so you should think about the stuff you want."

"I have what I want," she said under her breath.

"You should really contact your son, Frank. He is confused by all this." This statement made Frank furious.

"He aint my problem Kate. You made sure of that by turning him against me over the years. That's your burden now, not mine!" he said.

Noting her anger and sadness, he tried to shift gears.

"But you know, if you want to split the house, we can probably work out something. I mean joint custody, you know, so he can still have a dad."

She bit down on her lip in anger at the absurdity of his statement.

"It's just like the woman in the book," she thought to herself. "If I shot this man right here, right now, no one would blame me. No cop would arrest me, and no court in the land would convict me!"

"See you later, Frank," said Kate, closing the door firmly.

"Fuck you!" he yelled at the house.

105

The last chapter of Vida's book shocked Kate. As had happened in every mystery before, Daisy McQueen figured it all out. Yet at the classic sleuth-and-murderer confrontation scene, when she goes through all the facts and forensics revealing the telltale clues that point to the murderer, she amazingly states, in the traditional crime-solvers soliloquy, that the woman's alleged alibi and timeline prove without a doubt that she is not the murderer.

"NO WAY!" Kate shrieked as Vida rattled off the final words of the chapter.

"She totally let her go! I can't believe it. I know I sound like the leader of the 'Crazy for Daisy' fan club, and look at me telling you," said Kate, "but I can't believe she tanked the investigation to let her go free! I mean I have read every book, and I never saw it coming! How did you decide to do this? It is soooo different and so exciting."

"I don't know, Katie... sometimes it just comes," said Vida, brimming with pleasure.

"I am so happy for you! This is going to be a bestseller!"

"You don't think it's too dark?"

"No way, and I'll tell you why. One, people get away with murder all the time. And two, sometimes people deserve what they get! Unlike most endings, it works out in this story! People will love it, and I don't think it's dark at all. If anything, it might give people hope that justice comes in all forms!"

Kate and Vida jawed about the book all the way home from the chemo session and carried on through two cups of tea at Vida's house, where Kate had stopped off so they could take the garbage out together. Kate felt worn down, and the latest chemo cycle's thirty-hour clock to misery was ticking, but she was very excited for Vida's new book and felt the new twist was brilliant.

Kate was a bright woman, having inherited her mother's intelligence and her father's intuition. After listening to the plot unraveled by Vida, she couldn't help but draw a parallel to her life. A rotten guy gets murdered by the woman he had treated so horribly, and the crime is never solved. It was the stuff of fantasy.

"It's enough to make someone wonder," she thought to herself.

Kate had thought of killing Frank many times. The first time he punched her twelve years ago she'd thought of it... anyone would. After being ground down by constant verbal abuse for years where Kate suffered particularly cruel attacks by Frank, she'd thought of it. When Frank had beaten Anthony mercilessly on so many occasions, leaving the young boy bruised and damaged, she had fantasized about it in a way that made her ashamed, and she was compelled to quietly confess it in church. She had even thought about the guns that sat so close, and how easy it would be to shoot him. And when Frank abandoned her at the hospital to face the biggest battle of her life all alone, she'd absolutely thought about it. She wished it true.

"Who does that?" she had asked herself. "Who would leave someone to undergo a life-threatening operation, just drop them at the hospital and disappear? Never mind what husband would do that to a wife... what human being would do that to another?"

She had asked herself repeatedly from the isolation of her hospital bed. She'd thought about it so many times. She daydreamed about him entering the hospital room as she lay there recovering, him spewing his smug comments while she lay seemingly helpless. She actually envisioned the thin stream of smoke rising from a hole in her pale-blue blanket after firing a bullet from a pistol concealed beneath, striking him in the gut and dropping him to the cold linoleum floor where he would bleed out in the one place that could save him, because her friend and fellow human being, Nurse Odna, had pushed the door shut and masked his cries for help. Yes, her mind had taken her to places far darker than a mystery novel ever could, and she was ashamed. She wished again and again that someone else would do it, but knew it was not likely to happen.

How could she kill him and get away with it? She was stunned by her own diabolical curiosity, afraid someone would read her mind or that God would know her sinful thoughts. They had been planted in there for years, small seeds sprouting tendrils growing to a strangling mesh that gripped her soul and begged her to take action.

How could she kill anyone? It seemed so easy in movies or on the mystery shows, but what did it feel like? How did the killer handle the guilt? Despite someone being evil or in some instances deserving it, it must be tough to cope with. Soldiers who face a kill-or-be-killed dilemma still struggle with having taken life. Yet there is so much murder, so many homicides every year.

"Clearly, some people can live with it," she reasoned in her mind.

Kate calculated that the possibility of getting caught was the greatest deterrent. All the upside of her world rid of Frank posed the threat of being found out, of going to prison or worse. The vision of Anthony left alone as she was sent off to jail for killing his father.... It was all too hard to imagine. She could not bury another life to liberate her own.

No, there had to be a better way. The divorce would get Frank out of her life, and she could raise Anthony on her own. Perhaps she could finish school when she got healthy again and could get a job to support them beyond the alimony she was likely to receive in a divorce settlement. As tough as it would be, she could sell the house and downsize, perhaps finding a place with a yard for a smaller garden. Frank didn't seem to care about either of them, so she felt like things were certain to get better. In fact, in light of her health and his cowardly timing, a divorce was growing appealing. She and Anthony would be happier without him, and if she could just win the cancer war they could start a new life, maybe move to New York with Patrick.

106

Vida had enjoyed reading the book to Kate. She felt Kate genuinely enjoy the story and appeared thrilled with the new ending. Vida trusted Kate in a way she trusted no one else, and it meant so much to her to share the work. She also respected Kate's opinion as someone who represented what the readers would like, what Daisy McQueen fans would want. Many times, Kate shared tough feedback in her own gentle way. In Vida's opinion, that feedback made the work better, and to her it was more valuable than that of her editor.

Vida knew she was in the twilight of her life and believed she had lived a good one. She looked back over the years with fondness. She wished she and Hank had been given more time together, but she was grateful for what they had. Vida had roughly twenty-three million in the bank, and no one except her lawyer knew the exact amount. Her publisher knew how much she earned and speculated how little she spent, but even he, as a close person in Vida's life, did not know the number.

She did not care much about the money, and her attorney and she had already plotted out how to give the majority of it away, but lately her focus had shifted slightly. Vida had known Kate Bruno for about ten years, and their relationship had blossomed from early interactions that consisted of small talk about gardening into a deep and meaningful friendship. Vida believed Kate had an old soul, and she never felt inhibited by their forty-plus years in age difference. She had shared with Kate her perspective on life, and Kate was enthralled by its sensibility. Vida believed in God, but she took a very scientific approach to it.

She first began to share her life's lessons and ideologies eight or so years ago when she was a bit more mobile and used to walk the neighborhood about as frequently as Walter Heaney. Vida would wander down the street most days in the summer and find Kate kneeling in her garden.

One particularly perfect day, as the radiant summer sun stretched out to explore every contour, Vida walked down and sat on the front porch as Kate edged the ridge of the beautiful rose bushes that lined the front left section of the house. She reminisced about Hank with Kate and mentioned "an old soul."

"Hank's sister Margaret was a real old soul," she said matter-of-factly.

"What's an old soul?" asked Kate.

"Have you not heard that before?" Vida replied, a little surprised.

"Nuh-uh."

"An old soul is one that's been here before."

"You mean like reincarnation?"

"Yeah, I guess. I mean, I don't think they know it or have recollection, but it seems that heaven and hell would fill up awfully quickly if they didn't recycle," said Vida, rubbing her hands together.

Intrigued, Kate stopped her work, took off her gloves, and came over to sit next to her on the steps.

"The story goes like this: you live your life, and when you die the Lord determines how things went. Young souls invariably make some real big mistakes and perhaps even live pointless lives. So barring them being truly evil, in which case he sends them to the guy with the pitchfork, God sends them back to try again."

"How many times will he send them back?"

Vida replied, "I couldn't speculate, but I think it is a bunch.

"You just keep going back until you get it right. Each time progressing, driven by some internal force, some inherent knowledge that keeps folks from repeating the mistakes. When a soul has been back a number of times, it just makes better decisions earlier on in life. It shows maturity beyond its years indicating that these lessons have already been learned!"

"That's wild."

"Hank's sister was that way. She just seemed to know how things would turn out, and she never got too high or too low about anything. She was an old soul."

"That is so interesting. I hope it's true!"

"It's gotta be, otherwise I am in trouble."

"I'll say. I must be a first edition!" Kate joked back with a grin.

"Ha! You are definitely an old soul, Katie. Definitely."

The two ladies often had conversations like this, and over the years, their kinship grew strong. Eventually as Vida neared eighty, she become less mobile, and Kate began to visit her instead. It was just a natural progression that Kate began to informally care for Vida, performing a lot of tasks around the house, helping with bills, tending to the yard, and such. More than anything, they became dear friends, two old souls who shared many smiles and laughs together. They possessed a connection that made an often challenging life brighter.

107

Joe Bertucci had driven by Kate's house just as he had promised Patrick he would. It was a Tuesday night and he parked out front. He thought briefly about Kate and checked himself in the rearview mirror to make sure he looked presentable. He was about to get out and walk to the door when he heard a door slam and saw Frank exit the right side of the house with a large box in his hand. He was instantly on alert. Frank was very animated, yelling back over his shoulder in a heated exchange with someone, and he had two rifle cases slung over his shoulder.

Detective Bertucci slid instinctively out of the warmth of his unmarked police vehicle and felt for the firearm at his side. He cut across the front of the car and made his way south towards the driveway on the street but just feet from the curb. His eyes were trained on Frank, who placed the box noisily into the back of the truck and then slipped the two rifles into the back of the truck's cab. He seemed agitated.

Joe made his way all the way to a large oak on the tree line at the far corner of the Brunos's driveway that created a good lookout. He leaned into the tree's icy bark and peered around for a closer look. He now saw that Kate was standing at the side door looking out, and

a frame for flowers

Frank stood in a defensive posture by the truck. The neighborhood was very quiet, and he could hear the exchange between the two with reasonable clarity. He took note of the conversation:

"You hate everything about me and I get it."

"No, Frank, I don't think you do."

"I'm leaving. My lawyer will be see you with papers shortly."

"I figured that, Frank."

"They count up everything and split it in half. Think about the stuff you want."

"You should contact your son, Frank."

"He aint my problem, Kate. You turned him against me for years. That's your doing, not mine."

"See you later, Frank."

Joe watched intently as Kate slammed the door shut and left Frank standing alone in the driveway.

Frank then clearly yelled, "Fuck you!" back at the house as he jumped in the truck. Joe peeled off and moved farther south to hide as Frank tore out of the driveway in reverse. Joe was taken aback by the exchange and could assess that there was clearly some marital friction, but he also felt he could report to Patrick that Kate was okay. Considering the heated exchange, Joe decided it was probably not a good time to call on Kate, so he climbed back into the unmarked cruiser and drove away.

108

After he drove away from Kate's house, Joe dialed up Patrick from the car but got voicemail and left a message. He was thinking more about Kate. He wished he had let his feelings be known so many years back and had kept her away from that guy. He didn't know Frank well at all, just knew about him. He knew his brother Leo was a crooked guy, but only in a small-time way. He had never heard much about Frank, but what interaction he had gave a strong indication the guy was a jerk. Just then, his cell phone rang. He recognized the number was Patrick Kelley.

"Patty."

"Hey man, only got a minute for ya, but picked up your message and wanted to get back."

"So I went by Katie's house, and it was pretty interesting."

"Oh wow. Thanks man. So you talked to her?"

"Not exactly. Your hunch might have been bang on."

"Why? What's up?"

"Well, I parked out front and was going to go to the door, when all of sudden the husband—I should say, Frank—comes out the side door and he and Kate were in a heater."

"No shit?"

"Yeah, and I could hear them pretty clear from where I was."

"Were you hiding in the bushes? Nice work, Detective!" Patrick said in his best police chief voice.

"It's almost that pathetic! I was hiding behind a tree! But seriously, I heard them, and it was pretty interesting dialogue. Basically it seemed like they might be splitting."

"What? No shit! My sister hasn't said one word about it."

"They mentioned lawyers and some guy, Anthony, whoever that is, and Frank was loading some stuff into his truck."

"Huh. Well Anthony is my nephew, so nothing there, but Frank was loading stuff? Like packing his bags kind of stuff?"

"Oddly enough, it was a couple guns and a good size box of stuff I couldn't make out. But no, not like suitcases."

"Son of a bitch. I knew something was up. Was he threatening? And by the way, he is a gun freak. He like sleeps with his guns, so I am not surprised he took those first. What an asshole!"

"I didn't know that about the guns. I was pretty clear on him being an asshole." They both laughed.

"Wow, I gotta talk to Katie. Did you?"

"No. It was too heated, so I just left, and by the way I just left there ten minutes ago, and she is there so you can catch her."

"Okay. I'm in a total rush, but hey, let me try her and I'll call you back."

"Yeah go, no problem. Call me whenever."

Joe hung up the phone and went back to thinking about Kate. Patrick quickly dialed Kate, but she did not pick up.

109

Kate got a call from the doctors first thing Monday morning before Thanksgiving. She would finish her fourth cycle of chemo that morning, giving her an outside shot at feeling somewhat normal by Thanksgiving afternoon. She was looking forward to finishing it. Due to the advanced nature of her cancer, they had to hit her hard with the chemicals, so while some people report few side effects from the process, Kate got hit with most all of them.

She stood naked before the mirror in the bathroom upstairs, still damp from a shower as goose bumps spread across her pale skin. She would begin the process of facing another day with cancer, a process with many more steps than life had ever required. She looked at her body, scarred and uneven in the reflection, still unfamiliar. There, before the mirror, it was too real. She was not as she had been. So much now was different, and she missed her former self.

The six-hour sessions had certainly been arduous, and while she got used to the feeling of smooth skin on her scalp, the rest of the hair loss, nausea, headaches, swollen feet, blotchy skin, and the feeling of being cold all the time had proven to be another battle. All the positive thinking in the world couldn't make a weakened everything feel better. Yet she kept on smiling, though.

"Hi, Mrs. Bruno. It's Dr. Lynch. Do you have a minute?"

"Yes, Doctor. Good morning."

"Yes, good morning to you. Okay, so we are headed to the last cycle in this round of chemotherapy and we think the chemicals have been working hard to clean up anything left behind from the surgery. The incisions have closed up and healed nicely, and so we are pleased with that as well. In fact, you can consider a consultation for some surgical reconstruction if you are ready for that," he stated in the factual manner that Dr. Lynch always seemed to deliver.

"I do want to run some additional blood tests, though, while you are in your cycle this morning. The white blood cell count from your visit Friday is showing some slightly irregular numbers, so we should check it again to make sure it's accurate."

"What does that mean?" asked Kate, feeling a flash of anxiety.

"Hard to say. Likely it is nothing. You're in the trenches of this battle, and the body is fighting like crazy not just against the cancer, but now against what it construes as poison in the bloodstream from the chemotherapy. It is hard to say, but we will test it further. It could be an early nadir."

"I know nadir means low point, which kind of makes sense, but is it a medical term as well."

"Yes, it's both, really. The low point of your blood cell counts. The chemotherapy kills good blood cells along with the cancer cells, and it is normal to see. It just generally comes weeks after you're done with the therapy, so it is just a bit unusual. It's probably nothing to worry about."

"Okay."

110

Kate went to her last cycle of chemo, and Vida sat by her for the entire session. Having finished the book, they had less to do, and the six hours felt much longer. The nurse would come and go, administering the injections, and the two women spoke about all kinds of things from silly to serious.

Kate drove home and dropped Vida off.

"I am going to try and get extra rest and hopefully the attack wave comes early or at least on time. It is about 3:45 right now," said Kate. "I expect to get whacked at about 10:00 p.m. or so tomorrow night, so that is going to stink, but if I can sleep into Wednesday, I have a good chance of feeling better on Thanksgiving, and by that afternoon might even feel hungry enough to eat a piece of turkey!"

"Well, I will come down on Wednesday. I have a meeting with the editor tomorrow to go over the manuscript. She was very optimistic and loved the book, by the way."

"That is awesome! I just know this is going to be big."

"Yes, well, anyhow. I will be free Wednesday, but will wait until the afternoon to pop down and check in. You get as much rest as possible. I can help cook the turkey, but it's going to take both of us and a crane to lift the dern bird!"

a frame for flowers

"I got the smallest one I could find, and Anthony gets out early from school on Wednesday and is off Thursday and Friday, so he can help us."

"That's perfect," said Vida, climbing gingerly out of the car. Once out, she turned and held the door, leaning in to speak. "I'm really excited for Thanksgiving, Kate."

"Me, too. It will be a little strange, just the three of us, and I hope Anthony can eat a healthy share, or lots of food may be wasted! The Pilgrims would be ashamed of us!"

"It will just be nice to be together."

"For sure. Thanks, Vida. Here is to Thanksgiving, 2003!" Kate said, pretending to raise a glass to toast.

111

When Joe Bertucci and two backup officers took down the suspect in his homicide case, they confronted him as he walked out of his work office. This was the same place where his business partner of many years had allegedly taken his own life. When he saw Joe and the officers, he made no attempt to run. He did not act indignant, nor did he become violent. In fact, he raised his hands over his head then slowly back down to cover his face. As they put the handcuffs on him, he wept. He said nothing, but the tears were a confession, each drop confirmation of guilt. Joe had little sympathy. He thought only of the victim, the person who suffered at the hands of another human, a human who showed no humanity.

112

Kate's thirty-hour post-chemo-misery bill arrived on schedule, and Tuesday night into Wednesday morning was brutal. She drank buckets of water as it seemed to help, and she took some pain meds. Her blood was thin, and she was vulnerable to nearly everything. The doctors had warned to beware of cuts or bleeding. She would suffer through vomiting, diarrhea, and headaches, but the sleeplessness was the worst. To be forced to stay awake through misery was perhaps the worst part. She was exhausted, but her restlessness proved a formidable foe. Just enough to stir her from the twilight sleep anytime that true sleep seemed within reach. The previous three cycles proved that the bout would last about ten hours, then subside. She would just need to grind through it. She thought of Anthony, of life, of her long since passed parents, and of her garden—the bulbs that lay in the now frozen earth patiently waiting for their time, waiting for a warmer time, a brighter time to spring forth. And so, too, she must and would wait.

113

It was Thanksgiving morning, and the storm had passed. Anthony was not up yet, but Kate made her way gently downstairs after finally sleeping for several hours. She was weak, but she was resolved to make this a good day. She had applied some makeup instinctively after brushing her teeth, but had forgotten to put anything on her head and caught a glimpse of her slight self in the hallway mirror as she drifted past toward the kitchen. She hardly recognized herself. She thought she looked like Norma Desmond in Sunset Boulevard: old and rundown, hiding behind an overly made-up façade. Her knees buckled at the sight, nearly dropping her. She froze dead in her tracks, mesmerized by her own visage.

"How can you not recognize yourself?" she whispered aloud to herself.

Kate lingered at the mirror for several minutes at the cusp of tears, but the sound of Anthony stirring upstairs and King tapping his way downstairs behind her shook her from the moment.

"Get it together," she told herself. "Don't fall apart now."

She made her way to the kitchen, gathering strength on the way. She did not make coffee, and she missed doing so. Coffee had oddly been affected by the chemotherapy and tasted horribly bitter. In fact, many foods had been reduced not just to a general dullness, but quite the opposite. Certain foods, like tomatoes in particular, took on a bitter or even metallic taste that she could not seem to shake. She would chew spearmint gum often to try and escape it.

Kate went to the sink in the kitchen and stared out into the front yard and beyond into the street. The trees were all bare, and the cold of old man winter had clamped down on everything. The suffering blades of grass, once thick and green on her lawn, were now christened with a shimmering coat of frost from the evening's snap. A silvery lawn was framed by a window, itself rimmed with a curl of frost.

"We need a Christmas tree," she said to King who had taken post next to her by the sink.

"But first you need your breakfast, huh, big boy?"

114

There was lots of ice outside, so Kate sent Anthony up the street to get Vida.

"Can't I drive up and get her? It's safer than her walking," Anthony stated as a matter of fact.

"Oh sure, safer than an unlicensed teenager behind the wheel. Absolutely, but be sure to drink a couple beers before you go!" Kate said with a laugh so hearty that Anthony had to join her.

"C'mon, ma?" he chuckled.

"No, seriously, walk up there and get Mrs. Mudgett, will you please?"

Anthony looked over at his mother and was instantly reminded of everything. "Yeah, of course. Sorry, Mom. I was just kidding."

"I know you were, sweetie. You'll be driving soon enough!"

Anthony found Vida waiting just inside her front door with her overcoat and headscarf on. He held out his arm to help her down the front steps, and she held on tightly for the entire walk down.

"Your mom is a brave lady, Anthony," she said.

"Yeah… I know."

"She is getting her rear end kicked, and I don't think I've heard her complain once!"

He was silent, thinking of those words. Anthony had certainly recognized his mom's struggle, but he had also been focused on his dad leaving and school's usual challenges along with emptiness it provided… and the big art exhibit. He had only visited his mother's suffering when it dawned on him.

"What can I do to help her?" he asked, feeling a twinge of guilt, accompanied by emotion gathering in his chest.

"Love her with all your heart, every day. It is all she wants and all she needs, but understand also, it is all she has."

These words pierced his ears and seeped into his heart. He turned his head away from Mrs. Mudgett as the tears bubbled up from his eyes and his nose swelled shut. He said nothing, nor did she.

Back at the house, Kate was busy. She was carefully washing the potatoes to make a batch of mashed, and scrubbing sweet potatoes as well for a casserole that mixed fresh ginger, cumin, and coriander with chopped cilantro on top. Many of the ingredients had come from her garden and had been dried or frozen for this very occasion.

The three of them had a wonderful Thanksgiving, each assisting with their individual strengths to prepare the meal fit for a group three times their size and five times their appetite. Anthony lugged the turkey, which was a ten-pound bird and certainly smaller than years past, but still heavy and slippery. Kate reached in to remove the innards as Vida prepared an onion and stuffing to fill the turkey for baking. They worked well together, laughing and joking. Vida even sipped on a glass of whiskey.

Anthony prepared the dining room, spreading a clean white cloth over the old wood table, then meticulously assembling three perfect settings, the pristine white wedding china place settings with diamond-cut crystal glasses alongside the silver forks, knives, and spoons, each in their proper location. He even placed the two small silver candelabras in the center, flanking a foliage-themed centerpiece his mother had made many years ago. Everything looked amazing.

After hours of preparing together, they sat together to eat and bowed their heads in prayer. Vida spoke. "Thank you for this the ability to prepare such a bounty of food, and for allowing us to gather such special people together to share it with one another. Thank you, God, for our health, although I think you could do more on that front."

Anthony and Kate both chuckled at that, but Vida remained steady, head down, continuing.

"Thank you for life, for allowing us to open our eyes each day in this remarkable world. Despite its many flaws and challenges, this is a world of wonder with endless joys to be discovered. We appreciate this gift, and despite so many of your creations, perhaps missing or ignoring it, we recognize you have put it here solely for us to enjoy. Lastly, thank you for the human souls we share this life with, for with all the bounty, all the beauty and wonder, the world is just a painting without friends to share it with. For this we are grateful. Amen."

"She's a successful writer for a reason," Anthony thought to himself.

"She is a beautiful soul," Kate thought to herself.

"Let's eat!" said Vida.

So they did, enjoying this small Thanksgiving of three with smiles and plenty to eat. Kate was scarcely hungry, and the residual impact of her rancorous fourth chemo session lingered, but she ate the meal and partook in the conversation with joy.

Across town, Frank had thought of bringing Tricia to Thanksgiving with Emilio and Theresa as she had begged him repeatedly to do so, but he decided against it. Not in a respectful way, but rather that he thought his mother would be critical. The Bruno family ate and drank heartily and celebrated Thanksgiving like everything was normal. Everyone but Frank was unaware Kate had just labored through a month of chemo and sat at a table just fourteen miles away with a bandana to obscure her bald head.

115

The Friday after Thanksgiving was the big show at the Kennedy library, and Kate dressed herself in a black dress that hugged her thin but still shapely body and wrapped a fancy black-and-gold Givenchy silk scarf she had treated herself to around her smooth head. She misted perfume on her slender neck and applied makeup that filled out her face and highlighted her pretty eyes. She had gained a few pounds back, and it filled out her face. She felt hope.

Anthony put on a white dress shirt that didn't quite fit and a tie that looked like it had been knotted for a year. He shaved his mostly clean face and parted his hair to the side. It seemed ironic to Kate that her son looked less like her vision of an artist than ever as he nervously adjusted his tie in the hallway mirror. He seemed excited for this in a way she had not often seen since he had clicked past puberty and became a young man.

Vida joined them in her best Sunday dress, and the three piled into the Volvo with Anthony sitting in the back. Their breath burst clouds in the frigid air, and the sky was once again gray.

"Looks like it's gonna snow," said Vida.

"The weather man said it will. Maybe only a couple inches, but winter's here, no doubt!"

"How you holding up, Picasso?" Vida asked Anthony.

"I'm in a blue period," he said, staring out the window.

Both Vida and Kate gave a short laugh. "You're going to be great. I can't wait to see your work!" said Vida.

"I am so proud of you, Anthony," said his mom, looking back through the rearview mirror.

Anthony smiled to himself as they drove north on Morrissey Boulevard providing a glimpse out to the cold water of Boston Harbor and a good shot of Thompson Island. Apparently there was a school out there that took on some of the troubled youth of Boston, and it was rumored to be a tough place, or even as a destination for juvenile delinquents. On numerous occasions, his father had threatened, "Don't think I won't send your ass the-ya if you don't shape up!"

The car was warm, but the sight of the island gave him a shiver.

The three parked and walked together into the event. They weren't there five minutes before they were approached by Mrs. Devoy. She looked stunning in a red dress, tall and attractive in the crowd of well-dressed people milling about.

"Mrs. Bruno, you look absolutely radiant!" said Mrs. Devoy as she walked over smiling wide. She knew the whole story and knew that the compliment would feel good, but she meant it nonetheless.

Kate was flush.

"Thank you so much. You look lovely as well. This is an exciting night for us!"

"It should be, " she said, turning to Anthony.

"Everyone is here: the mayor, the superintendent of schools, and pretty much anyone who is anyone in art or society here in town. It's an amazing turnout."

"Yikes," said Anthony, feeling a bit small.

"Yikes is right. You know why?" asked Mrs. Devoy, pivoting to Anthony.

"I don't know. Cuz lots of stuffy people make me nervous?" he asked jokingly.

Mrs. Devoy looked at him and glowed. "No, it is because your work has gotten the most attention of any artist in the exhibit!" she said. "These artworks that surround us have come from all over New England, Anthony, and there is a crowd next to your triptych called"— she turned to Kate—"'Mother.' Karl Arghast from the Boston Globe couldn't believe a teenager had painted it! Can you believe that?"

"I can," said Vida, chiming in. "He's a bit of a windbag!"

Mrs. Devoy burst out laughing. "And who are you, madam?" she asked Vida.

"I am just a friend of Anthony and his mom," said Vida, lightly defensive, still unsure who the woman was.

"Well," said Mrs. Devoy, looking left to right then whispering. "I can't disagree with you on that, but he does know art and has a lot of pull in Boston."

"This is Vida Mudgett, Mrs. Devoy," injected Kate. "A bit of an artist herself. She writes the Daisy McQueen books," said Kate proudly of her friend.

"Which you probably never heard of!" added Vida.

"Get outta town, really? I love those books, and so does my daughter, Shannon. That is incredible. Wow it is nice to meet you. I'm a big fan! You didn't tell me you hung out with famous people, Anthony."

"Oh heavens, this is Anthony's night. Let's focus here, girls!" said Vida, mildly flattered by her recognition from a fan.

"True, true. I am Pam Devoy, Anthony's art teacher," she said, extending a hand to Vida.

"Oh!" exclaimed Vida, having heard good things from Kate. "It's a pleasure."

Anthony had been happy with the subject changed to Vida's books and was suddenly more nervous than ever that people, or at least this art critic guy, was talking about his work. He felt instantly awkward in the tall hall brimming with well-dressed Bostonians.

"Let's head over to your paintings, shall we, Anthony?" asked Mrs. Devoy to the group.

"Okay," he replied.

Anthony liked the way Mrs. Devoy spoke to him like an adult.

She actually asked him questions and had conversations with him in a way that so few older people did.

They made their way across to the main exhibit hall past the soaring windows supported by scaffolding-style iron framework. There was a smell of fresh flowers in the air, and an enormous flag hung majestically above them, along with a statue of the former President whose name was on the building. Anthony was astute enough to recognize this was a moment in his life, a snapshot not soon to fade. He looked at the former First Lady portrayed in a large painting on the wall, and it reminded him of his mother, who with her black dress and scarf stood out in the crowd—not for being bald or having the cancer badge—but rather that she looked so pretty and regal to him. She had not seen the triptych he painted in her honor, and his palms grew damp as they approached.

All the artwork had been done by high school students throughout New England, but the audience that evening was 95% adult. Anthony did not see one kid he recognized.

When they arrived at his work, it was as stated. There was a notable group gathered before the triple canvas painting whose colors popped off the wall in the hall's perfect lighting. The large canvasses sprawled with a perfect kaleidoscope of color and shape. Angelic figures swirled around the central character a floating body, ethereal and soft, hands extended palms up with a perfect oval face that lay amidst a halo of light, head tilted slightly with her eyes closed. It felt as if you could step up and receive a hug, and it looked as though the patrons were doing just that. Kate stood in the middle of Vida and Mrs. Devoy in complete awe. The painting was heavenly.

The evening was like a dream to a boy who had felt so rarely like he was the center of attention, who felt ignored most of the time by most of the world. It wasn't as if Anthony felt sorry for himself or like he was the biggest outcast at school. He just fell into the upper lower class, and that felt lonely. That evening, though, with his work on display, he felt purposeful. It was true that there was a real buzz around his work, and Mrs. Devoy stopped to introduce him to half a dozen or more people who marveled and fawned over his work. Kate and Vida sat back and drank it all in, basking in the sunlight of his big evening. Kate could see him growing before her eyes, the fresh sprigs of a young man pushing out from the shell of small seed drawn to the warmth and light. His time had begun.

116

The doctors had taken the blood samples drawn at Kate's last chemotherapy cycle and run additional tests. Dr. Lynch conferred with Dr. Johnson in the confines of their office at the cancer institute. The late afternoon sun cast an orange hue over the room.

"I really don't like the way this looks," said Dr. Lynch austerely. "I think we need to get Mrs. Bruno in here sooner than later. This in particular has me concerned," he said, pointing to a specific reading on the chart that was sending a negative signal.

"I hate to say it, but I agree," echoed Dr. Johnson. "I will phone her on this."

117

It was Monday morning, and Anthony had already left for school as Kate sat in the living room on the makeshift couch bed that she occasionally slept in, on evenings she was too tired to head upstairs. She wasn't feeling great that morning, as her entire body seemed to ache, but Vida was due to visit shortly and she was looking forward to it as always. Kate had enjoyed the entire weekend, reflecting in the afterglow of the art exhibit. Mrs. Devoy told them to plan for a trip to New York in the spring, as she was confident Anthony would be selected to represent the state at the national event. Kate was thrilled with the idea, as it would allow them to get down to Patrick's place just as they had discussed. She knew she was going to have to share a lot of tough news with Patrick when he arrived, but this could be the good note to end on.

Just then the phone rang.

"Hi, Kate. It's Dr. Johnson. How was your weekend?"

Kate told the doctor all about the art show with a notable pitch of pride in her voice. While Dr. Johnson paused to share her excitement for Kate's son's accomplishment, she knew she had to also share the discovery that concerned her and Dr. Lynch. She was conscious not to step on Kate's happiness, but eventually had to bring up the issue.

Would A DucTor Deliver This over The phone

"There is some news on the follow-up blood tests we took at your last cycle, Kate, and it is a little disconcerting to Dr. Lynch and me."

Kate felt her heart sink, and her chest fell heavily, instantly recapturing the fear and anxiety that had gripped her the majority of the last few months. Doleful as she felt, Kate was rapidly becoming a veteran of this war. She composed herself swiftly.

"What kind of treat are we in for next?" she asked.

"We both feel that we need to step this up to targeted radiation, and beyond that, consider a second round of chemo."

The radiation was an unknown which posed a fear for Kate, but perhaps worse the notion of enduring another series of post chemotherapy attacks devastated her.

"Why?" she asked.

"Well, Kate, the blood tests tell us the cancer is on the move, and it is still multiplying in some capacity. While we have greatly slowed it, we have not stopped it. Our goal here has always been curative not palliative treatment, and we prefer to stick to that."

Kate tucked the phone between her shoulder and head and looked down at her hands, as if to look for the new cancer cells.

"I forget what that means, Doctor. Palliative?

"It means to reduce the symptoms but not cure the problem. It means just extending life, Kate."

There was a moment of silence on the phone between the two, and Kate could suddenly hear the doctor breathing into the receiver.

"You mean, like, the winter's coming and your flowers and plants are going to die. You can leave them out to die, or bring them inside to enjoy them for a bit longer, but that's the best you can do?"

"Well," Dr. Johnson paused, as she was going to give a doctor's answer to the question, however she recognized that this was in fact the answer, just posed in a light that made the most sense to her patient.

"Yes, that's basically it, Kate."

"Okay. So we want to avoid using the word palliative, huh?" she asserted bravely.

"Yes, we will all fight to avoid that."

a frame for flowers

Kate was terrified when she hung up the phone, the fear and reality of her mortality leapt cruelly back into her mind, and she sensed somehow it would be staying for a while this time. She was alone in the house, although King was sleeping nearby. She stared out the window from her makeshift bed in the living room. Kate had enjoyed the last few days, having begun to feel hopeful about recovery, yet now it was all thrust back to negative. All the thoughts about the impact were immediately revisited. What would happen to Anthony if she died? How would she see to it that he was cared for?

Kate knew that Frank was not reliable as a husband or father. Vida was just too old, and besides she couldn't ask that of her. Who would take care of him? She supposed her in-laws would at some point step up, but she also knew Anthony could not stomach spending even Sunday with them, so it was sure to be a tough life if they raised him. She could imagine him burying his artwork along with his creativity and being isolated. If only Patrick still lived here.

All of these questions and thoughts had been drawn out and turned over a dozen times in Kate's mind, and she faced the realities of it very logically. She knew she had a life insurance policy for $200,000 to be paid out upon her death, but she also knew the surviving spouse got the money. Their lawyer, Tom Whalen, had explained it years ago.

"I need to ask Tom what happens in the event of a divorce," she thought.

"Frank has no idea how sick I am, and it would be karma for him to divorce himself right out of the money without knowing it."

She was pretty sure she could not simply change the beneficiary to a minor under eighteen without the consent of the husband, but again she would need to ask her lawyer.

Kate knew it was spiteful, but it made her furious to think that Frank would stand to get the house and $200,000. In fact, he would get it all if she were to die.

"He would get everything he wants, except that he would have to take care of Anthony," she muttered to herself, sitting hunched forward on the couch with her elbows on her knees.

That was what really mattered, and the one part that would help her overlook all the upside for him should she lose her battle to cancer. If Frank would actually step up and raise Anthony, perhaps it could turn for the better, but she knew it was impossible. He had never shown an indication or inclination for it, and to wish it so was foolish. Even if the courts mandated it, her son would suffer at the hands of Frank. The thoughts of him beating Anthony or verbally tearing him down year after year, or even simply ridiculing him into submission... it all ricocheted through her mind. It was a fate worse than death.

"I'd rather go to hell," she murmured to herself. Kate looked heavenward and asked aloud: "How is this God? He gets the house, he gets the money, he gets to fulfill his dream and buy out Jim Star, he gets to carry on with his girlfriends, he gets his life, his dreams, and I... I get to die?"

Her face fell into her hands, and she cried quietly, alone, with the dead of winter closing fast, in her white house atop a hill.

Conversation with lawyer on life Ins. Divorce

118

The following day, when Anthony walked in from school, he noticed his mother seemed down, so he searched for a way to cheer her up. Vida had not been over that day, as she was busy with the editing of her latest book, so he figured she was just lonely or bored. He was home early, and there was plenty of daylight. A bit of snow was falling and drifting slowly to the ground in big, fluffy flakes.

While enjoying an afterschool snack of graham crackers and peanut butter, Anthony was struck with an idea sure to lift his mother's spirits. He ran to his room and rifled through his desk for some money he had tucked away, and then barreled back down the stairs and down another flight to the basement to begin rummaging through the Christmas decorations that were tidily stored in plastic containers. He foraged around and pulled out the things he needed, then darted back upstairs. Then he pulled on a warm jacket and zipped out the side door, yelling back to his mother, "I'll be back in a few."

Smiling ear to ear, he galloped down the street to the local grocery market, clutching tight the small bundle of dollar bills.

Every year since Anthony could remember, Mr. Priore had worked the parking lot at the market selling Christmas trees. In recent years, his son Paul had taken up a place beside him. The two men were there as expected, braving the cold in their coveralls, bright orange knit caps pulled down tight. Paul was dragging some snow-caked trees still wrapped in mesh, a cigarette dangling from his lips, as Mr. Priore attended to a young couple trying to decide between their two finalists.

"What's up, Tony?" asked Paul when he spotted Anthony running up to the lot.

He had been introduced as Tony by Frank Bruno ten years ago, and it was just what Paul assumed he went by.

"Not much, Paul. How's business for you and your dad?"

"These Vermont trees pretty much sell themselves," he said with a rugged grin, his bare, reddened hands drawing the cigarette to his chapped lips.

"You need one?"

"Uh-huh," answered Anthony excitedly, explaining he wanted to pick out a perfect tree for his mom.

"Well, let's see what we can find. You know what, I just got some new ones. Let's unbundle these and see if there is a diamond in the rough!"

Paul Priore liked Anthony: he reminded him of himself at that age. He stood up for the boy one time many years ago in an awkward situation at the baseball field, which was across the street from that very market. They had never once discussed that day.

Years back during a little league game, when Frank was maligning Anthony for striking out, Paul was coaching the other team. Frank ran Anthony's team, but he didn't want to. Star Builders sponsored the little leaguers, and Jim Star had asked his foreman to coach. Frank hated every second of it, but did it to appease the boss. He pulled on a t-shirt with Star Builders stamped on the back, Monday, Wednesday and Saturdays in the summer. Frank sniped at most of the kids and incessantly berated the umpires during games, but he was particularly snide to Anthony, who was not a great ballplayer. Anthony also had little interest in participating, but he too had been forced to play. Frank's explanation on why Anthony needed to play was, "If I gotta do it, then so do you!"

a frame for flowers

Anthony had struck out looking, and Frank was irate.

"Jesus, Tony! That's the girl's way to whiff. Fa Gawd sakes you can't even strike out like a man," Frank barked from the chain-link dugout as Anthony slumped back to his team.

"Maybe take it easy on the kid, Bruno?" suggested Paul Priore from the opposite bench, having heard one comment too many from Frank.

"Why don't you mind yer fuckin business?" Frank snapped back, glaring across the diamond.

"Hey!" said Paul, looking back to signal to Frank. "The language okay?" he whispered. "They're ten, Frank," he continued, moving closer to keep his voice low.

"Exactly... time to grow a pa-ya," said Frank.

Both men had by then exited their respective dugouts and advanced towards each other. "What, ah you gettin froggy, you prick?"

"Just keep it down," said Paul, getting heated.

The umpire, an older gent from the neighborhood, made a mild attempt to separate them, but it was clearly on, and in South Boston everyone knew what to expect next. Frank marched right into the fray and took a swing at Paul right there by home base in front of twenty-four ten-year-olds and a few horrified parents.

Paul's dad had been a boxer in the Navy and had taught him to fight as a boy. With a graceful dodge, he ducked easily under Frank's blow and counter-punched him to the ribs, driving his hardened knuckles into Frank's mid-section, then straightened and shifted, digging the ball of his right foot into the malleable dirt of home plate and hauling over his shoulder with a lightning right. His tight fist cracked Frank's chin with a thud. Frank's knees buckled, and he dropped to the ground. It was over in a second, and everyone stood dumbfounded. Frank recovered and jumped to his feet quickly, ready to go more, but several parents and the umpire now intervened and it was done. Anthony couldn't remember how the game ended, but he would always remember what had ended: his belief that no one could stop his father.

"This one looks promising," said Paul, slipping a box cutter blade from his waistband and cutting back the mesh casing.

The tree sprung to life instantly and sat perfect in the cold parking lot with Paul Priore propping it up with a hand and a smile.

"This is the one," Anthony replied. "I'll take it."

"Alright then," said Paul, sharing the boy's excitement.

"How much is it, Paul?" he asked, as Mr. Priore walked up to the two of them.

"How much ya got, Tony?" the elder asked.

"Oh, hi, Mr. Priore. Ummm, I got twenty-umm…" He dug the crumpled dollars from his pocket and began to count. "I am pretty sure it's twenty-eight bucks. Is it enough?"

"Well, let's see," Mr. Priore said, looking at the tree as if he could see the price tag. "Whatta you know! This one is on sale for twenty bucks!"

"That's a sweet tree," said a voice from behind.

It was Joe Bertucci smiling from his car that everyone in the neighborhood recognized as an unmarked cop car.

"Hi, Joe," said Paul with a wave.

"Hey, Tucc. Can you catch the guy who stole my life?" joked Mr. Priore, cracking himself up. Joe pulled into a parking space and hopped out. Anthony did not recognize him.

"Is your mom here, Anthony?" asked Detective Bertucci.

Anthony looked at him cautiously and answered, "You know my mom?"

Paul interjected. "This is Detective Joe Bertucci, Tony. He is your Uncle Pat's friend from growing up. He's cool—for a cop, that is!"

Paul Priore had played some pickup hockey with them growing up, but his sport was always baseball.

"That's right, I know your mom and her brother, your Uncle Patrick. Sounds funny calling Patty an uncle," he said back to Paul.

"She's not here," Anthony finally answered. "Oh, yer with your dad?"

"Pffft," exclaimed Paul.

"No," Anthony responded curtly.

"Oh. Then how you getting that tree home?" asked Joe.

"You walked here, Tony?" asked Paul.

"Uh-huh, and I actually go by Anthony, if that's okay."

"Shit, of course, sorry about that. Well I can give you a lift," Paul said, taking Anthony's money and looking over to his dad who had gone to tend to yet another customer.

"It's alright, Paulie, I got this," said Mr. Priore from across the lot.

"Thanks, dad," Paul said.

He then bent down to Anthony's height to shake his hand and confirm the sale, the sticky sap on his hands locking their hands in a tight grip.

"You know what, Paul, let's strap it to the Chevy and I'll drive you up the hill, Anthony," Joe Bertucci interjected, recognizing Paul and his dad were pretty busy.

Having not really thought it through, Anthony considered taking a ride from a stranger might not be his best option, but he figured that with a cop the whole stranger danger thing went out the window. Besides, Paul and his dad knew the guy and said he was Uncle Pat's buddy. Seemed safe enough.

"Will you do that, Officer?" he asked.

"It's 'Detective,' actually," he said with a smile. "But call me Joe, and sure, it's no sweat.

"As long as the taxpayers don't report me!" he said, raising his voice so Mr. Priore could hear.

"Hope it's your only ride in a cruiser, kiddo!" added Mr. Priore. "Have a great Christmas, young man. The best to yer mom!"

"Yeah, Merry Christmas, Anthony," said Paul, having picked up on his dad's lead.

"Thank you, Paul, and thank you, Mr. Priore. Merry Christmas," he said.

Joe and Anthony worked together to tie the tree to the car, the fresh cut of the trunk kicking off the strong smell of pine.

"Your mom is going to love this," said Joe.

Anthony smiled widely.

119

Every Christmas Jim Star and his wife Myra hosted a small gathering at his house to celebrate the holidays. Not a big deal, but Frank was invited every year, and Kate had accompanied him each time. It was now the second week in December, and he knew he had to level with Jim about his situation.

"How we doing out at the Mulvaney lot, Frank?" Jim asked from inside his warm office.

"We just have some inside finish work the-ya and should finish totally in two days. We could close pap-ahwork next week fer shu-ya!" Frank replied.

He was leaning over the long desk in the front room of the two-room office and tossing paperclips into Tricia's cleavage as she pretended to be annoyed. "That's great work, Frank. Hey, come in here, will you?"

"Shu-ya, boss," he said, making his way along the desk and around to Mr. Star's office. He made faces to Tricia all the way up to walking in.

"It's nice and toasty in he-ya, huh?" said Frank upon entering.

"I might say it's just cold out there!" said Jim with his usual happy face. "Please, have a seat," he said, gesturing to the chair in front of his desk.

Frank plopped down and sprawled his legs out as he stretched his arms with an improvised yawn. He was pretty sure what was coming, but did not want to appear anxious.

"We had a good year, Frank," he said with a grin, "and you were a big part of it. I want to give you a little something early this year so you can do some special things for the family for Christmas."

And with that Jim Star slid a stout manila envelope across the shiny wood of his desk, the envelope appeared flush with cash. Years back, Frank had convinced Jim to pay some or his entire bonus from the petty cash fund that was rarely used. It generally had several thousand dollars in it by year's end, and Frank contended it was sunk cost that should be spent. He had read about sunk cost in a magazine, and it sounded logical to Jim. Of course, the big incentive was avoiding the taxes on the income, and although Jim realized that, he did not feel it was a big deal to conceal a little something from Uncle Sam.

"Geez, that's awful generous, Jim," said Frank, prying open the flap and thumbing through the bills. "Maybe get that pretty Kate a new dress for our Christmas party?" Star said in an innocent yet old-fashioned way. Frank winced at the comment, knowing the moment had come.

"Well, about that, Mr. Star," Frank began, straightening in his chair and bowing his head a bit.

"I am gonna struggle to make the pahty this ye-ah," he said, peering up slightly to gauge Star's reaction.

"What... why?" asked Jim, instantly concerned and leaning forward.

"Kate and I... she booted me out. She wants to get a divoa-ss."

"Oh by god," proclaimed Jim, clutching at his head. "How did this happen, Frank? You must be devastated."

Frank craned over his shoulder to gauge how the voices might carry out to Tricia in the front, but he could hear she was on the phone. The coast was clear.

"She broke my hea-ht, Mr. Star. She's gonna win custody too, ya know? It is just a real ha-hd time."

"Oh by god. Is that enough money? Do you need some extra help?"

"Oh no, Mr. Stah. I mean, I might, you know, if it gets real ha-hd, but, no, this is generous. I'm lookin for some place to stay right now. She's got me livin in a hotel!"

"What happened?"

"She says we been growin apaht fer ye-ahs"

Jim Star drew back in his chair and rubbed his chin in thought. He had been married to Myra for forty-two years and could only imagine the pain of it ending badly.

"Do you want to get her back?"

"Oh, I'd like to get her back," Frank retorted, mocking a sinister laugh.

Mr. Star chuckled a bit, but stiffened quickly, sensing Frank was sure to be in a vulnerable place.

"It's normal to feel hurt and even angry about it, Frank… very normal, just don't do anything rash. Maybe she'll come to her senses," Jim said in a fatherly way. He was certain Frank had been emotionally crushed by this turn of events.

"It's just ha-hd on a guy… you know?"

"Sure, of course it is. Especially around the holidays, but you take care of yourself now and let things sort themselves out. And Frank, you let me know if you need anything."

"I will Mr. Stah, and thinking about it. I guess we are going to have to change my health policy right? I mean if we're not married, you shouldn't have to pay."

"I am pretty sure that's not how it works, but I'll have Tricia look into it with our agent."

120

J oe Bertucci turned up Anthony's street with the Christmas tree
loosely bound and bouncing on the roof of the black Chevy. He
pulled up to the front of the house to drop Anthony off, but climbed
out to help lug the tree up to the front door.

"If you have the stand ready, we can bring it in, or do you want to
just leave it out front?"

"Yeah, I got the stand out before I went," Anthony answered, then
considered his next words carefully. "My mom is not feeling well, and
she can't really help, so it would be great if you can help me carry
this in."

Joe was more than happy to assist, and he quickly unknotted the
twine to release the bushy pine. He didn't think too much about
Anthony's comment and figured the boy just wanted some help. Joe
brushed away some pockets of snow that were tucked into the boughs
and shook the tree as he pulled it from the roof, dropping it to the
cement sidewalk on its trunk, with a thud to jar loose remaining bits
of ice and snow. The tree was taking shape and appeared full and
healthy. The rich smell of pine cleared his nose in the crisp air. He
felt, at that moment, like he was bringing home the family's tree, and
it felt good.

Anthony nervously brushed at the branches and tried to assist as Joe hoisted the tree and started up the front walk. It occurred to Anthony that he should try and give his mother some warning that he was coming in with someone.

"I gotta get around the side and open the front door, so I'll meet you there."

"Okay," replied Joe, making his way up the front porch.

Anthony scurried swiftly around the corner and slipped in the side door, then bolted directly to the living room were his noise had woken his mother from some light sleep.

"Oh hey, honey," Kate said, sliding up on the couch to see what he was up to. "You got the tree stand out?" she asked, noticing it in his hand.

"I got more than that! I got us a tree. Mr. Priore totally hooked me up and we got a wicked awesome tree! Mr. Bertucci is out front with it!"

"Who?"

"Mr., I mean Detective Bertucci. He said he knew you."

Anthony stopped, suddenly concerned he had led a stranger to the house.

"Oh god," Kate yelped. "Joe… I mean Mr. Bertucci is out front?"

"Umm, yeah, is that okay? He gave me a ride with the tree from the market."

"Mr. Priore sold it to you, huh?" she said, peering out through the living room window to look for Joe on the porch.

"Paul, actually," Anthony replied, busily unwinding the screws on the tree stand.

"Such nice guys they are," she said, exiting to the kitchen to go the long way to the staircase, allowing her to remain unseen.

"I will be back down in a moment. I look frightening!" Kate said suddenly, forgetting the doctor's call from earlier and rushing upstairs to freshen her face for the handsome Joe Bertucci.

Anthony said nothing as he was preoccupied with the tree, and he headed to the front door to let the detective in. The house was warm, but the cold air rushed into the foyer as Anthony opened the door. Joe stood smiling and holding up the perfect Christmas tree, looking like something out of a TV ad.

"Your tree, sir," he said, bowing slightly.

Anthony smiled.

"C'mon in. My mom said she'll be down in a minute. The tree stand is in the living room, back this way."

"Should I take my boots off?" he asked.

"No, it's no big deal," Anthony replied.

Joe Bertucci admired the obviously well-kept home with its old Victorian style, yet modern flair. The hard wood creaked a bit as he lugged the tree across it, mindful not to scrape the wall with its branches. The tree carried an aura of cold, as if it were trying to keep the outdoors with it. They quickly got it situated and tightened into the stand, setting it upright and positioned in the corner by the fireplace. It was instantly picturesque. The comfort of Christmas settled in.

"Hi, Joe," said Kate from the doorway of the living room.

Anthony was astounded how quickly she got dressed and made up. She wore jeans and a sweater, and she had pulled a ball cap over her bandana, obscuring her smooth scalp. Joe brushed himself off, scattering pine needles to the floor and nearby throw rug, and took a step closer. He recognized the hat and bandana as unusual, but did not ascertain the truth behind it.

"Hi ya, Kate," he said, flashing a smile. "Sorry for the intrusion!"

"Not at all. Thanks so much for helping Anthony with the tree. I have no idea how he thought he would get it home!"

"Yeah, the surprise seemed to be a good idea at the moment. I guess I was lucky you came along, although Paul did say he would've driven me," Anthony said, turning to his mom.

"Anthony said you're sick?" Joe asked, changing the subject and thinking she looked okay for having the flu or something.

"He did, huh?" Kate responded languidly, assuming Anthony had for some reason told him the truth. "I guess it is still obvious, even with the Sox hat."

Joe paused and it instantly dawned on him. He was a detective, so observation was a strong suit. "Oh shoot, what is it, Kate?" he asked timidly, wondering if it was a boundary he ought not to cross.

"I have stage three cancer and had to get an operation. It was... umm, I had a mastectomy a little over a month ago, and then I went through... I should say I am going through chemotherapy."

"Yeah, but it's done now. My mom finished it and her hair should grow back. That's what the doctors told us," Anthony added with an upbeat tone.

"Oh wow, shoot, Kate. I'm sorry you're going through that. You know my Aunt Joanne went through that. Boy, geez, I'm sorry. How are you feeling? Cuz you look great," he said, ambling and unsure of when to stop.

"Thanks, Joe. I didn't know about your aunt. That stinks. Is she okay?"

"Yeah, she's good. Five years now, totally good!"

"You see, ma!"

The three of them stood smiling and admiring the perfect pine tree that now anchored the living room.

"Can I make you some coffee, Joe?"

"I should get back to my job," he said wistfully, "but I did just bust a big case, so maybe a cup on the taxpayer's time is not a huge deal!"

They all laughed, and Kate led Joe to the kitchen, while Anthony scrambled back downstairs to the basement to haul up the boxes of decorations.

Kate made Joe coffee, which he took black, and they talked a bit about her illness as she moved around the kitchen. He reflected how she still looked healthy, if a bit thin. She told him about the operation, the chemotherapy, and had given him lots of detail when it occurred to her that she had told none of this to her brother. The one real common connection between the two of them was her brother, Patrick, and now she had revealed more to a man she hardly knew than her closest living relative.

"Patty doesn't know any of this," she said solemnly.

"Really?" Joe asked, trying quickly to conceal his surprise.

"I wanted to tell him a bunch of times, you know, but we're finally talking again regularly, and it has been so nice. I just… the time wasn't right."

"Yeah, but Kate…"

"I know, I know. I had planned to discuss it with him in person, you know, like this. It's so much easier."

"No, of course, that makes sense," he said.

"Now that you know, though, I gotta tell him."

"Yeah, you probably should. What does your husband think? How is he handling this?"

"Frank? Oh, that's another story not worth sharing. He decided it's a good time to leave me, smack dab in the middle of the biggest scare of my life."

"Are you kidding me? He left you?"

"Yup. Class act, huh?"

"That's unreal. Does Pat know that?"

"Ahhh, nope, hadn't gotten to that either."

"Sounds like you two need a long sit-down."

"I know, you're right."

They chatted for almost an hour, and it felt so nice. Talking with Vida was one of Kate's favorite things in life, but it felt good to talk to Joe—to talk to a man. She felt whole for a spell, and that was comforting.

"Well, I really should be going, but thanks for the coffee," said Joe, pulling his leather coat back on. "I hope you feel better, Kate. You'll be okay. You're tough just like your brother and your dad!"

"No, thank you for the Christmas tree and the help. He is a good kid, you know."

"Definitely, anytime. Anything I can do to help you, please let me know. You'll do that, right? Call me for anything, Kate. You still have my number right?"

She was embarrassed to admit it was still tucked in her wallet, despite having long ago given it to her brother as was intended.

"Sure, I still have it," Kate said as she walked Joe to the door. She was exhausted, but felt happy.

121

With just a couple more weeks until his trip to Boston, Patrick was out shopping in the buzz of New York City's December. He was way ahead of schedule on work and feeling very optimistic that he could leave without any worries and enjoy his time back in town. He was so excited to see Kate and wanted to pick out something nice for her and Anthony. Not knowing it was irrelevant, he had already scratched Frank off his list, wrapping him a black turtleneck from the Christian Harford "Everyman" collection. He was quite confident Frank would never consider wearing it.

Midtown Manhattan was teeming with a swarm of shoppers from every corner of the earth, and the energy was effusive, a velocity of good cheer that buffeted the bite of the subfreezing temperatures. People hustled from shop to shop, flanked by their square bags bulging with gifts. Others ducked into a local eatery for a bite, hot chocolate, or even a cocktail to warm the soul. It was a perfect holiday shopping moment.

As Patrick slipped his way through the crowds like a Yellow Cab on Broadway, he came up behind three women who appeared to be a generational triplet: daughter, mother, and grandmother. The women had dressed to fend off the city's bite, tucked snugly into their puffy jackets, stretching down to their calves and hugging them safe. Multi-colored hats and scarves wrapped around their heads and necks. It felt warm to just be near them. They stopped for a moment at the corner, and Patrick walked right into the middle of them, realizing they had paused for a picture. Knowing the visitor element only too well and the risks associated, he offered to take the photo.

"You ladies need some help?" he asked with his handsome smile.

"Gosh, would ya?" The middle woman responded with a Midwestern twang.

Patrick looked at their faces as they pulled back the knitted wraps for a photo. He could instantly see the similarities: their eyes each borrowing from the last, the curve of the mouths, and the shape of the face lending to one another. The eldest woman looked unwell and more aged than her offspring's years would project.

"Hey, mom. He's going to take a picture of us, okay?" she said, helping her mother pull back her scarf, the old woman nodding with a thin smile.

"She's really sick, but insisted on seeing Manhattan at Christmas one more time. We came down from Edina, near Minneapolis in Minnesota," explained the youngest, unwrapping a stark moment of truth with a stranger on the curb of New York City. She wasn't embarrassed or apologizing; she was sharing in a way uncommon for that city even at its holiday zenith.

"Take off your hat, Sharon. Show your pretty face," interrupted the mother, chiding her daughter and clearly noticing the good-looking photographer they had tripped into.

"Mom," she responded as if annoyed, yet a smile stretched across the three like a string of garland. Patrick framed the photo and squeezed off a couple of shots. The camera was older and a bit beat up, but it captured the moment on the small square screen. The cold chewed at his fingers as he steadied the camera again.

"Let's take another, just to be sure. I think we got a great moment," said Patrick, enjoying himself.

"That's all that life's about," said the old woman with surprising resonance.

355

"Don't wait til it's too late to realize that, young man," she added.

"Grandma, good gracious, the guy doesn't need life advice for taking a picture of us!"

Patrick smiled and took two more pictures, then handed the camera back to the mother. "Enjoy your shopping, ladies, and happy holidays," he exclaimed.

Then he was off as quick as he'd arrived, sinking into the crowd. "Thanks!"

"Thank you! Happy holidays!" they cried out after him as he moved away. With a wave and a pivot, they vanished into his past.

After a bit more shopping of his own, Patrick took a walk past the school in his neighborhood. He grabbed a brochure.

122

Frank took Tricia out for dinner at a nice Italian restaurant on the North End. He had the separation papers in his briefcase. He had filed a Complaint for Divorce, as his lawyer instructed, and Kate would soon be served with the papers.

"So it's done?"

"No! It will be done, when it is signed and done."

"Yeah, well, it's stahted anyways."

"Oh, it's stahted, but you just can't believe this bullshit. The whole thing is decided by some cou-ht-assigned idiot. They look at how long ya been married, reason for div-oss, all kind a gahbage. I'm gonna have ta give em my tax fohms so they can fig-ya out child suppoht and alimony... such bullshit. Like this fat bitch at the cou-ht knows anything about me being ignohed fer ye-ahs... that's neglect!"

"Ya, but it's ov-ah Frankie!"

"Yeah, my bank account's ov-ah. You know the medical bills from her being sick, like we ah way ov-ah the deductible. Like I can't tell you how much this shit is gonna cost. I may be havin to staht ov-ah, Trish."

"I don't ca-ya—"

"Yeah, well I do."

They ate dinner together like a couple, and that always made Tricia feel good. When Frank finished eating, he checked his watch.

"It's Wednesday, you know. I gotta go do the payroll."

"You and your schedule… Can't you just skip one night?"

"Trish, for the love a Gawd. If I ev-ah have to say this again, it's ov-ah between us, you und-ahstand? This is how I do things, and it is how things ah gonna be, now and fa-evah!"

He wiped his mouth with his napkin and stood up indignantly. "Time to go."

123

Christmas was a week away, and Vida was excited that her book was done. It was not going to be published by Christmas, and her agent was disappointed that sales could be affected, but Vida didn't really care. Christmas was going to fall on a Saturday, and Vida knew Kate's brother, Patrick, was arriving in a couple of days and would be staying at the house for a bit. She made it a point to head down every day to help her friend get the house ready. Kate seemed worn down to Vida, and she wanted to help her. She was excited for another get-together, having thoroughly enjoyed Thanksgiving.

124

Kate was busy getting the house ready for Patrick's visit. She was tired, and the latest reports from the doctors confirmed that she would need to undergo a second round of chemo accompanied with targeted radiation treatments. She had begged to defer the start until after the holidays, and the doctors had begrudgingly agreed. It was only another week or two, and the last chemo was still staving off most of the metastasizing. She prepared the guest room where they had scarcely ever had a guest and did her best to tidy up around the house. She was sad that after so many years apart, Patrick would see her yard and garden looking so barren.

125

Patrick arrived Monday afternoon, having spent the morning assuring that his week was squared away. The early numbers on his "Everyman" collection sales had beat expectations, and the entire team was excited about having big holiday season sales. He landed at Logan airport right on time at 3:16, touching down on a frozen and snow-banked runway. The sight of Boston out the window made him feel welcome. The dark, cold waters of the harbor were starkly juxtaposed against the town blanketed in white. It felt like Christmas.

Patrick hopped a cab to his hotel and got settled in. He unpacked and changed into a sweater before walking out into the evening. He headed straight to the Green Dragon near Quincy market for a pint and some shepherd's pie. The air was snap cold as he marched, head tucked with his hands jammed into his coat pockets. It was a short walk before he was into the warm confines of the bar that was older than the United States and was said to have been the location for the planning of the Boston Tea Party. The familiar barkeeps from many years gone were no longer there, but equally kind servers made him instantly remember why this had been a favorite haunt.

Patrick spent the first evening alone with a hearty meal and a few cold beers before retiring to the hotel for a good night's sleep. He did not think of work or even New York.

The next morning he phoned Kate at home. It was about 9:00 a.m., and he presumed Anthony was already up and gone to school. He figured she could probably come pick him up for a visit. He still had no inkling of her sickness. Despite Kate's indication to Joe Bertucci that she would share the information prior to his arrival, she could not bring herself to do it.

"I am ho-ho here," said Patrick, laughing through the phone.

Kate felt an instant spike of energy at the sound of his voice. It was now so close. "Yah! What do you want to do?"

"I don't know. I need to shop a bit."

"Okay. I can come get you. Give me the address. Can you be ready in an hour? I have a doctor's appointment at two o'clock,, then Anthony's home at 3:45, so I want to be home around then."

"I have no schedule except some hockey tonight, but that is not until nine o'clock, so I can do whatever!"

126

Kate picked up Patrick outside the hotel and saw him standing just inside the door. She knew the time had come to tell him, and she was nervous. She never liked to share bad news, and in particular, she never wished to burden someone with her problems. Kate never wanted to feel like reconnecting with Patrick was a result of the illness, but she recognized how wrong it was to have kept him in the dark.

She watched him stride confidently to the car with his hat pulled down tight and a smile ear to ear. Patrick jumped into the Volvo, leaning in immediately to embrace his sister.

"God, I missed you."

She exhaled. "Me too. I'm sorry… it has been so long. It's horrible and I know it. No excuses…"

"None needed," she comforted her brother who looked so familiar, but his scent and the maturity in his face felt still somewhat foreign.

His hands on her shoulder, he withdrew to look at his older sister. He was struck abruptly by her thin face. Something was different, even wrong, he sensed. Kate bowed her head in his gaze. She said nothing, but reached up to pull off the hat and bandana that covered her head, revealing her scalp, which had begun to spring small sprouts of fuzz for the first time in many weeks. He was shocked by the sight and sat speechless... even breathless.

"I know. It's ugly," she stated sadly.

Patrick's hands slid from her shoulders, smoothly up to her neck and then to her head, cupping her pretty face in his hands.

"Oh my god, Katie. What is this?"

"I have cancer, Pat."

His eyes fell deep and silent, staring into his sister's.

"When did you... how did you find out... how long have you had it?"

"I..." she began, but he spoke over her compelled by emotion.

"Kate how long have you been sick, and how serious is this?"

"It hasn't been long, Pat, but I have a lot to tell you. I... I just wanted it to be in person."

"Oh my God. I was upset you kept the Frank stuff from me, but now this... I guess I understand, just tell me what is happening, please."

And so Kate explained it all to her long absent brother, right there with the car motor running and parked on the narrow street in front of the hotel. She told him everything. How she found out she had cancer, the operation, the chemo, Vida's help, Anthony's struggles, the update on her illness, and Frank's incredibly gutless and callous departure. Patrick sat quietly listening and riding a roller coaster of emotion from anger to deep sadness. He was moved near tears listening to the story, frustrated that he had not been there, that she had suffered so greatly while he toiled over his self-perceived stress, having been consumed by what now felt like trivial or even pointless issues.

Kate certainly hadn't planned on having this important conversation in the car, but she knew the moment he saw her, there would be no alternative. She knew the best way to get herself to tell Patrick was to create a situation where she would have to. Like so many times in her life before, she cornered her courage in order to do what she had to do.

They talked through the cancer, the treatment, and Kate's future plans. They remained optimistic and vowed to beat the disease, but

364

prudently touched upon the worst case scenario and how it would be handled. He grew more emotional as the love and sorrow for his sister—and the rage towards Frank—burned in his mind.

"I could kill him," he said softly, shaking his head.

They tried to gather themselves and did some shopping, but Patrick had trouble concentrating. All he could think was, "How can I help?"

I could Too

127

They went to the house that night, and Anthony was reunited with his Uncle Pat. The two instantly bonded as they caught up on life. Anthony was intrigued by Patrick's alter ego, Christian Harford.

"So you just created another person and became them?"

"Kind of. Who could imagine Patrick Kelley, Irish hockey thug from Boston, as the next Calvin Klein?" explained Patrick to his wide-eyed nephew. "Sometimes you have to really break away from life to find your potential," he said, and Anthony hung on every word.

Kate spurred Anthony to share his artwork, news of his honors at the local exhibit, and his invitation to New York.

"Tell him about the exhibit, honey," she said.

"What is it? Tell me!" Patrick encouraged.

"It's nothing, really. I was in a local art show for some paintings."

"Ha. It is way more than that, Patty. It was so cool. Anthony had these huge paintings, a triplet—"

"—triptych," Anthony respectfully corrected.

"Right, triptych. Anyways, it was real big, and I swear you got the most attention in the whole place. I mean, the Kennedy Library, are you kidding me, how cool is that?"

Patrick rubbed elbows with celebrities and supermodels in his career and could have easily been unimpressed with news that a mayor and some local Boston art yahoos were impressed with Anthony's paintings, but it never crossed his mind. Pat swelled with pride for his nephew, again ashamed for having been away for so long and recognizing all he could do to help the young man. Anthony scrambled upstairs and emerged with sketches and paintings he had in his bedroom. Kate glowed, watching Patrick's eyes widen at the sight of these talent-driven pieces.

"This is really good stuff, Anthony. Really good!"

"You think so, Pat?" asked Anthony, perhaps happier than Kate had seen him in years.

"I do, and I would shoot it straight. You are legit, my man!"

"I told you, honey, and Pat knows this stuff, believe me," said Kate as she left for the kitchen, leaving Patrick and Anthony alone in the living room by the decorated Christmas tree.

"Well, if we can pull off the trip to New York City, I hope you can meet us for the exhibit. I will be sharing space with kids from across the country, so my stuff may not hold up to that, but we'll see, I guess."

"Heck yeah, we will. I wouldn't miss it for anything. And what's this 'pull it off'? When is it, and why could you not pull it off?"

"It's in March… the weekend of March 13 and 14th," said Anthony as he slowly lowered his voice.

"I am not sure we can pull it off because of money, and because… well, you know mom is sick, right? So, I mean, who knows with that. You know she has to go through treatments and stuff."

"Of course, of course, but I can handle the trip's cost and take it off your mom's plate. Don't sweat it. March 15th, huh? And you said it's a Saturday?"

"Yup, and it's at the Guggenheim in New York City."

"Anthony, some artists spend their whole lives trying and don't get in there. That is awesome! March 15th. That means St. Patrick's Day is Monday, so cool. We can go to the parade and make a real trip of it. This will be perfect!"

"You really think so, Uncle Pat?"

"I know so. I mean, as long as it works with your mom."

Kate walked back in with some early evening hot chocolates and a contagious big smile. She was tired but filled with joy.

128

Kate convinced Patrick to stick to his schedule and play hockey, and so he did. He connected with so many of his old buddies, and he and Joe Bertucci reunited like they had never been apart, instantly good friends once more. They had a great time skating, and although the wheels were a bit slower to turn, they still could play. They had a spirited game. Though Patrick missed New York, he once again remembered all he loved about that great place called Boston.

129

Christmas trees had arrived daily for weeks, dragged to door steps with a wake of needles strewn in the white snow. Boston's winter skies accommodated with fresh blankets of snow that made the lights in the yards beam with an added glow. Kate and Vida managed a fun but exhausting day at the mall together, knocking out their gift lists. Now the presents lay tucked beneath the perfect tree wrapped in bright colors. Kate had hung the stockings over the fireplace in the living room and stuffed them full of chocolates and little gifts, candy canes sprouting out of their furry rims. She had hung one for Anthony, Vida, and Patrick, and the sight brought happy tears to her eyes. She feared it may be her last Christmas, but quickly pushed the fear below.

Simple tasks like wrapping a gift or hanging the stockings were exhausting. Just digging in the basement to find the stockings had worn her out. She had paused for a rest in the basement and found herself staring at her father's old Navy trunk where she had folded and tucked away the American flag months earlier.

She thought about her parents, Ted and Moira Kelley, and how much she missed them. It was her mother who had filled the stockings for her and Pat, and they loved waking up those mornings when it always seemed to be snowing outside and warm inside. How their dad would work hard to take days off around Christmas, and how he would drink beer at the house and smile and laugh a lot. How she would sneak into her tiny room to wrap gifts for her family, folding carefully and taping the corners neatly, tying ribbons around the red-and-green paper, which she trimmed to perfection with her small red scissors. She smiled back at her life, concluding it had been good, a life worth living... and she was grateful.

130

Christmas morning arrived on a Saturday, and the first gift was the fluffy flakes of soft snow that drifted down into a pure white blanket, tucking the house in for a perfect day. Anthony sprang from bed like he was five years younger, anxious to see what Christmas morning had brought, bounding loudly down the stairs and stirring the house to life. King was a moment behind, leaping from Kate's bed, where he'd taken up residence on the night Kate decided to just stay downstairs on the couch.

Anthony found the tree was still lighted from the evening before, where he, his mother, and Uncle Patrick had sat up late in front of a roaring fire talking. They had opened a single present together, just as they used to do as a family in his earliest and happier memories, and as Kate and Patrick had done as children. The tree glowed as its white lights flickered off of the ornaments and tinsel. The house was warm with a light smell of pine in the air.

Patrick's body ached from back to back nights of hockey, but he woke with the first light that crept in the window that morning in the second floor guest room. He felt warm in the rarely used bed that Kate had fit with a thick white down comforter. He felt a twinge of joy, as in that moment, he'd drifted back to the Christmas mornings of his childhood when he would wake to sprint into his sister's room, so they could share the first glimpse of the gift-packed tree.

The last decade of life had wrapped him up in layers of obsession and conviction, a swirl of insecurities, challenges, triumphs, and lessons learned, a journey and battle for success and acceptance. It was a battle he seemed to be winning, finding himself successful, well-off, and respected amongst his peers. He had dared to leave the neighborhood, to shun the path most had already chosen for him in hockey and to pursue a passion for clothing design that was sure to invite ambivalence and likely ridicule from those he left behind. The wall he'd built between South Boston to New York City had crumbled. It felt odd and perfect all at the same time to wake up in Boston on Christmas. He rose from the bed, happy to spend the day with his family. He knew it was the part of life that was missing.

Kate was the last to get up, although she had lain awake in her bed for over an hour before she heard Anthony rise. She could hear the house's creaks, fending off the cold and warming itself for the holiday. She could feel the blood moving through her body, and she hoped it was winning today's battle. When she heard Patrick stirring, she thought back to being a young girl when he would barrel into her cramped room in his pajamas to wake her up for Christmas, and how most years she would be awake, but pretend to sleep so he could wake her. Those were days she would never forget, and she wanted this day to be such a day for Anthony. She had gone a little overboard shopping, and the tree was laden with gifts.

Kate wrapped her slight body in her pink, fuzzy robe and stepped into her slippers, then headed towards the kitchen. She could smell coffee brewing and was surprised to find Anthony busy at work, having brewed a pot and now messily glazing some cinnamon rolls on a cookie sheet for breakfast.

"Look at you!" she said as she entered the kitchen.

"Did you see the snow, ma?" asked Anthony.

"I did. So cool, huh?"

"How'd you sleep, Patty?" she asked her brother, who was hunched over a cup of black coffee like a camper on a cold night.

"I slept so good," he said. "That comforter is amazing!"

Kate made her way over to stand next to her son, leaning into him. "Did you feed King?" she whispered.

"Oh shoot, I forgot," said Anthony.

Kate knew this was a graceful way to move him off the cinnamon rolls that he was crucifying. Sure enough, he dropped the knife and went to pour King some food. Kate slipped in to resurrect the breakfast rolls.

"You hungry, Pat?"

"I feel like I'm a hundred years old! My legs are so thrashed from skating."

"I bet, but was it good to be on the ice again?"

"Oh, it was awesome! It was so great to see all the guys again and just to be out there getting a sweat. Playing, you know, like kids again."

"Was anyone still really good, or are you all in the master's program now?"

"Honestly, I had the most goals and may have been in the best shape, but everyone was still pretty good. Tucc might even be better than he was! Which, oops, by the way, I hope you don't mind I told Joe and Mr. Bertucci they could stop by later if they have time."

"Huh? Oh, yeah, of course," Kate said, thinking quickly about what she had picked out to wear.

"Detective Bertucci's coming over?" asked Anthony.

"Yeah, you know him?" asked Patrick, not sure of how the connection existed.

"Kind of. He helped me with our tree."

"He's a great guy. His dad and our dad—your grandpa—used to be best friends. Him and one other guy, they were all cops and inseparable. The three musketeers. It was a long time ago."

"Geez, I haven't seen Mrs. Bertucci in forever. How is she?" asked Kate.

"Not sure. I mean, Joe said she's good, but she is tied to the kitchen today, so he and his pop are making the rounds to say Merry Christmas to friends. I thought it would be fun if they drop by here."

"That will be fun! Remember Mr. Bertucci used to dress up like Santa when we were kids?"

"Yeah, and he smelled like Scotch," said Patrick, as they chuckled over the memory.

The three of them sat together at the kitchen table and enjoyed the moist, sweet cinnamon rolls as well as scrambled eggs, fresh orange juice, and crispy bacon. Kate's medicine made her blood real thin, and when she accidently sliced her finger cutting oranges to squeeze, the blood gushed out uncontrollably from a seemingly small cut. Patrick helped her get it wrapped up.

"Man that is bleeding a ton. must have hit an artery or something."

"It's my meds. It's like that kid, Steve Grimaldi, who lived on Wayne Street when we were kids. Remember the kid who could bleed to death from a little cut?"

"Yeah, he was a hemophiliac."

"Exactly. My medicine has a similar effect. My blood doesn't clot very well."

"Well, you better be more careful then, ya fumble bum!" Patrick said with a smile, as he taped off the small bandage on Kate's finger.

After breakfast, Kate went upstairs to get dressed and ready to cook a big meal for a small group. She stepped into the spacious walk-in closet to get her outfit together. She had picked out a gray skirt and a red sweater. She was going to wear white tights and a white silk scarf on her head, but needed to pick a pair of shoes, so she knelt down to get a closer look. As she looked, her eyes strayed to the metal box that was tucked back next to the shoe rack. The metal box still contained the shiny silver handgun, the only one Frank had forgotten to take. She lifted a shoebox, placed it gently on top of the metal box, and picked out a pair of black Mary Janes.

Kate took a shower, got dressed, and headed back down stairs. The snow was falling even harder now. Anthony had disappeared into his room, and the door was closed, which probably meant he was wrapping presents. Patrick had obviously taken a quick shower, and he was dressed in tan slacks and a plaid shirt. He was back in the kitchen when Kate walked in.

"Hey. 'd you get a shower?" asked Kate.

"I did… feeling much better now. I took some aspirin to numb the aches and pains, but I may need a beer to get me in the right place!" he joked.

"I have some in the fridge, so help yourself!"

"I will for sure, but I think I'll wait til at least noon to start drinking alone."

There were several minutes of silence as Kate began to pull items from the refrigerator and wash the dishes from breakfast. Patrick came over to the kitchen sink to stand next to her, and they looked out the window together. There was Mr. Heaney right on schedule, walking the two Yorkies, and he had cornered the neighbors across the street. They were engaged in a Heaney chat. Patrick began aimlessly scrubbing the greasy bacon pan and turned to ask Kate a question.

"What does it feel like?"

"What, my head?" she asked, running her fingertip across the light blonde fuzz.

She had not put on her scarf yet and was just walking around with her head exposed. Kate told Anthony the constant head wrapping was annoying. He had gotten used to it and told her to not worry about it when they were at the house.

"No, the cancer, I mean. Like the scars from the operation and stuff," he clarified awkwardly.

"Ugh," she exhaled, with a pause.

"It's weird, I guess. I mean… geez… where to start? It feels bizarre to have one breast, to be perfectly blunt. It feels bizarre to have no hair and to know that right now chemicals are inside me killing evil cells along with good cells in some crazy war to try and stop the cancer from killing me. It's all bizarre, but doesn't hurt really as much as it aches."

Patrick instantly realized his groaning about soreness from hockey must have seemed so trivial to his sister, whose daily aches were due to unthinkable tumult inside her body.

"You feel sick to your stomach all the time. You can't sleep real well, you're not hungry, but your digestive system is a twisted car wreck," she stated solemnly, staring out the window.

"The worst, though, is the anxiety, the fear that this is it."

"What do you mean?"

"Ah, come on, Pat. You're my brother, my only family. I can take the rosy optimism from strangers, but come on. I mean, look at me. This war inside of me that we're talking about, that you are asking me to explain. It's not just metaphor. Certainly you recognize it's a war that can be lost."

"Kate, don't," said Patrick, shaking his head and stepping towards her.

"I'm not being dramatic, Pat. It's life, and we all go some time. This is serious, and I accept it that way."

"Yeah, well, we can beat this thing. You… come on, you gotta stay positive."

"Stay positive? I am positive… what are you talking about? I have remained upbeat through all of this despite losing 17 pounds, despite all my hair falling out, despite my husband walking out on me… I have remained very positive. Look Patrick if you want to help… and I believe you do… then be by my side, understand where I am and help me deal with the outcome good or bad… ok? That's it… that's what I want," she said.

"That is what I need from you most."

She turned to face him fully standing up to his chin and leaning into the heat of his health, she spoke without looking up.

"I am afraid to die Patty… so I'm telling you, I am positive I will fight this until my last breath… ok?" Patrick stood silent. He now recognized the last ten years that he had been so distant was his doing.

That his desire for more time with his sister was equal parts selfish. He wanted the time back to do some things differently, while she just wanted time. He could no longer hold in the bottled sorrow that had been pent up since they spoke those first hours in the car in front of the hotel. It gushed forth from him in tears.

"I am so sorry Kate," he wept. "I love you so much…. I am so sorry for running away. I left you with that horrible guy and mom and dad gone. I'm sorry. I just figured we had lots of time."

"Pat... it's ok... I'm ok. Just be there for me no matter what. That's what I need. Do you understand?"

"Yes of course."

They embraced in the kitchen, the tears cascading to her shoulders and sinking into her red sweater as he held her tight. They lingered there for minutes before they both heard Anthony descending the stairs.

"Let's pull it together for your nephew... ok?" she asked. "Yeah of course... I'm a mess."

"He needs to know you more"

"I know... today. I mean... we are getting there."

Patrick darted to the bathroom pulling the old wood door behind him by the brass knob. He drew close to the mirror to view his reddened face and damp eyes.

"Pull it together, Pat," he whispered to himself, so close it fogged the mirror slightly.

Clenching his hands he bowed slightly to murmur forth a prayer, asking God to please help his sister... asking God for the strength to help her himself. He stared for a moment longer and gathered his strength knowing this was something he was more than capable of. He splashed cold water on his face and was flush with a sudden awareness... a feeling of appreciation he had not known. He had long suspected, but never knew so clearly, how strong his sister was.

131

Patrick drove the Volvo up to Vida's house with Anthony to help her with the presents she insisted on bringing. The two sat for a moment in the garage, rubbing their hands together as the car mumbled its way to warm.

"You like New York, Uncle Pat?"

"Heck, yeah. It's a great city. I can't wait to show it to you."

"Yeah, me too. That trip is gonna be wicked awesome."

Patrick clicked the car into reverse and backed slowly down the snow-covered driveway, his arm over the passenger seat and his torso twisted to look behind them.

"I could never have done it without your mom. You know that, right?"

"Umm, not exactly. What do you mean?"

"Your Grandpa and Grandma Kelley passed away before you were born, and Kate and I were pretty young, too. It was a hard time. Your mom became the parents of our house. She got me through high school and helped me get into NYU. If Kate hadn't shared her inheritance, I probably would have had to go to a lesser school. I never would have made it the way I have. Her sacrifices paved the way for me."

"Really?" Anthony responded. He wasn't being coy; he really had no idea. No one ever told him any of it, and even if Frank had cared, he didn't know the half of it. "It's funny how we don't wonder about things we don't know," he continued.

"Ha!" Patrick laughed, but felt the weight of the young man's observation. "I owe her a lot. That's all I can say."

"Yeah, well, me too. That's why I spent every penny I've saved to buy her this necklace," said Anthony. He pulled the piece from his jacket pocket and pried open the blue, square, felt box. In it lay a shiny silver cross necklace with a green, glowing emerald at its crux.

"It's a Celtic cross, called the 'warrior's cross,' and it is pure silver."

"It's beautiful, Anthony. She's gonna love that."

"You think?"

"I am sure of it," said Patrick, as they turned around and pulled up in front of Vida's.

She was waving wildly from the porch with about as much excitement as one could imagine.

"Nice lady, huh?" asked Patrick.

"The nicest," said Anthony. He leaped from the car to go help Vida.

Back at the house, Kate prepared the ham, vegetables, and various accoutrements for the big Christmas feast. She had prepared some appetizers and laid out some crackers and port-wine cheese like her dad used to love. The kitchen smelled delicious, and the house felt like Christmas as the three rumbled into the garage. Kate could hear the thud of the car doors and the trunk as they emptied the car of Vida's bounty of carefully wrapped gifts. The familiar sound of the doors opening and closing made her smile.

"This Christmas will be the best ever," she whispered to herself.

132

There were only four of them, but they filled the rooms with holiday cheer: eating, drinking, and being merry. They enjoyed the food, shared presents, and sat down for a perfect meal. Kate was overjoyed by all the giving and particularly thrilled by Anthony's necklace, which she immediately put around her neck and frequently reached up to rub between her fingers.

Vida had gone a bit overboard, buying several gifts for everyone. She was in great spirits. She bought Kate a collection of precious flowers for the garden: tulip bulbs, Casablanca Lilly, and Hydrangea. Kate was overwhelmed. Vida had also bought a virtual artist's studio for Anthony: canvasses, brushes, oil and acrylic paint, and an easel. He, too, was overwhelmed. Even Patrick had been blown away when he opened a box to find an expensive lens for his camera. The best gift Vida received was the unyielding smiles from each of them.

Vida enjoyed a single glass of whiskey, which she sipped regally. The early reviews on her book were positive. The fans responded with fervor at her latest twist. She was eighty-two years old, but she felt much younger, and her happiness was ageless. The snow subsided in the early afternoon, and the four of them sat back in the living room, enjoying the warmth of a nice fire and basking in the glow of a brilliant day.

a frame for flowers

"Thank you all for a perfect Christmas," said Kate.

Patrick, Anthony, and Vida responded with heartfelt smiles.

Kate couldn't keep herself from thinking of Frank and his cruel ability to ignore them completely. She hated to let thoughts of him sully a perfect Christmas. She hadn't told any of them about the battles with utilities leading up to the holiday that had nearly left them in a cold and dark house. Frank had called to get his name off the gas and electric accounts. When they told him they would need paperwork from both parties to change the name on the bills, he just told them to shut them all off. Kate would not have known if the gas guy hadn't shown up to cap the meter. It took her hours of battling on the phone and paying up bills to straighten it out.

"I just wish I could get rid of him, lock him up, and throw away the key," she thought to herself.

133

Frank spent Christmas at his parent's home. He brought Tricia with him, and everyone tried to act like everything was normal. Tricia drank too many beers and flirted a bit too openly with Leo, leading to a near fistfight in the family room of the Bruno house. Emilio was irate, and Theresa was distraught. It was a fairly standard Bruno Christmas.

134

As dusk settled in on Christmas, light flakes of snow fell from the gray sky. There was a knock at the door. It was Joe Bertucci and his father, who was not dressed as Santa, but did don a Santa's hat. Patrick met them at the door as the two men knocked off the cold and snow.

"It's Christmas now," said Patrick happily.

"Great to see you, Mr. Bertucci. Merry Christmas."

"Merry Christmas to you, too, Patrick. Damn, it's been a long time."

"It sure has."

"Ten years, pop, this jackass has been making dresses down in New York and barely a visit!"

"It's true. I mean, everything but the dresses thing. I actually make men's clothes."

"Oh yeah, that makes a difference," Joe said with a hoot.

"Well, you look great, Patty, really great. Merry Christmas," announced Mr. Bertucci with excitement in his deep voice, perhaps seeing his old friend Ted Kelley in the face of a grown Patrick.

"Get in here," said Kate, ushering them into the living room from the foyer. "What can I get you boys to drink?"

"I'll get it, Katie," said Patrick. "Beer, Scotch?"

"Beer me," said Joe.

"Scotch would warm me right up," howled Mr. Bertucci.

The group became a party in the living room as Patrick returned with the cocktails. They all sat around laughing and telling stories of years gone by, Vida and Anthony laughing along to the funny tales of Kate, Patrick, and Joe as youngsters. Joe had warned his dad about Kate, so they just ignored the whole subject, but Mr. Bertucci couldn't help reflecting on the two adults he best remembered as his best friend Ted's handsome young children.

"Well, your parents would be proud to see the two of you," he began. "They were great people, your mom and dad… and your grandparents," he said, turning to Anthony. "I miss them, but they are smiling. I am sure of it."

"To the Kelleys!" said Joe, assuring things didn't turn melancholy.

"To the Kelleys!" they all cheered, and Patrick kept the spirit going.

"One more toast for you, Detective. For solving the crime you were working on and putting the bad guy where he belongs!"

"I second that!" said Mr. Bertucci.

"Joey nabbed the rat before some technicality got him off!"

"What do you mean, Mr. Bertucci?" asked Anthony.

"All kinds of tricky legal stuff stop us from actually putting criminals in prison. Technicalities, crime scene mistakes, or stuff like the statute of limitations lets 'em walk free," said the elder Bertucci.

"What's a statute of limitations?" asked Anthony.

Joe chimed in with the answer, sensing his dad may have reached his Scotch limit.

"After a certain amount of time, you can't be held responsible for some crimes, even if they catch you."

"That doesn't seem fair," said Anthony, thinking about the impact.

"Sometimes life aint fair, Anthony," said Mr. Bertucci, "and that's a fact, but cheers to my boy. I'm proud of you, Joe!"

The people in the room clinked glasses and went on to cheer several things throughout the evening. They hung around for hours, talking and laughing. It was a day of good tidings.

135

Patrick headed home after a trip he thoroughly enjoyed. He was happy he'd made it back to Boston to be with family for the holidays and vowed to make it a tradition. He missed Kate and Anthony as soon as he boarded the plane, and he began plans to bring them down to New York in March, which already felt too far away. He committed himself to helping his sister get past the cancer and the divorce, to help her forge a new and better life. His work, which he had hardly thought of during the trip, seemed suddenly so irrelevant.

136

Kate's appointment with Doctors Lynch and Johnson was on Tuesday. There were only a few days left in the year, and Old Man Winter seemed to be trying to make a point. She listened to classical music as she drove alone across town to the cancer institute, and it had a soothing effect. Christmas's excitement hangover was ebbing to make way for the real hangovers of New Year, and the buzz was already building. Frank had never surfaced during Christmas. No gift for his son, not even a call, his cowardice redefining itself with each new low.

The hospital smells and sounds yanked her back quickly as the phantom feelings in her chest crept back in, boring their way to her center. She had become accustomed to seeing herself in the mirror after a shower, and though the emptiness in her blouse was still depressing, it was less alarming. The scars had turned a softer pink as the sutures faded, but what wasn't there was stark, part of her womanhood missing.

She made her way through the familiar halls, past patients who were just learning their fates or veterans who had the same steely gaze as she did. She reached the office door and paused for a deep breath before heading in. Like a principal's office in high school, this place did not lend itself to upbeat news.

a frame for flowers

Drs. Johnson and Lynch were in their respective offices when Kate entered, and she went to have a seat, but Dr. Lynch emerged before she could.

"Hi Mrs. Bruno," he opened.

"You know, Doctor, I decided I'm going to go by Kelley from now on."

Kate could tell the Doctor was confused, wondering if she meant Kelley as in a different first name. "That's my maiden name, Dr. Lynch. Kelley: K-e-l-l-e-y."

"Ahhh, I see. Okay.. Well then, how are you, Mrs.... or Miss Kelley?"

"I'm fine, Dr. Lynch," she said with a sarcastic laugh. "Some hair is growing back, just in time to zap it again!"

"Hmmm, yes. Well it does always grow back eventually," he reasoned. Just then Dr. Johnson peered out from her office.

"Hello, Kate. Why don't we meet in here?" she asked in her typically soothing tone.

Dr. Lynch and Kate filed into the office and took familiar seats. Kate's eyes moved around the room as Dr. Johnson began.

"Kate, we know you have been through a lot. This is terribly difficult. The fact is, we are only blunt for the patient's benefit, so we can get to the healing and not deliberate over the findings."

"I think it's dying," Kate said abruptly.

"I'm sorry?" replied Dr. Johnson, taken aback by the comment.

"Your Weeping Fig. I think it's dying."

"Oh," said Dr. Johnson, shifting uncomfortably in her seat and looking over at the small tree-like plant in the back corner of her office.

"Are you sure? It has been doing so much better since your advice."

"It likes the light, but they don't like being moved, and it has been in a different spot every time I've been in," stated Kate, suddenly glazed over and speaking in a monotone. "It also may be overwatered," she added.

"It has been losing lots of leaves, but I thought it was just the season."

"Yes, it will do that if it's unhappy, but it has no idea what season it is inside."

"What should I do then?"

"At some point, you just need to do nothing. Let it run its course," Kate said ominously, slowly craning her head to look into Dr. Johnson's soft brown eyes. "It will find the right place."

The doctor paused and stared at the plant, but recognized how inconsequential it was compared to the information she needed to share with Kate. She quickly snapped back to doctor and patient.

"I am sorry, Kate. Let me get back to you," said Dr. Johnson as Dr. Lynch leaned forward to speak.

"Mrs. Kelley, we have assessed, based on tests and the impact of your treatment cycles, that we need to re-stage the cancer. Regretfully, we are going to classify it as stage four. The cancer is moving, and we have detected cells in your liver and lymph nodes, as well as other locales."

"Okay." Kate swallowed hard. "So this is it?"

"No... no, we're just fighting a tougher battle."

"Is this the palliative treatment we spoke about?" Kate asked Dr. Johnson.

"Not necessarily. It's not good, Kate, but let's stay positive on this. You have done remarkably well,"

Dr. Lynch added, "You are one of the strongest cancer patients I've had. I've seen people beat this."

"Oh, I won't give up. Don't misconstrue my response as giving up."

"Capitulation is the worst thing you can do, Kate, so we are grateful to hear that," said Dr. Johnson. She stood and walked over to Kate's chair, and the doctor slowly knelt before her. "We're in this together."

"Not really," she said with stark honesty, "but I know what you're saying, and I thank you."

The three spoke for twenty minutes more about scheduling the next cycles of chemo, as well as the radiation treatments that Dr. Lynch would perform. They talked about what to expect, and the alternative steps and treatments to consider. They talked about keeping her alive. When they were done, Kate quietly left, and the doctors sat alone in the silence of sadness, the steady tick of the clock on the wall the only sound.

"She wasn't talking about the plant, you know," said Dr. Johnson, looking solemn.

Dr. Lynch ran back over the conversation that he had perceived as a delay tactic and recognized in the exchange exactly what Dr. Johnson had already picked up on.

"She knows she's terminal, doesn't she?" he asked his colleague.

"I believe she does," said Dr. Johnson, staring at the Weeping Fig. "I believe she does."

137

The drive home was a blur. All Kate could do is revisit the same film clips, the same themes that had haunted her for months.

"Why, God? Why me? What will happen to Anthony? How much time do I have? Will it hurt? What will it be like on the other side? Will I be able to watch over Anthony from wherever I go? Will I see my parents? Why does Frank always slither away untouched? Why can't it be him who dies? Why can't I find the courage to shoot him through the heart? Why, God?"

Each mundane street took on relevance as she toured short moments of her life on the way back to the house: the pages of neighborhoods that illustrated her years and memories. The bridge and river, the sky line, the harbor and its history, tufts of snow set atop the distinct architecture like so many winters before, now so important, so noticeable.

"We all know this day is coming, yet none of us seem prepared," she said to herself. It felt strange to think so much about something she really didn't want to know. She continued to speak to herself.

"I want to handle this well. Everyone appreciates someone who is brave in the face of death, so that has to be the way. I think it makes it easier on them. Mom never cried about Dad, and she never complained as she died. It has to be that way."

a frame for flowers

She thought about the fact that the doctors had never actually told her she was dying, and she tried to encourage the hopefulness. She may have driven for hours or minutes, but she recognized the familiar streets and turned where she ought, winding toward the house where they lived—the house where she feared she would soon die.

The Drive home
- No words.
- Flashbacks?
- Be strong!

138

That dark winter night, sitting in her room in the silence of her thoughts, Kate decided to kill Frank. The barrier of getting away with it had now been removed. The tale that Vida had written portending the empathy, channeled through the once unmovable Daisy McQueen, seemed so lucid. She still struggled with the moral dilemma: that murder was a sin. But this was about the alternatives: justice and the consequences. Frank had filed for a divorce, but she was now convinced she would not live long enough to see it through. He would inherit the life insurance, the house, and all their assets.

Her attorney, Tom Whalen, told Kate that Frank had taken up with Tricia from Star Builders. Frank had told Tom to "fuck himself," after he explained he could not represent them both and that Kate had approached him first.

"I hope you know that bitch will never pay you," were Frank's parting words, so Tom looked forward to helping Kate through the divorce. However much he wished to help, though, it would take at least a year under Massachusetts law, and that was if Frank cooperated. The will would have to be negotiated, as it was a joint document, and again it was unlikely she would get any cooperation.

Kate recognized that she was helplessly pinned between miserable and unthinkable. Frank was to get everything, and she was to be quietly buried. She thought about the hit and run from a decade earlier, Charles Edward Stuber who died alone and cold on a random early morning, left to die by Frank. She felt shame for letting it remain hidden all these years, protecting a killer.

Kate had thought about going to the police, to identify Frank's crime all these years later, yet she considered closely what Joe Bertucci had explained at Christmas, that maybe something like the statute of limitations would protect Frank. So he killed someone, lived a crooked, self-serving life, and gets rewarded. She felt empty to think these thoughts, but she was swarmed and overwhelmed. It's a rather easy to say "Life ain't fair" when you aren't facing your own mortality. The nightmares about Anthony's future plagued her, the thought of him being alone in the world with that monster of cruelty and neglect. She was afraid and petrified. It was no longer fantasy or whim; it was real. Her life was ebbing away, and she had to make choices she'd rather defer and delay, but the realities were all consuming. She rose from the bed and walked to the closet, where she once again knelt before the metal box, moving away the shoebox that covered it. She tumbled in the code to unlock the container and reveal the weapon, which she lifted and held easily balanced in her hand. So easy: just pull the trigger.

139

K ate's yard and garden was frozen, and the snow had hardened
to a crust, locking in the green beneath the white. Deeper still,
her flowers waited, stirring in their sleep in anticipation of the warmer
times that lay ahead, the warmth that would call them to burst forth
and claim a new season, to give hope to birds who would sing, telling
all that the sunny days had returned. The weeks of winter marched
forward into the darkest of January and February, as the bitter cold
of the Nor'easters licked the coast and punished those who would
not retreat.

Kate had once loved Frank, back when summers seemed to last
forever, but now the winter seemed to be half the year. She had planted
her bulbs as she had each year before, with the hope that a new sym-
phony of color would unfold. To be truly committed to a garden is
to work year round at it. The preparation for the following season
was paramount, and for a serious gardener, it was the differentiator.

"What would you do if you knew it was your last performance, your
last dance, your last everything?" she asked herself.

The setting up and organizing of the following spring during the
dark of winter was the key to delivering summer's presentation. Each
color and contour needed to match and accent the others, timing the

blooms, like notes on a score of music, to sustain the vista. The soil was critical, as was the environment that served as the foundation. To Kate, it wasn't just the presence of good ingredients, but also the absence of bad. For the average weekend gardener, weeds were a visible menace, but to Kate they were a virus, an unwanted scourge, a cancer whose role was to strangle and stifle the beauty. They were a negative presence that, if not eradicated beneath the surface, would spread rapidly and ruthlessly, choking the colors. Kate patrolled the yard like a sentry for early detection, pulling up and cutting to the base of the unwanted. She would never let weeds mar the beauty. That was just common sense.

140

Kate labored quietly through a second series of chemotherapy cycles, again ravaging her body and mind. The targeted radiation treatments burned lesions and delivered searing shots of pain. Vida was by her side as she battled on, forging to the front to face the shrapnel, often trembling to exhaustion, pale and drawn as she pushed on, leaning towards spring, leaning toward deliverance. Her hands, similar in appearance to her old friend's, clasped Vida's for hours through the sessions. Thirty hours later, the poison's storm would descend.

"You would think I'd get used to it!" said Kate through teeth that were now a slight shade gray.

Vida could scarcely hold back the tears at the sight of her beloved friend. Watching her fight on each session, the smile more strained as she just survived.

"Next one is the last one," said Vida with encouragement. "There is a light at the end of the tunnel."

"I thought they tell you to stay out of the light," Kate chided through a thin-lipped smile.

"Oh, sweetie," Vida said as her wrinkled eyes squeezed. "You are so amazing."

"Yes, but I think my modeling career is shot."

Sitting in the ward of battles at the Farber Institute with other stricken people all around, the sounds of machines doing their part, there was a long silence as the two women, friends separated by forty-four years, stared into each other's tired eyes. "I'm afraid."

"Me, too," replied Vida, as a tear dropped from her wise eyes.

"It's not so much fear. I just don't want to die," said Kate as Vida gripped her hand tighter. "I am gonna miss you. I am going to miss Anthony so much," Kate whispered.

"Try not to be afraid. It just burns up moments that can be spent happy. Be sure that the time you have left and the things you do, the things you leave behind matter. I am sorry to sound negative or be so blunt, but I am afraid of how much time we have."

"That is why I love you, Vida. "

"I love you, too."

The two women leaned into each other as they wept quietly for several minutes before Kate drew back and spoke with an abrupt purpose.

"Please promise to do something for me. If I do lose this battle, please find a way to bring Anthony and Patrick together. That is where he belongs… it is where he needs to be. Can you do that?"

"Of course."

"I am not going to give up, ever, but I am not going to be blind to nature's will, either. Things will happen the way they are supposed to."

The rest of the session was spent sitting quietly. Both women knew what was coming and how the chapter would finish: how peace would come again.

141

Kate picked out the day. She had already laid the groundwork with Patrick about the new treatments and how it looked improbable that she would join Anthony on the art exhibit trip to New York City in March. She set aside the money and booked Anthony's travel, allowing him to spend all of spring break with his uncle. The art show was March 13th to 14th, so her day would be March 15th, Monday: the beginning of the week. Everything was falling into place, assuring her this was destiny.

Kate would invite Frank over to sign one of the endless documents. She would get him to come over in the early evening, which by his schedule should be 5:30 on the nose. She would lure him into the living room. She would shoot him twice in the chest.

Kate was petrified of what it would look like to see a person shot, or how it would feel to pull the trigger, or whether, when it actually came time, she would have the strength mentally or physically to do it. Her head swirled with the conflict of the decision, and she found herself standing alone in the living room, walking through the logistics of a murder. Every bit of her life seemed more implausible and foreign with the events of the past six months. She tried to repress the guilt and convince herself of the justice. He had killed someone and never gave a damn about it. The vivid memories of his abuse fueled her to act out the event again and again, to practice. Conversations played out in her mind daily.

"You must keep your distance in case it takes multiple shots," she calculated. "I should check the gun and make sure it still works," she considered.

"No, then there is proof. Remember that everything can be evidence," she argued to herself. "Who cares? They're gonna know it was you," she justified.

"Oh my god, what if Joe is the arresting officer?" she considered as her mind skittered about. "Self-defense against him is very plausible. Maybe I could get him to hit me," she wondered.

"I don't know if I can do this... what if I miss," was usually how the conversation streams subsided.

Kate read Vida's book again, her now slim fingers carefully turning each page. This time she ingested it like a text book, studying for the final. The character had done many of these same things: talking to herself, plotting, practicing. She described exactly what to do and how she would likely feel doing it. It was like a manual.

It was so awkward to plot it out, and her willingness to continue defined the depths of her hatred for Frank, hatred that had been stacked neatly and methodically, brick by brick, for so many years. Despite everything in her life, her beliefs, her morals, the underpinnings provided the compass that had compelled her through the years. This was strong enough to overcome. It was, of course, bolstered by her belief that she was terminal and going to die, despite the doctor's tepid optimism. She believed in her soul that it was her calling to bring Frank to justice. It was so clear, that she feared she might be losing her sanity.

142

School did not get any easier for Anthony. Not surprisingly, the big art show did not provide a boost in popularity amongst his fellow students, but he no longer cared. He now walked with the expression of someone who knows a great secret. Strolling from class to class, he was insulated from the cruelty.

"What are you smiling at, faggot?" asked a faceless bully on his regular route. Anthony just moved forward.

"Everything's temporary," he recited to himself.

Anthony was consumed, however, worried about his mother whose recent chemotherapy sessions had broken her down harder than ever, leaving her sicklier than he'd ever seen her. Some days, he did not recognize her as she stood in the kitchen, so thin she seemed to be floating. He would ask regularly whether he should stay home, but his mother always smiled through the assurance that he needed to be at school. He believed his mother would heal soon, but he had dreamed about her death, and often awakened feeling desolate in his room.

In one such dream, he was lost in the woods. It was dark and cold, and he was alone as he strained to identify a distant light or hear a sound of humanity that could provide a path to follow. Wandering aimlessly as the forest grew thicker around him, he felt surrounded by the pointed needles of pine trees and brush. It was as if he were in an endless field of Christmas trees, and somehow the trees were growing, swelling around him, slowly constricting the path until his legs were buffeted and he was unable to move forward. He would pivot and move in any direction that provided an opening, but each led to a new impasse where he would again need to shift and re-direct. He made no progress. This imagery persisted until he shook himself awake.

Once at school, all he could think of was his upcoming trip to New York. He couldn't wait to see all the amazing things that his Uncle Pat had described, the wonders of the big metropolis. The trip was booked for the evening of the 12th of March, and he was going to be flying from Logan to LaGuardia, then spending nine days in the city with his Uncle Patrick. Mrs. Devoy was making the trip for the weekend to see the show, despite the school not paying for it.

"Are you excited?" she asked Anthony as the last of the students filed out for first period.

"Heck, yeah. This is so cool, and my Uncle Pat lives right in the city and is going to take me everywhere."

"Are you nervous?"

"Not really. I mean, I look at it like a free trip, you know? It's one thing to get some attention locally, but my stuff is not gonna really get noticed in a national exhibit."

"Well, it's healthy to be humble, but I think you're going to be surprised," she said with a smile. Anthony noticed a small smudge of her ruby-red lipstick on her front teeth.

"Thanks for all your support, Mrs. Devoy. You're a great teacher!"

She smiled. Several folks had come back years later to share such platitudes, but she had only heard that once or twice from a current student.

"I wish you nothing but the best, Anthony, you and your mom, and of course that kind and talented white-haired dame!"

"Ha! Vida Mudgett? She's the greatest, huh?"

"A special person… and we only get a handful in our lives."

143

Frank was told by his new attorney that it was unlikely he would get custody.

"I don't care. That doesn't mean shit to me," he replied cavalierly. "Just split up the stuff and tell me what my monthly nut is, okay? That's all I need you fo-ah."

The divorce papers were filed, but it took a period of separation to validate that both parties wished to finalize the forfeiture of marriage.

Theresa Bruno told her son he needed to get this approved through the church.

"Frankie, you gotta get this annulled through the church. They won't even let you get ya communion. Did you know that? You gotta ask the church to let you out of this mistake."

"Ya, I'll get it taken care of. Don't worry, ma."

"And don't ya go marrying this other Irish girl quick either."

"Please, ma. I'm nev-ah getting married again."

Life had gone on pretty normally for Frank. He had to stop by the house a few times to collect additional things, but he was moved into his new place and now spent his time with Tricia. The year had ended well, and Frank had managed to rake in more tax-free money. Despite claiming otherwise, Frank ended up attending the holiday

a frame for flowers

cocktail party where Jim Star told him he was retiring the following year and that he would be providing Frank with a buy-sell agreement, so they could finalize the deal for Frank to slowly buy Star Builders. Everything was looking up.

KATE

FRANK

Anthony

VIDA

Heaney

Bertucci + FATHER

PATRICK

TEACHER

FRANKS FAMILY

Jim star + Employees

Tricia

Tom whelen - Attorney

144

Frank took notice how horrible Kate looked when he visited. He suspected she was having trouble adjusting to the single life. When he went on a Wednesday to remove a file cabinet and a desk from the office, he spoke to her for the first time in weeks.

"You don't look too good, Kate. You gotta cold?"

"A cold? Jesus Christ, Frank. I always suspected you were not that bright, but is that an ignorant comment or just a typically cruel one?"

"What?" he asked indignantly.

"I have stage four cancer, Frank, not a cold. It doesn't just clear up!"

"You had that operation months ago. I thought you were better. It got worse?"

It dawned on Kate that her demise may seem convenient to him, so she avoided the truth.

"No, I am much better, as far as the cancer is concerned. It's just the medicine beats you up for a few months. I will fully recover in the spring."

"Yeah, see. Well, that's good."

"Yeah. It's great."

Kate stood with her arms crossed, leaning against the kitchen counter as Frank struggled to get the table out through the side door and over to his truck.

"How's the kid?" he asked, walking back in, dragging as much cold as he could with him.

"The kid… hmmmm, let's see who could that be. Oh, you mean your son, Frank?"

"You don't gotta be a bitch, Kate."

"You're right. How crass of me."

"Crass? What, do you just make this shit up? And I don't know what that means, as usual, so don't be a bitch. I'm just askin how Tony's holdin up."

"He's holding up fine. Are you almost done?"

"It's Wednesday. I got payroll tonight, so I gotta go."

They did not speak again. Kate stood silently and imagined shooting Frank as she watched him lug each piece out and load them into his truck. She imagined the surprised look on his face when he realized it was he that was going to be buried. When he finished tying down the furniture, he drove out of the driveway without acknowledgment, leaving the side door open, cold air streaming into the house.

"Enjoy being an asshole while you still can," Kate whispered, pulling the door shut.

145

March approached, and it appeared it would come in like a lion. The winter was holding firm with temperatures hovering in the single digits and the skies belching bad weather. Kate finished her last session, and Dr. Lynch waged a battle with his radiation. Some days he looked as exhausted as she felt. They also began testing an unproven medicine on Kate's liver, which had been under attack by the rapidly expanding cancer cells. They smiled at each other and spoke in terms of fighting the good fight, but they all knew they had reached the palliative treatment phase, and their actions were about extending life and minimizing pain and discomfort.

The doctors were visibly saddened at times. They were always professional, but they had developed a deep affinity for Kate and an admiration for her fortitude. She had always dealt with every piece of bad news with courage. She rarely cried or broke down, and was quick-witted and jovial amidst the often painful procedures. They also felt as though they were failing. It was against all the codes of the medical profession to blame yourself for your patient's declining health, but they wanted so much to help her… to save her.

146

Patrick could be impulsive at times. He bought a comfortable double bed, just for Anthony's visit, and set it up in a lofted section formerly used by a roommate. The loft was built atop steel girders and had likely been an office that overlooked the work floor in the old days. It was reached by a steel staircase and set about twelve feet above the floor. For a while, Patrick had used it as his own bedroom, but it seemed silly for him to walk up to a bedroom when he lived alone, and he had abandoned it years ago for a bed on the main floor. He figured he was long overdue for guest accommodations. More than that, he really wanted Anthony to feel at home. He had sketched out a fun itinerary.

Patrick also planned to take Anthony to the school nearby. He couldn't help thinking how cool it would be if Kate moved them down to New York. Kate could sell the house and get a place in the neighborhood, and Anthony could finish school in an environment that would cultivate his talents. He had been appalled when Anthony shared stories of the bullying and the fact that he had hidden his artwork from virtually everyone. Patrick remembered feeling closeted by his creative side in a world that seemed to favor sports over arts. He had to run away to be himself, and that was not something he wished for his nephew.

147

Despite missing the holiday rush, Vida's latest Daisy McQueen mystery was flying off the shelves. The winters were the toughest time of year for Vida. She was a tough bird, but most people her age, if they were still alive, had moved to Florida or at least wintered there. The cold was hard on her skin and amplified the aches and pains her years had accumulated. Worst of all, though, the cold kept her inside. She could not take her walks or wander down to join Kate in the garden, things that made life worth living.

Vida hobbled down to Kate's every day she could, which depended mostly on the weather. Some days Kate would drive up to get her, but recently Kate was getting frailer and could not stay awake for very long. She slept much of the time or drifted in and out on her makeshift bed in the living room on the first floor. Sometimes Kate would not make it upstairs at all. On more than one occasion, Anthony told Vida that he had to carry his mom up to bed. He remarked at how light she was to lift up and how strange it felt to tuck his mother into bed. When the young man described the scene, it made Vida cry.

148

It was Monday March 1st when Dr. Johnson admitted to Kate what she already knew.

"You should get your things in order" was the standard language she expected to hear when Kate got to the doctor's office at the cancer center.

Dr. Marchand was there. She knew exactly what it meant. "Hi, Kate," he said, almost immediately emotional.

"It's okay, Dr. Marchand," she said, standing like Molly Pitcher as the three doctors assembled slowly before her, standing in the office where the war had waged for many months.

"We are sorry, Kate. We have done all we can," began Dr. Lynch, who seemed near tears.

Dr. Johnson could not contain herself and stepped forward for a deep hug, pulling Kate's weakened body close. "We fought so hard, but I can't tell you it's okay anymore. I am so sorry."

Kate had no reference, but none of these doctors had ever experienced this with a patient, not to this level. Each had been overrun by emotion, by the stark reality that this woman in their care was almost certainly going to die. They discussed the time left, the medicines that could make it tolerable, the eventual hospice, and the need to make arrangements for her estate beyond her life.

It was overwhelming for Kate, despite knowing all her life this would happen, despite suspecting for the past six months it was possibly approaching, despite believing for the last thirty days that it was upon her. She wept at the reality that her life was drawing to a close.

149

The final days leading to March 15th were spent as happily as they could be. Kate mustered all her strength to gather Vida every day, and they had long conversations about so many things. They drew pictures of the garden, listened to music, and watched movies that made them laugh.

Kate sat down with Tom Whalen and told him most of the truth. She explained she was sick, and it was prudent to make certain her things were in order should she get sicker. She did embellish when explaining to Tom that Frank was getting increasingly erratic and threatening, and that she was concerned for her and Anthony's safety. She shared some of the trials over the years, with Frank's abuse physically as well as mentally. Tom asked if they should speak to the police. She suggested they hold off.

"He's a lot of bark," she told her attorney with a nervous smile.

"Well, you let me know, Kate," he said.

She also spent every minute possible with Anthony and actually took him up on the offer to stay home from school a couple of days. They talked energetically about the future and quite a bit about the upcoming trip to New York.

"I am so psyched, but totally sad you can't go. I mean, I understand you're not feeling great, but I think you've looked better lately. Probably still time to reconsider," said Anthony wishfully.

"I wish I could, baby. I will be there in spirit, like I always am. You know that, right?"

"Yeah, of course, mom."

"I love you, honey, and I'm so proud of you," she said, staring into his handsome eyes. "I am sorry for your father, but without him, I don't have you, so it must have been fate."

"He doesn't matter to me. He is just a donor, as far as I'm concerned. I know it's wrong, mom, but I haven't missed him one bit. Not for one second."

Kate looked at him reassuringly.

"I don't even miss Grandma and Grandpa or any of the Brunos. I know it's wrong. Am I going to hell?"

"I think God is so much bigger than any of us give him credit for. I'm pretty sure God knows the whole story and that the line between right and wrong is a bit more blurry then we… than the church thinks."

"You really believe God sees everything?"

"Absolutely, and that means he saw all the things your dad did, all of it."

"Even the hit and run?"

Kate was instantly stunned to silence.

"I know about it, Mom."

Kate did not know what to say. She felt a twinge of guilt that it was a secret she had kept, but she was shocked to consider for the first time that it was a secret her son had maintained as well.

"How?" she asked.

"He told me, drunk one night, like a year ago."

"He told you?" she asked, betraying her surprise. "He told you the man died?"

"Yeah, and he actually said the guy deserved it. Those were his words. He said he shouldn't have been out in the snow like that, and that people that old shouldn't drive. He said he tried to help, but the

412

guy was already dead, because he was old and it was his time. He also said that he tried to stop the truck and it wasn't his fault. Yeah… he told me everything."

"Oh my God, I didn't—" Kate reached up and rubbed at her temples, as if it would jog free an explanation. "What did you say to him?"

"Nothing, I never said a word. I just hope God sends him to hell for it."

Kate knew that despite any DNA that ran through his body, her son would grow up to be a good man. It made her smile to look upon him, a young man with so much potential and such a bright future. Everything would be okay.

150

On Thursday, March 11th, Kate called her brother Patrick to go over the plans. Anthony would board the flight, and Patrick would meet him on the other side. Kate was calm as she went over the details carefully with her brother.

"One more time to be sure. Anthony's flight lands at 5:40, and you can meet him right outside security of B Terminal at probably 5:50 or so. He will have checked his bags. They are kind of over packed, but I wanted to make sure he had enough clothes to get by for the whole trip."

"I will be there, Kate. Don't worry!"

They discussed all the specifics, and Patrick shared his lengthy list of places he planned to take Anthony. Kate could tell he was very excited for the adventure.

"It's gonna be awesome. Just me and Anthony. Man, I wish someone had done this for me when I was young. It is so cool you're letting him come, Katie. I don't mean to be too dramatic, but it will change his life, you know?"

"I agree, and I hope it does. Anthony had such a good time with you when you were here. He needs a father figure. I mean, you know Frank never was good to him or for him."

414

"Yeah, I figured. God, I just wish I had done this earlier, realized this potential earlier."

"It is what it is, but there's time to make it right."

"For sure."

They talked and talked as conversation drifted to memories.

"Remember when Mom and Dad gave me that magic kit for Christmas one year?"

"Yeah, you made me watch your terrible tricks over and over, then tried to convince me to be your assistant!"

They laughed as they recollected performing a magic act for an audience of stuffed animals: Kate in her sparkled-red leotard and her Irish dance shoes, Patrick in his top hat and long-tailed coat.

"I loved that thing. Best gift ever. I knew even then I would not play hockey. I knew I would do something creative."

"You're lucky to have known. I never knew what I wanted to be."

"Really?"

"Well, I mean, I knew I wanted to be a mom. I knew I wanted to be a good person, and I pictured myself in a house with a family, and I pictured having a perfect garden, so I guess looking back, I did have a plan after all."

"Well, like you said, there is still time."

"Hmmm, you're right, and I am going to do my best with it. I love you, Patty."

"Thanks Kate. I love you, too!"

Kate cherished his voice and held his image in her mind: her smiling and happy younger brother in his top hat, in his hockey uniform, in his Red Sox pajamas on Christmas morning, his kindness, his creativity. She gathered his life in her mind, and it felt so warm. She knew he was okay, and that helped.

151

Vida was concerned about Kate driving in her weakened state, so she rode with her and Anthony to the airport on Friday, March 12th, after school. It was a sunny day and a bit warmer as they parked in the concrete garage. Kate and Vida walked Anthony all the way to the security checkpoint, and it felt short in time, but long on their bodies. Kate watched every step that Anthony took as he strode happily forward.

"Do you have everything?" she asked her son.

"Yep."

The walk seemed eternal as they passed countless blurred people hurrying through their lives. She held emotions in check as she held Anthony one last time before he left, his smile topping off her confidence. Lingering in embrace, she felt her son's strong heart beat through her frame.

"I will call you when I get there."

"Okay, good," Kate said, releasing him.

Anthony went off to join the line and began the shuffle forward. Kate and Vida retreated to the pale-gray wall of the terminal to watch him through.

"I will be there with you the whole time," Kate cried out to him.

"Okay, thanks, ma!" he replied, a little embarrassed by the strangers in earshot who flanked him in line.

"He's beautiful," Kate whispered to Vida.

"He's part of you," she whispered back.

Vida knew this was hard for Kate. She sensed that her friend was envisioning her final goodbye to her only son. Vida leaned in to wrap her arm around Kate's waist.

"He's going to have a great time."

"He's going to have a great life," she replied softly, but surely.

152

Kate spent the available hours of Saturday and Sunday arranging the house, writing notes, listening to her favorite songs, holding pictures, and thinking. She had planned everything out, and she was ready. She confirmed with Frank that he could stop by on Monday at 5:30 to sign the papers. She had taken the pistol out of its metal box and familiarized herself with its shape and feel. Point and squeeze.

Kate prayed every day. She spoke with God about her life, she prayed for Anthony's future, for Patrick to have the strength to provide support during the aftermath and to be his family after she passed. She prayed for forgiveness for the things she'd done and the thing she planned to do.

The sun blazed bright in a clear blue sky, and on Sunday, it was warmer than it had been in three months. The remnants of snow that had long crusted on the roof and ground melted slowly. Water dripped steadily like tears from the corners of the house, winding down small icicles then falling to the earth, drops of water that would seep into the ground and find the seeds below.

153

Kate received a message on Saturday after the first day of the New York art exhibit from an ecstatic Anthony, who had received an award for his triptych.

"Hi mom! You are not going to believe this." He paused for effect, then continued. "I got a gold ribbon at the event," he shrieked into the phone. "Uncle Pat took me to a fancy restaurant to celebrate, and he said it's really a big deal. Can you believe it? I am so happy, mom, but I miss you. I hope you're feeling okay. I am so happy," he repeated as his voice sailed up and down, his words a song in her mind.

Kate was flying in the clouds for hours after hearing the joy in her son's voice.

On Sunday afternoon, Kate tried Patrick's apartment to hear how the art show ended up, but she too got the machine.

"Hi, Anthony. I hope you enjoyed another great day. You sounded so happy yesterday, and it made me smile all night. I am so overjoyed for you and not surprised at all that others are seeing the beauty you create. I am sorry I missed you. I love you, sweetie."

154

For much of the day, Vida visited, and they took advantage of the warmer weather and wandered into the backyard to view the dark soil that now revealed itself from beneath the winter's coat. They spoke about the arrangements, about where the flowers would grow and how things were meant to be.

"It is going to be beautiful," said Kate with a calm confidence.

"There is no doubt," responded Vida, steadying herself on the rapidly softer ground.

"This is something I will miss so much, being in the garden. Do you think there is anything like this after we go, Vida?"

"I think so. I think heaven contains what we cherish the most. It's all there. I don't really think we float around with wings and harps, mind you, but I believe this is there. Just seems there is too much to us, for us to simply be worm's food."

"What about paying for the things we did wrong?"

"That is about forgiveness."

"From God?"

"Maybe, but I think it is equal parts from yourself and those around you as well. We all do bad things, or at least things we regret, certainly things considered wrong in the eyes of God."

"Huh. Yeah." Kate sighed.

"The key is the forgiveness. I forgave Hank for his indiscretions, and I believe he died at peace and free."

Kate stood over the patch of dark ground, envisioning the brilliance of its future. Remembering where she had carefully placed and planned each bulb and seeing clearly exactly how it would burst forth from the earth, each one to play their role in the bigger picture.

Kate wobbled a bit as she hit a soft patch of earth. Vida noticed. "Let's head in before the two of us topple over!"

"I could stay out here forever," said Kate with a smile as she nodded to Vida. The two locked arms to walk back in.

Kate had not told Vida about her dire prognosis or even the relative certainty with which the doctors had forecasted her time. She had shared that she was terminal, but never the brevity of time she had left.

155

Kate told Vida she had errands all day Monday and could not get together, so Vida stayed on into the evening. The two women shared supper together, enjoying a wonderful piece of Kate's favorite fish and a nice glass of red wine. They talked until late, in a way that only the closest of friends can. Vida sensed the time was limited, perhaps for both of them. They spoke endearingly about all the good parts of life and steered clear of the darker things. Kate walked Vida up the street to her home after dark, and though the cool of evening had descended, it was still the warmest in months.

They paused at Vida's porch to say goodnight.

"Thank you for a wonderful time," said Vida.

"The pleasure has been all mine!"

"I love you, Katie."

"Thanks, Vida. I love you, too. You are a great soul, and my life is better because you're in it."

"Try not to worry about Anthony. He will be great."

Kate could not contain herself at this statement, and tears slipped from her eyes. She leaned in and embraced her friend, gripping her as tightly as her starved muscles could muster. "I am not afraid," she whispered to Vida.

"Don't be," Vida replied, as she held her like a child.

They lingered on the porch for twenty minutes more, then separated.

156

It occurred to Kate that remaining calm and focused was the key to achieving something that seemed impossible to endure. It was how she'd approached childbirth, which had also frightened her so many years ago. The shooting of someone seemed to be that type of overwhelming scenario. She thought about the heroes in war, or the cool demeanor of seasoned bank robbers, the poise of a star athlete at the free throw line when the game is on the line. They all looked calm, and so she sensed that was the key: bury the emotion, the fear, or even pain, and focus on doing what you must to achieve the outcome.

It was Monday and the warmest day in months, even warmer than the previous day. The sun no longer melted the snow, but instead penetrated the moist earth. She was sure it was stirring the bulbs in the ground.

The hours of the day moved neither slow nor fast, and she noticed the motions of the birds, the taste of warm-buttered toast, the smell of good coffee, the sounds of the music, and the colors of the house. She again held the pictures of her loved ones, and images of a life worth living drew tears of joy and sadness to her face. She prepared with each breath.

Kate took the pistol from the metal box one last time. It was warm as she carried it down to her makeshift bed in the living room. She wore a white nightgown, which she had put on after showering that morning. She took her medications and even some extra pain medicine to make it easier. She placed the pistol carefully on the small, wood-carved table that sat just out of reach from her blanketed couch. The weapon lay alone, except for a small box of tissue on the round wood surface.

As the hours passed, she prayed and finished another of the notes she had been recently writing in the event she died. Everything had to be ready, as it was sure to get crazy after. As the day wound down and the warm sun slowly began its descent, she settled into her bed in the living room. The warm weather had her retrieve the flag from the basement, and she had also retrieved the dark blue wool Navy blanket from her father's trunk where it had rested with the flag over the winter. One last dose of medicine and the shot of whiskey she needed to pull this off had her sitting awash in warmth beneath her father's blanket, staring at the clock on the wall. She knew Frank would pull into the driveway at 5:30 precisely, just missing Mr. Heaney. Then it would be the opening and shutting of doors as he made his way from the truck through the side door of the kitchen, then eventually back into the living room to confront her.

Kate had checked the weapon earlier to confirm it was capable of firing and had wiped it clean to assure it was as shiny as it could be. She wanted to be sure he saw it.

As the clock clicked to 5:30, the last of the sun flickered away and the doors opened and closed as was expected. She heard the footsteps, and her entire life seemed to parade through her mind. She held strong, despite the pain and stress. She thought of everything from the night they met to the night he killed Charles Edward Stuber, to the first time he had hit her, to the endless cruelty to her son—the light of her life—and Frank hitting him. She begged God for the strength to make it through this exchange. She felt that strength slowly draining from her body as Frank marched confidently into the room, his dirty boots clomping across the wooden floor.

"Theya you ah. What the fuck ah you hiding in heya for?" he asked with his typically brutish delivery. "I'm not hiding," said Kate, calmly tucked beneath her blanket.

"Okay, so where are the pap-ehs?"

"I decided I am not going to sign them," she said casually.

"What," he said, clicking quickly but expectedly into the first phase of irritation.

"You heard me. I decided to not sign them."

"Is this some kind of joke?"

"No, Frank. You're the joke."

And with that, the snorting and fidgeting began as he started to pace left and right in the room. His nervous, annoyed laugh accompanied his twitching.

"Kate, look. No time fa bullshit he-ya. Stop playing your little power trip, get your skinny, pale ass up out of ya nap time and sign the fuckin papehs!"

Frank's voice rose with each word, but Kate sat quietly, smiling at him.

"What's that stupid fuckin grin for? Are you kidding me, I'll smack it right off ya face!" He paced the room, aggressively rubbing his hands and face.

"Stop huffing and puffing, you fool," she said with a wry smile.

"What, have you lost yo-ah mind?" he barked, now amplified to a full-blown rage.

Kate let him twist in the wind as he paced the floor, sputtering insults and profanity at the full capacity of his furious lungs. He stomped his feet and knocked items to the floor in spite, even loudly shattering a picture frame.

Kate sat softly laughing to instigate him further.

"I will fuckin kill you, bitch!" he screamed, but Kate calmly stared at the shiny pistol that sat on the round wood table until he took notice.

When he did, he froze in his tracks like an animal in the cross-hairs. He stood, instantly sensing he was in danger, but perhaps still convinced he could get free.

"Oh, what's that fo-a? Huh? Don't just stare at it. If you got any guts, pick it up. Come on, bitch. You know you want to. You have aaaalways wanted to."

Kate simply kept her eyes fixed on the weapon, but made no move to reach for it. Frank was about ten feet away, and she was sure she could reach it and fire before he got to her, yet she did not move. She looked up for a moment at him, then past him through the front windows and out to the street where the streetlight flickered on. It was time.

As Kate began to move, she first sat up slightly and painfully in her bed, drawing her right arm out from beneath the blue blanket, her thin fingers slashing the air as they shot towards the table. Frank made his move, lunging forward toward the table and covering the distance quickly. Kate was sure she had the drop on him and was inches from the gun's black handle when she suddenly and unexpectedly stopped, pulling back slightly, then averting to clutch a tissue from the box that lay just beside the weapon. She winced as she slowly returned her hand to her side. Frank was now standing above her, panting, considering how foolish he must look, having thought she was going for the gun.

"Oh, and by the way, take that godforsaken gun out of here," she said casually as his eyes darted furtively from her face to the pistol and back again.

Frank was a bit disoriented.

"What?" he asked to clarify what he thought he heard.

"Take the gun, Frank. It makes me sick, having it here."

"Huh, yeah, okay," he said, feeling insecure.

He laughed nervously as he spoke, picking up the pistol and pressing his hand around its familiar grip.

"Jesus Christ, Kate, I thought you were reaching for the damn thing. What the fuck… you ah fuckin… Jesus." He muttered on, not sure what to make of it all. "I'll tell ya… You're fuckin lucky you didn't try that shit, cuz I woulda shot you dead right here."

"Look, I am. I'm just gonna leave," he said.

"Good," she replied curtly. "Don't let the door hit you on the way out."

a frame for flowers

Still perplexed, Frank resorted to overcoming the embarrassment of having sprinted across the room to stop his wife from getting a tissue. "I'm leavin, but I… we're gonna sign the pap-ahs, you understand. You enjoy this for now, but we'll see what happens."

"Frank, I am sure you will get all you deserve, whether I sign the papers or not. Just take your gun and go," she said, straining a smile.

"Fuck you!"

Those were his last words as he stomped back out through the kitchen, his thick mitts clutching the pistol as he tucked it into the back of his pants. The doors opened and closed, then gravel spit as he rumbled back down the driveway.

Kate's face looked not happy or sad… just satisfied.

157

Kate sat for a good thirty minutes, until she began to feel faint. Then she pulled aside the blue blanket and attempted to rise. Kate's white nightgown was a thick ruby red from the waist down, and she reached to her side to clutch the wound that sent pain messages through the haze of medication she had ingested. The blood continued to flow from the wound as she clutched at the couch and pushed herself to her feet. As she rose, blood splashed to the wood floor from small pools that had accumulated in the folds of her gown and bedding. She had sat wounded for over an hour. She bled out as she expected, her blood thinned from the chemo poisons.

Each step was strained as she moved slowly away from her resting place, a thick train of blood trailing her thin and weak frame. She held her chin high as she floated through the kitchen and towards the side door, each step an effort as the blood flow sapped her strength, rendering her in a twilight of consciousness, moving only on instinct. The pain medicine made it tolerable, but she knew her life ebbed out with each step, so she pressed on.

As she pushed open the side door and turned toward the backyard, the evening's air felt pleasantly warm on her skin, though the cement path was cool beneath her bare feet. She made each step with purpose, and as her hand slid open the white-slatted gate, she drifted forward into the yard, the small sprigs of grass tickling her feet and pushing up through the spaces between her toes, lifting her with their tiny strength and urging her forward. She floated on, reaching the six-by-twelve-foot rectangle of fecund soil eager to give birth to the colors of life that spring promised each year.

Kate knelt down before the bed. Her knees felt the warmth of her blood mixing with the cooler moisture of the grass. She folded her hands and prayed to God. She spoke to her son and asked for his forgiveness. As she felt her body slowly drain of its warmth, she leaned forward and lay her body down softly into the earth, the ground welcoming her. She closed her eyes and said her final goodbye to a life worth living.

As the sun rose on a Tuesday that would again bring warmth to the city of Boston, its rays fell onto the quiet backyard to discover the still body of Kate. She was gone, but a sprout too early for any season pushed up from the ground like the finger of an angel reaching to touch her, to let her know she was forgiven.

158

There was a swarm of activity surrounding the white house on the hill, and the flicker of red-and-blue lights bounced off the white colonial and ricocheted to neighboring homes. There were throngs of black-shoed people milling about, heads down, taking notes, huddling for conversations, pointing, taking photos, and crouching on the ground, looking at and marking things with little flags.

Detective Joe Bertucci was on the scene, and from the moment he had gotten the call, he had a pit in his gut. On arrival, his worst fears were realized. This tough cop and good man had to duck into a bathroom to hide his emotions upon seeing Kate's body in the garden. He cried quietly as he fantasized about having saved her, protecting her from this outcome—and, even for a moment, about spending his life with her. Yet now he faced her death, her murder, and it was shocking to see her limp body, despite having encountered dozens of lifeless bodies in his time.

Joe knew the only thing left to do was to do what he did best: hold the person responsible for this crime accountable and put the guilty person away for the crime.

"You the lead on this one, Tucc?" a uniformed cop asked Joe.

"Yes," he replied, not even noticing he'd not been addressed on a crime scene as "detective."

"You okay?"

"Yeah," he replied blandly, pretending to flip through a small notebook he clutched in one hand. He cleared his throat.

"The victim is a very good friend's sister."

"Oh God, I'm sorry, Joe."

"Yeah, thanks. What we got for evidence?" he asked, snapping back to duty as they moved from the body in the backyard, following the clear trail of blood back into the house and ending at the couch in the living room.

"Okay. So, as you know, the female victim is the resident and owner: Katherine Kelley Bruno. Thirty-seven years old, died of a single gunshot wound."

The officer took a step forward, pointing to the couch where a large blood stain marred the couch, then bent his knees slightly and mocked pointing a pistol at the estimated location of the shooting. "It looks like the shooter popped her at fairly close range as she lay or sat on the couch. Not much of a shot: only hit her in the lower left side of the abdomen."

"One shot or just one hit?"

"Well, we only uncovered one shot, already pulled the bullet from the couch. We're pretty sure it's a .38 pistol slug," said the cop, holding up a clear plastic bag with the small chunk of a bullet in it.

"Any witnesses?"

"Oh yeah, multiple people saw the husband here. We got new tire tracks in the driveway that we will need to match, of course, but we believe to be from his truck. Pretty sure we got his footprints in the house. Thanks to the warmer weather, we got some real good tracks."

"Really? Jesus. Let's get a warrant together for this guy."

"Oh yeah, we're on it already, Detective."

"Good. What else you got?"

"Another witness, this guy outside giving a statement right now says he was walking his dog and heard the whole thing: an argument, yelling, stuff getting smashed."

"Is he credible?"

"That's the thing. This is the same guy who helped us nab a thief out this way a while back. One of the local beats kind of knows the old-timer. He's a bit of a busybody perhaps, but yeah. Solid witness."

"No weapon, though?"

"Not yet."

A photographer entered the rooms and began to snap pictures, interrupting the detective and officer.

They walked to the front window of the living room.

"The dog walker says he could see and hear the husband in this room through this window," said the cop, using a pencil to pull aside the thin, see-through curtain.

"Hmmm."

"Looks pretty clean, If we have a motive and no alibi for the husband," stated the cop.

"Yeah, well, I've seen cleaner scenes fall through," said Detective Bertucci, turning to the uniformed officer. "We need the weapon."

Just then a second uniformed cop entered.

"Detective, we got the guy. Picked him up at work. Arresting officer says they got the gun, a .38 silver snubnose. It was in this idiot's glovebox! Guy just goes to work. What an asshole."

"Hmmm," said Detective Bertucci, biting into his lip.

"Find out where we're booking him, and I can head there."

"Will do," said the officer, quickly exiting the room.

Joe Bertucci put his hand on the uniformed officer's shoulder and applied enough pressure to get the man's attention.

"I want every statement, every drop of blood, every speck of evidence on this scene processed flawlessly."

"Sure, Detective, of course."

Joe Bertucci said nothing else as he stared back at the blood-stained couch. So much blood there. It indicated that Kate had bled on the couch for quite a while and then exited the home.

"Why would she do that? If you could reach the yard, you could reach the phone. Why not call for help?" he asked himself. In his mind, something didn't add up.

159

Frank went to work, and the suddenly warmer weather was a good development. Star Builders had nine new home builds already set, and he was sure this would be the best year yet for him. He was still hacked off at his exchange with Kate the evening before, but it didn't really matter much. He would get the divorce eventually, and he was free now to do whatever he wanted.

Tricia was late to work and apologized with an impish allusion to sex. He didn't really care. He was thinking about breaking it off with her. He could just hire somebody new. It would be easier. Jim Star had only been coming in a couple days a week since the first of the year, and Frank was actually sitting in his chair stretched out and thinking when he heard the police come in the front door.

"We're looking for Frank Bruno, ma'am. Is he here?"

"No, he ain't here," Tricia responded defensively.

Frank got up from the desk and marched out of the office. He was the soon-to-be proprietor, and he had no reason to fear the cops.

"I'm heya, I'm heya," he said, marching confidently out of the office and past the long desk. He reached out to shake the one of the two officers's hands: the man of the male-female duo.

"What can I do foh ya?"

"Are you Frank Bruno?"

"Ya."

"Mr. Bruno, I'm Officer Glynn and this is my partner, Officer Thomas."

"Yeah… how ya doin?"

"Can you tell us where you were last night?"

"Me? What the fuck is this?"

"Please just answer the question," said Officer Sharon Thomas, her forearm resting on her holstered weapon.

"Ahhh, okay, Kojack. I was… let's see. I was at home doing the payroll for this company of which I am part owner."

"Were you anywhere else, anywhere before that?"

"Last night? No!"

"So you did not go to your house in Dorchester last night? We have witnesses that claim they saw you there."

"Oh yeah, well, that was like 5:30. Not exactly last night. Yeah, I was the-ya. Seriously, what is this?"

"So you confirm you were there?"

"That's what I just said. So what, I own the fuckin place."

"Do you also own a gun, Mr. Bruno?"

"I got lots of guns."

"You went to see her," chimed in Tricia.

"Stay outta this," Frank said and continued with the cops. "What about the guns? Seriously, what ah you getting at?"

"Do you have a .38?"

"A .38? Yeah. It's in the cah, and I got a permit."

There was a pause as the two officers briefly conferred.

"Don't say nothing else, Frankie. Somethins fucked here," said Tricia.

"Mr. Bruno, we're gonna need to take you downtown with us to answer some more questions."

"I think I want my lawyer," said Frank, realizing the cops were serious.

"That is your right under the law," said the female officer as she reached for her handcuffs.

160

Vida got up a little late that Tuesday, and she could feel the warmer air outside as she went about her business getting ready for the day. She planned to walk down to Kate's after a small breakfast.

The review for her book had come out in the Boston Globe the day before, and it was perhaps the first truly glowing critique she'd gotten in her career as a writer. She looked forward to sharing it with Kate. The critic was particularly favorable to the plot twist, where Daisy McQueen, the "relatively predictable character" had "found a personality" and "delivered compassion" in a "truly plausible murder plot." It was perhaps a backhanded compliment, but the critic said it was a "thoroughly enjoyable read," and they "looked forward to the next adventure."

The overdue write-up made Vida smile. She had waited a long time to get a little recognition from those folks.

"It's a shame I am not going to write another one," she said to herself, pulling the front door closed behind her and heading down the street toward Kate's. Vida was still several houses away when she saw the cluster of emergency vehicles in front of Kate's address. She felt a shiver and feared immediately she had lost her friend. She stood, frozen, staring from afar, picturing Kate's pretty face. Slowly she bowed her head to pray.

161

When the news reached Patrick, it came directly from his old friend, Joe Bertucci. Joe was emotional when he explained that Kate had been found dead and that it was almost certainly a murder, but kept himself together.

"I'm so sorry, Pat," Joe said, grinding back the tears. "We will hold the person responsible for this and lock em up forever. I promise you."

"Why? Who would do this?" Patrick sobbed loudly through the phone. "Kate's just getting better. She is getting healthy again. Why would anybody hurt her?"

"Pat," he said, followed by a tensioned pause. He knew he wasn't supposed to discuss what he was about to say. "We're pretty positive Frank did it. We already picked him up, and he is being held without bail."

There was silence on the phone as the words seeped into Patrick's mind. Frank, this rancid man he had tolerated all those years, the person he knew had knocked around his sister and thrashed his nephew. The thought of her dying at his hand was too much to bear.

Patrick fell to his knees in the New York loft and moaned loudly, a frightful wail like a siren of pain that pierced Anthony's ears and drew him running to Patrick's side, panicked. Awash in misery and helplessness,

a frame for flowers

Patrick broke the news to the young man. Anthony was stunned to silence. Just days before, he had felt such great joy for the recognition at the art exhibit, and now his whole world collapsed around him in a crushing canvas of darkness. The thought of never speaking to his mother again beat against the side of his brain: the thought of never holding her, never hearing her, never seeing her. He was thrust to swift misery and sadness, made only tolerable by Patrick's presence in the same, dark place.

He did not yet know she had been murdered by his father. Patrick did not have the strength to tell him. The two huddled on the smooth cement floor of Patrick's loft, weeping as the pipes of the radiators whistled loudly and overheated the space. Their sadness was incalculable.

162

Walter Heaney gave his testimony at the trial, calm and precise like the engineer he was. The air in the courtroom was thick and dusty. Walter had worn his favorite brown tweed sport coat that day and had shaken hands with half the people in the room by the time he took the stand. He identified Frank Bruno in the courtroom as the man he had seen that evening. He had easily recounted the timelines that matched the forensics and placed Frank at the scene, which Heaney described with dramatic detail, including hearing a heated argument between Mr. Bruno and the victim.

Walter relayed earnestly to the court that he had been witness to Mr. Bruno's bellicose nature for many years. Describing his own experience with the briar-tempered man, he recounted seeing Mr. Bruno leaving in a hurry that evening, screeching out of the driveway and down the street at considerable speed. He detailed Frank's big, white truck with great specifics, even knowing the brand of tires on the vehicle.

When asked in cross-examination if he had heard a gun go off, Mr. Heaney explained he heard lots of loud, banging noise and could not be sure whether or not he heard the actual sound of a gunshot, but he recited specific words heard above the din: curse words and expressions of anger between the two. He described hearing the crash of glass amidst the exchange. The attorney pointed dramatically to the enlarged photograph pinned to a corkboard: evidence from the crime scene showing the shattered picture frame found on the floor just feet away from the couch where Kate Bruno had been shot, forensics proving the bullet had passed through her and into the couch in the room they had argued in. The attorney made clear that there was no way Mr. Heaney could have known about the broken picture frame, and the noise he heard matched the event as it unfolded.

The defense lawyer tried to discredit Walter as an old man with a faltering memory, but Heaney's recall was shockingly astute, and his detailed answers captivated the jury. There was little doubt Mr. Bruno could be placed at the scene of the crime in a timeframe that coincided with the coroner's time of death and estimation of the gunshot wound. He also served as a character witness, relaying years' worth of belligerent behavior from the chronically tempestuous man.

COURT ROOM
MR. Heaney

163

Joe Bertucci took the stand. He had to recuse himself from the investigation to avoid any conflict of interest, but a seasoned homicide detective taking the stand provided the prosecution potency and he knew it. Joe remained connected throughout the entire investigation, assisting the detective in charge. He was a convincing witness on the stand, testifying about the fight he had witnessed and the guns he had seen. He validated the victim's brother Patrick's testimony about Frank's history of abuse by explaining how he had been asked to check in on Kate when his childhood friend Patrick Kelley expressed concern about his sister.

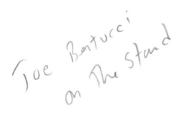

164

ODNA on The Stand

Nurse Odna was also called to the stand to explain to the jury how Frank had failed to be there for his wife during her life-threatening operation, and when he finally did show up, he was curt and irritable. She also delivered particularly damning testimony by recanting a conversation that she and Kate had the day Kate left the hospital.

"She said he would kill her!" Odna stated, speaking directly to the jury of peers.

"Kill her?" repeated Kate's attorney. "Can you be more specific, ma'am?"

"Not just that he would kill her, but she said he'd kill her slowly. I thought she was kiddin me, cuz I was kiddin when I said he'd throw her out the window."

"What was her response?"

"Miss Kate said he wouldn't throw her out the window cuz it'd be too quick, that he'd want her to suffer."

The jury wasn't listening when the defense attorney took Odna apart for unpaid parking tickets. They had heard enough.

165

K ate's attorney, Tom Whalen, was also called to the stand. He
explained how Kate had warned him of Frank's threats of
violence. He wept as he explained that he had followed instructions
from Kate to "hold off going to the police," despite feeling he should
do otherwise.

He explained the financial motive for Frank to want Kate removed
from the picture. He explained the conversation Frank had with him
regarding the life insurance.

The jury was riveted as the white-haired lawyer recounted his testimony. The motive seemed to be clear: Frank Bruno stood to gain
financially if Kate was gone.

"Well, Mr. Whalen, if Frank was motivated in this way, as you say, and
had gone to the home with the intent of murdering his wife, don't you
think he would be a bit more careful? Don't you think he would have
done something to provide an alibi? Does this really make sense to you?"

There was a significant lapse as Tom panned the room briefly until
he met the gaze of Frank Bruno, who sat leering at his former attorney.

Tom Whalen ended with one sentence: "In my thirty-five years as
a lawyer, I have learned one thing with absolute clarity, sir. There is
no defense for being stupid."

166

Vida Mudgett was an endearing witness who cozied up to the jury and deflected the defense lawyers with time-sharpened wit. She explained the years of abuse of Kate and Anthony at the hands of Frank Bruno, describing with dramatic detail the wounds she had witnessed firsthand. Vida unfolded for the jury many of the secrets Kate had shared with her over the years, stories of being punched and beaten by Frank as well as the endless ridicule and relentless berating. She explained Kate's quiet admissions of fear and concerns that something "horrible could happen." She also told of the abuse to young Anthony, describing Frank as "an angry and self-absorbed man, seemingly fueled by contempt of humanity."

Vida told a compelling story of a woman who lived an enviably wholesome life, dedicated to her son. A woman who quietly bore the pain of a cruel man whose deplorable behavior only served to create sorrow. How Kate had few friends, but no identifiable enemies. How Kate was selfless, helping an elderly woman live a respectful life, liberated from the eldercare she was prescribed again and again.

"I couldn't imagine anyone in the world wanting to kill this beautiful child," Vida told the court.

"The world has lost a great soul," she pronounced, staring right at Frank.

The defense again tried to discredit the witness, painting her as an infirmed woman with signs of senility. Vida needed no assistance dismantling the paper-thin attack, easily wrapping the young attorney around his own axle. Much of the jury was smirking or even smiling as she tottered down from the stand. Frank sat wagging his head and grinding his teeth.

Vida immediately established a trust for Anthony, assuring he was financially squared away through college and beyond. She donated the rest of her considerable wealth to her favorite charities. One contribution went to the Arnold Arboretum, to whom she gave five million dollars to establish a small garden with a white picket fence around it and an American Flag flying in the middle. The fund would make certain the space inside the fence was to be filled with gorgeous blooms every year until the money ran out, which it never did.

Vida's farewell Daisy McQueen novel outsold every one of its predecessors and was a tremendous success. Much to her fans' joy, Vida went on to write just one more novel, "The Garden Gate Murderer." In the farewell book, Daisy stepped away from solving crimes to go to law school, but in this encore emerged from retirement to solve a local mystery the police could not. An abusive husband had killed his wife and gotten away with it using an elaborate scheme to provide a tight alibi. Daisy's crafty sleuthing cornered the man, who tried to flee, but was done in during a shootout by a handsome cop with a bullet to the chest, "a fitting end to a wretched character," said a Boston Globe critic.

In Vida's mind the real story played out much better. "Sitting in prison and thinking about it for the rest of his days is a much better penance." She thought. At 92, Vida peacefully went to see her friend Kate in the garden.

167

When Anthony finished on the stand, there was not a dry eye in the court—except perhaps the judge, whose years on the bench gave him an objective filter and emotional detachment. Anthony spoke timidly but convincingly about the years of abuse at the hands of his father: the physical abuse that had left him bruised and scarred, as well as the deeply damaging verbal abuse that had chiseled away at him for years. Anthony was genuine in a way that only the truth can be. He was not vindictive and remained focused on the life of his mother, who he spoke of in such glowing terms that it made the jury visibly emotional. Anthony recognized the magnitude of his testimony, knowing he would condemn his own father to prison. It was a burden he handled with immense maturity as he recognized the justice in the proceedings.

Anthony looked to Vida who sat in the courtroom quietly supporting him through the difficult testimony. She had supported him in so many ways since he lost his mother, providing short term financial support and encouragement as he made the decision to move to New York to be with his Uncle Pat. Vida knew she would see less of the boy who reminded her daily of the beautiful friend she had tragically lost, but she knew this was Anthony's path and she wanted to help him fulfill his potential.

168

Frank sat throughout the entire trial basting in his own smug frustration, vacillating from arrogance to bewilderment. He could not believe he was being held without bail for the murder of his soon-to-be ex-wife for a crime he knew he didn't commit. He found himself as toothless as his lawyers, overwhelmed with damning evidence. They labored to gain any traction and scrape up a character witness who would testify on his behalf. The legal team gobbled up his money as they defended him for a crime he didn't commit but had irrefutable evidence proving he did.

Frank's mother and sisters sat vigil in the courtroom every minute, and made themselves readily available for comments to the press.

169

The prosecutor orchestrated a brilliant presentation of the case, walking the jury methodically through the portrait of a murder and connecting the dots of evidence that proved the guilt of Frank Bruno. In the closing arguments, there was no Colombo moment, no Daisy McQueen revelation. This was real life. The prosecutor articulated in no uncertain terms the formula for a guilty verdict: the murder weapon with perfect prints, a motive to kill, lack of an alibi, and eyewitnesses placing him at the scene. She explained that the only reasonable conclusion was that Frank Bruno shot his wife in rage, and the only justice would be a conviction and punishment to the fullest extent of the law.

The defense clung to the notion that this just didn't add up and didn't make sense. Their flimsy message wilted before the jury, and as the attorney returned to sit next to Frank, they looked at one another as if to say that this doesn't look good and a conviction is really happening.

170

In the end, the jury returned after just thirty-eight minutes of deliberation and delivered a unanimous guilty verdict for Frank Louis Bruno. He would be sentenced to life in prison, and although he might someday get out on parole, he would most likely die in jail. He was going to prison for all the crimes he committed. He may have been one of the only convicts who was telling the truth when he claimed he was innocent, but he was serving time for a murder: the murder of Charles Edward Stuber. Finally, there was justice.

171

Anthony enrolled in the charter school in Manhattan, and he could not believe the curriculum they provided or the classmates that now surrounded him. He had been transported to the summer camp of his dreams, a welcoming place for creative young people mostly devoid of pretention, and the bullying element was noticeably absent. He woke each day with a feeling he had scarcely ever felt—an anxiousness to participate. He also bonded with his uncle, who he found infinitely interesting and talented.

Anthony missed his mother desperately and thought of her daily. Her image was etched in his mind and resting softly on his shoulder. He spoke to her quietly at rise and rest, and he often sensed her response. He never communicated with his father again, although many years later, Frank would write and even express some remorse.

Anthony became a great man, husband, and father. He went on to be a successful artist and collaborated with his uncle for many years. He also was fortunate to marry a strikingly pretty and kind New York girl who shared his life. They had a great apartment on the Upper West Side that overlooked Central Park, with a spacious patio that, in the warmth of summer, spilled over with flowers and plants, the fragrances of a hundred petals serving as a reminder of a special soul. He had long since reverted to using his mother's last name, and they named their first child Katie Kelley: a beautiful tow-head girl with garden-green eyes.

Acknowledgements

Huge thanks to my family for their support, and my wife Teri for her patience and insights. To my Dad for his editing and great advice. To my mom for her endless encouragement. To Paul McCarthy for his awesome cover art. To all my friends, thanks for your honest feedback. To E.M.P... I miss you. Thank you to J.I. and E.H.: you inspired me to write. To O.C.—thanks for the push. I know you didn't mean it, but it helped.